# DEATH OF A LADIES' MAN

# ALAN BISSETT

First published in 2009
by HACHETTE SCOTLAND, an imprint of
HACHETTE UK

First published in paperback in 2010
by HACHETTE SCOTLAND, an imprint of
HACHETTE UK

2

Cataloguing in Publication Data is available from the British Library

ISBN 978 07553 1942 8

Typeset in Walbaum by Avon DataSet Ltd, Bidford on Avon, Warwickshire

Printed and bound in Great Britain by Clays Ltd, St Ives plc

Hachette Scotland's policy is to use papers that are natural, renewable and
recyclable products and made from wood grown in sustainable forests.
The logging and manufacturing processes are expected to conform
to the environmental regulations of the country of origin.

HACHETTE SCOTLAND
An Hachette UK Company
338 Euston Road
London NW1 3BH

www.hachettescotland.co.uk
www.hachette.co.uk

For Kirstin

**You must at all costs** distinguish yourself from every other male in the room. Animals use **visual stimuli** to attract a mate: frills, colours, elaborate **patterns.** Sometimes they are blue. Sometimes they are, say, **yellow!** You too should stand out from the crowd, be a unique, startling creature. Make them **laugh!** Prepare funny **anecdotes!** Be the centre of **attention!** This theory is called peacocking. Be a **peacock!** Women will look at you from across the room, fascinated, wondering, Who are you?

**Who *are* you?**

neck exposed like a glacial pass slopes sweeps to the shoulder
fingernails clamberover lift her bra-strap she softens mmmm skin
*warm* incisors *press* Julie leans in we touch tongues flic flick flicker
everything slow everything slooooow Julie giggles *Oh Charlie*
thistinyweeroom *Careful now Charlie* hair smells of cigarettes
andisthatstrawberryshampoo Dust in the air she leans on a full shelf
!the books! !careful! slowlymoveherround My Hands her waist My
Touch she BITES me the minx OW move upgear *now* nails drrr aag
on the small of her back spreads herself against me softpit of her
neck rolling shifting she whispers *Come on Charlie* earlobenibble
playing like a lioncub testing teeth I grin *What?* she says *Your eyes* she
raises her skirt holds her breath knickerflash the sheerlacypeach she
squirms I look stare up/down thinking What in the name of god am I
doi

Bell rings.

*'Shit.'*

Julie fussed with her skirt, pulled and hitched, quick as a phone-
box change. 'We'd better go,' she said, lowered herself from her
position against the bookshelves and took her marking, instantly
vocational.

Charlie felt cold showered. 'Okay,' he said. 'Quick. Before the wee
bastards break out their cages.'

They looked at each other. He narrowed his eyes. Hers smiled slyly.
Something pulsed in the space between them and he felt it begin
again, felt the air melt again, become globules between them, but just

3

as she leaned forwards to kiss him, just as she inclined her head and touched his mouth with hers and he closed his eyes and she raised her hand to his hair again, the doorknob rattled.

Julie froze against his lips.

*Gavin?* Charlie whispered.

Julie frowned.

Keys at the other side of the door. Charlie panicked. *I have to hide!*

She went *no no no no no.*

His hands made claws: *What, then?*

The key shook in the lock. She shooed Charlie behind the door – *Move! Move!* – then opened it, smooth as a hostess welcoming guests. He heard corridor noise bloom and Gavin's voice, surprised, say, 'Oh. Julie. I didn't think anyone was in here. The door was locked.'

'Sorry, must've shut behind me,' Julie said, and her voice pinged, professional. 'Looking for *Animal Farm?*'

'Yeah,' said Gavin. 'Set Text time again. Whoo!'

Books shifted. Julie grunted.

'Cheers,' said Gavin. 'More at the back there, I think.'

'These?'

''S okay, Julie, I'll get them.'

'No! I mean. It's fine.'

Charlie heard her walk into the depths of the book cupboard and Gavin come in after. He squeezed behind the door so tightly he felt tubular.

'There.'

'Thanks.'

Books were being passed. An international resolution, it seemed, was being passed. C'mon, c'mon.

'So, Julie, what is it you're starting with the third-years?'

'Um . . . *Of Mice and Men.* Just popped in here to pick them up.'

4

Gavin said, 'Oh.' And the sound hovered like a soap-bubble. 'That's in my room.'

'Is it?'

'Yeah. I told you that this morning. You asked if you could borrow them.'

'Did I?'

'You did. So, uh, why did you come here to get them?'

'Must've forgotten.'

After a while, Gavin said: 'Let me guess. You didn't want to come to my room?'

'What?' said Julie. 'Course not. I forgot, that's all.'

'Julie, we can't let this be awkward. We still have to work together.'

'Well, Gavin, it's chats like this, *in book cupboards*, that make it awkward.'

'Right. Sorry.'

There was silence for a few seconds. *Get rid of him, get rid of him,* Charlie's mind drummed, like fingers on a desk. This *really* isn't the time to negotiate the terms of your break-up. Then something occurred to him, sat there in the front of his psyche like a grimacing Imp of the Perverse. He wondered if she'd motioned to Gavin: *Charlie's here. Be! hind! the! door!* He suddenly felt convinced that a game was being played here, at his expense, which Julie and Gavin had rehearsed beforehand. The feeling was so strong and unexpected that he nearly pushed the door from in front of him just to see what they'd do. Ha! I'm *on*to the two of you! But then he heard Gavin say, 'Okay, good, so you know where the books are,' and Julie trill, 'Right, thanks,' and a few words were exchanged about some kid who was playing up in the third year ('Fucking Darren Clarke *again*?') and Julie and Gavin chatted out the Many Tribulations of Darren Clarke and Charlie's mind reeled, reeled, and he wasn't breathing. Eventually Gavin said, 'Send him to me, we'll sort him out once and for all,' before he was gone into corridor noise, and Julie shut the door.

She bent. Exhaled.

'That was close,' Charlie said.

When she stood her eyes accused.

He laughed.

'It's not funny,' she said.

'Yeah, I know.' Charlie tucked in his shirt. Julie started pacing up and down the book cupboard, a general whose troops had just been decimated.

'Think he wondered why the door was locked?'

'Nah,' Charlie said, doing his tie.

'I mean, why would the door be locked? Why would I be in here myself with the door *locked*?'

'Did you mime something to him, Julie?'

'What?'

'Did you point to me?' he said. 'It went quiet for a second there. You tell him I was behind this door?'

'As *if*, Charlie,' she said. 'Why the hell would I do that?' Then she folded her arms across her marking, stood on tiptoe and kissed him, primly, on the nose. 'Young man, we need to be more careful.'

They kissed on the mouth. A tackle.

'Not at school, Mr Bain,' she said. 'Okay?'

'Yes, Miss Carell.'

She left.

Adolescent chatter in the hall: laughter catcalls spats. Charlie adjusted his suit, went into the noise and colour of the corridor, the cackling masses and swaggering schoolbags. He strode. He was the Colossus of Rhodes. He strode past Gavin's room. Gavin stood. Gavin looked up as Charlie passed. Their eyes met like those of rival salesmen chasing a buck. His glance snapped from Gavin's like a business card. A first-year said, 'Morning, Mr Bain,' dragging itself to

6

class, a nuclear mutant. 'Oh,' Charlie said. 'Morning.' He was already thinking through the lesson – Shakespeare – mind dancing – Shakespeare – wondering how he was going to make Shakespeare interesting. His snappy title was 'Montague v. Capulet: the Grudge!' The kids were in the class, and Charlie's entrance struck a note through waves of noise: bobbing boys settled, turned, started to take things out from their bags – grenades? guns? deodorants? He still couldn't think of any jokes! The one about the crack-addicted hamster? That it mugged for—? For—? Punchline? Perhaps he should *teach* them something. He could always fall back on that. The class swarmed and moved as one: faces, a shore of them, and he was Canute, keeping them at bay. King Charles. King *Bain*. He liked the way you could say it: *Baaaaain*. Arms outstretched and proclaiming. 'Okay, everybody!' he said, a meaningless utterance with no other purpose than to announce that he was there, in charge, that education was about to commence: all eyes on me, if you please.

For I Am Present.

The class quietened. Bums shifted as he called the register. He ticked off their names – Here Here absent Here – moved down the list, adrenalin beginning to ebb now, to adjust: he was teaching.

He was a teacher.

One late night in Berlin, curled around an Irish backpacker, curled smokily around her accent and the thickish fact of her body, her *superb* thighs, he'd learned something about himself. The cannabis on her breath. The lovely stonedness. She'd harangued him – 'Ye're a feckin ladies' man! I don't believe it! Go on, *tell* me ye were never feckin loved as a child' – trying to read him, chart him, irritatingly sexy. Their love-making was light and dream-like and she was right

she was *right*

He hated those guys, with their expensive shirts and their false laughs and their sleekness and pearls-before-swine eyes. But when she'd detailed the evidence, there it was. Sex was the lens through which he, Charles Bain, BA (Hons), perceived the world. Gave it clarity, colour, sparkle.

Warmed it.

Receiving head didn't do much for him but, man, he loved to give it. That kissing and touching, the tapping, the stroking, the circling, all that want and heat and presence. The *eeriness* of an orgasm. Like someone leaving their body. The mounting roar as Possessed became Exorcised. The rearing, stiffening and softening. This was what hurtled him through life: the clutch and collapse; the network of feints and signs and sighs to navigate in getting there, a map of the stars. When he saw a woman – in the shopping-centre or coffee-shop or, God, the *library*, c'mon, readers were *sexy* – he wondered at the moans and gasps she might make, how easy or difficult it would be to arouse her. He wanted to please her, this stranger, fall onto her lap like a gift—

Happy birthday!

Make no mistake, there was nothing of the misogynist in him. He'd never drooled to 'guys' in 'bars' about 'chicks' he'd 'banged'. It was a force for good, all this flirting, a simple recognition of humanity. It was UN Peacekeeping. It was naturalistic. It was jogging or reading great books or clubbing – coked! Totally In The Moment. It was game theory. Functional. Fun. Fucking wonderful. It was planned or it was unplanned. It was *hell, honey, let's just spend it*! If someone wanted to have sex with him, he would; if they didn't, he'd persuade them that they *couldn't*.

Then they did.

In such ways seduction takes place, a natural order of events. Hearts are injured occasionally, yes, but love is a messy business. Surely everyone knows that. And, for Charlie, it was always about love, a *kind* of love, this bringing of human beings together. This mingling of desires. This telepathy between bodies. Recognise it? The connection? The rush of blood? The sound of men and women fucking like animals? Like *jaguars*? How can these things mean *nothing*?

Nonetheless, he still lived with his mum.

At the age of thirty.

A generation ago on a teachers' pay: *faux*-baronial. But this market. Nights in front of the telly upstairs in that same bedroom he'd had till uni, its shifting dreamscape of wallpapers: pirates, clowns, Hulks, Rangers FC crests, simple blue stripes then deep, sad, adolescent black. Then the uni years

then the married years

Now here he was again. The same TV. Same endless TV. Weed from a little hash-pipe cos he hated tobacco: hack hack, fuck that shit, man. Dense-scented smoke coveted richly by the lungs that made soap operas and *The Simpsons* and *Batman Begins* an orgy of fulfilment and brilliance, of narrative fascination, of of of sound! and colour! and action! and fuckin thigh-slapping fuckin hahahaha oh man that's funny, that is so *funny*, fuckin

Yeah, man

The darkness of the *Nine o'Clock News*, brooding upon his monged brain. Iraq. Iraq. The weight, the weight of it, down down down on his swirling consciousness, the gravitational pull of a giant global capitalist conspiracy somewhere. Probably. Then switch like roulette to:

Lydia, cant stop thinking about when I pushed deep inside you, and you held me there without moving. On the verge of coming. Been on my mind all day. x

Hey Jackie, still enjoying the 'modelling portfolio'
you sent last week...x

Was just thinking, Marie, that it's the fact that we're
virtually strangers that makes this exciting. x

Nothing.

He flicked through Saved Messages for the greatest hits. Ursula.
Trixie. Moira. Hot Moira. I want you. I want you to. Feels so horny
when you. Across my thighs and over my. To remind himself. Just to
remind himself.

His mother also sat in a chair in a room before a screen. Downstairs.
Sometimes he'd sit up with her at nights, and she didn't mind. Having
him there meant she had her dinners made and her clothes washed,
and her clothes ironed, and the rooms cleaned, and bread and milk
and papers waiting obediently for her in the morning, and her baths
run, and someone to go to the supermarket for her, and her telly
programmes recorded, and her breakfast prepared and cups of tea
brought to her – No sugar, Mum; More sugar, Charlie – and lightbulbs changed and keys found and birthday/christening/
anniversary cards signed on her behalf and her back scratched and
her shoulders massaged and her lottery ticket bought and her lottery
ticket *checked* and her toothpaste changed when it ran out. If it ran
out. She just used his. Till it ran out.

Dinner. Soup. Chicken. He coughed and said, 'So!'

His mum looked at him. 'So.' She chewed.

He said, 'It's the truth.'

She said, 'Expect me to believe that?'

'What?' he said.

'Charlie,' she said. 'They're a pair of women's socks.'

'No, they're not,' he said. 'Look. Grey. Grey socks.' He shook them. 'Grey. Men wear them all the time.'

'Not ones with pink toes.' She swallowed a piece of bread. Her eyes alert as a meerkat's. 'Look. Son. I really don't mind.'

'But I wouldn't bring anyone back *here*, Mum.'

'It's your room, Charlie, you can have who you like in it.'

'It's not my room! I won't be staying here for long.'

'You said that three years ago. And c'mon. I heard the door going last night. Giggling, Charlie. You don't giggle.'

'I giggle.'

'Go on, then.'

He giggled.

She shook her head like a concentration-camp guard.

He took out the newspaper and smoothed it onto the table. It crackled. He looked up at her.

'Just how many are there?' she said.

He shook his head and the paper and fucking *Scotland*.

'Look at this,' he said. 'Fully furnished flat in the West End. Double glazing. Near to Hillhead subway station.'

'Charlie.' She took his hand. 'I understand that young men have. *Needs*. I'm just saying I hope you're taking precau—'

'Mum.' He stood. 'We are *not* having this conversation. I'm a teacher for godsakes, give me *some* credit.'

He hadn't been able to find the sock, hurrying Ashley? Ann? Andrea? out of the door as dawn broke, raking his sister's clothes for a sock for Ashley? Ann? Andrea? because his mum would be getting up, but he hadn't counted on the toes, the pink toes. A pink-toed tarantula, splayed in his bedroom, incriminating as porn. He put the paper away. His mum smiled. He dipped his roll, watched soup bleed through it, and on the wall was a calendar of stags and hills.

11

She poured more wine.

'What are you doing?' he said.

'What do you mean what am I doing?'

'Are you going to have a meal with your wine?'

'The doctor said an occasional one was okay.'

'Glass, not bottle.'

She shrugged and topped up her glass. It glugged delicately. His mother sipped. They cut and ate food. She laughed a little again, reached for the salt.

'Go easy on that stuff.'

'It's salt, Charlie. Edible. The Romans ate mountains of it.'

'Yeah, well, they all died, didn't they?'

She put down her knife and fork. She tugged her jumper sleeves. He dipped more bread into the soup and chewed. After a long time she said, 'American *Wife Swap* is on.'

'I'm just looking out for you.'

She got up from the dinner table, went to the living room. Charlie cleared the plates, took them to the sink. American *Wife Swap*. 'Take my wife ... please!' (Laughter.) 'I take my wife everywhere, but she keeps finding her way back!' (D-doom! tsh!) He filled the sink. He made some tea. Brought it through to her. Kissed her head. Then he stood and watched the programme. They'd swapped a militant organic family with a designer couple. The Militant Organics grew their own food, killed their own animals, and would use nothing at all with chemicals in it. They did nuclear-attack fire-drills. They were prepared. That's what they said. 'Prepared.'

Designer Couple told the Militant Organics: 'You've been brainwashed.'

One of the kids screamed, 'No, you have!'

Like sci-fi.

He went to the sink, placed his hands either side of it. In there

12

were plates and cups; he should wash them. Do this: wash them. But Julie. That flash of peach knickers. That smile. That bell ringing at just the very worst time and the sheer stupidity of what he'd done – at school? At *school?* The look on Gavin's face if he'd found Julie there, thighs spread coolly, Charlie grunting away between them, her fingers making indents on his butt as they bucked. The two of them turning and grinning at him like in a horror film . . .

He texted Gavin: Hey mate fancy going out tonight?

. . . twenty seconds . . .

Nah mate not in mood.

Charlie stared at the phone. Tasted each syllable. He considered those moments behind the door, when he'd thought Julie was gesturing to Gavin. He went to call, sighed, slammed closed the phone. Then he opened it again and birled past Abi, Chrissy, Jenna, Jessica, Kirsty, Monica, to *N*. Nadine. *Select.* A thumb-tapped sonnet. *Send.* He went upstairs to his bedroom and took some coke, some fuckin COKE that's what we need here fucking COKE my man understandwhatimsaying it's Friday night oh yes it's

**Always go with women to clubs,** don't go with men. The company of women makes you seem attractive and **popular,** especially if you are making them laugh. **Make them laugh!** Big loud guffaws so **everyone** can hear. Others want what your companions have and you have **status.** Status is everything. What is a man without **status?** He is like a **state** without status. Take state from status and you get **us.** And why are **we** going to a club? We a couple of **fags?!** Take a dame. Take **two dames.** Take a **bag of dames!** If you get lucky, you aren't leaving a friend on her own.

You are a **winning barbarian** and you know it. If chicks don't bite you can always go home with one of the **hotties** you brought with you. That is because they are **still** laughing at your jokes, my friend.

# Int. Nightclub. Glasgow

*CHARLIE and NADINE are dancing. A poster behind them says: 'National Pop League'. The whole floor stutters with scenesters. There should be a vague prettiness about the way this is shot, an industrial light and magic. These people are Full Strength Indie. The Zoey Van Goey song 'Foxtrot Vandals' is playing: 'I dreamed we danced upon the walls/And on the ceiling dear ...' CHARLIE, coked-up and feeling like a movie star, is wearing a cowboy hat, a blazer, jeans and a Karate Kid T-shirt. NADINE looks every inch the Glasgow School of Art student – pixie-like, bobbed hair, fashionable yet utterly out of step with fashion. Charlie often thinks she looks like the novelist Donna Tartt.*

| | |
|---|---|
| CHARLIE: | Hey, be honest. Will this hat make people think I'm a knob? |
| NADINE: | You're totally working it, honey. |
| CHARLIE: | What about the eyeliner? |
| NADINE: | Applied it *myself* so I know it's good, soldier. Relax. There's loads of women checking you out. |
| CHARLIE: | Really? Where? |
| NADINE: | (*Glances conspiratorially*) To your right. Knee-length boots. Stripy dress. Remember the drill? |
| | CHARLIE *salutes.* |
| NADINE: | First day of basic training? |
| CHARLIE: | Never Hesitate. Keep it Light. Smile. |
| NADINE: | You still owe me for setting you up with Gail Cullen. |
| CHARLIE: | That was fifteen years ago. We were still at school. |
| NADINE: | *The*. Gail. Cullen. |
| CHARLIE: | She. Dumped. Me. |
| NADINE: | Not my fault if you blew it. What do I keep telling |

17

you? Girls that age, *any* age, don't want 'nice guys'. Took you long enough to figure that one out.

CHARLIE: Hm.

NADINE: I created a monster! (*Whispers*) But *a fabulous* one (*winks*).

CHARLIE *walks like a fabulous Frankenstein creature.*

NADINE: And what about that hen party I got us talking to in Barcelona? Told them you were my shy wee cousin? You fucking were that night. What was *wrong* with you?

CHARLIE: I think a hen party was the last thing I needed at that stage, Nadine. Given the circumstances.

NADINE: Oh. Yvonne. Forgot. Sorry.

CHARLIE:

NADINE: Heard from her recently?

CHARLIE:

NADINE: Right.

*They dance in silence for a bit. The song changes to 'Loneliness Shines' by Malcolm Middleton.*

CHARLIE: Couldn't even summon the energy for a wank on that trip.

NADINE: Ha. You liar!

CHARLIE: What do you mean? How would you know? You've never seen me wank.

NADINE: I shared Eastern European hostels with you for two months, darling. I didn't have to *see* to know. (*Peers*) Charlie Bain, are you *blushing*?

CHARLIE: I. Don't. Blush.

NADINE: But. You. Wank. (*Grins*) So who's been checking me out, then?

CHARLIE *does a quick sweep.*

CHARLIE: *Clockwork Orange* T-shirt. Behind you.

NADINE: Cute?

CHARLIE: He has 'creative' hair.

NADINE *checks.*

NADINE: Me like! Bet he's a bass player. Hope he's a bass player.

CHARLIE: Thought you went for singers?

NADINE: Too obvious. Bass players are totally in this year. Okay, how am I looking?

CHARLIE: Like a fucking Exocet. Target locked, soldier?

NADINE: Locked and loaded, Sarge.

NADINE *flicks her hair and dances, sexy-lazy style, to* CLOCKWORK ORANGE GUY. CLOCKWORK ORANGE GUY *sees* NADINE, *grins and starts dancing with her.* CHARLIE *dances for a bit on his own, watching the lights, blissed out. The lights are magical. Glasgow is magical. Everything. Everything. When next he looks at* NADINE, *she is kissing* CLOCKWORK ORANGE GUY. *Twice she flicks her eyes at* CHARLIE, *something about it like flicking fag ash. He stares at the two of them.* NADINE *glances back. Then someone takes the hat from* CHARLIE's *head and he turns. It is the* STRIPY DRESS GIRL *whom Nadine pointed out to him. He narrows his eyes and smiles at her.*

CHARLIE: 'Scuse me, young lady, I believe that's my property.

STRIPY
DRESS GIRL: Well. Now it's back on the market.

CHARLIE: Trust me, you won't be able to afford the repayments.

STRIPY
DRESS GIRL: Oh, no? And then what?

CHARLIE: I'll own your ass.

*He takes the hat back.* STRIPY DRESS GIRL *laughs and*

> *starts dancing with him, neat, cool, indie-girl moves.*
> *Close-up on her eyelashes: like the skinny, regal legs of*
> *synchronised swimmers.*
>
> NADINE *is staring at the two of them.*

CUT TO:

# Int. Taxi. Night

CHARLIE *and* STRIPY DRESS GIRL *are kissing in the back of the taxi.* CHARLIE *strokes her hair. Beneath his hat she looks small, with her stray curls and those eyes. She looks right at him. They've clicked into place now, we can see it. Something inevitable has happened, deep in the DNA. He kisses her. Hard. A subliminal shot: Dracula preparing to bite the neck of a young virgin. They stare into each other's eyes.*

STRIPY
DRESS GIRL: So who was that girl you were with all night?

CHARLIE: Nadine? Ach, she's an old mate of mine.

STRIPY
DRESS GIRL: Where did she go to?

CHARLIE: Dunno.

STRIPY
DRESS GIRL: You left her in there on her own?

CHARLIE: (*Laughs*) Hardly. She left with someone before I did.

STRIPY
DRESS GIRL: Oh. That's quite some ... arrangement.

CHARLIE: Yeah. So what?

STRIPY
DRESS GIRL: You guys were out on the pull together?

CHARLIE:      What's so strange about that? She's a mate.

STRIPY
DRESS GIRL:   You don't go out on the pull with guys?

CHARLIE:      Well, who would you want more? The guy standing with
              a big group of pissheads, or the one with the hot woman?

STRIPY
DRESS GIRL:   Hm. Got it all worked out, you pair, haven't you?

CHARLIE:      Basic psychology. Nadine the Machine, I call her. You
              should see her turn it on. There's no guy she couldn't
              get. At school she had half of the teachers crying
              themselves to sleep.

STRIPY
DRESS GIRL:   She sounds charming.

CHARLIE:      That's. Why. It. Works.

              STRIPY DRESS GIRL *nods slowly*.

STRIPY
DRESS GIRL:   Has she had you?

CHARLIE:      *(Pauses)* None of your business.

              *He leans forwards. They kiss again. He touches her face.*

STRIPY
DRESS GIRL:   Smooth.

CHARLIE:      I thought so too! Where do you live?

STRIPY
DRESS GIRL:   South Side.

CHARLIE:      We're going to fuck. *(Smiles)* Aren't we?

              STRIPY DRESS GIRL *purrs. He shifts against her.*
              *Streetlights pulse.*

STRIPY
DRESS GIRL:   My bedroom's a bit of a tip, though. Can we go to
              yours instead?

CHARLIE:      No. My mum might still be up.

> STRIPY DRESS GIRL *laughs. She looks at him, blank and disbelieving.*

STRIPY
DRESS GIRL: Your mum? You're kidding.

CHARLIE: (*Pauses*) Obviously.

STRIPY
DRESS GIRL: Cos I was going to say ... still living with your mum is *sad.*

CHARLIE: Is it now?

STRIPY
DRESS GIRL: Yeah. Talk about not letting go of the apron strings. What's *with* that?

CHARLIE: Hm.

> CHARLIE *turns away to the window and stares. After a few seconds he asks the driver to stop the car. He throws some pound coins onto the seat, glances at* STRIPY DRESS GIRL, *then gets out and starts walking.*

STRIPY
DRESS GIRL: Hey, Charlie, where you going?

> CHARLIE *hails another taxi. It pulls over. He gets in.*

STRIPY
DRESS GIRL: Charlie, wait! What about your hat?

> *Close-up on* STRIPY DRESS GIRL *holding the hat. Yeah, make sure you get that one. Right close-up.*

Over the years he'd come to loathe the company of straight men. Straight *Glasgow* Men. It was their relentlessly dull conversations about football and football and football and cars and football – like this stuff mattered? *Still?* To *adults?* He hated the way they talked about women too, in the pub, safely out of earshot, Viking-like about their conquests. Leaning over pints, foot up on the rail at the bottom of the bar, namechecking the hardware – tits, ass, cunt – not a *hint* of psychology, of the softcore fizz of consciousness beneath. Are women automobiles? Are they garden furniture! Detail for us, gents, that delicious push-pull of attraction, that melting of inhibitions, the dazed, heavy-light spiralling down into the sheets. Were Charlie an art teacher he'd be begging this crowd of blokeish dilettantes: show us *process*. Eh, they'd reply ... hump them? No! Wrong. Eh ... grab their tits and that? No, you dolt! You have the sensitivity of a drunk elephant. To be a ladies' man you must be a feminist. You must think like a woman. A straight, male woman. Groomed and fucking *immaculate*. Feminists are a turn-on. Feminists are *feminine*. Read the literature, lads, even the crazy stuff from the seventies about forswearing men and different societies for each sex and sons being given away like curses, the might and power and drama and opera!

Men, you are too content just to have dicks.

To move them backwards and forwards a bit.

But women weren't down with the feminism thing any more, even Charlie knew that. He'd ask them straight out over dinner, on dates: 'Are you a feminist?' And more and more often they'd hesitate guiltily, the candlelight illuminating their unease, then sigh, 'I'm all in favour of equal pay, y'know, don't get me wrong,' and stutter something about men not being the enemy now, it's women who are harder on women, then say, 'Well, y'know, I'm probably a *post*-feminist if anything,' because they were being pulled in two different directions. To say you weren't a feminist would seem disloyal to your sex. Those battles had had to be fought and they were grateful for the opportunities afforded them by the previous generation of women, etc., etc., blah blah. But when it came down to it, they simply loved men more than they loved wo

simply loved men more than they loved wome

Yvon

Ha! But they were wrong. The feminists, the *real* ones, keeping the faith, had discovered their own selves – beyond confectionery – nurtured deep inside and crystallised. They were what happened, spectacularly, when you split the atom of a woman – boom! They'd worked it out: clocked guys like him long ago. Being a woman was heave and haul and storm and blood, was quicksilver survival instinct, was a fight against history and destiny. They didn't give a fuck if he fancied them or not. They didn't give a fuck full stop. That drove him *wild*. Powerful women. Bring 'em on. A team of Amazons, of Wonder Womans, of She-Ras and Boudiccas and Pankhursts, lugging the weights of their slavery into the ring and dropping them, clanging, to the floor and staring. Come on then, fucko, they will. With their *teeth*. Let them pit themselves against him. Let them pit themselves against him and *win*. He couldn't stand the weak, needy ones, just did not want to sleep with any of them. There was nothing sexy about weakness: it dripped and sniffed and stooped and apologised for itself. Fight, woman, fight! he wanted to bark. And when they told him they weren't feminists he'd think: Well, y'know, good luck.

You're going to need it.

He also loved the company of gay men, but knew they regarded him the way he saw other straight guys: typical, monochrome, boorish. That pissed him off. He was the gay man's non-gay friend. He would have made a *great* gay man if only he'd *been* gay. But as it was they made jokes at his expense, about his straight dancing, straight clothes, straight haircut. He even resented the word 'straight', implying as it did something linear and rigid and *dull*.

He wasn't dull. Was he dull? He wasn't dull.

*It is raining. Yvonne is on Buchanan Street. Yvonne, sodden, coming towards you on crowded Buchanan Street. 'Baby?' you say. She won't*

*look at you. 'Yvonne?' you say. 'It's me, baby. Stop. Please.' She still won't
look at you. Her wedding dress clings to her legs, face dripping with
rain, as though she is melting. She is melting. She is melting into water.
The giant video screen above Buchanan Street shows cruises, shoes, home
furnishings. Your legs slow and slow. She is coming towards you. She is
crying. You will console her. You will protect: this was your pledge, that
you would protect her, all of her life. Open your arms and feel her body
beside yours again, its warmth and heartbeat, its life. She walks right
through you. Liquid. She is gone.*

    *she is gone*

*sh  e  gon*

    *s e  is g*

        *n*

*e  s*

   *h*

      *o*

    *o*

The sch *o* ol day jived around Charlie, to its iPod, in its uniform and
trainers. Trainers DESPITE SCHOOL REGULATIONS!!! It was Monday.
What was Monday like except Monday? Monday Monday Monday,
fucking magnolia man. The school walls, covered with notices about
drugs prevention that featured hooded kids armed to take over society.
To smash in your windows and kick in your doors. Hitler Youth. He'd
just taken a double-period of such kids. Their chewing-gum and
folded arms and porn-slack eyes. He'd virtually had to breakdance for
them. 'Whuh?' they'd said, to every last joke.

    'Darren, are you *stoned*?'

    'Whuh?'

    Wandering past the science block he spotted Monise Ferguson,
standing with two of her friends. They were all eating crisps and
texting, and probably talking about boys, as though in an actual

comedy-sketch about teens. 'Hiya, Mr B,' said Monise's friend. Her voice went up and down, girlishly, gratingly.

'Oh,' he said. 'Hi.'

'Aren't you going to say hi to Monise?'

Monise tutted.

'Hello,' said Charlie.

Monise nodded.

'None of you girls have seen Miss Carell, have you?'

'Miss Carell,' said one, elbowing another.

Charlie looked at them. He couldn't believe how bristling and brazenly sexual the girls were these days, the extent to which they openly flirted with him.

terriffuckingfying

'Yes,' he said. 'Miss Carell.'

'Hmm,' they said.

'Find that funny?'

'No, sir.'

'Then kindly cease.'

'Yes, sir.'

They did eyebrow innuendo for a while.

Another tack. 'Monise, have you seen Miss Carell?'

Monise wriggled in a chamber of embarrassment. 'Came past about five minutes ago, Char— I mean sir.'

'*Charlie?*' said the girls.

'Oh, shut up,' she said.

'Thank you,' he said, then: 'Are we looking at your creative writing tomorrow? My room?'

Monise nodded.

'Good.'

He turned to go and she said, 'Mr Bain?'

'Yes?'

'I read that novel you suggested.'

'Which one?'

'*The Bell Jar*. Loved it.'

'You did?'

'Oh, yes,' she said. 'It's amazing. I could *so* relate.'

'Didn't find it too grim?'

'No! It was *heart-breaking*.'

*Heart-breaking* fought *grim* with its waves of fuchsia. He let it go. Grim was washed away on a surf of romance, leaving bits of stars as litter. Such was Monise's world.

'I mean, Mr Bain, I just thought it was so . . . *powerful*. And, like, *moving*. Just gives a sense of her *emotional*, like, *dislocation*.'

'Reckon?'

'Yeah! I can't believe that Ted Hughes. What a bastard!'

'Hm,' Charlie said, thinking: This is a woman who, the first time she and Hughes met, *bit him on the face*! But he recognised that the Plath Stage was a necessary one in Monise's development as a nascent thinker and feminist and that its appearance now was a Good Thing. Probably.

Monise's friends were tugging sleeves and pointing to her. Monise touched her hair, shrugged. 'Anyway, uh,' she said, 'see you in class, Mr Bain.' He nodded, smiled, and left, rather burnished of face. He straightened his tie. An English teacher. A talented pupil. He felt full with literature. Ah . . . ah – *sonnet!* – choo. Why didn't it always work like that? It would no more occur to some of these kids to read than it would to take a trip to the zoo. 'I mean, c'mon!' he'd say. 'The zoo! You're missing out on elephants. And hyenas. And giraffes. *Giraffes*. Do you know how cool a *giraffe* is? Up close? An actual *giraffe*? Their necks are *huge*. Look at those necks and see how huge they really *are*. You know they have long necks, but you don't realise they'll be *that* long! Stare in wonder at the neck of a goddamn giraffe!'

Then he'd pause and say, 'Well, kids, a book is also like a zoo . . .'

And still. After *that*? When *To Kill A Mockingbird* doesn't do it? And *Catcher in the Rye* doesn't do it? And *Lord of the Flies* and *Sunset Song* and *The Kite Runner* and *Curious Incident of the Fried Green Grapes of Gatsby on a Hot Tin Roof* and 'If the Characters in Animal Farm Were Part of the Marvel Universe . . .' and 'Iago: The Original Gangsta!' doesn't do it, how long do you keep going before you face the fact that, y'know, *maybe most kids just don't like reading*?

So when you found one who did.

Who reallyreallyreallyreallydid.

*Check you, Monise*, they clucked behind him, and *Ooh la la* and *You so fancy him* and *Miss Carell's a fat something something* and *Mr B's soooooo fit*, but he didn't hear Monise say a thing.

Good girl.

Charlie went looking for Julie, formulating plots to meet her after school. But Gavin was always walking past her class, glancing in. Tap tap tap, went Gavin's shoes. Blind Pew. Searching. Searching for him and Julie. Sensing them. A thriller: the plans passed in each kiss, the espionage of the where? the when? the what'll you be wearing? Julie hadn't been around at break. Charlie pushed through puffy jackets and schoolbags, crunched through their undergrowth.

Kong!

He found Julie in her room, mussing with jotters and looking kind of fearful about what her desk could do. When she saw him she brought her paper opera to a rest. He shut the door. It clicked softly. They stared at each other.

'Man,' he said, 'I can't believe those girls sometimes.'

'I've been their age,' she said. 'Believe. Believe every bit. What'd they say?'

'Nothing. Just the way they hinted.'

'At?'

'Och, you know the way girls drop hints,' he said. 'The kind of hints that destroyed Hiroshima.'

'About?'

'Just gossip. Boys. It's nothing.'

'Nothing is nothing. What did they say?'

'Monise Ferguson's pals?' he said. 'Names?' He click-clicked fingers. 'One sounds like a car?'

'Haley Davidson. Wait, hang on, that's a bike.'

'So I've heard.' He smirked.

'Careful.'

'Tegan!' he said. 'Tegan McGann. And the other sounds like she was born in a boutique.'

'Oh. Kinsella Clarke.'

'Where do they get them? American first names, Scottish surnames. Exotic spices slapped on top of mince.'

'Shut up and kiss me.'

She was a dame from an old film. Busty and glam.

'Grrr,' he said.

'Oh!' she said.

'Kong!' he said.

She hammered his chest. 'Unhand me, you beast!'

He started to kiss her — smooch — and she smiled against his lips.

'Crystal Duncan,' he said. 'There's another.'

'Hm,' said Julie, and pulled him in.

'Sofia McPhee . . . Yasmin Murdoch . . .'

'Are you kissing me or them?'

After work they drove back to Julie's flat in Hyndland and smoked some weed. They listened to Julie's stoner folk music, like Bob Dylan and Joni Mitchell and Leonard Cohen. Taking its time to unfold. The sixties, man, the fucking sixties. But when she played that Beatles song, 'Something'?

'What?' she said. 'This is a beautiful song. It's about how George Harrison Loves Pattie Boyd Oh So Very Much.'

'Yeah,' he said, 'but you know who else was in love with her?'

'Eric Clapton?'

'Exactly. Listen to "Layla". About the same woman. But written by a man who couldn't have her.'

'*Raw*.' Julie grinned.

'On *fire*,' Charlie said. 'Now listen to "Something".'

They listened to 'Something'.

Floaty floaty nice nice.

'That's the difference between love and pain,' said Charlie, 'right there.'

He put his arms around her, in her softly furnished flat – bean-bags, drapes, beads. The place felt as though it had collapsed under a narcotic weight, undulating prettily. She rose and played *Songs From A Room*. 'I love Leonard Cohen,' she said, snuggling into him again. 'He was sexy.'

'Was,' Charlie said.

'Even now.'

'Julie,' he said, 'he was, like, forty when you were born.'

She wriggled and said, 'Uh . . . not . . . really.'

'Seriously?' he said. 'How old *are* you?'

'Why? Difference does it make?'

'Well, for a start, Gavin's a lot younger than you . . .'

She wriggled out from his arms and stared at him. 'Gavin's *five* years younger than me.' She pulled on the joint then breathed a dragon. 'Your point?'

'I'm six years younger than *him*.'

'So what?' she said. 'So *what*? That matter?'

'Not really,' he mused, and touched her hair. 'Not really.'

The weed was making her a bit paranoid. The lines at the side of her face: a narrow fan. Her Lucy in the Sky with Diamonds eyes.

'I don't believe you sometimes, Charlie. Way to give a woman a complex. Don't you think I reckon this is weird enough between us?'

'What?' he said. 'You're not old. Not *old* old.'

'Oh, not *old* old. Just normal old?'

'Exactly,' he said. 'But everyone's normal old.'

She looked at him. Then: 'Ha!' Then: 'Ha ha ha ha ha ha. That's so true. Oh, Charlie. Yeah. Hoo. *Everyone*'s normal old. Hoo.'

Monged.

Julie took another draw, then blew upwards. It spread through the air, ornamental. 'Older women are *defeated*,' she said. 'Age feels like *defeat*.'

He considered it. 'That's rubbish. Older women have got it going on.'

'How?'

'Well,' he said, 'young women just don't *know* enough.'

'About sex?'

'About anything.'

'That's true,' Julie said.

'Age makes people smarter.'

'But slower,' said Julie, and toked on the joint.


He stroked and licked her, then they fucked. The sheets pooled around them as he moved inside her. Their kisses. Limbs. He could feel each tingling moment of it, the stonedness making her skin starry, cosmos-alive. Her fingers in the dip of his back. His cock, deep. She coaxed him further, tensed, and they came, clutching. He eased and held her and they lay wrapped around the sheets for a while. They talked, weed-animated. About singers Julie had fancied in school. Adam Ant and Tony Hadley ('*Never* Simon Le Bon'). About how much they both hated beetroot ('Stains everything on the plate!'). About terrorism. About work: the endless endless teaching endless marking endless reports endless. About who whups whose ass: the Brontës or Jane Austen ('Is it three-on-one *Kill Bill* action?'). About a play Julie had just seen at the Tron. *Marvin's Something Angry*. They talked about two divorcing film stars.

They talked about divorcing.

Julie's Married at age, Divorced at age.

Charlie's Married at age, Divorced at age.

they talked about what it felt like

'Like dying,' said Charlie.

'Like waking up,' said Julie.

Saturday morning started to fade in. Daylight. They kissed. He bent his head to her ear and whispered, 'Aye, older women aren't sexy.' Her body stretched and grinned. Her laughter lines: brilliance. They kissed. He dressed, because he had to get home to make a healthy breakfast for his mother; if he didn't, she'd just get up and make herself something fried. 'I'm really sorry,' he said. 'She doesn't keep well.' 'Don't worry about it,' Julie muttered into the pillow. 'See you on Monday. You coming to the union meeting?' 'No,' he said. 'Look, Charlie,' she said, 'we can't *avoid* Gavin, y'know?'

'I know,' he said, and stared at the duvet.

He looked for his socks. He couldn't find his socks. Fuck was it about socks? In the half-light he roamed for socks, suppressing that guilty, slinking-out feeling because, no, this was Julie. This was *Julie Carell*. This was not slinking; she was not That. And when he located a sock he fell putting it on and his head cracked against the bedpost and she gave a sleepy thumbs-up, the side of her face pressed into the pillow and smiling.

'Like waking up,' she'd said.

'Like dying.'

What is the trick to teaching a class? Tell us, maestro. Well. Now that you ask. You've just made your first mistake. You don't *teach*, my young apprentice. You simply tune them up, conduct, and a hymnal music cometh forth. Tappeth your baton. Taketh the register. Daniel McIntosh? Here, sir. Tori Walsh. Sir. Now, today we are going to think about Voices, class. Voices, sir? Yes, Daniel, the Suppressed Voices of the Working Class. Like funny voices? Daniel does Funny Voices off the Telly. Comedians, sketch-shows, catchphrases. 'Am I bovvered?

Face? Bovvered?' The class laugh. *Now*. They have opened, the tenor of their wee thoughts buzzing in the air, but you must bring them under control, and quickly. You must also do a Funny Voice off the Telly, to prove that you understand their youth-culture frame of reference, and if you succeed they will laugh and you can grasp the threads of their attention – from the air, fine, like spider-silk – draw them away from Daniel and towards you. Maestro, you have your orchestra. You have them *in*. Now you should hear the lovely sound of their listening – pitch-sharp, dog-sharp, *sir*-sharp, the edge of their attention singing – and you sharpen those notes *further*, grind them against the whetstone of your knowledge – so that by the end of the lesson they are in harmony with each other. Like *so*. (Pinch the thumb and forefinger like this, no, like *this*.) You have five minutes. A lesson is five minutes. Always five minutes. This is because after five minutes they begin to lose interest. So you move on. Control your orchestra. You are a Conductor. Hit them. Tame that tempest. *Hit* them. Hit their childish souls with your passion! For lit-er-at-ure. Make them laugh! Make them *question*. Make them Think. Think about the structures that surround them every day. Class. Sex. Race. Religion. Screw religion, my young apprentices, a religious brain is a closed brain. Your minds are not closed, what are they, class? Open, sir! Indeed, class. You are individuals. What are you? Individuals, sir! Bring them up. *Up*. Lower. Toccata and Fugue. Some kid'll fart a bassoon – Wagner? – neutralise him, cover it with a joke of your own and move on. Don't give them an opening. This ain't freeform jazz! You are the conductor. Keep it going. Te-tum te-tum te-tum.

Fuck, yeah.

When Charlie had been a trainee teacher he'd heard this talk from the headmaster of a Catholic school. A Catholic school, for godsakes, those goddamn Catholics with their stupid *stupid* guilt-then-sin-then-guilt-for-desert-based 'ethics'. What could Charlie learn from *them*? But he was giving practical advice, this guy, which the trainees wanted to hear. 'Tell us what to do when kids set fire to the desks,' one of the students asked. Everyone laughed. The headmaster smiled and leaned into the lectern. 'Listen, guys,' he'd said, 'you learn to come and go with the kids. It's not a war. Order must be maintained, certainly, you need to get the class under control. But teaching is all about love. You cannot expect to be a good teacher if you care more about discipline than love.'

Charlie had thought: Yes. Yes. *Yes*.

'Stuart Anderson, do I have a head like a peanut?'

Stuart Anderson said, 'Aye,' and it was echoed by the class. Faces flashed mirth like parakeet wings.

'What are we going to read today, class?'

'Poetry, sir!'

'And is poetry cool, class?'

'Naw, sir!'

'That is correct, class, poetry remains deeply uncool. And so it should. Because cool is the refuge of the insecure. People think in herds, my friends, and you are all unique. You make up your own minds. You must never think in a herd. This is how they will *trap* you.'

'Moo!' said one.

'Ha ha. Very good, Steven.'

Steven put horns to his head and stuck out his tongue.

Charlie said: 'Quite finished?'

'Aye, sir.'

He nodded. 'Suited you, though.'

The class laughed.

'Now, what day is it on January the twenty-fifth?' said Charlie.

'Burns Day, sir!'

'That is correct,' said Charlie. 'And what does Burns Day celebrate?'

'Robert Burns's birthday, sir!'

'And who was Robert Burns?'

'The greatest Scottish poet who ever lived,' they said, in a mass mumble.

'Exactly. Poet. Songwriter. Genius. Ladies' man. No Burns, no Leonard Cohen.'

'Leonard who, sir?'

'Ask a geek. Now you all should have memorised by now the song we're going to sing at the school Burns Supper.' He tapped an imaginary baton and held his hands in the air. 'So. When you're ready, class . . .'

The class shuffled, cleared throats bunged with embarrassment.

'"Twas on a Monday morning,
Right early in the year,
That Charlie came to our town –
The young Chevalier.'

'Chorus.'

'An' Charlie, he's my darling,
My darling, my darling;
Charlie, he's my darling –
The young Chevalier!'

'Sing up, can't hear you!'

'As he was walking up the street,
The city for to view;

36

O, there he spied a bonnie lass,
The window lookin' through.'

'Chorus!'

> 'An' Charlie, he's my darling,
> My darling, my darling;
> Charlie, he's my darling —
> The young Chevalier!'

'*No* reason why I picked this song. Next verse!'

'Sae light is he, jimped up the stair,
And tirled at the pin;
And wha sae ready as hersel',
Tae let the laddie in?'

'And!'

> 'An' Charlie, he's my darling,
> My darling, my darling;
> Charlie, he's my darling —
> The young Chevalier!'

'On your seats! Up! Stand on your seats!'

'He set his Jenny on his knee,
All in his Highland dress;
For brawlie weel he ken'd the way
To please a bonnie lass.'

37

'On the tables!'

> 'An' Charlie, he's my darling,
> My darling, my darling;
> Charlie, he's my darling –
> The young!
> Chev!
> a!
> liiieeeeeeer!'

Sunlight rang through the window. He looked at them all standing there on the desks, their faces quick and thrilled. 'Poetry!' he announced, a rallying to war, 'Scottish *poetry*, people!' The class grinned. 'With this, boys and girls, we shall overcome. We shall overthrow the tyranny of the British state! And capitalism itself!'

He stared at them, panting. He raised his sword.

'Soon, my friends. Soon, my brave soldiers. We shall crush the aristocracy, and establish the great Scottish socialist republic! On this very spot!'

The door opened, and there was Baldy Paulson, eyes hawkish, talons clinging to a folder as though fresh from a swoop.

'Everything all right in here, Mr Bain?'

'Oh, absolutely, Mr Paulson.' Charlie smiled. 'Just practising our song for the Burns Supper.'

'Ah,' said Paulson. 'That'll be what the noise was. And why it's all gone a bit *Dead Poets Society* . . ?'

'Indeed,' said Charlie. 'Projection. All to do with the diaphragm. You want them good and vocal, don't you?'

'Of course,' said Paulson, and lingered a bit before he retreated, surveying the kids. 'Well, first year, I look forward to hearing you.

Good and vocal.' Then he retreated, turning for his eyrie, to feed on raw, Charlie-tanged meat.

The door closed.

'That's *you* telt, sir,' smirked Steven.

'Art is the enterprise that stops
the mind from spinning.'

Leonard Cohen

Charlie's sister and her husband visited at tea-time, when *Countdown* was on, which was strange since Deborah never visited during the week, encumbered by the pageantry of marriage, motherhood: the changing, the feeding, the teaching of numbers and shapes, the firework tantrums, the gurgle and splash and stream-of-piss at bath-time. Deborah carried wee Elizabeth into the living-room while Jordan looked round with that Napoleonic air of his. He was a car dealer for fucksakes. A *second-hand*-car dealer.

Mum kissed Deborah and said, 'Hen!'

Jordan kissed Mum and said, 'Hi!'

Mum kissed Elizabeth and said, 'Aww!'

Deborah kissed Charlie and said, 'Charlie!'

Charlie kissed Elizabeth and said, 'Twinkles!'

Charlie and Jordan shook hands.

'Charles,' said Jordan, prolonging it.

'Jordan,' said Charlie, ending it.

'How's the teaching? Still filling the kids' heads with socialist propaganda?'

'No,' said Charlie. 'Doing the Qur'ān with them now.'

'Wouldn't surprise me,' said Jordan, draping his leather jacket over a chair, a skin fresh from the hunt. 'All that politically correct stuff in schools. Like how it's great to be a poof?'

'Maybe it *is* great to be a poof.'

Jordan crossed meaty poof-barriers.

They broke out of their foursome into tea and newspapers and polite talk. *Countdown* babbled quizzically in the background. Consonant. Vowel. Vowel. Consonant. 'So, Jordan, how's the business

43

coming along?' said Charlie's mother. Eight letters. *Largesse.* Jordan grinned and bounced Elizabeth on his knee. He toyed with her and talked to their mum about his dealership. He told a story about a young couple who'd come in, the male trying to outsmart Jordan, knock him down a couple of grand, show off in front of the girlfriend, about how Jordan had outsmarted *him* and how the guy — meekly, willingly — not only paid the going price but signed up for warranties, waxing extras, a car stereo: 'Bought the lot.'

'He's not the only one,' whispered Charlie to Deborah, gesturing to their mother.

'Very clever,' said Charlie's mum. '*Astute.*'

'Well, you know me, Linda, I'm a businessman.'

'You're running a business, Jordan.'

'It's not a charity operation.'

'Nope.'

'Gotta make a living.'

'Bills have to be paid.'

'By hook or by crook.'

'You've always provided, Jordan. You've always provided for our Deborah and the wee one.'

Deborah's eyes rolled and she looked at Charlie. Charlie grinned.

'That's a good man,' said their mother, gesturing theatrically with her wine glass, 'That's a GOOD MAN you've got there, Deborah.'

Deborah whispered to Charlie, '*Why don't they just get a room?*'

Charlie whispered: '*Cos Jordan's too busy haggling with the manager.*'

'I mean, what am I, Linda? A socialist?'

'Heaven forfend,' said Charlie.

Jordan looked at him. 'Aye, well, it's a bit easier in the public sector there, Charles, with your seven-week holidays in the summer and your two weeks off at Easter and Christmas and your guaranteed pensions. I'm out making it work for myself.'

'Working for himself,' nodded their mother, sipping.

'You'll be all right as the credit crunch hits, Charles, but joes like me?'

Joes? thought Charlie. You're not a *joe*. A *joe* fathered fucking *Jesus*.

'And I tell you, if my business goes under, I'll be straight back out there making it work for my family. You won't see me in a dole queue. Never taken a handout in my life, have I, Deborah?'

'Pish,' said Deborah. 'I make your dinner for you every night.'

'He's a worker,' said their mother. 'Least you can do, Deborah, is have a man's tea ready when he comes in.'

Charlie noticed some wine slosh out of the glass as she waved it.

'And while you're at it,' said Jordan, 'the three Rs, Charles. Apprentices coming to me, hardly even got the basics. What are you learning these kids?'

'*Teaching* these kids,' said Charlie.

'Are you?' said Jordan. 'Sometimes I wonder!'

Elizabeth bounced up and down on her father's knee like a marionette, fists gripping his big forefingers. She giggled and gurgled. 'Unca Chally!' Charlie smiled at her as he rose to go to the bathroom.

Deborah followed him out into the hall. 'Psst!' she said.

'No, I'm not. But I want to be. Your man talks some amount of shite, by the way.'

'I know. Humour him, Charlie. He only does it cos he likes you. It's just banter.'

'His kind of banter is banned in Germany,' said Charlie.

'Stop it,' she said. 'Charlie. You know him better than that. Just because he's not a socialist doesn't make him Attila the Hun.'

'Really?' he said. 'Does he still have his season ticket for Ibrox?'

'Och. Why can't the two of you just? See you bloody *boys*.'

45

'Yeah,' Charlie said, 'I should be more like Mum. *That*'d solve it. Look at her in there!' His finger flew stage-left. 'Lapping up his patter. That *pish*. Just like she used to lap up Da—'

He stopped.

Deborah folded her arms. 'Think you should leave that one right there, Charlie.'

'Well.'

'He's *not*. Okay? He is just *not*. Take it easy, bro.' She checked to see if he'd rebuke. He did not. 'Now, where did I get to? Before the bloody Alpha-male Off.'

'*Psst.*'

'Yeah,' Deborah whispered. 'Explain. *What* is Mum doing drinking wine in there?'

Flowers nearly erupted from his face. He wanted to grab Deborah and shriek: *I've tried to tell her!*

He shrugged and shuffled. 'Dunno, Debs. Dunno. Y'know.'

'You're supposed to be taking care of her.'

He looked at the end of the banister.

'I've got a family of my own, Charlie, I can't see what's going on.'

'I've got a teaching job, Debs, I can't see what's going on.'

'Is she still taking salt?'

'What? No! Well. Kind of. No.'

'Butter?'

'Not *much*.'

Deborah placed her hands on her hips and shook her head. She stared at him as though he was a disobedient kid, the same way he stared at disobedient kids. Yet he was her older brother. By four whole years. He remembered a face smeared with Marmite, her holding his hand, singing: *I wanna hold your haa-a-aand, I wanna hold your*

'I'm trusting you to be my eyes and ears, Charlie.'

He nodded. 'It's fine. She's fine. We're fine.'

Deborah seemed to roll a heavy steel thought round her mind.

'Okay,' she said.

They went back in. Their mother stared at them. She made a point of lifting the wine to her lips and taking a large drink.

Charlie cracked open a couple of cans: one for him, one for Jordan. Elizabeth pottered around the living-room, babbling something about Postman Pat or Peppa Pig or physics. Deborah and their mum watched *Countdown*. Jordan turned to him and said, 'Got a glass for this, Charles?'

'You can't drink from the can?'

Charlie gave Jordan a pint-glass and Jordan poured the lager. Then Jordan drank and gasped, 'Glass makes all the difference. Aah.' The drink flowed down over his big Adam's apple. His thick neck swivelled round to Charlie. 'So. *Charles*. Seeing any new lady friends?'

'No,' Charlie said, and scratched.

'No sexy student teachers?'

'No.'

'Must be tempted by some of them wee sixteen-year-olds in uniform?'

'Jordan,' tsked Deborah.

'What?'

'Shut yer face.'

'Having a laugh. Charles knows the score. You know the score, don't you, Charles?'

*Aye, two-nil to you, ya prick.*

Deborah frowned and bounced Elizabeth on her knee. Charlie scuttled across the floor and put his face to the baby's. 'Ooh-ooh-ooh,' he said, 'I'm the monkey.' He made a monkey-face. Elizabeth laughed. Charlie mashed his tongue and crossed his eyes and Elizabeth cackled. He tickled her belly. He picked up Elizabeth and whirled her, going,

Wheeeee! and Elizabeth gurgled and swallowed. He spun. She whined.

'Put her down,' said Deborah.

Charlie spun her some more. Elizabeth started to cry.

'Charlie,' said his mother, 'put her *down*.'

He brought her to rest on the floor. He wanted to sink into it with her, and beyond, into a kingdom of softness. 'She must have gas or something.'

'Imbecile,' said Jordan. Charlie looked at him, bristling.

'Eight letters,' said one of the contestants. '*Imbecile*.'

Jordan slurped from his glass.

Charlie had his Advanced Higher class. He rushed to it, folder under one arm, tie trailing behind him. Past the lockers, where the kids yakked and texted and slackered and Magic-Markered. But not this class: *Classic*. Three girls. One boy. Monise Ferguson: she'd read everything, was a terrific writer, so obviously bound for Oxford or Cambridge, and was a smashing girl, a cracker, so humble about everything, not an attitude. Even though she was from one of the posh families, there wasn't anything like the *attitude* you get from some of those other rich kids. He rushed past colleagues, who said, 'Morning,' and, 'Everything all right with Bryan Fisher?' 'Fine,' he said. 'He's just easily influenced by others, that's all.' Monise. Bethan. Jenny. Simon. Top of the hit parade. The Big Four. Queen Monise! Monise turned up, did the work, talked intelligently, even though she had a mighty crush on him (everyone said it, even the teaching staff, sniggers and jokes and nods and winks), and Charlie respected that, because she could have been really arrogant about things the way Simon was.

The Way Simon Was

'. . . help us understand the characters, and so pay *attention* to the characters. The, uh, *characterisation* of the, uh, characters. And that's what I think, um, sir.'

Simon stopped talking. Simon realised he'd stopped. He frowned. He blinked. He scratched arms fresh from an indie band.

'Thank you, Simon,' said Charlie. 'Bethan?'

Bethan looked up through thick, thick, thick glasses. Bethan hadn't a clue how to apprehend Chaucer, or perhaps things like orange juice or the wheel. 'Um,' said Bethan, 'I don't know what we were . . .'

'Show her, Monise.'

Monise showed Bethan whereabouts on the page they were.

Bethan swallowed and said, 'Sorry I hadn't realised that we'd been . . .'

It wasn't going well today. They were dreary. He was dreary. Drear *seeped*.

'It's fine,' smiled Charlie. 'Don't worry about it. Monise?'

Enter Monise, as though onstage, draped. She swept the hair away from her face. She blinked into theatre lights. 'Well,' she began, with an intake of breath, 'love didn't even really have a place in the Middle Ages — it was all about the acquisition of land and titles, or else child-rearing — so the idea of writing love poetry to your wife was a little, well, irrelevant. Only mistresses were the objects of that, some unattainable dream of a girl that the poet can't have. Y'know? He's prostrate before her, wounded by her beauty. The more she dismisses him, the more he wants her. One smile is reward for night after night of sweating and rolling in the sheets, thinking about her. Love is this beautiful agony for all of Chaucer's heroes.'

In his head, Charlie stood and clapped thunderously. *Bravo! Bravo!* Roses were thrown and he was turning to friends and grinning, *Wasn't she great tonight? Wasn't she just great?*

'Good, Monise,' he said. 'Anyone else?'

The catcalls came from Jenny. Throughout Monise's speech, Jenny had been shaking her head, knees drawn up to her chest, staring.

'So Chaucer doesn't believe in marriage?' said Jenny. 'How does that explain the Wife of Bath?'

'The Wife of Bath *doesn't* believe in marriage,' said Monise, meeting Jenny's gaze with a wall of intellect.

'She must do,' said Jenny. 'She's had five husbands.'

'Du-huh,' said Monise. 'Ex*act*ly.'

He could see where this was going. Jenny was the Christian in the group.

WHY DID EVERY GROUP HAVE TO HAVE A *CHRISTIAN*?

'Explain what you mean, Jenny.'

WHY DID THEY HAVE TO INFILTRATE THE FUCKING *ARTS*?

Jenny shrugged. She still had her knees up to her chin. 'Well, Chaucer believes marriage is the natural state of being between men and women, sanctioned by God.'

YOU DON'T BELONG IN HERE, AMONG ALL THESE *FREEDOMS*!

'Okay, guys,' said Charlie. He turned to Bethan and Simon. 'What do you think? Is the Wife of Bath advocating marriage or promiscuity?'

'Both?' said Bethan.

Bethan always quivered with question-marks, uncertain.

'Go on.'

'It's, like, Chaucer seems to be in favour of marriage? Just as long as the husband is, like, the wife's servant?'

Charlie snorted.

They all looked at him.

'Good point, Bethan,' he added.

'She's right, though,' said Monise. 'Listen to this.' She scanned the page, an advocate, slick and professional, appealing to the court: 'But wel I woot, expres, withoute lye,/God bad us for to wexe and multiplye;/The gentil text kan I wel understonde./Eek wel I woot, he seyde, myn housbonde/Sholde lete fader and mooder and take me;/But of no nombre mencion made he,/Of bigamye or octogamye;/Why sholde men speke of it vileynye?'

Jenny rolled her eyes.

Simon made a quiz-show-host face. 'Ladies and gentleman . . . Monise Ferguson!' He did quick applause. 'Translate, Fergie, translate.'

*Fergie?*

'What it *means*, Simon,' said Jenny, tutting, 'is that a husband is under God's command to leave his parents and take a wife, since God instructed us to go forth and multiply.'

'Be a bunch of slappers,' said Simon. 'Cool.'

'Yeah,' said Jenny, 'But *within the confines of marriage*.'

'Not quite, Jenny,' said Charlie. 'You're only looking at part of the quotation. The Wife of Bath is careful to specify that there's no limit to the number of husbands you can take over a lifetime. So she *is* advocating multiple lovers. Just in a way that she believes God will recognise.'

'That's my point.' Jenny shrugged. 'Marriage is still sacred to her. Because it's sacred to *God*.'

OH, GO AWAY AND PERSECUTE SOMETHING, WHY DON'T YOU!

'Man, that Wife of Bath,' Simon snickered, 'I'd *so* do her. She rocks.' Simon did the devil-horns sign.

'And?' said Bethan. 'She thinks wives who can't master their husbands are pathetic. So she's kind of a feminist?'

Yes, thought Charlie. Thunderbirds are *go*!

Jenny tsked. 'More like an *adulteress* who doesn't live up to the ideals of marriage.'

'Oh, come *on*,' said Monise. 'Enough.'

Jenny placed her hands on top of her head. Monise glanced at him, as though for back-up.

'Actually,' said Charlie, 'Jenny may have a point here. Queen Anne of Bohemia was so offended by Chaucer's poem "Troilus and Criseyde" and its implication that women were more faithless than men that he had to publish a retraction.'

'There you *go*,' said Jenny. 'The Wife of Bath is an adulterous, deceptive, manipulative, greedy control-freak. Hardly a positive portrait of the woman.'

'Or of marriage . . .' Monise muttered, unusually cowed. She'd taken a hit, and Charlie felt strangely disloyal now, gifting Jenny this opening. Then Monise coughed and closed the book, and her eyes. 'Of tribulacion in mariage,/Of which I am expert in al myn age –/ . . . Be war of it, er thou too ny approche.'

Jenny started flicking through for counter-quotes.

'So she's saying beware of marriage?' Charlie said. 'As an expert herself? But does that make her a feminist? Bethan?'

'Uh,' said Bethan, 'we can't really . . . judge it like that? It's a six-hundred-year-old poem. And it's only showing what they would have thought in that *time*, in Chaucer's *time*?'

The gulf. Bethan peering at the hieroglyphics of Jenny and Monise's dialogue – their Big Civilised Thoughts – running her fingers over it, trying to decipher it, while exam-sand filled the chamber, poised to swamp her.

'The Wife of *Bad-ass*,' grinned Simon, who, Charlie reckoned, could see the same weird hieroglyphics that Bethan saw, but just whistled 'Walk Like An Egyptian' and considered himself on-topic.

'Anyway,' said Monise, 'she's doesn't *need* a husband. She's a strong, sexually confident woman.'

'So is it sexist or not?' said Simon. 'Just tell me if it's all right to dig this chick!'

The girls laughed.

'Simon,' said Charlie. 'Please.'

'Sorry, Mr Bain.'

'Depends what we mean by sexist,' said Monise.

'Good,' said Charlie, trying to bring it back. '*Good*.'

'What do you mean, though, "Depends what we mean by sexist"?' Simon sat back, chuckling. 'What do *you* mean by sexist, *Ferg*uson?'

Monise made a comedy scowl at him.

The unsure way they used these terms – sexist, racist, homophobic – bits of adult culture they'd found, picked up, feeling the heft and blade and danger. But in time they'd wield them with dexterity. There'd be essays, theses, whip-smart as rapiers. They would march from the universities into the cities, overthrow the dull dull suits and greed and create an *Arts Scene*, be whole, dreaming people raised on the ideals of humanity.

And they would save the world.

Or that was the idea.

'Um,' Bethan said.

'My *cherie* amour,' Simon sang, clicking fingers.

'Come on, guys,' Charlie said, 'don't lose it.'

'Ba ba BA ba ba ba . . .'

'She's got a gap between her teeth,' said Jenny, seizing a line: '"Gat-toothed I was, and that bicam me weel/I had de prente of Seinte Venus' seel."' Isn't that code for being a *slut*?'

Her gaze slammed straight into Monise's.

The word *slut* reverberated in the collision.

Bethan chewed her pen. Silence.

'Hey, you two, does any of this matter?' said Simon. '"Is the Wife of Bath a Slut?" Hardly an exam topic, is it?'

'So?' said Jenny.

'So...' said Simon '... why do we need to worry about it?'

Charlie looked at him: his skinniness and fizziness and music-mag hair. His boyful buoyancy. But there were parents at home with arms folded, *locked* – he's the arty one, okay, that's great, Mr Bain. Our child is a romantic. We get that. But We Want The Best For Him And Have Entrusted Him To You AND WHERE THE FUCK IS POETRY GOING TO GET HIM EXACTLY?!!! *Cough.* 'Scuse my husband, Mr Bain. It's only because he *cares* so for our son, you understand that, don't you? Are you married, Mr Bain? Do you have children of your own? What's that? Div—? Divor—?

Oh. I'm sorry.

There's no need to be. It was a mutual allforthebest fucking amicable justoneofthosebloodythings, you see.

Uh. Of course.

'Mr Bain?' said Simon.

Charlie looked at him.

Charlie looked at the exam hovering phantomly in Simon's future, shaking its parchment of Predicted Grades. Beyond: a ceremony; a graduate afterlife; a resigned just-gimme-the-fucking-money-now Purgatory.

'Okay then,' sighed Charlie. 'Let's move on, shall we? Simon has decided. The Knight is due for some attention at this stage, so let's meet him. Please read his character introduction in the General Prologue, Monise. Line forty-three.'

Monise turned pages, ran her finger down then started to read, pronouncing the Middle English correctly, *superbly*, as the daylight churned with tiny motes of dust, with the dead hair and skin of pupils and teachers long gone:

> A KNYGHT ther was, and that a worthy man,
>    That fro the tyme that he first bigan
>       To riden out, he loved chivalrie,
>    Trouthe and honour, fredom and curteisie.
>    Ful worthy was he in his lordes werre,
> And thereto hadde he ridden, no man ferre,
>    As wel in cristendom as in hethenesse,
>    And evere honoured for his worthynesse

Charlie sat back and closed his eyes, listening to Monise read in this clean, clear voice. He was on a horse, riding towards Canterbury, back straight, armour jangling, shield before him, and Monise atop the horse next to him, reading in her sweet, crisp, posh Scottish accent, and up ahead the hills were old with thunder and the valley rippled with green — he raised his sword! He galloped!

When he opened his eyes again Simon was staring at him.

And Jenny was staring at Monise.

And Bethan was just staring.

At the end of the class Charlie stooped over his papers, felt weighed-down and dense as a fog of argon. The desks were in lines. For little people. He was too big for them. Too *Gulliver*. Heavy and adult and flailing at wires. He sighed, fulminating into thin air. Something had gone wrong with the lesson, but he didn't know what. The more he sat there pondering it, the more he became shrouded in clouds of thought, so he took out his phone to text a girl, slice through it with the trusty, hard edge of sex.

Helen?Eleanor?Corrine? Text text. When you touched my cock with your. Message has been sent. *You still exist.* He stared at his phone, drooped and insubstantial and sad for a few moments until — blink! — a figure materialised: Gavin's skinny frame dangling in the doorway.

'Gavin,' said Charlie.

'Charlie,' said Gavin.

They stood. Gavin held a folder across his chest. Eventually Charlie said, 'Hear Baldy Paulson's assembly this morning?'

Gavin grinned. 'The knob.'

'Thought I was dreaming,' Charlie said. 'Did he actually say the words *Thou shalt not*? Referring to problems in the *bus* queue?'

'Religious nutcase.'

'It's bollocks.'

'Knob-head.'

'Twat!'

Baldy Paulson, Headmaster of Disaster, had united them in a high-five and soon there was water-cooler action and bitching about Baldy Paulson and *dumb-ass* union reps and *toss-pot* chemistry teachers, and there was *Hey see that game last night*ing and Charlie wondered if he should crack a beer, a joke or a fart, until Gavin said, 'So you coming to the union meeting? Crucial vote.' And Charlie said, 'I dunno about strikes, man. They're so unfair to the kids.' And Gavin thinned his lips. And Charlie said, 'They've got their exams coming up, remember.'

And Gavin said:

'Still on the right side, Charlie?'

And Charlie said:

'I'm still on the left, if that's what you mean.'

And Gavin said:

'But you're not voting for the strike?'

And Charlie said:

'Different kinds of socialism, dude.'

'What's your kind?' said Gavin. 'One that's not social?'

'No,' said Charlie. 'One that's not an *ism*.'

They fell silent, and Gavin put his hands into his pockets and stepped around the floor a little bit. Then he looked up at Charlie. 'Big night out on Friday?' he said.

'Yeah,' Charlie said. '*Yeah.*'

'Good time had by all?'

Charlie made Tourette's sounds: yups, *fucks*, whistles.

'Should've texted me.' Gavin stood there, napkin tucked in, poised to carve into juicy detail. Charlie felt edible. Uncomfortable. 'I need to get back out there, in the field. Now that . . . y'know . . . Julie's . . .'

Charlie waited, but Gavin didn't finish the sentence, so he said, 'I asked but you said you weren't in the mood.'

'Did I say that? I wonder why. Maybe I was pissed off.'

'About what?'

Gavin placed his triangular chin in his hand, stroked it. Shrugged. 'Good night, though?'

'Grand.'

'Score?'

'Nah, was with a girl.'

'Anyone I know?'

'Her you met at my party that time? Old school pal of mine?'

'Nadine?'

'Yeah.'

'Artist? Everything's "retro" or "so cute"?'

'That's her.'

Gavin drew in air between his teeth. 'Niiiiice. Shagging her?'

'Naw,' Charlie said. 'It's not like that. Known her since we were wee. She's just a mate, y'know?'

'Right. Sure.'

Charlie narrowed his eyes.

Gavin sat on one of the kids' desks and crossed his legs. His knee pointed out like the eraser on the end of a pencil. 'I mean, I didn't think you *did* female pals, Charlie. Seeing as you're such a ladies' man. That Nadine's hot.'

'She's. All right.'

Gavin placed hands behind his head. 'She's all *right*? The last of the great Romantics! Where's that famous spirit of beauty that dost consecrate?'

Every fucking time.

'Um,' said Charlie. 'Byron?'

'Shelley.'

'Shelley,' said Charlie. '"She walks in beauty, like the night/Of cloudless climes and starry skies."'

Gavin sucked air through his teeth. 'That's Byron.'

'Aw, so it is.'

Poetry chess. Knight to A6.

'Byron,' said Gavin. 'Fact: he wanted only one word on his gravestone.'

'And what was that?'

'*BYRON.*'

'Wow,' said Charlie, etching a word onto Gavin's that wasn't *GAVIN*.

'Speaking of beauty, see Julie when you were out?'

'Our Julie?'

'Well,' said Gavin, light flashing off his specs, 'she's not *my* Julie. Not any more. But yes,' he said. '*Her.*'

He said *Her* as though coughing up a hair-ball.

'No,' said Charlie. 'Didn't even know she was out.'

'Well,' said Gavin, took off his glasses, cleaned them, returned them to his face, 'I think she's seeing someone else.'

*stag*

*g   er in*

　　　　　*in g*

　　　*g*

　*ing*

　*with Yvonne,*

*staggering back　　　to her Hall of Residence, leaning booz　　ily into each other, and you both spot an urban fox prowling the bins of the campus – sleek and pristine in the moonlight.*

　*Scavenging.*

　*You'd met her that day, during your Shakespeare and Theory class. The lecturer tapping a screen.* A Midsummer Night's Dream. *The theatre intimidatingly large, full with learning bodies: row upon row upon impressionable row, intellects bristling like spears. The clean pure thrum of education. 'Shakespeare's Comedies' onscreen. 'This play is structured as a world within a world within a world,' the professor says. 'It deconstructs itself.' The next ten minutes are an aerial barrage of big words, landing like cluster bombs – structuralismBOOMpost-structuralismKA-THOOMpostmodernismBLAMdeconstructionBOOM – before someone touches your arm and you turn and she whispers, 'Do you understand this?'*

　*'What?' you say. 'Yeah. Of course. Don't you?'*

　*'No. Fuck is he talking about?'*

　*You take this in: good-looking. Good-looking and asking for help. For your help. You are a stranger witnessing a domestic on a train, a bus driver hearing screams from the back on the night shift. You are wearing a cape.*

　*BLAM!*

　*KA-THOOM!*

　*'Well, post-structuralism is what came after, uh, structuralism. Obviously.'*

　*'And what about Postmodernism?'*

59

'That came after Modernism.'

'Modernism. That's, like, stuff that's just been released?'

'Uh, no. It's stuff that came out mainly in the 1920s.'

'That's not very modern.'

'I suppose that's why they had to invent Postmodernism. Cos Modernism wasn't modern enough any more.'

'This is complicated.' She expels a troubled breath. 'I'm going to fail this, I know it.'

'You've read the play?'

'Not exactly.'

'No wonder you don't understand it, then!'

'Tell me the plot.'

'The entire plot?'

'The edited highlights. The York Notes. The Greatest Hits.'

'Now?'

'Yeah.'

She has a full-cheeked, pleading face, like a toy left behind in the removal van. You glance at the professor. The room still and poised and listening to him. Your whisper feels loud as artillery but it's a straight choice at that point between Shakespeare – his world within a world within a yaaaawn – and this girl who looks as if she'd be brilliant with a whisky. Something about her eyes. Something about her eyes, here, cutting through this overgrown, pretentious thicket of words and theory, lost in it. She is extending a hand.

'It's pretty complicated,' you say.

'What isn't?'

'Okay,' you sigh. 'Theseus, the Duke of Athens, is preparing for his marriage to Hippolyta. This courtier tries to get his daughter, Hermia, to agree to his choice of Demetrius as a husband, but she loves Lysander. The Duke tells Hermia to obey her father, or else accept a life as a nun. Lysander and Hermia plan to elope, so they tell

Helena, who is in love with Demetrius, but he hates her and loves Hermia.'

'I thought it was about fairies!'

'It is. The lovers run away from Athens but get lost in the woods.'

'Where they meet fairies?'

'And rude mechanicals rehearsing a play.'

'There's rude stuff in it? If I'd known that, I would've read it.'

'And someone gets turned into a donkey.'

'Rude stuff with a donkey!'

'Excuse me?' says the professor.

You both sit up straight.

'This isn't Burger King. If you want to chat each other up, do it on your own time.'

The room looks around at the two of you. A tide of eyes. The girl waves at everyone. 'Hi,' she says.

Yvonne.

Yvonne, she's called. Afterwards, when you're trotting from the lecture theatre and she's saying, 'Man, we got soooo busted,' and you're agreeing, shyly, you're thrilled by the proximity of her. You're waiting for her to say, 'Okay, well, thanks for the help,' and, like Nadine, skip off to lunch with some trendy new uni-pals, who have found just, like, the cutest vintage clothes shop. But she doesn't. She walks alongside you, hands behind her back, and you're forced to grope in your pockets for the loose change of conversation. 'Um,' you say, 'so. Not into Shakespeare?'

'Nah,' she says.

'Milton? Blake?'

'Douglas Adams,' she says.

'The Hitchhiker's Guide to the Galaxy?'

'Him. And Terry Pratchett.'

'Um, Yvonne?' you say. 'Are you sure English lit is the subject for you?'

'Hey! There's more to Douglas Adams than you think. He's looking at the complexity of the universe, and, like, chaos theory. 'N' shit.'

'Uh-huh,' you say.

'And, like, the origins of life on earth and, uh, forces behind the course of history. 'N' shit.'

''N' shit.'

'Think I can convince them of it?'

'I'm sure you can charm anyone.'

She smiles, and looks at you. Then your cheeks start to burn and you look away.

Attention?

Actual attention?

From a girl?

ATTEN . . . SHUN!

You've grown used to being the perpetual friend. 'You're such a nice guy.' 'You're such a nice guy.' 'You're not like all those other guys.' 'Let me guess — I'm a nice guy?' 'You are!' Nice, nice, nice, like a nice bow or a nice treat or a nice cheese. Every one of Nadine's friends at school politely knocked you back (an ability to pick yourself up, dust yourself off, and ask all over again) and though you'd hoped that Glasgow Uni would be the Great Reinvention, all through first year there was no sign. There was no Nadine either, since she'd twirled off to the art school with all of its myriad bourgeois charms. At the end of each Friday night after the Queen Margaret Union, huddled with twelve strangers in a stranger's room, you were regarded sweetly, with serene, trusting eyes. You were pecked and ruffled, passed round, patted, tickled under the chin, the baby at a baby-shower. You were asked for 'advice' on 'guys'. And yet here is this girl, this giggling, glinting slip of a thing — herself Puck-like — and she is saying, 'Families are so fragmented these days, I don't think it's a bad thing for people to be close to their parents,' and you say, 'Parent. It's just my mum,' and she says, 'Oh, uh, right, I didn't

*mean, uh,' and you catch her looking at you with little flecks of*
*curiosity, trying to work*
*out*

    *who*

        *you*

            *are*

                *Dad once gave you advice on women. Oh, the irony. Make*
*them laugh. Be able to dance. Women love men who can make them*
*laugh and can dance. Never get drunk in front of her. You imagined*
*your father and mother out on some perfect date, dressed up dapper like*
*in the 1950s: he's holding doors open and laying his jacket over puddles,*
*dancing a tango while whispering witticisms.*

    *Aye, right, Dad.*

    *ya fuckin*

    *More: when escorting a lady (he actually used the word 'lady',*
*wiping oil from the car he'd tried to get his bookish son to work on with*
*him in an attempt to 'bond'), walk on the side closest to the road. You*
*remember this one. Walk on the side closest to the road. So when you*
*walk with Yvonne you're on the side closest to the road. You've no idea*
*why you're supposed to do this, but it makes you feel gentlemanly,*
*upstanding. Walk on the side closest to the road.*

    *A week later you and Yvonne make love in her dorm room. Among*
*her Garfield books and* Lord of the Rings *posters and Terry Pratchetts*
*and Douglas Adamses.* Life, The Universe and Everything. *It is your*
*first time. It is fumbling and artless. You even laugh – though you*
*shouldn't, you definitely shouldn't – when she pauses to mimic the guitar*
*solo that comes on the radio. The sex is useless. Hilarious.*

    *'What?' she says. 'It's a great guitar solo.'*

    *'It is,' you agree. 'It really is.'*

    *Afterwards, she admits that she too had been a virg v ir    vir*

                             *i    rg    rg*

*rg in    n   ir*

         *i     r n*

    *v*

       *i*

'You're seeing a woman who's over *forty*?' said Nadine, leaning against the escalator rail, hands locked on hips, bags either side, black coat buttoned up, red beret angled like *so*. Leaning there, she looked part of the shopping centre itself, smoothly ascending, foot tapping the rhythm of flattening steps, shp shp shp. She pronounced the syllables 'for-ty' as though they were separate components of machine-code. She slid her dark glasses down her nose and said, '*Well?*'

'I am,' Charlie said. 'So?'

'Doesn't she *smell*?'

'Tsk. Nadine, I expected better of you. You might not like people talking that way when you're forty.'

'I'll never *be* forty.' She raised her nose in the air.

'Or fifty, or sixty, or seventy . . .'

'Not listening!'

'You've got her all wrong,' he said, as they skip-stepped off the escalator. 'She smokes more weed than anyone I've ever seen. Great taste in music. Experimental in bed. She's cool.'

'She'd have to be *very* cool to *remotely* still have *anything* over forty. Despite her disgusting habit.'

'More disgusting than coke?'

'Coke is the drug of the young and the exciting. Weed is the drug of the fucked and feckless. Let me guess. Hippie music?'

'Yep.'

'Neil Young. Nick Drake. Joni Mitchell.'

'Yep.'

'I *hate* Joni Mitchell. So drippy.'

'What? Just because you can't dance to it?'

'You can't dance to *anything* when you're stoned, Charlie. What does this creature do for a living? Besides vegetate?'

'She's a colleague.'

Nadine stopped with a suddenness that made the eyes of a security-guard flicker.

'My GOD, Charlie, you're shagging a *teacher*?'

'Yeah. So?'

'*Soooo*. You're committing the cardinal sin. *Never* people you work with. Next you're going to tell me she's married. Or, worse, *divorced*.'

Charlie's jaw shifted.

'Ooh,' said Nadine. 'Sorry.'

Charlie narrowed his eyes. Then he carefully said, 'Speaking of cardinal *sins*. Why are you wearing shades indoors?'

Nadine raised her hands in an *I-ask-you*.

'Don't you understand,' she said, 'that when *famous* people do it, it's *fine*?'

'But you're not famous.'

She tilted her head at him. 'Charlie. Only thinking "I'm not famous" makes you not famous.'

'You're so Audrey Hepburn.'

'Really? I was going for Lennon. Anyway. Back to the succubus.'

'Nadine,' he said, 'stop that. I quite like her.'

'You like *everyone*,' she said. 'That's why it's so easy for you to fuck them.'

'And you like no one,' he said. 'That's why it's so easy for *you* to fuck them.'

Nadine took off her shades. When she spoke it was with a Stasi officer's insistence. 'Careful, Charlie. You just rethink some of that shit right there.'

'I didn't mean . . .' he said.

She stared at him for a bit – the tiny veins her shades were hiding – before pushing the black wall up her nose, obscuring her gaze again.

She stood straight ahead. Her face: sculpture.

Neither of them spoke, until she said, 'I'm not some kind of slapper, Charlie.'

'I know,' he said. 'I'm sorry.'

'Okay.'

'Primark?'

'Primark.'

'Now you shall become my most *fabulous* creation.'

They quick-stepped.

Shopping never used to make any sense to Charlie, seemed as alien and frivolous a thing as kids dressing up. It was functional, not recreational. You needed a shirt, you bought a shirt. A cash exchange took place for which you were given a receipt. There was no *pleasure* in it. A shopping-centre felt cavernous in its cleanliness, like a shiny, steel-and-glass Mordor, himself a tiny Frodo venturing in. It was the rib-cage of capitalism – girdered with steel – where the fat thump of a black heart was concealed by chatter, chart music and the beautiful yawns of shop assistants. It all made him feel sick.

But this was before he went shopping with Nadine.

Not long after his divorce, he'd met up with her and sad-sacked. Over coffee, damp and weak, he'd split himself open: spilled to Nadine the tale of him and Yvonne, the marrying young and, suddenly, the gradual decline, the tears and fights, divorce – screeeeeech! Crashtinkle – the dazed, wounded walk away. There was a great deal to tell. Yvonne, having viewed Nadine as a threat from the start (she saw threats, she saw plots and, as it later transpired, was right to), had shut the friendship down. His boat was carried one way, Nadine's another, and soon there was an ocean between them. He sat with Yvonne for years in the Good Ship *Matrimony*, drifting, drifting, rations dwindling and the band winding down, until that cold bright morning he'd awoken to find Yvonne had leaped into the sea rather than face another day with him. The tide had swallowed all traces of her, had forced him to scan the horizon of his life for old friends, for bobbing bottles, for signs scattered across his vast and empty life.

Who did he have now?

Where should he go now?

What. The. Fuck.

So he'd phoned Nadine, out of the blue, his hello awkward and gangly as a teen's. She'd sounded surprised to hear from him, not quite welcoming, jettisoned as best friend once love had come slinking by. Charlie. Um. Hi. Nadine. How's it? Um. But the friendship was slowly punted from the shore it had been docked against. Nadine's stories. Oh, Charlie, I was on this date last week and we! Then when he returned from the bathroom he! But I couldn't touch his! It wouldn't zip open cos it was! And he was laughing, and she was laughing, then he told her all about Yvonne and they were not laughing.

She agreed to see him immediately.

Over coffee next day, Nadine had listened ('Oh, Charlie,' she kept saying, 'oh, Charlie') and after only a few minutes it felt as though they were back at school, and he was round at her house – the smell of her mum's burned dinner drifting – and they were sitting cross-legged on her bed and he was telling her about Eleanor Cameron and what he'd overheard her saying about him in the bus queue ('Charlie Bain's gay, I'm sure he is') and Nadine would only pause to get up and change the CD – Idlewild, Mogwai or Arab Strap – and come back and say, 'Okay, continue. What else did Lady Fuckface say?' Then when he'd finished she'd pick the bits of him up and stuff them into back into his skin. 'You've got to stop being so *nice*, Charlie,' she'd advised him at school. 'Girls don't *want* nice.' And he'd said, 'I don't understand. Why not? Nice is *nice*,' and Nadine would growl and go dreamy and say, 'But there's just something about a *bad boy*,' and then they'd watch *Dawson's Creek*, lying on Nadine's bed, still in their school clothes, and talk about the difference between bad boys and nice guys.

because Charlie didn't want to go back to his mum and dad's the Fuckoffyouyersuspiciousfuckingmindthat'swhat'stheproblemnever mindthefactthat

Now there he was with Nadine again, in their mid-twenties, fully paid up members of the professional class, drinking coffee in a trendy West End coffee bar (a place that was just close-but-not-quite pretentious enough for a socialist like him to hate) and he was telling her not about what someone had muttered in the bus queue but about his divorce.

A divorce, by Christ. He was a fucking divorcee.

At twenty-six!

Oh, Jesus, Nadine, he'd said. Oh Jesus fucking Christ.

Twenty-six.

Nadine's eyes, sympathetic and liquid while he told her about him and Yvonne, snapped with decision when he'd finished. She'd paid for the coffees and marched him to the Buchanan Galleries, into Gap and TK Maxx and River Island – 'Baby steps first, baby.' He'd whined like a kid forced into school shoes, while Nadine's heels clicked dictatorially and she said, 'Retail therapy, Charlie, my boy. We're going to make a whole new you from this mess.' It was talk from a chick-lit novel. The wounded twentysomething. The frothy best friend wielding her Day of Fun like a weapon, bullet-pointed with Chardonnay stops and waiter-flirting. Fucking retail therapy?

Consumerism was not therapy! It was the absence of therapy! It was a filling of the void with sweetie wrappers!

The first time, she'd discovered him slumped in a corner of H&M, pressing his head against his fist and saying, 'Twenty-six. I mean, *twenty-six.*'

The second time, he'd schlepped and sighed and shrugged through the racks, through safe denims and dad shirts, and she said, 'Fucksakes, Charlie!'

But they'd found a jacket in Top Man. Really sharp one too.

The third time he'd actually heard himself saying, 'Can we go back and look at that thing in Watermelon? That had, like, the cool motif on the shoulders?'

It was as gradual as coastal erosion, but once begun seemed inevitable, pre-ordained. He tried on a jacket in Urban Outfitters, felt its strange mass and shape around him, while Nadine scuttled off, hunting, only to return with fresh miracles draped over her arm. She stood there while he hmmed and emmed – her eyes sipping at him. 'It's not the right cut for you.' 'The medium, try the medium.' Then she stopped some shop assistant, drifting on an air-cushion of boredom, and said, 'What do you think of this?' The guy had paused, frowned, but before he could reply Nadine said, 'I'd like to see it on *you*,' and the guy's eyes had sparked like flint and Charlie had willed Nadine not to say, *But I'd prefer to take it* off *you*. He stood, arms outstretched, doll-like and prissy, while Nadine flirted with the shop assistant. Charlie looked round to see if there was a passing female member of staff – match Nadine's ante – but in these clothes was a crustacean stepping awkwardly on the sea-floor. So he had to endure it, staring at his reflection, willing change, while the guy's lame chat pattered on his brain.

'Quite finished?' he said, once the guy had gone.

'No, actually,' she said, and lifted an eyebrow. Then she shook her

69

head, dislodging pantomime-filth images, and focused on Charlie.
'You know,' she said, 'I think I preferred the yellow.'

'The yellow?' he said. 'What's wrong with the dark blue?'

'Dark blue is too male.'

'Too male?' He laughed. 'Why don't I just go for pink?'

Something clicked in Nadine's gaze. 'Got it.'

'What?'

'Put those down,' she said. 'C'mere.' She took him by the hand and
led him to the escalator.

'It's women's clothing up here, Nadine.'

She faced him from the step above, hands on either rail, a Primark
priestess.

'Wait,' he said. 'No.'

'Trust me!'

'Nadine . . .'

'It's an adventure. You're an Indiana Jones fan, Charlie, you like
adventure.'

'Not ones that end with me being taken up the arse.'

She tutted. 'You've a lot to learn. Do you understand how sexy a
straight guy is who's confident about his own sexuality? So much so
that he can pull off women's clothes?'

'I can certainly do that. Just not from *me*.'

Nadine skipped from the escalator and plunged into a jungle of
clothing, a native leading a dazed colonialist: Here Be *simply
delightful* Tigers. The day whirled by thereafter, a tropical storm of
fabrics. 'Look,' Nadine would announce, holding some artful little
number. 'Isn't that cute?'

'They just fit better than men's jackets,' he found himself
muttering. 'They taper at the waist and flare at the hips.'

'Figure-hugging,' Nadine concurred. 'How do you feel?'

'Like David fucking Bowie!'

'Something for the lady with everything,' she'd said, proffering new treasures, and while he posed and preened, she'd winked, 'Girl . . . you'll be a woman soon . . .'

'Check me out!' Charlie trilled. 'Don't I look *ace*?'

'Sharp as Jack the Ripper.'

'Oh, yes,' he'd said, and his reflection smiled. '*Yes*.'

What it brought back was the fact of his body: that it existed, physical and unadorned. Without doing something *to* it, he could do nothing *with* it. His body was a canvas, across which he could paint himself, his wild desires. For Nadine, he realised, shopping was not passive consumption – the pull of the tractor-beam from lumbering retail giants – but creative. There was an aesthetic in checking colour, fit and style with body shape, skin, eyes, hair, a quicksilver thrill in finding the combination, as all elements fell into place with the brush-stroke of a tossed scarf.

He felt like art.

Previously he'd step into a clothes shop and be filled with socialist disgust, see the chain of exploitation like an X-ray: the shop assistants on miserable-an-hour, the Third World sweatshop labour, the insecurity spell it cast upon *Heat*-mag-racked women, all of it ugly and illusory. Now he stood back and saw what Nadine saw: the opportunity to remake himself. What was wrong with dressing up? It was play. It was fun. It was fuck it.

Soon he even began to see a different Glasgow, a hidden treasure-map of vintage clothes shops – their myriad *ta-dah* moments – and boho-chic watering-holes where bands and film-makers and art-school grads clicked nails against tables and planned a velvet uprising. Watermelon. Mr Ben's. Starry Starry Night. Beneath hard-man Glasgow lurked beauty: an androgynous torch-singer waiting to be born. She would save the city. She would get the bastard dancing.

She would *seduce*.

It was surprising for a socialist to learn that there were different kinds of revolution.

He stood before Nadine in this: a woman's leather jacket, a woman's pink shirt with roll-up sleeves. A flat cap. Skinny jeans and Converse All-Stars. He was slink. He was panther. He was Charlie and Charlene. He was making his own cock hard.

Nadine surveyed her canvas, thrilled. 'Know all you need now?'

'What?'

'Eyeliner.'

'Piss off.'

'You've trusted me this far, and look at you.'

'Nadine, are you sure this is me?'

She'd placed her hands on his shoulders, stared into his eyes. 'You have no idea what you're about to become. By the time I've finished, believe me, Yvonne won't even recognise you.'

'Okay,' he'd said, unable to imagine anything worse than Yvonne not recognising him.

Often now, after school, Julie drove him to her flat and cooked dinner – steak or chicken – the table set with candles. Leonard Cohen singing with that sepia voice of his. Julie had large house-plants that reached the ceiling. A teacher's house. Tea in the colonies. Why, *thenk* you. Veh decent of you, eld chep.

Beyond, Glasgow howled.

She poured them wine, twisting the bottle at the end so that it didn't drip. Silence, ticking purely. He watched her pour. 'Ever been a waitress?'

'I *have* actually,' she said. Then, after a few seconds, 'Want me to be one again?'

'Hmmm . . .' he said, lingering on the image.

'I could get your order wrong. You could bring me into line.'

'I could put you over my knee and spank you.'

'Make me suck your cock?'

'Yeah.'

She grinned. Then she cut her food, mused, and said, 'I'm too old to be a waitress.'

'Julie,' he said, 'hardly matters if it's role play.'

'But it does, doesn't it,' she said, 'if you've got, like, some fat forty-one-year-old woman pretending to be a sexy wee young thing? I mean, who's going to believe it?'

'But it's not about that,' he said. 'It's about the fantasy. It's about losing yourself in . . . pretend.'

'You shouldn't have to *pretend* to be sexy,' she said. 'You either feel it or you don't.'

'Yeah,' he said, 'but, Julie, good sex is this little sphere where you remove yourselves from the world. When you take off your clothes and your job and your responsibilities and your kids' demands and the economy and the fucking Iraq war and all that crap. You just. *Indulge.*'

'You make it sound like eating chocolate.'

'Eating chocolate is *sexy*,' he said.

Julie's eyes flash-narrowed. 'Oooooh,' she said. 'We've got some for dessert too. Chocolate cheesecake.'

He groaned and clawed the table.

'Do you, Charlie?' she said.

'What?'

'Feel sexy? In your life, I mean.'

He stopped. Julie was looking over her glass at him, fingers cradling the stem.

'I don't suppose it's something I've ever stopped to think about,' he said, 'but since you ask, then yes. I do.'

'Well,' she said, '*quel surprise.*' Her eyebrow was mock harsh.

'But I think everyone is sexy,' he said, 'or has the potential to be. They just don't get the chance to *realise* it very often.'

Julie shook her head. 'You're such a smooth talker. Where do you *get* this stuff?'

'It's true, though,' he said. 'It's when someone's turned on that they're most completely themselves. When there is absolutely nothing else to think about. What age or class or even *sex* you are doesn't matter. When two people want to fuck there is literally nothing between them but that. They stand before each other completely naked in every way. And I think that's quite beautiful.'

Julie clapped tinnily. 'Wow,' she said, 'the voice of youth.'

'I don't know if I still count as youth,' he said, 'at thirty.'

'Younger than me.'

'You, Julie Carell, are utterly sexy.'

'Thank you,' she said. Then she touched her mouth with her napkin and smiled.

After a while he said, 'Think Gavin knows?'

Her eyes did a flick away.

'You're not worried?' said Charlie.

'A little,' she said.

'How did things end? Between you and Gavin.'

She looked down. Her voice dropped, and in the candlelight she seemed tired again, probed and prodded by the school day again. He'd broken the spell. Damn. 'Charlie,' she said, 'I only went out with him for five months.'

'Six.'

'Five. Six. Does it make a difference? We weren't married.'

'I know. But I think he saw it as something more than you did.'

'Look,' she said, 'I know you're friends. And we all have to work together. This is a bit tricky for everyone. Gavin's fine. He said he'd be okay about seeing me with someone else.'

'But he didn't know it'd be me.'

'Well, I *prefer* you. End of story. He has no claim. I'm nobody's *possession*. I don't like this. I was married once to a possessive man. Used to hate other men even talking to me. I don't owe anything to Gavin. Or you.'

'Okay, Julie, but I'm just saying. He really likes you.'

'Really "likes" me?' she said, and placed her fork down too heavily. 'What is this – school?'

Charlie paused. 'Yes.'

She shook her head and gulped her drink. They ate for a few seconds. The clashing of cutlery. Candlelight.

'Come back to me,' he said.

She stared at the table. He took her hand.

Her eyebrows flickered. Then she focused. The clouds passed from in front of her face. The eyes of older women – deep and sharp with experience. They were urban foxes. Decades of Glasgow life, hunted through relationships, hunting through the detritus of the singles scene: there in her eyes. And here she was now, forty-one and *just not standing for it any more.* He remembered first seeing her. At a union meeting, a borrowed maths classroom attentive with bodies. Gavin warning them about new government policy – he was *always* warning them about new government policy – and heads were nodding and hands were going up. Charlie was new to the school, wanted to look keen by going to the meeting. It was the only way a younger teacher got any respect with the older ones: you either attended union meetings or played football with the guys.

He wasn't playing football with the guys.

There was Julie at one of the desks, doodling on her pad. The sheer calves of her crossed legs. The pulse of her throat as she'd swallowed. Julie had glanced over, caught him looking. Twice more

75

they'd caught each other's gazes in the meeting, and each time: a little spasm of electricity in Charlie's breastbone.

All his older-woman fantasies from when he was young: Randy Teacher, Foxy Librarian, MotherOfYourBestFriendWhoWantsYou ToSpreadSuncreamOnHerTi

Gavin had asked for a show of hands, then a forest of them obscured her.

Julie touched her cutlery and said, 'You know, Charlie, in school today I was thinking about . . .'

'What?'

'That.' She squeezed.

He smiled. 'Really?'

The thought of turning someone on was still strange. Obscene puppetry in her head. Where he wasn't real.

'Yes,' she said. 'Know what I did?'

'What?'

'Went to the ladies' room at break and . . .'

She grinned.

'What?' he said.

'You know . . .' she said. 'I . . .'

'Took coke?'

'Don't be ridiculous.'

'Was it a good one?'

'I don't do *coke*.'

'No,' he said. 'I mean the . . .'

'Oh,' she said. 'The . . .'

'Was it?'

'Yes.'

'And did you manage to . . .'

'Yes, I did,' she said. 'Twice.'

*'Really?'*

76

'Uh-huh.'

'And were you thinking about . . .'

'I was,' she said, 'and the time when we . . .'

'Oh!' They both cackled.

'And I kept picturing your . . .'

'Right,' he said. 'When I . . .'

'In my . . .'

'Wow,' he said.

After the dessert, and part-way through their second bottle, Julie rose and started to undress. Shoes, blouse, skirt. Underneath she was wearing red lingerie, which she revealed like a winning poker hand.

They moved to the bedroom. The curtains were open. Charlie closed them. 'No,' she said. 'Keep them open.'

'What?' he said. 'Why?'

'It's exciting that someone might see.'

He looked across the street. Mute lives in tenements: watching telly, clearing dishes. Glasgow. Streetlight burnished the huge dark blue. Julie stepped towards him, the soft sound of her feet on the floor. Swishing. Hand to his face: they kissed. Leonard Cohen sang about Suzanne. His Suzanne.

'Can anyone see?' Julie said.

He glanced beyond her.

'Yes.'

'Man or a woman?'

'A man.'

'Is he good-looking?'

'Yes.'

Julie nipped at his ear with her teeth. 'Can he see you running your hands over my tits?'

'He can.'

'Think he's enjoying himself?'

Charlie drew down her bra-strap. Kissed her shoulder. His teeth touched her skin. 'Yes,' he said.

'Think he's getting hard?'

'Very.'

'Want him to see me do this . . . ?'

When they finished he was dripping with sweat and Julie was sighing, thigh muscles softening, and the room seemed to exhale. Ghosts in the air. Their bodies were slick. 'Thatwasgreat,' she said. 'Thatwasgreat. Thatwasgreat.' Their breathing slowed and she wrapped her arms around him, and when he looked up he almost expected to see Gavin at the window across the road, spectacles – teeth – gleaming.

They listened to music and drank wine and Julie cuddled into him. He was snug among the house plants. He shifted on the couch. He felt small. Animal. Nocturnal.

TV flickered.

'Charlie?' she said.

'Yeah?'

'We are together now, aren't we?' She looked at him. 'Y'know, *together*.'

'Of course,' he said, and kissed her.

'Will people mind the age thing?'

'Who cares?'

'I mean,' she said, 'you're thirty. We're both *divorced*. It's not like you're a probationer. Some fresh-faced kid.'

'I used to be. But it's difficult to stay fresh-faced after a divorce.' He made a comedy sad face.

'You don't have to tell *me*, hon.' She touched his cheek.

He bent into the touch, bubbled like Stan Laurel, then turned it into a laugh. 'Thank God I'll never see her again!'

Inside something whispered: *evil*.

What? he replied. Who said that?

*You loved her*, it hissed, insistent.

So who asked you? Get outta here!

'Wow,' said Julie. 'She really must've done a number on you.'

'Hm,' he said, and stroked her face in silence. After a while he said, 'So are you telling me that if I wasn't divorced you wouldn't have done this?'

'I would,' she said, eyebrow rising, 'but I'd have been much more gentle with you.'

'Why's that?'

'Because divorce toughens you.'

'True,' he said, and his fingertips on her face felt the way eyes feel on colour.

They cuddled, not talking.

Her fingers stalked his body. Eventually he shivered. 'Tickles.'

'What if someone says something?' she said. 'Y'know. At work?'

'Just tell him how great the sex is.'

'Him? I'm more worried about the women. Don't want them thinking I'm just going round the male staff. Like some frustrated middle-aged slut.'

'Men are worse,' he said. 'Men are cunts.'

She slapped his leg. 'Charlie Bain, watch your language.'

'Sorry. Men are *dicks*?'

'That's better.'

'Dinkles? Winkies?'

'Much better.'

He reached over her body to the floor. He found his wine and sipped. 'Want me to roll a joint?' he said.

'Not when I'm drinking.'

'Mind if I roll one?'

'No,' Julie said. She kissed his cheek. She rubbed her nose against his. 'Hey, want to come round again this Saturday?'

'Uh . . .' My sister's coming over to visit me and my mum.'

'Tsk. I can't believe you *still* live with your mum.'

'Yeah,' he said. 'So?'

'Never thought about moving out?'

'I did move out. I was married, remember?'

'I mean, moving *back* out?'

'She doesn't keep well,' he said. 'I'm responsible for her.'

'I suppose,' she said, 'we all have to be responsible for somebody.'

Charlie looked at the glass he was holding. There were clear smudges all round it. Smudges with purple tints. Manky.

'Julie, do you ever clean these?'

'What? It's fresh out of the dishwasher.'

He held it. 'Look.'

'At what?'

'*Look.*'

She peered.

'You can't see that it's covered in fingerprints?'

Julie shook her head and frowned.

'What?' he said.

<sub>'Charlie?'</sub> she said, as though from down the end of a long corridor.

'What?' His voice felt heavy, echoing. 'Did you say something there, Julie?'

<sub>'Charlie, are you really sure you want to</sub> have the rest of that

we   e   e   e   e

we   e   e   ee d ?   d

w ? eed? e

e    d

?

?

e    ed?

ee?

ed?

?

*N ? x weed*

*t t      x     t    n t the rest of that we ed ?*                    *Char ie ?*

*t t a ? y e      x x e ?rest*                                      *Charli ?*

*?ext day N        e Xt   a of  tha wee d*

*a ?      x weed*

*t      weed*          *Charlie?*

*Yvonne?*

*ext day, nst inst instead of  s tu dy stu d yin*
*Next day, instead of studying, as you promised you would, you walk*
*through Kelvingrove Park, a Glasgow Saturday, with Yvonne. She is so*
*very*
*her company, excited,*
*fidgeting around your responses to her*
*as though worried that her jokes will fall through the air and land*
*clunking*
*at your feet.*
*When one does she picks it up*
*wipes it off,*

*and says,*

*'Ach, sorry that was a crap joke.'*

*She's not even conscious of this as a compliment! She actually cares what you think! No girl except Nadine has attempted to make you laugh; all the others from school sat there, sullen and funless, while guys pecked and squawked with their lame wisecracks all around them. But Yvonne is this. She is sweets or hats or scooters. She brings you out. These simple, useless things you discover about each other, disconnected to work and career plans and mortality, like elements of sky. Here, in the second week of your second year at uni, you are born. What is this strange element of you? Your thoughts are confetti: light and tiny and celebratory. You keep your hands in your pockets to stop yourself floating off.*

*She has attuned you to the world.*

*The two of you stop into Tchai Ovna, warm your fingers on the cups. Yvonne asks you who your favourite philosopher is and you say, uh, Nietzsche and she says, 'Eh, I was thinking more along the lines of Yoda,' and then you try to impress her with your knowledge of philosophy – existentialism? utilitarianism? solipsism? – but forget which is which so it stutters, feels mannered and barred. She furrows her forehead and looks at you as if to say, I was trying to talk about Yoda, dude. Fuck are you on about? This half-studied foreign language of isms is not what the scene requires. Love is reconstituting things as you speak, a stagehand arranging the scenery and lighting round the actors. This is what it means, you find yourself thinking, when they meet and fall in love in movies. This is it! This must be what it's like! And even though you've known this girl less than a week, you've lost your virginity in that week, so you do not doubt that this is love, knew it even as you were making it between you, like something precious from the senses, sweating and moaning, slickened against each other's bodies, then laughing at a guitar solo – okay, a great guitar solo, as she'd forced you*

to concede – a dreaming mammal in your arms. At school you were
hopping in and out of crushes, a cat seeking (but never winning)
attention from a crowded room, but now you are here, your chilled
fingers around a hot chocolate, listening to her talk about the time she
visited the Sistine Chapel in Rome and the security guard hushed her
because there has to be silence in the chapel and she said, 'Listen, man.
Don't let people in here to see this beautiful fucking ceiling if you don't
want them to talk about it,' and you find yourself touching her hand,
lifting it to your lips and kissing it. She stops and stares. And you feel the
molecules of your self slip and rearrange, slide in and out of each other
like a 3-D jigsaw, settling in some new shape.

    This shape.

    A boy. Talking to a girl.

    In the centre of a forest, the fairies whispering.

            and you realise

            *y o u r e a l i s e*

            that you too are a world *Within* a world within a

world within a

                                 *w*

                                          **o**

withi

                    *wO o*

                *with     i  n  a*

                  *w orld*

                      *orl    rl*

                          *o*

                           *r d*

*within*

night!of!champions! amorous stretched princely *Get dressed* mirror
hey it's Travolta *champagne for the lady* Dancemoves WHOO cheeky
line? chopchopchopchop snort GRIN hey Saturday Night Fe-vah! You
should be danc-ing *Yeah* coke-wrapping texting onefluidmovement
text blindly looking for contact out there some late-night radio DJ
going to the phones Helen? Jackie? Penny? Clara? sniff Kirsty? Jada?
Sophie? sniff Maria? Jo? sniff Nadine texts me back CLASSIC Fancy
Jupito? she texts – p-tchoo! – Where? text back quickstyle – tchoo!
tchoo! – gunslinger she replies GET WITH THE PROGRAMME CHARLIE!!!!
IT'S LIKE THE COOLEST CLUB NIGHT IN GLASGOW!!! WE'LL TOTALLY BE
STARS!!!! stares stares stares at the text but for some reason
thisiswaytoomuchinfoformybraintotakeinman cos I remember that
every atom inside me comes from an exploded star somewhere in the
universe millions of years ago whoah

**HEA       VY       HEA       VY       HEA       VY**

deep breaths deep breaths don't panic I can *deal* with this I can *deal*
with this I can *deal* with this SHUT THE FUCK UP CHARLIE YOU
MISERABLE TWO-TIMING PRICK I can *deal* with this It's who I
am now I can *deal* with this IT'S WHO I AM NOW 'kay take some
COKE my man if it's worrying you *that* much fucksakes sniiiiiiiiiiiif
now Let's *go* Gangsta mon

Muthafuckah

Flashes     of     saturday

Night       contact lenses make the ole blue eyes into !BLUE EYES!
dazzling peacocking Nadine wearing a flouncy dress hairband a sixties
chick dancingdancing eyesSTARBURSTbright she's a girl from real
life who inspired some famous song Dear Prudence See Emily Play
Ruby Tuesday NADINE LOOKS FUCKING BEAUTIFUL she leans
in to point out some member of an upandcomingGlasgowindieband
Endor or Errors or How to Swim or Wake the President the indieband
look being the dominant cultural system of signification and suchlike

in this here fuckin bourgeoise Glasgow fuckin MY SHA-RO-NA!
WHOO! don't you love this SONG? Nadine raiseseyebrow tap tap taps
her nose: separate toilets *pour Nadine et moi* MY! MY! MY! MY! MY!
MY! WHOOH! chopchopchop antiseptic smell snort Gasp
starscollapsing brightness in Nadine when she emerges we !GRIN! at
each other Dancefloor oh man Nadine looks beauuuutiful gr grr rinds
against me SEXY AS HELL got a headful of angels cockful of come
Girls looking Boys looking How did that loser get with such a *hottie?*
Cos friends I am from TRANSYLVANIA aah aah aah Nadine slithers
up down stares I reach down touch her hand say Nadine remember
that time in Barcelona? and her panthereyesflash her mouth
opens/closes she presssssses her body against me wrap fingers round
hers breathe onto her neck she kisses my cheek I bite her neck *Charlie*
she says I move my hand down her back we lock eyes can see her
tongue touch her teeth gently *Oh Nadine* soft curve of her ass she
pulls !AWAY AGAIN! dance dance dancing *I'm bored* she says No keep
dancing Nadine guys are checking you out and women are checking
me out! Nadine says *This song's crap Charlie* Keep dancing! but
they're looking away now *No Charlie can we sit down for a bit?* GET
THEE TO THE BAR rounda shots *one two three* Down them cocktails
Dancefloor whoomp whoomp whoomp I am RISEN from the fucking
GRAVE *ma chérie* arm round Nadine glance round the bar at
dresseshairshoes gaze dra dra ggs something with it No don't believe
it: school pupils! In the sixth year! Not mine phew but what do I do?!!!
What's a boy to do?!!! Hustle quick get Nadine *outta* here

OHFUCKWILLTHEYBEABLETOTELLI'MONCOKE! must
protect One's Teacherly Reputation or should one brazenly display
oneself with a young lady stunner !STUNNER! to *enhance* one's
reputation? what does the modern gentleman do in such a dilemma?
If *you* Charlie had seen one of *your* teachers on a Saturday night with
a corker !CORKER! laughing uproariously at everything

!EVERYTHING! what would you have thought? Good luck? Good riddance? MY COCK IS HARD AND BROODING AND SHAKESPEEEEEAREAN Nadine over her straw stares stares at me *Charlie?* she says *do you think I'm pretty?* I say aye to the max! but I'm not sure if people still even SAY to the max she says *Do you think I'll be famous one day?* I say aye bigstyle! but I'm not sure if people still SAY bigstyle but she goes all fucking WEIRDOOOO *Well I don't care* she says *I don't care what you think* so I just turn away Don't then and after a while she goes *See when you're on coke you're a fucking nightmare* stare at her Okay Nadine let's talk about this (sigh) she says *I don't want to talk about this with you THINK in future* About what? then she says *What's all this?* mimics us slithering *Feeling my arse? What's wrong with you?* mumble thought this had been sorted out in Barcelona *What was that?* she says an animal flashglittering from the forest I go I THOUGHT THIS HAD BEEN SORTED OUT IN BARCELONA

she narrows her eyes

sleek and wild

SLAMS! down her drink, it
SMASHES! she's pointing pointing
*Know what you are Charlie?* I sigh A miserable cheating bastard? She says *Afraid* and I say of what? she just shrugs turns away drinks her cocktail fast GULP *You're going to end up in a black hole Charlie* I just frown she shouts *Black hole* SLAPS me leaves wiping eyes hissing *fucking bastard* Nadine? I say but !SHE'S GONE! sip drink Dancefloor

light whoomp whoomp whoomp remembering a song by Burnt Island that goes *I've been reading that what matters most is how well you walk through the fire But I didn't know I was on fire until the flames engulfed me* heading into the dance-floor swearthisgoddamncokeisflirting withme hypnotic You Cannot Fail repeat You Cannot Fail and the flame engulfs me and I am the

D      R      A      G      O      N

## Int. Next day. Charlie's bedroom

CHARLIE *staring at his mobile phone, hand over his mouth. Eventually he picks it up, hesitates for a bit, then presses 'ring'.*

| | |
|---|---|
| CHARLIE: | Hi. Nadine? |
| NADINE: | Hi. |
| CHARLIE: | Hey. How did you, uh. How did you get home last night? |
| NADINE: | Taxi. |
| CHARLIE: | Oh. You got home okay then? |
| NADINE: | Yes. |
| | *Pause.* |
| CHARLIE: | Good. |
| NADINE: | You didn't even come after me. |
| CHARLIE: | Nadine, uh. Uh, Nadine. I was way fucked up last night. Took far too much coke. Some shit going through my mind. I, uh . . . I . . . |
| NADINE: | Yeah, I was high as well, but y'know. I'm sorry for slapping you. It's. Look, Charlie. We can't. I can't . . . |
| CHARLIE: | I know. |
| NADINE: | It's not that. It's. We, uh. I mean. |

87

| | |
|---|---|
| CHARLIE: | What? |
| NADINE: | I can't even. No. Listen. Just listen. Let's not treat each other like we're one of those others, okay? *This* isn't *that.* |
| CHARLIE: | No. |
| NADINE: | That's all I ask. |
| CHARLIE: | Yeah. |
| NADINE: | I mean, *Charlie.* |
| CHARLIE: | Got it. |
| NADINE: | We couldn't. |
| CHARLIE: | No. |
| NADINE: | And we won't. |
| CHARLIE: | Of course not. |
| NADINE: | Let's just be a bit more careful. I've got stuff going on inside me too and it makes me frightened. And I lash out. There's darkness, Charlie. Y'know? There's so much darkness inside both of us, and we can't afford to start *using* each other. |
| CHARLIE: | |
| NADINE: | And lay off the coke. It brings out the worst in you. |
| CHARLIE: | Can I still smoke weed? |
| NADINE: | You can still smoke weed. Just lay off the coke. |
| CHARLIE: | |
| CHARLIE: | |
| NADINE: | I mean, is everything okay, Charlie? |
| CHARLIE: | |
| CHARLIE: | |
| CHARLIE: | Yeah, totally. |
| NADINE: | Cos you can talk to me. I'm your friend. If it's all about Yvonne, then I— |
| CHARLIE: | By way of apology, I was wondering, uh, if you wanted |

88

to come and have dinner with me, my mum and my sister on Sunday.

NADINE: Oh. Well. Yeah. That'd be nice. Thank you.

CHARLIE: Yeah, I just thought. Y'know.

NADINE: Be good to see your mum again.

CHARLIE: Been a while.

NADINE:

CHARLIE: Great then.

*Pause.*

About four?

NADINE: We're on.

CHARLIE: Cool. Oh, Nadine?

NADINE: What?

CHARLIE: I really do think you'll be famous one day.

*Pause.*

NADINE: Thank you, Charlie. (*Pause.*) Charlie?

CHARLIE: What?

NADINE: Does your phone do this?

NADINE *hangs up.* CHARLIE *swears, presses the end-call button too late. Then he stares at the phone, shaking his head and smiling.*

He drove his mother to the library, and on the way they listened to Radio 4. *The World at One.* Radio accent and the smell of the car making elbow-room in his nostrils. The day was bright and cold, and the sun reflected on the windscreen made him wince. Solarium. Pub. Bookies. Take-away. A feature came on about the cultural renaissance in Scotland, exciting new artists. Take-away. Bookies. Pub.

'Watch how you're driving,' his mother said.

'Sorry.'

They parked near the library and he helped her from the car. She was wrapped in a coat, scarf and gloves. She was a bit stekky when she moved. *Stekky*. He imagined a line of Stegosaurus, walking doomed plains.

'All right?' he said.

'Yes.'

He kissed her cheek. They entered the library. In the evenings, all alone, she liked to read. Inhabit elsewhere. The lamplight on, nursing her wine. Usually some murder mystery. When he came into the room she'd recite the plots, foretell the ending: 'Well, this body's been found upside down bleeding and Detective Warsaw thinks he recognises the marks from a case he worked on decades ago and the killer was never caught. Basically I think it's the girlfriend. Imitating the original killer. Probably *killed* the original killer. Maybe even *is* the original killer.' Then she'd say to the librarian when returning it: 'Don't you have any of the *harder* stuff?'

'Mum?' Charlie had asked her once. 'What did you want to be when you grew up?'

She'd mused on this. Touched her chin. The TV babbling while she'd thought. Then she'd said, 'I'd like to have been a horse.'

The chair, which changed with furniture fashions. Her hair, growing longer, shorter, longer. Her clothes, flashing further and further out of style – green, yellow, brown, white – the colours of seasons changing. Book. Wine. Lamp. Just getting her out of the house now required some kind of necromancy, the arcane ritual of the library trip. Then back to unblackmagic reality: a chair is a chair is a chair. Sometimes when he saw her there he wanted to sit in it with her. Oh, Mother, whatever will happen to us here on this earth? What horrors will visit us one day?

My son, I am your mother. No ill will come to you, I swear it.

Oh, Mother, my very first friend and love. I am frightened of what I am becoming.

When you were a child I nursed you. Now you are a man and I need you with me.

Oh, Mother, dear Mother, my purpose is you. Do not die.

One day—

Do not die!

'Just going to check the crime shelves,' she said.

'What exactly is it you're *planning*, Mum?'

'The greatest bank job in history.' She grinned.

'I won't cover for you,' he said.

'You bloody well will!'

Charlie went to the politics section, looked vaguely at a book. *The Future of Socialism*. Its cover featured Hugo Chavez, finger accusing some off-stage rich bastard. The array of women in the library: distracted housewives, hippie idlers, mothers who reached for the self-help books. *The Only Thing Stopping You Is You*. Students with iPods and T-shirts and chewed pens. Ladies of a certain age with their Mills & Boon, their hankies and a hankering. The Ages of Woman, moving, shifting, becoming each other, before his eyes, every day, all those sleek or plump or tattooed or smartly dressed figures merging into shapes, smiles, scents, memories. Beds. Living-rooms. A wind-chime at someone's window. A birthmark on someone's thigh. A toe-ring. A pill-box hat. A La Senza bra dropped carelessly. These things. The women they summoned. He wanted all of those moments again.

all of these moments again, every one of th

He wondered what Yvonne was doing. Who she was w i t h

whether or not

she'd

*marry again*

Charlie glanced at the librarian: pretty. A uni graduate with her hair up. Their gazes caught before they both unclipped them politely and glanced away. He'd seen her a few times in this library. She had that indie look which he homed in on. Alt.sexy. Booksmart. Eye-contact, smiles — something more? edgier? — and there'd been some banter when he'd spoken to her at the desk that last time. His mother chose *The Da Vinci Code*. She wanted to read it *again*. When he took it to the desk the librarian said, 'Hello there,' and he said, 'Hi,' then, 'It's not for me.'

She smiled and scanned the book. 'That's what they all say.'

'Mm,' he said then: 'Take off your glasses.'

She looked up. 'What?'

'Are you self-conscious about them?'

'Um,' she said. 'What makes you say tha—'

'You *are*,' he said. 'You're self-conscious about them.'

'Maybe a wee bit,' she said. 'They're a boys' style. Can you tell?'

He nodded. A flicker crossed her forehead. He took his own glasses from his pocket. 'Swap.'

'Uh, okay.' She gave him her glasses.

'Put them on,' he said.

She did. She blinked for a bit. 'Suit me?'

He said nothing and simply regarded her.

'I said, do they suit me?'

'They suit you like a tattoo across your forehead.'

'Sod off!' She laughed. Then neither of them spoke, and he let her paddle awkwardly in the silence. Waiting. She reached for the scanner, then realised she'd scanned the book. 'Seriously?' she said. 'I don't suit boys' glasses? Oh, no. However am I going to cope?'

'It's the truth,' he said.

'You know of no such thing as truth, sir. May I have my glasses back?'

'No, you may not,' he said. He looked at her, then away, and then back at her.

She lowered her gaze. 'Please?' she said.

He placed his thumbnail in his mouth. He looked away, then back at her again.

She touched her hair.

It was starting to feel fugitive.

'I would *so* kiss you,' he said.

She opened her mouth, then closed it. 'You would *what?*'

'If you'd let me.'

'Well, I won't.'

'I could learn from you. You could *teach* me.'

'About kissing?'

'It's always better to know. I've never done it before. I don't want to mess it up.'

She laughed again. 'Oh. Really.'

'Look,' he said, 'I'm just thinking of you here.'

'You can't *kiss* me. I'm at *work*.'

'If you weren't?'

She shrugged and smiled.

Charlie held up his hand as if to say *okay* or *don't move* or *trust me*. Then he leaned forward, fingertips pressed to the desk. The librarian inhaled a little but didn't move. He could see the muscles of her neck roll lightly.

'Maybe,' he whispered in her ear, '*you* can't kiss *me*.'

She raised an eyebrow. 'Is that right?'

'Can I have my book now?'

She stood looking at him, *into* him. He gave her glasses back, then took his book. When he moved aside, the queue nudged up and she said, 'Oh,' and reached for the next one. Charlie folded his glasses into his pocket. He turned to a pensioner with a walking-stick.

'Don't trust this woman.'

'Eh?'

'Mr Smith,' the librarian said, introducing Charlie, 'this is the devil.'

'Eh?'

Her gaze touched Charlie's – iridescent, lingering – until she started scanning books again and he felt himself disappearing out of the moment, back into solid physical libraryspace. Oak panels. Pot plants.

A pang.

He found his mother, who was talking to a woman Charlie recognised from somewhere. He stood behind her while they spoke and the woman said, 'Mm,' and 'Oh,' and 'Well,' and, 'But it must be hard for you, Linda, being on your own.'

'I'm not on my own,' said his mother. 'Charlie's with me.'

'Oh,' said the woman. '*This* is wee Charlie?'

Charlie bowed.

'Remember Doreen?' said his mother. 'She used to babysit when you were wee.'

'Of course,' he said. 'So it's your fault.'

'Charlie Bain,' gasped Doreen. 'Haven't seen you since you were about that height. What a cheeky wee bism you could be. Mind, he used to sit on my knee, Linda, and tell me he was going to be Indiana Jones. That's what you said, Charlie – Indiana Jones.'

'Hey,' he said, 'the whip's at home.'

'Oh!' said Doreen. 'Cheeky!'

He did a tap dance. Doreen laughed and touched Charlie's elbow. His mother noticed, eyebrow twitching.

'Taking care of your mum now, are you?'

'That's one way to describe it,' said his mother.

'But I thought . . .' said Doreen, hesitating '. . . weren't you . . . married?'

Charlie nodded slowly.

'They split up,' his mother said, and then, before silence could wash it away: 'She was cheating on him.'

'*Mum*,' Charlie said.

'Well!' Doreen said.

'Yep,' said his mother.

'Just goes to show,' Doreen said.

Charlie touched his forehead.

'Charlie,' Doreen said, 'what a shame for you.'

He clenched his teeth.

'The poor laddie,' said Doreen, strident. 'It's not right. It's just not right.'

'That's what we thought,' said his mother.

'*Sex in the City*. Ever since that show came out lassies just gallivant about and do what they like.'

'Yep,' said his mother.

Inside was magma, molten rock.

'Right, Mum, we going?'

'I'm talking to Doreen.'

'I've a lot to do.'

'No, that's fine, Linda,' Doreen said, batting a gloved hand. 'You get yourselves home.' But she stood for a while, shaking her head and sighing, 'Poor souls,' as though to stray puppies on her doorstep. 'I'm so glad you've got each other.'

Charlie stared at her. Breathed deeply then released. 'Well,' he managed to say, 'nice to meet you again. Doreen.'

Doreen waved as they left, and Charlie smelled the grave off her, then walked with his mother to the bus stop and looked at the tops of trees while she spoke to him, and there were crows, so many crows, so many fucking crows, and the noise of their flapping wings disturbed him, and when they got to the bus stop Charlie fussed, 'Mum, please,

you're not wearing your gloves. Wear your gloves, Mum, please. For
me.'

s

o

o

*n you become*

      *e*    *bec*  *o me Charlie and Yvonne*        *Y*    *C*

                                                         *v*    *h*

                                                          *o*    *a*

                                                          *n &*    *r*

                                                          *n*    *l*

                                                          *e*    *i*

                                                                                       *l*

                                              *you become Charlie and Yvonn*  *e*

*Neither exists without the other*

                *neither exists without the othe*

*n ei the r*

                        *neither exxxissssssts without the other remember you*

                                            *bassssstard*

*friends just groan at your*

*longing*

                *looks at each other over pub tables, the way they have to ask you a*

                                      *question two or three*

                              *times before you hear it. Oh, sorry! you both say, realising,*

                          *This must be sickening for you. Yeah, your friends laugh,*

                                                *It is!*

## *neither exists*

'God,' you say to Yvonne later. 'Don't tell me we're that *kind of couple?*'

'Well,' she says, 'I don't mind. I think that kind of couple is nice. Some couples hate each other.'

'True,' you say, and kiss her. For – what? – the millionth time that week?

There is nothing beyond this sealed-shut universe of the two of you, the breathable atmosphere of yourselves, your own psyche gliding into the other's, memories merging, futures flickering. You slide without fuss into the rhythm of it (you make her less stressed, she makes you more tidy; while your consciousness swarms invisibly between the two of you), shared routines (you make casseroles, she makes punk compilat she makes punk makes punk ions compilatio

She listens to them sometimes when she gets angry. Sometimes she gets angry. At how 'stupid' and 'ugly' she is.

'What are you talking about? What do you mean stupid and ugly? Where's this coming from?'

'I'm failing this English degree. I'm skint. And look at me.' At which point, she'd step back to expose the supposed facts of her ugliness: a slight tummy and exaggerated waist flab, pressed between the fingers.

'Yvonne,' you say, 'stop this. I wouldn't love you if you weren't beautiful and clever.'

Then she'd look at you and the levee would break: 'You wouldn't love me if I wasn't beautiful?!'

'I didn't mean it like that,' you say. 'I mean you are beautiful. I mean—'

And even though you do mean it – she is beautiful – the words sound wooden and unnatural in your mouth, like an Elizabethan stage script.

'I'm hideous!' she'd weep. 'How can you love me?'

*No one is surprised when you move in together. It has the same impeccable logic as the next date on a long-ago-booked tour. A tiny flat, top floor, White Street, off Byres Road. The door flaking with paint. But on this moving-in day, the day of your new life starting, you feel the absence of your father, who should be here, standing with hers by the car, talking about football and how your kids are graduates* already *and the slow, sweet pain of watching them disappear up those stairs. Your mother comes along instead, to check out the flat, but they somehow seem to irk each other, she and Yvonne; both overplay their speeches ('REA-lly?' 'I KNOW', 'Is that SO?'), like two actresses vying for the lead. Deborah is seventeen and uninterested in whatever ('Or whoever,' she'd smirked) her brother's doing.*

*Your first night together in your first home together. You lie in front of the electric fire surrounded by dust-balls and tall, unpacked boxes of things you can barely afford, the handful of essential albums, all the student bric-à-brac, her PlayStation and your oversized headphones, all the nothing and next-to-nothing you own, and feel the soft clutch of happiness pressing you together in the dark.*

*'Do you think we should be worried about the future?' she says.*

*'Why?' you say.*

*'We don't have any money. Or careers. Or furniture. Or a car. Or a mortgage.'*

*'Who needs them?'*

*'We will, pretty soon.'*

*'It'll all come.'*

*'And if it all doesn't...?'*

*You shrug.*

*'Shrugging doesn't pay the bills, Charlie.'*

*'Depends how good you are at it. I could go professional.' You shrug some more to show her this. 'That's amateur level. This one... this is the one that'll hit the big-time.'*

'Stop it. Talk me down from this.'

'Darling,' you say, 'you're thinking it through too much. Let it all happen. We'll be okay.'

She cuddles into you, orange-peel close. 'This is why I like you, Charlie. You just never stress out about things.'

'You didn't stress about Shakespeare, I seem to remember. Turned up at your first class unprepared.'

'That's different,' she said. 'That's not real.'

'Neither is this,' you say. 'The trick is just realising that. We're only twenty-one. Jesus. And we've just moved into our first flat. Let's treat it like a game, Yvonne. Let's pretend there's no such thing as consequences.'

'But there are,' she says, covering her face.

Your life feels close to being complete, here, this early. Love screws with your ability to smirk at trash, at sentimentality, at cringeworthy soap-opera dialogue and the lyrics of pop songs. You plunge, breathless and torrid, into it. 'I want to hold your hand', 'You lift me up', and 'Everything I do, I do it for you' make perfect, almost metaphysical sense. Who could laugh at these things? You want to hold her hand! She lifts you up! Everything you do, you do it for her! These are mere facts of the world you now inhabit, a world of The Greatest Love Ballads In The World Ever albums and giddy, princely talk of marriage. You are twenty-one. Nothing seems ridiculous. Marriage is not ridiculous. Marriage is not r i    cu l ou

                             di

                                       s

ot ng  s ms

                             r i    cul us

*you are twenty-one*

**Let Her Come To You.** This is the cardinal rule, so drill it into your brain, **doofus!** Let Her Come To You. Feign **disinterest.** Not complete disinterest, of course, you have to throw the occasional **bait** out, just to keep her attention. But the second you tell her she's **beautiful** it's over. Think she wants to be told she's beautiful **yet again?** This is, like, her fifth time since **breakfast!** So keep her unsure if your remarks are insults or compliments. 'You're too intellectual for me.' 'I prefer older women.' 'I bet you're secretly a geek.' Keep her **dangling,** uncertain about whether or not you're totally disinterested or want to take her to bed and do wicked things.

**All the things she'll like,**
**bad boy!**

Monise sometimes visited his room to chat about writing. She'd peek round the door, curious, a wood-nymph near a human campsite. 'C'mon in!' he'd holler, and she'd approach his desk cautiously, as though tiptoeing towards the fire. Then she'd say, 'Hi, Mr Bain,' and proffer cakes and biscuits like gifts from the netherworld. He still had a sweet tooth because of all those hours when he was wee spent guzzling the Irn-Bru and liquorice and sherbets and jelly-babies from the ice-cream van, jammed with his sister before the otherworldly sheen of a games console, attacking. Blam. *Attacking*. Jerking, like, back and, like, forth and then

Blink!

Teaching.

How did that happen?

'Monise,' he said, 'that was great cake.' He dabbed sugar specks.

'Made it myself.'

'This? It's *delicious*. It tastes like *art*.'

Monise smiled and drew her hair over her ears. Charlie wiped his hands. He picked up her manuscript and read the title aloud, like God. It was THINGS TO DO WHILE WAITING FOR SOMEONE MORE POWERFUL THAN YOU TO SPEAK.

All capitals. Deliberately, he hoped. *Yes*.

'You like?'

At the start of the school year he'd asked the class for samples of their writing. It was the usual litany of teen woe, peer pressure, angsty images (roses, blood, thorns), parental divorce traumas, Goth-studded fantasies of crucifixion and crunching, leather-clad rock stardom. And then: Monise. Clear, crystalline lines. About a watering-

can. A watering-can, no less. A watering-can that had almost moved him to tears. It had been a bad week, right enough – his father had tried to phone – but that didn't stop it being one startling fucking watering-can. When the watering-can poured it *spoke*:
'plastic/rain/the scrabby earth/place back in shed/when nothing's left/things seethe and grow and writhe/And you are me/And I am you/And we are we/Unseen'. So he'd asked her to wait behind after class and as she'd sat there with her bag on her lap, hands demure, he'd held up the poem.

'You write this?'

'Sir?'

'Mr Bain is fine, Monise. Did you write this?'

'Is there anything wrong with it?'

'No,' he'd said. 'There's nothing wrong with it. That's what's wrong with it.'

'Sir?'

He'd offered her some herbal tea, which he brought out strategically whenever a pupil was upset.

'No, thank you,' she'd said.

'Tell me,' he'd said, folding arms, 'which poets do you enjoy?'

'Hm, let me see,' she'd said. 'Some MacNeice. Spender. William Carlos Williams. Yeats, obviously.'

That she'd referred to poets from the thirties. That she'd called them by their surnames. That she'd said Yeats 'obviously'.

'William Carlos Williams?' he'd said. Charlie often mixed him up with . . . Wallace Stevens Wallace?

'Totally,' she'd said. 'Especially "The Red Wheelbarrow". Sir.'

He'd sipped his tea. *Sir*. The taste of an apology stewed upon his tongue.

Soon this sharpened into a working relationship, a brisk, syncopated, sewing-machine rhythm. He fed her material – was

Joseph Conrad racist? Did Ted 'kill' Sylvia? Was Satan the true hero of *Paradise Lost?* – and she went away and read, came back to his room the next week, stitched their discussion with quotes, hmmed and emmed, before an opinion emerged, fresh, ready for her to wear.

Sweatshop conditions.

Their economy grew.

From her first year he'd seen her at the fringes of things, sitting on a bench near the lockers, away from the buzzing swarm of peers, head bent and arm scribbling, a flower struggling to twist from the earth. He'd witnessed dripped acid from girls her age – 'emo', 'Goth', 'weirdo' – but among the staff Monise blushed and bloomed, perpetually in season. Julie had taught Monise in third year and raved. Gavin had passed round her satirical playscript setting *Macbeth* among a high-school clique: *Macbitch.* Now she'd opened her mind to Charlie, absorbing the rays of his knowledge. Light-hungry.

'I liked it,' he said.

'You don't think it's too . . .' she said '. . . teenage? Y'know, with the bit about the sea?'

'The sea is teenage?'

'Um,' she shrugged, 'it is to me.'

'No posters of boy bands on your walls, then?'

'There are,' she said. 'The Beats. The Modernists. The Existentialists.'

'Oh, them,' he said. 'I've heard their second album's good.'

She smiled, but didn't laugh. It hadn't been that funny. He was conscious that it hadn't been funny. *Must do better.*

'So, Mr Bain. You like.'

Statement now, not question.

'I do. But—'

'No buts!' She cringed. 'Sorry. *Continuez tout droit.*'

'Hm,' he said, and coughed. Then coughed again. The content of her novel, in truth, had surprised him, and he didn't really know what to say. It was about an adolescent girl and a bereaved man, a chap who, being a kindly, neighbourly sort in his sixties, was teaching her how to play guitar. The widower and his student met in a café at the start of each chapter and over coffee he'd ask about her playing. The widower had calloused hands, usually pressed against the young protagonist's gawky wrists, guiding her over the frets. It was a mature work, sensitive, dignified. But, despite the subject matter, it was strangely sexless. And a little bit boring. There was just too much about guitars in it.

'I was going to say . . . Sometimes I think it's a little . . .'

She paused in her note-taking. Her gaze hovered.

'. . . *careful.*'

She slid the pen into the rings of her pad.

'How do you mean careful?'

'I think you could *let go* a little more.'

'Let go,' she murmured.

'The scenes are a bit uptight,' he said. 'Almost repressed. I mean, what's *really* going on between these people? It can't just be about music, can it?'

He knew, from her guidance teacher, about the cuts on her wrists.

The widower kept touching the girl's wrists.

'I see what you mean,' she said. 'Sometimes it actually feels like just "writing", you know? Like I haven't quite released the catch on it yet.'

'Exactly,' he said. 'Go deeper. You have to *feel* it.'

'Yeah,' she said. '*Yeah.*'

They looked at each other. In the playground, kids whirled and screamed.

'Have you ever wanted to be a writer?' she said.

'When I was at school,' he said, 'I wrote poetry.'

106

'Really? What was it like?'

'Ach,' he said, 'not as good as yours. Bit derivative, really. Love poetry for the many girls I fancied. I've been writing an "epic" for most of my adult life. In modern Scots dialect. Tom Leonard meets John Milton. It's called, um, "State of Independence". Political, y'know?'

'Sounds, um . . .' she said '. . . sounds . . .' Then she coughed and said, 'Why didn't you keep going?'

He tapped his pen on his leg. 'You know what it's like. Go to uni, get a job, get married, have to pay the bills. You never find the time.'

'You don't think you'd go back to it? Now that you're not . . .'

He waited. 'Not what?'

'Married?'

'No,' he said, and folded his arms. 'Not really, Monise. That was a different me.'

She nodded.

They talked a bit more, about the début novel by some trendy New Yorker. 'Too *arch*,' she said, waving her hands. 'Too *tricksy*.' Then she reached for her bag, started to pack up her manuscript, replete with his red-pen marks. Charlie noticed Simon through the glass, waiting, with his boy-hair and bounciness.

Simon waved.

'Simon's outside,' he said.

'Is he?' Monise slung her bag over her shoulder. 'What a sweetheart.'

'Are you and he, uh . . . ?'

She hesitated. 'No, sir,' she said, with a downwards note. 'We're friends.'

'Call me Charlie.'

'Mr Bain,' she said, 'we're friends.'

'Right,' said Charlie. 'Same time next week?'

'Count on it.'

sop's Fables Metamorphoses The Canterbury Tales The Thousand and One Nights Don Quixote Pilgrim's Progress Oroonoko Robinson Crusoe Gulliver's Travels Clarissa Tom Jones Candide Emile Tristram Shandy Les Reveries du Promeneur Solitaire Les Liaisons Dangereuses Les 120 Journées de Sodome The Adventures of Caleb Williams Camilla Pride and Prejudice Frankenstein Ivanhoe The Private Memoirs and Confessions of a Justified Sinner Le *Me!* Noir Oliver Twist The Fall of the House of Usher Mertvye Dushi Illus Vanity Fair Jane Eyre Wuthering Heights Moby Dick Bleak House Walden North and South Madame Bovary Oblomov Silas Marner Otti i Deti Les Misérables Zapiski iz Podpolya Prestupleniye i nakazaniye Idiot Voyna i Mir Middlemarch Alice's Adventures in Wonderland Erewhon Besy Anna Karenina Bratya Karamazovy Ben-Hur The Portrait of a Lady The Adventures of Huckleberry Finn Germinal The Strange Case of Dr Jekyll and Mr Hyde Sult The Yellow Wallpaper Jude the Obscure Dracula Sister Carrie Heart of Darkness The Wings of the Dove L'Immoraliste The

He woke early and looked at the ceiling. There was the ceiling. His bedroom was made of four walls. There were the walls. A dream about vampires chasing him retreated into the mist, ha ha ha ha ha ha. He got out of bed. There was the carpet! He shuffled through a fuzzy wall of alcohol residue. His date the previous night had liked to drink and he'd had to keep up. Bathroom. Picked up his toothbrush and stared at it. What a strange implement. How humans have evolved to make such things.

When he looked up the mirror said: So who are you?

You tell me, he replied. That's your job!

Charlie crawled downstairs to make his mother breakfast. She was asleep in her chair, the television still on and everything. He watched her sleeping there, head bent back, mouth open, snoring gently. He watched her. There is life here. There is still life. She exists at this time and has not been taken away from you. Once she has been taken away, you will never have her again. Remember moments such as this. He watched her sleep. Then went to the kitchen.

As he moved about, the floor seemed to creak in sympathy. Toast. Brown bread with low-fat spread. Eggs. Poached not fried. Bacon. Grilled not fried. Tea. Skimmed milk and no goddamn sugar, no way. Such nourishment he would provide. He would provide and provide and would continue to provide.

For her.

When he went into the living-room she was moaning in her sleep.

He woke her with a kiss and she opened her eyes and smiled and when he presented her with the tray she blinked wearily, winked blearily.

'Oh. Son. Thank you.' Her eyes narrowed against the light.

'What were you dreaming about?'

She frowned. The dream seemed to percolate in her brain.

'Well,' she said, 'um. Let me think. I was in a castle. Claymores and saltires on the walls and everything. And you were there, Charlie. You were teaching a class or something. And Deborah and myself and your father were watching you. And then it started to rain. It was raining inside the castle. And we all started dancing. All of your pupils stood up on their desks and we all started to dance. It was kind of . . . funky.'

He crossed his arms. 'Dad was in the dream?'

'Yes,' she said.

'Oh, yeah, Dad and his *dancing*.'

'Oh, Charlie, he was great. What a mover. The dancing's where we met. Dance-*floor*, in fact. He came shimmying up to me like this, didn't even have to speak. Just the way he moved. Like a . . . panther.'

'Panthers eat people.'

His mother looked up at him, gaze ringed with warning. She started to pick at her breakfast.

'It's difficult to imagine you and Dad happy together.'

'Charlie, we both *loved* to dance. You should've seen us. T. Rex. Bowie. I was very glam.'

'Really?'

'We were the best-looking couple in Glasgow!' She leaned forwards suddenly. 'Those dance-floors. That's where me and your dad were most . . . together. In our own wee world. Connected. Under those lights.'

Charlie smiled. 'Should've installed some in the front room.'

'Yeah,' said his mum. 'Maybe could've kept it going longer.' She sat back. 'Just all changes when you have kids, though, son.'

'How so?'

'Gradually,' she shrugged, 'the lights go out.'

She tugged at a loose thread on the cushion.

'Are you remembering Nadine's coming round this afternoon for dinner?' he said.

Her gaze hung for a second, uncertainly, before swooping into a smile. 'Yes,' she said. 'I can't wait to see her. I always thought she was a *lovely* girl, Charlie. Are you and she, uh . . . ?'

The question-mark took a while to hook into his thoughts. 'Nadine and m——? Are we . . . ?' Hook. Snag. Ow. 'No, Mum, we're not. Just pals.'

'Right.'

'What?'

'Nothing.'

That afternoon, he cooked a chicken while his mother watched *EastEnders. Easties*, she called it. *Beasties*, he called it.

'Smells lovely,' she shouted from the living-room.

He brought her some more tea.

'Is it nice?' he said, watching her drink it.

'Well,' she said, 'it's. Tea.'

'Need anything else?'

'I'm fine,' she said. '*God.*'

'What?'

'I'm not a cripple, Charlie!'

He stared at her. She matched it. He shook his head and turned to the telly. They watched *EastEnders* while waiting for the chicken to roast. Shutcha mouf yer caaaa. Gerrout moy pub! He wasn't really watching, as the intricacies of dinner ticked and danced in his mind: baste the, roast the, chop the. He'd made plenty of vegetables for his mum, and since 90 per cent of the fat in a chicken was in the skin, he'd skinned it. His meals were lean and fighting-fit. He and his mother sat watching telly together, supping, then from nowhere: 'Heard from Yvonne?' she asked. She was dunking a biscuit.

He blinked over his tea. 'We haven't spoken for about four years. Why would I hear from her now?'

'Aunty Betty saw her in Argyle Street.'

Charlie swallowed his tea. 'Did they talk?'

'No,' said his mum.

Charlie nodded. 'Was she with anyone?'

'Aunty Betty?'

'Yvonne.'

His mother looked at him.

Charlie sniffed. 'A man?'

As soon as Nadine rang the doorbell his mother became a dervish of worry, lifting, rearranging, scanning for carelessly left items. 'Mum, don't bother tidying,' he said. 'She's not one of *them.*' But, still, it put him on edge. When he opened the door he half-expected to see a clipboard in Nadine's hands.

Nadine curtsied and proffered a bottle of wine.

'Pisshead,' he said.

'It's not for me, it's for your mother.'

'That's the last thing she needs. But thanks.'

As he led Nadine into the living-room his mother was still opening windows and spraying air-freshener. Charlie hoped it wouldn't mask the smell of his cooking.

'Hiya!' his mother said, a bit too dramatically, and hugged her. Charlie watched Nadine do the same, the bottle of wine dangling from her fist. When his mother asked Nadine to take her shoes off, he suspected it was so she could check if Nadine's socks had pink toes. Nadine did so, then passed his mother the wine. 'Why, thank you,' his mother said. 'Chablis. Lovely.' She rolled the word 'lovely' and glanced at him. He locked up his irritation. Then she ushered Nadine through the rooms of the house. 'It's been such a while, Nadine,' she said. 'You haven't seen what I've done with the place.'

In the years since Nadine used to visit after school, badge-encrusted bag slung insouciantly, his mother's life had turned so inward that she'd forced the walls to offer infinite reinvention. The house, having felt the family's collective rage during his parents' divorce – its dark reverberation like feedback – instantly complied, terrified of her. Charlie's father had gone and walls had been knocked through, rooms had been 'converted', and now coving, Artex and cornices flowed, textured as ice-cream. The whole house, over time, had become an elaborate, layered fuck-you.

'Wow,' said Nadine, peering into a *fin-de-siècle*-themed bedroom, which no one but Deborah and Jordan had ever used. 'This is lovely.'

Charlie knew Nadine thought quite the opposite, but also that she would never say this. She was art school, but that didn't make her a dick.

'What's your mum done with her house since I last spoke to her?' said Charlie's mother.

112

'Well,' said Nadine, 'she's ripped up the patio.'

'Really?'

'Wasn't enough room for my dad underneath it.'

Charlie laughed. His mother's eyes did something and she opened and closed her mouth. Then Nadine grinned and his mother summoned a smile to trail the joke with. But it lagged behind: Charlie was guffawing now. His mother shifted her gaze between the two of them, as though wondering if the joke was at her expense or not.

'Doesn't matter, Mum. Show Nadine the spare room.'

For twenty minutes his mother leaned forwards in her chair to quiz Nadine about her progress since art school, concentrating on its bizarre curlicues – backpacking, documentary-making, nude modelling – while Nadine sat primly on display, in knee-length boots and a smock.

'Charlie tells me you're a working artist now.'

'Well. I stick things on top of other things and put them in a room for people to look at. Dunno if that makes me a working artist.'

'You saw the Vettriano in the spare room. Tell me, what do you think of him?'

Nadine gave an industrial-strength shiver. With a neat side-step, which reminded Charlie of the way she danced, Nadine said, 'He's very popular.'

'And boyfriends?' his mother said, then let the word drape itself around the two of them. Nadine glanced at Charlie. He covered his mouth and closed his eyes. Nadine smirked, then stopped herself.

'Yes,' said Nadine. 'Lots.'

His mother nodded slowly.

'And what about yourself, Linda?' said Nadine. 'Charlie tells me you haven't been keeping well.'

His mother sighed a truck. 'Well, Charlie likes to exaggerate.' She poured herself another glass of wine. 'A bit of heart trouble earlier in the year, but the doctor says I'm fine now.'

Charlie stood up so abruptly his mother stopped pouring.

'Going to show Nadine my bedroom.'

'Oh,' laughed his mother, 'it's just like old times!'

Charlie lit the block of hash and crumbled off an edge, while Nadine searched through his playlist and selected Strike the Colours, her new favourite Glasgow band. The snarling wolf of adulthood at the bedroom door and only music to defeat it with. It was why adults kept iPods at their hip every day: a chamber of silver bullets, indie-tipped and true. Eat some Bowie, you soulless corporate whores! Captain Beefheart, muthafuckas!! As for you, Take That . . . take *this*:

*BLAM! BLAM! ZAPPA! BLAM!*

You arm yourself.

'Aw,' said Nadine, 'isn't your mum sweet? I always liked her.'

'She's a pain in the arse.'

'Charles Bain, that is your mammy.'

'Did you see her pouring that wine? "*Charlie likes to exaggerate.*" Fuck is she trying to prove?'

'That you can't baby her,' said Nadine. 'It's her life.'

'Not for long, if she keeps this up.'

He tried to concentrate on filling the pipe, tamping just enough hash into the bowl, but found his fingers were trembling. He had to place it on the bed while a sphere of moisture crept along his eyelash.

'Charlie . . .' said Nadine.

He dabbed at his eye and lit the pipe. Then he took a long, slow draw and handed it to Nadine. She took a smaller draw, and by the time she'd exhaled it, he was still holding his in.

He let it go.

114

Nadine stared at him. 'Why are you living here, Charlie?'

He puffed a little more on the pipe while he thought, like Bilbo Baggins in contemplation of a quest. 'Well,' he said, 'after Yvonne kicked me out, I didn't have anywhere else to go.'

'But why are you *still* living here?'

He shrugged. 'Suppose I've just got used to it now. And it's nice to have someone to take care of. Also, my dad really did a number on her. I don't like her being alone.'

'You'll have to move out some time.'

'Says who? Want some?' He offered her the hash pipe.

'Charlie. Do I have a straggly beard? Am I tripping over my eyelids?'

He wove it around in front of her. He blew scented smoke at her.

'Fuck off with that stuff. It does *not* make you Beck.'

Nadine stood and crossed to the window. His bedroom looked onto the playground of a primary school. 'Remember we used to bunk off,' she said, 'and come here when your parents were at work to watch the kids play?'

'Yeah,' he said, as the room swelled and subsided.

'Remember that little kid who never did what he was told?'

'Wee blond one?' said Charlie.

'That's right. At the bell the kids would run into line and he'd still be there, hula-hooping or booting a ball.'

'What did we call him?'

'Gordy.'

'Gordy! The teacher would come out and bark and he'd drop his head and walk up to her and we'd see her give him a row. Then he'd traipse to the end of the line, dragging his feet.'

'Yeah,' said Charlie. He felt the colours emerge from the music.

'And the class would file in, holding hands with their partner and

115

putting their fingers to their lips. But he wouldn't have a partner cos he was last in line and he'd just kind of solemnly shuffle in behind them.'

Charlie looked at Nadine's back. She was a frontierswoman, staring out at the landscape, its ripples of raw beauty. Her dress had crinkles in it. He focused on the spot at her neck, where it tied.

'But just before he went through the door, he'd always do a wee dance. A wee final act of rebellion. And then disappear.'

'So he did.'

Nadine turned and tried to smile at Charlie, but something about it would not comply. Then he offered her the pipe again, smoke stroking the air. She shook her head. 'Charlie, I don't feel so good these days. I think I'm failing.'

'No, you aren't.'

'Then why am I not famous?'

He leaned forwards on the bed and touched her with a stoned hand. She looked at him. 'Nadine,' he hash-smiled. '*Honey*. We are *Hot 100*.'

Deborah and Jordan arrived as he was getting the plates ready, a wee plate for wee Elizabeth's wee portions, which she'd eat in her high-chair, watching *Thomas the Tank Engine*. Jordan grunted as he came in. Criticise one thing about this fucking dinner . . .

Elizabeth ran towards Charlie and he opened his arms and felt her small body in his. That brief ecstasy, then she was gone, to buzz around another adult like a summer bee. Deborah went straight for Nadine with a pre-emptive hug. He remembered Deborah, when she was a kid, being a little jealous of Nadine: this girl who monopolised her big brother with her weirdo music and clothes. There had been one time when he and Nadine had been smashing their sobriety before a night out, the same night Deborah had been having a sleepover with her pals. Nadine had barged into Deborah's room, red wine sloshing, and scanned the six startled bodies huddled before a Patrick Swayze film: paused.

'Oh, girls, pleeeease,' Nadine had sneered. 'Put baby in the corner, come out to the Arches, and *I'll* show you dirty dancing.'

Charlie had had to lead her, teetering, from the room, while flashing an apology at Deborah, whose words '. . . so that's my brother's slut friend . . .' failed to pierce Nadine's carapace.

Nadine and Deborah hugged and said, 'It's good to see you again,' at exactly the same time and with the same degree of formality. Then Nadine offered a handshake to Jordan, and Jordan took it, leaning in for the kiss. Charlie saw a pilot light in Jordan's eyes that he hadn't witnessed since the very first time Deborah had brought him home, and Charlie had caught him casually eyeing his sister's arse, right there in front of them. In her family's home.

Deborah sat on the sofa, smiling. Charlie wiped his hands on a dishcloth and described dinner with pornographic, bistro-menu precision. Braised shanks of. The charming, fruity tang of

Deborah was still smiling.

'What are you so chirpy about?' he said.

'Nothing,' she said. 'Just excited about dinner.'

'*Excited* about dinner?' his mother said. 'Remembering who made it?'

He could tell when his sister was keeping secrets, a skill honed over countless games of Monopoly and Cluedo and You Fat Lying Bastard, the game they'd made when they were kids, in which each tells the other various Factoids. Spot the lie and you get to call your opponent a fat lying bastard, and pummel them.

Charlie left them at the table to check dinner – oven beeping a distress signal, microwave humming flat *vvvvv*'s – and the weed in his brain thought about machines taking over the world. It could happen any day, he was sure of it. All these computers running everything? Until? Until! Don't move we have the house surrounded oh shit redlaserbeams trained then years down diamondmines to find preciouscrystal which will power the

When he drifted back, they were talking about Iraq. He didn't have to spend long guessing who'd brought the subject up, or who'd responded quickest. Jordan, mouth full of bread, was pointing at Nadine with a fork.

'I know it's a mess, but we have to finish the job over there. These bastards are ruthless. Fight fire with fire, that's what I always say.'

Deborah was rolling her eyes.

Nadine neatly spread butter on bread, balancing two olives on top. 'I agree,' she said, 'but that doesn't mean we lose our own moral compass. Torture is unacceptable in any circumstances.'

'Any circumstances?' said Jordan. 'So there's a bomb ticking and some prick with a Jihad Rocks T-shirt knows all about it, but you don't think it's fair to put pressure on him?'

Deborah explained to Charlie: 'There was a programme on last night about Abu Ghraib and Guantánamo Bay.'

'I saw it,' Charlie said. 'Disgusting.'

Jordan turned his planet-sized opinion towards the little moon of Charlie's.

'Well, that doesn't surprise me from a socialist, Charles,' said Jordan. 'What I can't understand is why an intelligent, well-dressed young woman like this hasn't thought things through.'

'Jordan, that's enough.' Deborah scolded. 'Nadine is our guest.'

Charlie searched and searched for the significance of 'well-dressed'. Monged and fumbling, he found only salesman's patter, and a synaptic link in Jordan's head between character and clothing.

'First,' said Nadine, 'well-dressed. Thank you.'

Charlie remembered she believed in the same link.

'Second, I fully accept that I haven't "thought through" why it's fine to deprive grown men of sleep for so long that they can no longer tell the difference between fantasy and reality. Then hang them up by the arms and beat them. Maybe stuff wet towels into their mouths to simulate drowning. Then put a dog-collar on them and drag them, naked, across the floor. You're right, I haven't thought through why that's necesary.'

'Is that what they do?' said Charlie's mother.

'That's only the stuff we know about,' said Charlie.

Jordan sighed. 'Yeah, but.' And in that pause minds at the table slipped from his grasp. When he spoke it was a sharp yank back. 'This is *war*. This is a *war* situation. They declared *war* on us when they started blowing up our buildings and subways. Think we should give a shit if one of them has an uncomfortable night?'

'Only three per cent of detainees in Abu Ghraib have been found to have links to the insurgency.'

'Insurgency?' said Jordan. 'Is that what you call terrorism these days? Tell me, how did we weed out that three per cent without asking them some tough questions?'

Images strobed in Charlie's brain. Beaten faces. Bruises – black, blue, yellow, purple – blotching the skin like dirty suns. Nude bodies stacked, an ugly avant-garde exhibit.

Detainee.

Interrogation.

Touch, kiss, lick, stroke the stations of her body. Find the moment to kiss here, press there. The moment to suck her nipples. The moment to stare into her eyes. The moment to ease your finger inside her. The moment to hold back. The moment to let go. The massive sensory collapse, blissful and echoing.

'Tha wheels onna bus go roun and roun,' sang Elizabeth, 'roun and roun . . .'

The body cartographed in units of pain, its points most sensitive to agony. The drilling into the mind – not an easing of inhibitions aside like soft drapes – but a brutal, bashing-in of consciousness. Good sex filled humans to the brim with themselves. Torture was an emptying, an evacuation of the soul. Hate's seduction. Wind howled in what was left.

fucking wished he hadn't smoked so much of the

When he returned to reality, for some reason, the subject had moved on to his own love-life. There was readjustment, before Charlie realised his mother – trying to tether her boy to an up-and-coming Glasgow artist – was behind this.

'No, our Charlie's not seeing anyone. Keeping himself for someone special, I suspect.'

'He did that once before, Mum,' said Deborah. 'Look what happened.'

His sister, clearly, was less keen on Nadine dancing into more family dinners, war-talk trailing like a flaming dress.

'You are so seeing someone, Charlie,' said Nadine. 'What about that forty-year-old teach—'

His glare.

'Forty-year-old *teacher*?' laughed Jordan. 'You're shagging one of your colleagues, you dirty dog!'

'No, I'm not,' said Charlie.

'*Forty?*' said his mother.

'Forty-one,' he said.

Nadine sipped her lip and avoided his eye. Telepathically he said, Thanks very much. Telepathically she said, Okay, but why expose me to this asshole brother-in-law? Telepathically they both shrugged. Fair enough.

'Charlie,' Deborah muttered, 'you're such a slag.'

'Seriously,' his mother said, 'this woman's a colleague of yours? And forty-one? Is she married?'

'Why does everyone ask that?'

Jordan chortled the scales.

'Okay, I've been seeing her,' said Charlie, 'but it's nothing serious. We're not, like, together. Not *together* together.'

Nadine raised eyebrows.

You shut it.

'Anyway,' said Deborah, 'never mind that. Jordan and I have got some bigger news.'

He saw Jordan's ego ripple while he unfolded his arms. This better not be about his business, thought Charlie. It just better not.

'I'm pregnant again.'

'Oh!' squeaked their mother.

'Hey,' said Charlie, sweating gratitude. He went round the table to kiss Deborah, then shook Jordan's hand and congratulated him. Deborah went to their mother, who, chair-bound, opened up her arms and accepted kisses, and Nadine hugged Deborah too, hesitantly shook Jordan's hand. His mother started firing out, 'Well!' every few seconds and dabbed at tears. All were smiling now.

'Is it a girl or boy?' said Charlie.

'Who cares?' said Deborah.

'We need a male.'

'What for?'

'To lead a rebellion against the machines.'

'Eh?'

'Nothing,' said Charlie. 'Um.'

Elizabeth was gazing round the room, baffled and chewing. She could feel, it was clear, a shift in mood. In the facial expressions and tone of voice. It was a pattern her software could not unscramble. She gave up, turned to the telly, slapped it. 'Pat.'

Charlie put on her *Postman Pat* DVD. She sat down, gooey and in love.

He went into the kitchen and checked the chicken. Jordan was standing in the doorway, arms folded, watching Deborah being clucked and fussed over by the two women. 'Man, that's great news,' said Charlie. 'So pleased for the two of you.'

'Cheers.' Jordan nodded. 'Strong juice in these Jaffas.'

Jordan grinned. Charlie found himself returning it. He shook Jordan's hand again, clapped his shoulder, and for a few seconds it was the two of them together. The title-card read:

## MEN

But it didn't last. At the dinner table, Jordan started on about how they were going to have to move again because the school in their catchment area wasn't good enough. 'Why don't you just go private?' Nadine asked (ironically, Charlie suspected), and before Deborah could respond Jordan had said, 'Well, that would be a logical step, wouldn't it, darling? We only want the best for our kids.' And Deborah nodded. And Nadine glanced at Charlie, because she knew as well as he did that, 'We only want the best for our kids,' meant 'We only want for our kids more than everyone else's kids have.' Charlie shot glances at Jordan, the sight of whom made stoned thoughts darken spiderly. He wanted to steal Elizabeth from Jordan. Elizabeth, his niece, *his* niece, and merely Jordan's daughter. Jordan Barr, with his four Barr brothers. 'Self-made' Jordan Barr, with his used-car business, all-male workforce and – Charlie had visited the place – topless calendars on the wall. It seethed and writhed with testosterone. With *Barr*. How could this man, this *salesman*, who spoke of 'race problems' in the UK and did not mean racism, who voted Tory, who admitted that his favourite book ever − *his very favourite book EVER* − was a biography of Richard Branson, how could this man love Elizabeth as much as Charlie did?

'Thought of names?' Charlie said, gripping onto beauty.

'If it's a girl,' said Deborah, 'we like Paige. Or Kayla. Or Alisha.'

'Oh, they're gorgeous,' Nadine said dutifully.

Paige Barr. Alisha Barr. Kayla Barr. Jesus. Why not just go the whole way and call her Candy?

'If it's a boy?'

'Well,' said Deborah, rubbing her hair, 'we were thinking . . . if it's a boy . . . then Charles.'

'Oh,' Charlie said. 'My.'

'I wanted Jordan,' said Jordan.

Their mother took Charlie's hand and gave it a squeeze that said, *See?* Then she continued eating. Deborah winked at him. Elizabeth waved a bit of carrot, glancing from Mummy to Postman Pat, Mummy to Postman Pat.

'Yum!' said Elizabeth.

'Oh, my,' said Charlie.

Then Deborah looked around the table and said, 'Reckon we should tell Dad?'

'I read about my reputation as a ladies'
man. For someone who has spent so
many nights alone, that has a special
bitter amusement attached to it.'

Leonard Cohen

Charlie visited Julie that lunchtime and took flowers with him. He didn't often buy flowers for women, but knew Julie liked them, since whenever he gave her flowers she yelped and gasped and cried her surprise. The kids thought her the school's strictest teacher, but she couldn't be a rock of discipline all the time, he knew. A striped swirl of girliness ran right through her. He stood in the rain outside her flat and rang the bell. Twirled his brolly. I'm singing in the rain, just

'Hello?'

'Hi, Julie, it's me.'

'Me?'

'Charlie.'

Crackle hiss crackle crackle.

'Charlie *Bain.*'

The lock buzzed and he went in, up the close into an echoing tenement. She was at the door to greet him in her dressing-gown. In her dressing-gown at three in the afternoon. In her dressing-gown, unshowered, hair still rumpled, with no makeup on, at three in the afternoon. The flowers bloomed hello. He kissed her on the cheek and she didn't return it.

She traipsed into the kitchen, hands stuffed into her gown, dragging slippers. She put his flowers into water. They became doomed soldiers, waiting for the rifle crack. He talked: 'So! Marking this book review, y'know, Graham Robertson? Fourth year? And he's only reviewed *Portnoy's Complaint.* And he's quoted, like, the worst bits. I mean the *very* worst. I mean, the bits with the wanking and his sister's bra and the *C*-word and all that. And I'm thinking has he done

127

this on purpose? Just so he can write these porno scenes and all these C-words? You know what Graham Robertson's like.' Charlie picked up a crisp from a bowl on the coffee-table. Why were there crisps in a bowl on the coffee-table? 'But what do I do, because it's, like, a *classic*, y'know? And I'm always on at them to read quality books and not just, like, football magazines or novels about boy wizards. But, I mean, *Portnoy's Complaint*? What do I—'

He stopped. Julie wasn't even looking at him. She was staring out of the window, hands deep in the pockets of her three-in-the-afternoon-but-I'm-entitled-to-look-like-shit dressing-gown.

'Julie, is something wrong?'

She turned, but didn't look him in the eye. 'Why would there be anything wrong?'

'Because you've barely spoken since I came in.'

'Oh, how rude of me,' she said, 'to interrupt your partying.'

He was not unreasonable. No, he was not an unreasonable man. 'Partying?'

'Didn't you tell me your sister was visiting on Saturday night?'

'I did . . .' he said '. . . but . . .'

His fingers waggled like little legs.

'What is this?' she said, mimicking.

'Uh?' he said.

'Does this,' she said, doing it again, 'mean you don't *know*?'

'No. It means I'm thinking.'

'What do you need to think about? Were you or were you not at your sister's?'

'How do you know this?'

It was the pupils. At Jupito. Had to be the pupils. The sixth-year pupils. The sixth-year *sneaks*. Gollums! He knew he should have neutralised them when he'd had the chance, slid up behind them with a needle – witnesses dropping one by one, while he hissed and scuttled away and fucked someone, since this was what he was being accused of, after all, wasn't it? When he'd done nothing. Nothing!

'Gavin saw you,' she said. 'At something called Jupito? With a woman. You had your hand on her arse.'

Nadine.

'Oh,' he said. 'Wait,' he said.

'I am waiting.'

'Gavin?'

'Yes,' she enunciated. 'Ga-vin.'

'I didn't see Gavin that night.'

'But Gavin saw you,' she said. 'In Ju-pi-to.' Her tone was *pi*-exact, to three demical points.

'But I didn't see Gavin,' he mumbled again.

'That's not the issue. *Were* you there with a woman? I don't mind, Charlie,' she said. 'I don't *mind* you going out with female friends. But it's the fact that you touched her arse, and so obviously lied about seeing your sister. Curious.'

'Wait,' he said.

'I *am* waiting. Still.'

A zoetrope of thoughts spun. He slowed it. The picture: Gavin. Gavin's eyes. Staring out in flashes. Charlie hadn't even seen him in the club. Had Gavin secreted himself among the wall of hipsters, polymorphed into some post-punk drummer with an ironic T-shirt? Had he been *spying*? Obviously. Prick! And he was going to tell Julie because he wanted her back, '*I want you back, Julie!*' he'd say, a pining, spurned, soap-opera lover. '*He's no good for you! He cheats! Like a dog!*' Then he'd follow Julie to the bedroom and grip her sheets and they'd make torrid, saxophone-soundtracked love. If Gavin had noticed Charlie at Jupito, he'd have come up to him, surely? Unless he'd tucked the sight of Charlie away, thief-like, for use in a later *coup de grâce*. Excuses were lacking. He panicked. He was slack-jawed and furious: Gavin had played it beautifully. Charlie thought and thought, the zoetrope spinning, burning, fast, and Julie wanted answers.

She tried to make an angular shape, but her body was too thick.

'So what?' He laughed.

Then stopped.

'Why are you lying to me?'

He waggled his fingers like wee legs again. Why didn't she think this was cute? 'Because,' he said, 'it was my sister I was *with*. End of.'

'You had your hand on her arse?'

This. This. This. This.

'Of course I didn't. I was consoling her. Our mother is recovering from a heart attack, remember. It affects us.'

Julie's eyes closed lightly.

'You don't believe me?'

'You touched her arse to console her?'

'I didn't touch her *arse*, for fucksake. I was cuddling her. I had my arms round her. It must've looked like I was touching her arse.'

'On the dance-floor?'

'Think it's up to me where she gets upset? Quite frankly, I'm starting to find all this offensive.' Bulldoze. Bulldoze. Only way out of the stockpiled evidence. 'So I don't know what Gavin thinks he saw, but I'd like to take up with him why he thinks I'm perving on my fucking sister when she's upset about my mother's health!'

Julie retreated, hands raised. 'Okay, Charlie, okay. Don't bring it up with him. I'm sure he'd be very embarrassed that he got it wrong.'

'He'd better be.'

She placed her arms around him. He was shaking, but not for the reasons that she thought he was. Her dressing-gown fell slightly open.

'Are you telling the truth?'

'Julie . . .' he growled.

'Okay,' she said, 'I believe you. But, Charlie?'

'Mm?'

'If I ever find out you've lied to me, or cheated, I will cut your dick off.'

He nodded against the top of her head.

'It'll make a nice ornament,' she said, 'alongside the dicks of all the other cheating bastards.'

Her hair smelled warm, unwashed.

'Understood?' she said.

'Yep. Can we leave this now, please?'

'Gladly.'

And he saw her here over the weekend, in her dressing-gown, watching TV, unshowered and throwing crisps into herself and used tissues into the bin and growing angry and hate-filled and wondering whether or not she should phone him, whether or not she should phone his *sister*, but no, cos that's what a *psycho* would do. He felt a slight bulge of fat creep beneath his fingers, and sensed, deep within Julie, nestled like a black pith-stone, a nurtured grudge somewhere in her past. Squeeze hard enough, he thought, and a defence mechanism, porcupine spines or something, will erupt from this skin.

*Sshk!*

She was weeping, and he was holding her and saying, 'It's okay, Julie, it's okay,' and her dressing-gown was falling further open, and soon she was kissing at his neck and ears, the potential energy stored all weekend become kinetic. They were there. He'd surveyed the lie of the land and the horses were cantering at the borders, and he could see trees and fields and vast lakes. And then they were fucking as the sun went over the hill, her lovemaking harder and angrier than his: they clashed and strafed and reared like cavalry.

\*

Afterwards she lay upon his chest and said, 'Why do you suppose Gavin told me that?'

He took the joint from her and toked. Smoke billowed. The battlefield slow and wreathed in Scotch mist. Culloden. Bannockburn. Glencoe. As the dope kicked in everything moved away about a foot.

Charlie frowned. 'Why do *you* suppose he told you?'

'Hm,' she said. Then shifted.

He kissed her hair.

He stared at the ceiling.

'Y'know, you should really get that redone.'

She glanced up. 'The Artex? What's wrong with it?'

'Look at it,' he said. 'What a botched job.'

'Why?'

'There's,' he said, 'like, fingerprints and stuff all over it.'

'Fingerprints?' she said, put her glasses on and strained. 'They're not fingerprints, that's the design.'

He stared into the map of Artex, its lunar landscape and pin-mountains. There were fingerprints, he could see them: five fingertip-sized indents, repeated endlessly. They raised themselves as though in a 3-D picture, a hologram, they were *right there* – why couldn't she *see* them?

But then they were gone. Lost among cracks and smoke.

He exha                    l                e              d
      *a*              *a*           *l*   *e*
   *a*      *a*      *a*          *a*       l      e   *d*
   *a*   *a*   *a*  *a*        *a*   l         *d*
*a*            *a* *a*   *a*                        l      *d*
   *a*                          l   e *d*
        *ex*      *h*   *a*   *l*   *e*        the sea
*the*      *s*    *ea the sea is hissing*    *and*    exhale    *touching your bare toes. It's a freezing day. A gigantic grey sky. All the age and power*

*of the world. Here on the lonely west coast of Scotland, midwinter. You have just come from eating ice-cream at Nardini's, choc-chip for you, butterscotch with Skittles in it for Yvonne. Long, silver horizon. You stand there, holding hands, and the tide creeps further up your feet, ankles, shins.*

*'So cold!' says Yvonne.*

*'Is this paddling?'*

*'This is Hopeful Standing,' she says.*

*'No,' you say, 'this counts. We're in. We're definitely in.'*

*'Paddling involves motion,' she says, moving forwards. 'A paddling motion.'*

*'What about crabs?' you say.*

*Yvonne shakes her head. 'You big jessie.' A smile tickles her face.*

*'What?'*

*She pushes you. Off balance. Cold: shock.*

*'Agh! Ya cheeky—'*

*'Watch out for crabs!' She's off and running, water leaping from her feet. You give chase. She squeals. Your clothes are dense with brine, thick round your limbs. You're both charging through the surf. You catch her – climb round her – haul her down. She screams. And then you just splash each other, yelling, getting no wetter than you already are. She gives chase this time* the system is finding its own shape *and you are running and her arms grip your waist and she tries to lift you and you say, 'You'll never do it,' and she does it, lifts you, barely, then lets go and you are under, submerged, the roar of water almost inside you. You emerge, grinning to see her grinning.*

*Car. Stripped and shivering with the heater on full blast. Under a blanket in the back seat, skin soft and salt-tender against each other.*

*You rub your nose against hers.*     *generations unborn*

*'You have a cute smile,' you say.*     *Gliding through the unive*

*She brushes her lips against yours.*
*'You have a cute . . . elbow.'*
*You rub elbows.*
*'You have cute nipples.'*
*'Good try.' She laughs. 'You have nice hair.'*
*You brush your hair over her face.*

*'Hee,' she squeaks.*          *we are animal*

*'You have a nice bottom.'*

*'You have nice shoes.'*          *m   e        a        t*

*'You have a nice toaster.'*
*'You have a nice tree outside your house,' you say.*
*'You have a nice . . . collection of books.'*
*'You have a nice . . . dog.'*
    *'My dog is dead!' she says. 'He died five years ago, you insensitive*
*bastard!'*
    *'Marry me, Yvonne,' you say.*          *pan*
*She stops laughing and looks at you. 'What?'*
*'Fuck it,' you say. 'Let's get married.'*          *panic*
*'Married?' she says. 'When?'*          *p   a   n   i   c*
*'Some time in the summer.'*
*'Boring,' she says. 'Let's do January. Good for January?'*
*'Have to consult my diary.'*
*'Nobody gets married in January. We should soooo do January.'*
*'January it is,' you say. 'Then we'll move to the seaside?'*

*'And collect crabs.'*

*'And shells and stuff,' you say. 'And in the winter we can go sledging. Fast!'*

*'And in the summer?' she says.*

*'In the summer we'll eat figs.'*    *panic*

*'What is a fig?'*

*'I don't know. But we'll have them at the wedding. Then do all the Happily Ever After stuff?'*

*'Deal,' she says.*

*'Deal,' y o u   s        a        y*


*panic!*

*!panic!*

It is a man's self. His essence. It has to be.

Your cock does not obey reason.

Does not philosophise.

It wants to fuck.

All it wants.

135

It fills itself with blood.

It is what she knows, in that moment. She can need your cock
more than your love or companionship, can want it like you want her
cunt. But still. Do not take off your jeans. Keep your jeans on.
Keep them on as long as possible. Bare yourself above the waist.
Strip her to her underwear. Cage her among your limbs.
From above, stare. Your fingers on her shoulders. You are male.
Let your belt whip from your waist. Let her feel your hard-on
between her legs, the thick ridge of denim against her. She
will writhe. Do not take those jeans off, but do everything to her,
all the things she loves. You are hers. You belong to her.
You are her plaything. Stack pleasure upon pleasure and watch her
become animal. Hear it in her throat, a creature's growl, and
Do not take off your jeans.
Not yet.
Let her wait.
A little longer.
You exist only so far as your cock exists, so much as your fullness
fills her, your fuck
and your roar – your souls clenching rawly.

it is who you are

what you have become

bad

## Bad

## BAD

Charlie drew on the joint and stared at the picture of his cock. He liked looking at it. The thick, wanting fact of it. In the picture his thumb was hooked into his pants, pulling them down. His pubic hair was a dark flame, his penis rigid and smooth. He'd been told by women that they preferred a circumcised cock. He'd notice the way they petted and stroked it, looking, letting their gaze lick even before resting their tongue upon it. It had taken a while for him to realise that women could feel desire for the cock itself, could want it in them, pulsing. Something so ugly. So beautiful.

He sparked at the joint again, pressed send.

His cock disappeared.

He scrambled down through his playlist: We Were Promised Jetpacks. He picked up the book he'd bought that day, *The Blank Slate*. Bookshops were a good place to chat to smart women. He'd been in Borders, browsing through pages, idly daubing his thoughts on them.

As he roamed, the names of great authors he hadn't read passed solidly through him – Begone HELLER! Have at ye, BELLOW! MELVILLE! – and he drifted through a percolating Starbucks haze. The psychology bay before him, men and educated guesses, their quantifying of the soul. A million mistimed thrusts into the numinous cloud of the mind. Damn it, lads, we missed again! Vell, gentlemen, I theenk you vill vind it has zumsin to do vith your muther. Oh, fuck off, Freud. Here, someone chuck him a dream about yellow penguins, see what he comes up with.

In the past century many people have assumed that we are shaped by our environment: a blank slate waiting to be inscribed by upbringing and culture, with innate abilities playing little part.

Steven Pinker's profound and essential book shows that this view denies the heart of our being: human nature. We are prepared for sex, aggression and jealousy – and also love, compassion and reason. Violence is not just a product of society; male and female minds are different; the genes we give our children shape them more than our parenting practices. To acknowledge our nature, Pinker shows, is not to condone inequality or callousness, but ultimately to understand the very foundations of humanity.

**£9.99**

He'd bought the book. He'd started reading on the subway back to Hillhead. He hadn't stopped, and now picked it up each spare minute, allowing himself a delicious, frightening glimpse into the history of consciousness. Then he'd glut himself on it one night, like a hand plunging into sweets spiked with drugs. Dangerous ideas boiling, hardening into argument. Logic. The Noble Savage. Species character.

Nature versus nurture. Reason. Genetic determinism. The grammar of consciousness. The mind/body divide. Humankind humming beneath his fingertips, its vast intimate drone.

The Ghost in the Machine.

He would understand what he was.

He would *find it*.

He noticed the ink kept smudging wherever he'd touched the print, though. Purplish fingermarks. Back to the shop with you, *The Blank Slate*! Your insights do nothing to offset the poor quality of your production!

fingerprints

Charlie's phone beeped and he reached across the duvet to pick it up. Download Message. Tiny slivers of adrenalin started to circulate; it was Annabelle, dressed only in bra and knickers. Annabelle was a girl he'd met in Borders. She'd picked up Toni Morrison and without even hesitating he'd said, 'Oh, go for *Beloved*, it's a much better book.' She'd glanced up; the rapiers of their looks. Hers prodded through a bit: 'What's that?' 'I must sound like a terrible snob,' he smirked, 'but seriously. Believe me.' He was gambling on the prediction that someone who picked up Toni Morrison didn't mind book snobbery. He was right: she'd smiled a little. She'd told him it was compulsory for her uni module, Contemporary American Fiction, and they'd scatted through the usual Glasgow Uni English-student chat – comparing modules, dissertation titles, favourite tutors. Where she stayed. What clubs she went to. What nights she went. Give me a text if you're going to be there, then, Annabelle. Uh, tell you what, I'll text you when I'm going. What's your number? He'd typed out, You are such a fox, pressed send. Her phone had beeped immediately and she'd opened the message, then looked up at him, a brief firework of a smile making its way across her face. It had begun.

hadn't shown her face in the pictures    just    skin

He stared at the bra, knickers, the shape beneath them. The body that had been there, all the time, during the chat in Borders. Waiting to see if he could punch the correct codes. It was etiquette to write That was a random, cheeky encounter! at one point and I want my tongue on your pussy at another. Annabelle's body. It was hers. It belonged to her. She had shown it to him. A connection. This act of unveiling. It had lain in wait for him her whole life. The pleasures he would bring to it. The things his cock would offer. For her: this imminent fuck. Right to the centre of each other.

Lazily, he began masturbating. With the thumb of his other hand he typed:

Sexy girl. Now take them off.

Two minutes later: Wish you could take them off for me...x

Tease.

You like it. x

Maybe I'll turn you down...

Maybe you won't get the choice...x

Naughty girl. Might have to bring you into line...

Oh I think I deserve it....x

A single line, or even word – 'cunt' where 'nipple' should be, or 'to fuck you' instead of 'to kiss your neck' – could veer off-target and shatter that tension, suck it down into a void of mere characters sent by strangers via telecommunication. There was one – Gail (his opening gambit: 'Who'd win in a fight between Spider-Man and Batman?') – who had warned him, too proudly, that she had a reputation as an ice-queen. He'd replied: Good, I like a challenge. But thereafter every ironic text-joke became a tumbleweed drifting across space between them. What are you on? she'd said, or just sent a confused smiley, mouth twisted like wire. End of the line. But this. This here Good Flirting! When it was moving this quickly? This was *art*. Imaginations unleashed and just going *at* each other, a mind that pours out of you, ahead of you, towards someone else, takes a shape, a form, a body, a cock, which they can recognise as pain, joy, frustration, soul, lust.

*This is who we are.*

*We are alive, you and I.*

*Look at us: this detritus of space-matter that has formed a human shape!*

*Look at us fucking on this here Earth!*

*What are we like?!!!!*

to have two women in the same bed    two    tongues slick round his

He listened to Leonard Cohen and thought of Julie. He flicked through the iPod shuffle function of his mind and found songs and scenes of girls he'd fancied. The sheer unrequited *longing* that draped things:

'Need You Tonight' by INXS – Nadine, as they both found music. Her purple, teengirl bedroom. The smell of her starter perfume: Sunflowers by Elizabeth Arden.

'Don't Look Back in Anger' – Sarah Gardner, fourth year of high school – !!!BABE!!! – bus on school trip to Paris. 'Yeah, Oasis, yeah yeah, cool, Sarah, love them. Will you go out with me?'

'Insomnia' – Megan Wright, fifth year, her back garden that summer, her thighs draped with heat, sweat shimmering on them, and you unable to tou—

'Shine On You Crazy Diamond' – Lesley Grant, sixth year, introducing you to hash. The music, the mong, making her pretty, pixie.

Brahms Fifth Symphony – Jennifer, French student, first year of uni. She'd smoked slowly and said, slower: 'Thees ees the only real myuzeek, Charlie. Everytheeng else is joos *trash*.'

'O Brother Where Art Thou' soundtrack – Angela Canterbury, worked beside him in Boots that other summer, that other time. She

141

had a boyfriend. She said: 'I have a *boyfriend*.' Making a rock-hard barrier with one word.

None of these girls had slept with him. No one till.

```
        v   n   e
Y           n   e
  v         o   e
```

He thought of the aftermath of Yvonne, the wreckage of it, when they'd split and he'd lurched off to Europe backpacking that summer – seven weeks between school terms yawning ahead of him, seven weeks of alone alone alone. So he'd called Nadine. The call. The 'Charlie!' The coffee. The night out. The going to a party together. The going to a wedding together (as pals, obviously!). The backpacking round Europe (*still* as pals, obviously!). You reconstruct. You reconstruct a reconstruction. Your mind acclimatising itself to the freedom of enjoying female company *guilt-free*. You and Nadine fishing old memories out from the rock-pool of childhood. You and Nadine creating new memories. Drinking. Taking coke. Taking ecstasy. Beach parties in Germany. Getting lost in Madrid. An albino ape at the zoo in Barcelona. Nadine had said, 'Doesn't that look like Graham Dempsey from our school?' and you'd both laughed – his huge Adam's apple! There there was that

one                          night st          a          n d

that neither of you talk about any more. But in the darkness afterwards Nadine had wept, slow and almost silently, like a lowing marine creature, and you'd placed your hand on her naked shoulder and she'd hissed, 'Don't fucking touch me,' and her sobs seeped their way into your bones and both of you just lay there willing the darkness to cleanse you.

Next night some guy felt her tit.

She smashed a bottle across his head.

She spat on him.

Other women on benches or against trees – these women who are not Yvonne! They are not Yvonne! They. Just. Are. Not. But *how?* – though she remained an ululating siren song in your mind, your soon-to-be-ex-wife, while you licked, smelled, tasted the rest of the world outside her. The sound of the wind in leaves at midnight, or silently kissing in hostels while strangers slept, snoring gently, all around you. Paris. *Montmartre feels red*, he'd thought. *Her lips feel red too!* Man. Monged. Dark. Paris. Crepuscular. He dreamed that he was in *Interview with the Vampire*. Stalking the night. The light on the walk back from a hostel he'd fucked in. Beautiful. *Pellucid.* The touch of a Canadian girl. Her baseball cap, its maple leaf, whydidCanadians ALWAYSwearmapleleaves? Nadine gruntingly asking about your lovebite next morning. A beach in Spain at midnight, the vast speaking shore. The hugeness of the moon, a gigantic piece of peace. Charlie's route had criss-crossed Europe like a bootlace, *tightened*. It was all there within his reach. But what was life for? When it could be so easily torn. Ripped asunder and made meaningless. Who was he? Shock horror! *Him!* The entity, the collection of molecules that was Charles James Bain, BA (Hons)? His lashes: dipped in the mirror. Hey. His body still in its twenties. Flexed. After those first few times with those first few girls, *new* girls, some drunk, stoned, some on coke, some with a vision so clear, *so seeing into him*, that it was frightening. 'I think you need help,' one of them – Emma? Mary? The Canadian? – had said, stroking his face. 'I am lost,' he'd wept. 'I'm slipping under.' Names and shapes and accents; fondness and affection and longing. Raw needy sex. Fucking. Fucking. Bodies that were *necessary*. Women who *liked* him. *Wanted* him. Thought it was worthwhile spending the *night* with him. *A whole night of their lives!* What were they – crazy? Blind? Were they doing this for a bet? Who'd put them up to it? Who? He demanded to know! What celestial japery was this?

They'd been in Barcelona, sitting in the sun, by a fountain, some gaudy Gaudí thing, Nadine reading a map, when he'd said it:

'I probably love you, y'know.'

She hadn't even looked up from the map, kept scanning it, and she had her shades on so he couldn't see her eyes.

ouldn't see her ey

speak to me

Then – right at that moment – some Spaniard had come up to them and said, 'You Eengleesh?' and he'd said, 'No, Scottish,' and the guy had said, 'Ah, bagpipes! Keelt! Ah . . . Weelliam Wallace? Mel Geebson? Free-dom! Loch Ness Monster! Yes? Scotchland? Haggees!'

Nadine never ever mentioned what he'd said to her by that fountain. And she never told him why she'd started crying in bed either.

Iden Bowl The Cabinet of Dr Caligari Death in Venice Battleship Potemkin Sons and Lovers Greed The Ragged Trousered Philanthropists Rashômon A Portrait of the Artist as a Young Man Women in Love Ulysses Un Chien Andalou A Passage to India Pandora's Box Der Zauberberg M Der Prozess The Great Gatsby Fantasia Mrs Dalloway Amerika Citizen Kane To the Lighthouse **Me!** la Recherche du Temps Perdu Decline and Fall Lady Chatterley's Lover Orlando Histoire de L'Oeil Look Homeward, Angel The Magnificent Ambersons Les Enfants Terribles The Sound and the Fury The Postman Always Rings Me Twice **Me! Me! Me! Me! Me!** Im Western nichts Neues A Farewell to Arms The Waves Brave New World Sunset Song Tender Is the Night A Handful of Dust **PLEASE?** Tropic of Cancer Absalom, Absalom! Murphy Notorious U.S.A. La Nausée At Swim Two Birds Finnegans Wake The *Me!* Wrath All About Eve The Power and the Glory Native Son *Me!* the Bell Tolls L'Étranger Brideshead Revisited La Peste Under the Volcano Se Questo e un Uomo Nineteen Eighty Four Molloy A Streetcar Named Desire The End of the Affair The Catcher in the Rye Invisible Man Go Tell it on the Mountain L'Innommable Lord of the Flies The Recognitions Rebel Without a **Pleeeeeeeease . . . ?**

\*

Charlie spun and revelled in class, on form, bantering and larking with the third-years, whip-crack strict with his first-years, who'd started acting up. Their hive mind swarming, stinging in short disruptive bursts. They laughed for no reason that he could discern. A couple of the boys made comments that crossed the line. He dealt with it, put out their fire, wondering, Was there a fight at break-time? Had some routine geek or nerd – blessed are the geeks, special are the nerds – been turned on by the herd, their slender, shivering genius-in-waiting demolished by a boot to the shin? Whatever, it was sunny outside and there were constant ripples of dissent whenever he asked them to do work.

'This isn't funny, first year!'

'I'm getting tired of this, first year!'

'First year, this is your last warning!'

Doled out like do-not-pass-Go cards. But when he told them his joke about penguins, they laughed. Before the bell, he said, 'Right, you, you and you – I want to see you after class. The others, be off with you.' The class scattered, but three boys hung around after like stains on the classroom floor. He went through the ritual of being Disappointed In Them. 'And do you think that's reasonable behaviour from a twelve-year-old at this school? No, you're right. IT IS NOT.' Then he let them go. Tiddlers. The real mean fish wriggled away from whatever barb you tried to land them with, only to resurface again later – fat, taunting, unintimidated.

But over the course of the day the kids' behaviour worsened. It seemed as though some kind of collective madness was at work, some mass-rage spell.

At break he interrupted a fight between two third-years, going at it like spitfires. Holding each of them at arm's length, he yelled, 'Enough! My room! Now!' A living tribunal.

*

Gavin stepped into Charlie's room during the lunch-break, that sort of precise, insectoid way he moved. Hands in his pockets, he circled the table that Charlie sat at as though sizing it up for a meal. Charlie considered simply continuing to work until Gavin spoke. Then Gavin spoke.

'So, how are things coming on with the Burns supper preparations?'

'Pretty good,' said Charlie. 'I've got them singing "Charlie Is My Darling".'

'Appropriately enough,' said Gavin, lifting Charlie's Glasgow University paperweight and inspecting it, as though inspecting Charlie's actual degree.

'What have you got yours doing?'

'Well,' said Gavin, 'not anything eulogising Burns's role as a womaniser, that's for sure. Just think that sends out the wrong message to the kids.'

Charlie folded his arms, picked his way back through the conversation they'd had in which Gavin had *actually said* about Nadine, *Charlie's close friend*: 'Niiiiiice. Shagging her?'

'I don't think we should whitewash Burns for them in that way,' said Charlie. 'It was part of him. The same creative energy that gave us those poems went into his women as well. You can't separate them.'

Gavin sniffed and pressed a peeling poster on Charlie's wall back into place. 'That's certainly one interpretation,' he said. 'I just prefer to de-emphasise Burns's more salubrious aspects. So I'm doing "A Man's A Man For A' That". Burns at his humanist, socialist best.'

Charlie waited for the quotation to come tumbling, and when it didn't he realised he was supposed to provide it. Charlie's move. 'Uh,' he said, closed his eyes, ' "Is there for honest Poverty/That hings his head, an' a' that;/The coward slave – we pass him by . . . " Uh . . .'

'Not bad.' Gavin smirked and sat on Charlie's desk, looked at him through his glasses, perched owl-like on the end of his nose. 'I'll give you that one.'

Charlie stared at him, then started moving papers away from him. 'Listen, uh, I've got something I want to talk to you about.'

'What's that?' said Gavin.

'I'm, uh. I'm seeing Julie.'

Gavin pushed his glasses up his nose, smiled. 'Oh, I know that.'

'You do?'

'Of course. I was just waiting to see how long it would take you to tell me.'

Charlie patted some papers on his desk into a neat pile. Gavin coughed. Then he lifted his bony arse from Charlie's desk and left the classroom, without another word spoken between them.

In the staffroom later Gavin, their union rep, told them to strike for pay. He delivered a confident, almost-searing indictment of the economic crisis, and told them that to protect their families and their livelihoods they would need to send a message out to the government about which they valued more: the financial sector or education. Everyone nodded and murmured. Charlie's laces kept coming out, he kept having to tie them. Charlie would, of course, strike. He *was* a socialist, despite what Gavin insinuated in his wee knight-moves. Outside, the gigantic capitalist economy tipped eerily towards recession, laughing as it did so, an overgrown toddler on a see-saw. Charlie had to equip the kids to fight it, and yet also? To become part of it. This contradiction gnawed at his skull. The corridors of the school thrummed as he walked, the hull of a spacecraft: the constant hum of activity and intellect, the radiation leaked from teaching. He felt sick with it sometimes. They were all *leeching* from him, Klingon-like; he felt slow and weak and empty, a drooped, physical feeling of unlife, all of it to find those kids, those glittering kids who Thought and Felt and Wanted. Yet in the newspapers, weekly: schools being attacked, with phasers full-on, for failing to educate the young. They were definitely educating them in *something*, but nobody knew what. Swearing? Drug-dealing? Kids every year, as he was propelled towards his thirties, had seemed more and more like that abstract thing *Youth* to which everyone referred, a concept he'd once felt in his soul *electrically* but which nowadays was merely sketched out before him each day.

He was having too much sex.

*There are too many women in my life!*

It was exhausting him; the constant cycle of their psyches in his brain. The things they wanted. Things! With their fingernails and pussies and hearts, they wanted Things. And here he was trying to haul the damaged hull of scholarship, howling, from the void. This will be a Good School. These will be Good Kids. Believe. *Believe*. It's what'll get you through. 'Charlie,' a colleague would say as he passed, 'could I have a word about the exams?' 'Certainly,' he'd reply, and they'd discuss the arrangements practically for a few minutes, and in such moments the power of the state coursed through him.

W    A    R    R    I    O    R

With his sixth-years, though. Ah, his sixth-years. There were only four. Four soldiers to train. Be brave, young people. I am with thee.

This'd scare 'em! He'd found a picture in a Sunday supplement, appearing as he'd schlepped through the papers, munching cereal. It had shocked him out of the morning, showerblink stark.

He handed round the photocopies.

They looked.

'Wow,' said Bethan.

'Jesus Christ,' said Jenny.

Monise had her hand to her mouth.

Simon stared.

The article had been about immigrants into Morocco. He didn't know much about Morocco, or the refugee situation there, but didn't really want to talk about that anyway. It was the picture. It was a photograph of a beach: a lithe, tanned couple beneath a parasol, looking at an asylum-seeker in the distance, dead in the surf.

Washed ashore.

'Anyone?' said Charlie, glancing round the class.

'God,' said Monise.

'Is this real?' said Simon.

Typical. Is this real.

'You bet.'

'Where?' said Jenny.

'Morocco.'

'I've been there on holiday,' said Bethan.

'We've all been there on holiday,' said Charlie, even though he hadn't and didn't know anyone else who had.

'We're the people in the picture,' said Jenny. 'It's condemning us.'

'No,' said Simon. 'It's condemning them. *We* wouldn't do this.'

'Wouldn't we?' Charlie felt almost debonair when he said it.

'Well,' said Simon, 'if we would then why are we shocked?'

'Because we're confronted by our own apathy,' said Monise. 'We ignore people like this when we walk past beggars in the street.'

'It's not Scotland, though,' said Bethan. 'It's Morocco.'

'No,' said Monise. 'It is about Scotland. It's about everywhere. We're watching them watching him. So the picture makes us complicit.'

oh good stuff, Monise

He liked this, could feel their adult minds emerge, glistening, everything New and Important and Needing to Be Discussed Right Now Before It Was Too Late, but soon he drifted. He started thinking about being admiral of a large trade ship in the nineteenth century.

And when he docked, they were talking about the singer from some band.

'I love them,' said Monise. 'Hard, angry and beautiful all the same time.'

'They are not,' said Bethan. 'Depressing. Miserable. Yuk.'

'See they're playing the ABC?' said Simon. 'Supporting Sons and Daughters.'

How had the conversation become this? How had music entered the fray? Charlie fumbled and grabbed the rope of discussion before it disappeared off the edge of the ship.

'The photo?' he said.

'Yes,' said Simon. 'It's horrible. Just like your taste in music, Monise.'

'Shut *up*,' said Monise, and slapped him. Simon guffawed.

'Simon,' snapped Charlie, 'show some respect. This is serious.'

Simon turned, smile draining. 'Mr Bain, it wasn't me who changed the subject.'

'The man in this picture is dead,' said Charlie.

'Sorry.'

'It's a disgrace,' said Charlie.

'Sorry,' said Simon.

'I expected better from you,' said Charlie.

'He said sorry,' said Monise.

Charlie looked at her. She frowned at him.

'It was actually me who changed the subject,' said Bethan. 'Simon was talking about the picture and I said the guy looks like that singer.'

'Which singer?' said Charlie.

'You wouldn't know him,' said Bethan.

'I know music,' said Charlie. 'I saw the Strokes play the Barrowlands. Try me.'

'Adam Stafford.'

'From . . . ?' said Charlie.

'Y'all is Fantasy Island,' said Bethan.

'Oh, yeah,' said Charlie. 'Of course. They did that . . . album. That song. That, um, video.'

'Yeah,' laughed Simon, 'that's them.'

Charlie blinked at him.

'But still,' coughed Simon, 'we should've kept to the topic. I'm sorry, Mr Bain, I know you brought the photo in so we could talk about it.'

Charlie nodded. He looked round at their sheepish, cartoonish faces, at Monise, adjusting her glasses, an inscrutable wee move. Then he stretched his fingers. They cracked. Satisfactorily. 'Don't make a mockery of death,' he said, mainly to Simon, comfortable, middle-class Simon, whose dad worked for an oil company in Aberdeen. An oil company whose rapacious demand for markets had caused havoc in the Middle East and whose corporate profits alone were larger than the economies of some small countries so WHAT THE FUCK COULD YOU KNOW ABOUT SUFFERING???!!!!!

He sniffed. 'Continue,' he said. While they got on with discussing the picture he listened, commenting encouragingly. But after a while he went back to his great big clipper ship, in his smart admiral's suit, and Monise glanced at Simon and Simon glanced at Monise and they both glanced at Charlie, and Charlie set sail to find Jamaica.

He decided to check out this Y'all is Fantasy Island. Nadine knew her Scottish indie, so he texted: a test. She responded with expertsharpness. O yeh fantastic. U dont know their stuff? x

He replied: What do they sound like?

She replied: Like Nirvana Unplugged. And Jeff Buckley. And Love. x

He replied: Are you sure? Then deleted it and wrote: R u sr?

She replied: Am I 'sir'? Dont try 2 write txt spk charlie it doesnt suit u!! x

He replied: Indeed. That is because I am an ARTIST! The shallow confines of short messaging suiteth not my boundless self!

She replied: U shld also put kisses on the end of a txt to me. x

Like this? X

Smaller. x

This? x

Havent u LEARNED this shit yet?!! x

I'm more used to sending pictures, heh heh. x

She said: Well now u know. Always put a wee kiss on the end of ur cock. x

Y'all is Fantasy Island were supporting Sons and Daughters in the ABC, and both he and Nadine loved Sons and Daughters, so they went. Simple as that. They met in Nice 'n' Sleazy's before the gig. His nerves were fluttering. Because he had a wee bag of coke on him. And he'd smoked a hit from his hash pipe before he'd left the flat and now he was growing all narrow and nervy and Smeagol-like, surrounded by Everything, with its noise and trickery and sudden movements and its . . . its . . . *Everything!* Scenesters huddled in colourful clusters, taking notes on jackets, sharp shoes, edgy hair – compliments where due: 'Is it vintage? It looks vintage' – but mainly, y'know, talking about how they're *totally* pals with Glasvegas, or navigating through the ironies, the retro, the pop-culture layered delicately into their banter and their clothes.

Just for once, he thought, why can't we all wear a T-shirt and *mean* it?

Nadine came bristling towards his booth, a sea creature traversing the ocean floor. Nadine: poised, prim, the male eyes fixed to her angles. Nadine reached his table then splashed Nadine all over it.

'*What* are you wearing?'

'Tartan jacket,' he said. 'Why?'

'That's right, Charlie,' she said. 'A tartan jacket. Say it with me. A. Tartan. Jacket.'

'What? Tartan's in.'

'Yeah, scarves. Skirts. Collars. Not full-on fucking Highland regalia! Where did you get it?'

'Old man's shop on Argyle Street.'

'Yeah, cos old men are so happening right now. This is like you still boasting about having seen the fucking *Strokes*.'

'But I've indiefied the jacket. I'm subverting the jacket.'

'Oh, I see! I did wonder why I was feeling so *subverted* all of a sudden. I'd thought I was maybe coming down with something.'

Nadine cracked her knuckles.

'Ow,' Charlie said. 'Ow.'

'Wheesht, ya big baby.'

'You'll get arthritis.'

'Not if you do it *subversively*. Stand up. Let me see the jacket.'

He stood before her, hands in the pockets of his tartan jacket.

'Hmm. Like the pin-badges. Bowie. Blondie. Emergent indie band. All present and correct.'

'And the skinny jeans?'

'And. The. Skinny. Jeans.' She sighed. 'But what are you trying to *say*, Charlie? What are you trying to *say* with the jacket?'

'Say?'

'It's reading its own press statement as we speak!'

'Look,' he said, 'the tartan jacket on its own, fair enough. But with the pin-badges and the skinny jeans? It says: See? The *rest* of me is indie. It says: I am doing this *deliberately*. The tartan jacket is *aware*.'

'How could it be *un*aware that *it's so fucking tartan*?'

He pointed at her over his White Russian. 'Just you wait. Just you wait till we get in there. Just wait till the *revolution*.'

'Yeah. March me off to the gulags. In *Brigadoon*.'

'Sons and Daughters are a Scottish band,' he said. 'I'm sure they can take a bit of tartan.'

'Not when they're all leather and sex. Just don't stand at the front, Charlie. You might blind the singer with *couthiness*.'

'Hey, it's the confident, new, modern Scotland. We're tartan and we're proud.'

'Think I'll stick with the crap, cringing one.'

'Huh, call yourself an artist?'

'I prefer *terrorist*.'

They crossed the road and trotted down Sauchiehall Street, tra-ing and la-ing. Charlie suspected she'd already taken some coke. He could see the little paper cuts on her personality: the speed she was talking, her fluttering hands, the way she'd scythed, without mercy, into his jacket. He remembered that guy in Barcelona

felt her tits

bottlesmash over his

*Kfsch!*

spit

'don't you fuckin *ever*

As they neared the ABC, indie fans swarmed, multiplied, stylishness bobbing out from the masses. Legs in brightly coloured tights. Silver shoes. Eyes: Look. Look: Eyes.

He was kinda horny.

'Charlie,' she said, 'know that girl I told you about? Dawn? Was at the art school with me?'

'Oh, yeah,' he said. 'Didn't you ... once ... sleep with her ... ?'

'I did,' grinned Nadine. 'I *did*. Well remembered.'

'Hardly likely to forget *that*. What about her?'

'She's coming up to visit me from Brighton next weekend. Wanna come out with us? You guys never met.'

'Is she a lesbian?'

Nadine frowned. 'I'm not sure what she is. *She*'s not sure what she is.'

'Human, at least?'

'I think so. Difficult to tell.'

'But I'll like her?'

'Oh,' said Nadine, 'you'll definitely like her.'

'Y'know something?' said Charlie. 'I've never met a lesbian I haven't liked.'

'You should put that on a T-shirt.'

'I don't know why. I just really get along with lesbians.'

'It's cos you can't flirt with them. You have to treat them like *real* people, not just someone you can fuck.'

He stopped. She was standing there, eyebrow poised whip-like. *Go on then, challenge it.*

Nadine's sobs; what he'd said at the fountain; what was happening behind her shades; all of it.

'You're probably right,' he said.

'Lesbians are your only salvation, Charlie. The only people who can stop you being a total prick.'

'Don't push it,' he said. 'Anyway, thought you told me she wasn't sure what she was.'

'I think she's half Vulcan.'

She offered her arm. He took it.

'Can't we all link arms?' she pleaded. 'Can't we just all for *once* link arms, in this goddamn world of insanity?'

They skipped a bit. They skipped through hipsters.

'It's like we're off to see the Wizard,' he said.

'Oh!' she said. 'Can I be Toto?'

'You're no dog,' he said. 'You can be the Tin Man.'

'Why the Tin Man?'

'If you only had a heart.'

Nadine stared at him. Then she spoke quietly. 'I have a heart.'

They arrived at the venue and there was Julie: fuck! He ducked away. About six people ahead of him in the queue. And here he was, arm-in-arm with A Girl.

But then he noticed that Julie had Gavin with her.

Ga? Vin?

In a Sons and Daughters T-shirt? As though *he* knew about indie bands? As though he was young? As though he was Julie's boyfriend? As though he was – let's be clear about this – as though he was Charlie?

Charlie unlinked arms from Nadine with the speed of someone caught wanking. 'What?' said Nadine.

Charlie shrugged.

Gavin would remember Nadine – the same girl Charlie had been with at Jupito that time, whose arse he'd felt. The same girl Gavin had grassed to Julie about. *The same girl who was supposed to be Charlie's sister!* That was the cool excuse delivered, with all the efficiency of a doctor's prescription: I was comforting my sister, who is recovering from our mother's heart attack. But he wasn't sure if Nadine would pretend to be his sister. He wasn't sure if Julie would perhaps one day meet his real sister and say, 'But you're not his sister! I've seen her live before!'

'Seen them live before?' said Nadine.

'What?' Charlie said.

'Sons and Daughters. I saw them in the Grand Old Opry, they were soooooo cool.'

Charlie nodded.

Charlie looked over at Julie.

Nadine looked over at Julie.

Nadine narrowed eyes.

He did an elaborate mime, which involved a key, an orange, some pliers and . . . dandruff? He mimed brushing specks of it from his shoulders. Nadine laughed. He turned his back to Julie so she couldn't see him. Nadine peered beyond his shoulders, frowned. He wanted to turn away from Nadine too. He felt thin. Thinning. He wanted to take some more coke before the gig. He wanted to shrink into invisibility and not have anyone see him again – ever ever ever – or else be so monstrously large that the entire gig would turn to him – him, *him*! – and he would open his arms and accept their love, perhaps pluck the prettiest girl from the audience and slow-dance with her while she swooned against his shoulder, nuzzled, kissed his neck, whispered, 'This is my dream come true. I love your poetry,' and the crowd applauded, and he waved an acknowledgement.

But instead he just stood there in the queue: smiling and ageing and, if he was being honest, needing to pee.

*wh 13 en you were 13 thirteen*

*y ou had to d o*

## *oh just fuck off*

had to do this experime nt     in c  hemistry with iodine
you can                                                      't   even reme
ou can                                    't   eve   n
mber what the experiment had been – heating something or cooling
something or dissolving something or adding something to something.
Science isn't your strong point. But it involved iodine. That much you
remember. Who had you loved at the time? Stacey Hill? Eleanor
Draper? Janice Cameron? Wendy Miller? Alison Jenkins? Tracey
Ashworth? Barbara Kerry? Adrienne Green? Claire Alexander?
    Rachel King?
    Jackie Yule?
    Louise Rae?
    Mhairi Graham?
    Dana James?
    Maggie Sloan?
    Katy Craig?
    Sarah Dougall?
    Clara Smith?
    Ellie Torrance?
    Sally Hammond?
    Helen Swift?
'Can't we just be friends, Charlie?' 'I'm not really looking for a
boyfriend, Charlie.' 'Can I think about it?' 'I'm going out with someone.'
'I've just split up with someone.' 'I'm not looking for someone.'
    'Oh, you're so nice.'
    'You're such a nice guy, Charlie.'
    'Isn't he nice?'
    'You've got to go after what you want.'
    'Don't come on so strong.'
    'You're just the sort of guy a girl wants to be friends with.'
    'You're a cutie.'

*'You're my best pal.'*

*'You're like a brother to me.'*

*'You should wear trendier labels.'*

*'I don't like boys who wear brands.'*

*'You don't really understand much about fashion, do you?'*

*'You're trying too hard.'*

*'Fail harder. Fail better. Succeed.'*

*'I like bad boys. Bit of danger. Ooh.'*

*'Yeah! A bit of danger. Some rough. He's in charge. You know it. He knows it.'*

*'Girls just want a boy to be good to them, Charlie.'*

*'Respect. That's all we want.'*

*'I don't think you're capable of falling in love.'*

*'You fall in love with* everyone.'

So you've been doing this experiment with iodine and the teacher has said, 'For godsakes, don't get this on your fingers or clothes because it stains and it doesn't come out,' and during the experiment you aren't really looking, not really, because Gail Cullen – Gail Cullen! – is at the other side of the class and you keep glancing at her when you're supposed to be squeezing the iodine into the mix using the rubber dropper from the wee brown bottle, and there is Gail Cullen – Gail Cullen! – laughing and joking with her friend and checking you out, and you're going to do it, going over there to ask her now.

You've had enou*tyranny*gh! Standing on your own at lunchtimes, edging towards the cool herd of creatures that exist coolly at the cool corner of the quadrangle each interval, and of which Gail cool Cullen is one, in her cool white jacket and cool tight jeans, so cool you put the cool dropper back in the bottle, cool walk over to her bench, place one cool hand coolly on the back of her chair, the other cool on the desk cool and say, 'Uh, Gail, I was wondering if you'd *like to go to the cinema with me on Friday to see, uh…'*

*But Gail isn't looking at you. She is looking at your hand on her jotter. 'Charlie,' she says.*

*'Oh, sorry,' you say, and lift your hand, only to find purple-brown fingerprints smudged there. 'Whoops, Gail,' you say. 'It's the iodine. I should have washed my hands …'*

*Gail's eyes travel up your arm, across your chest, and down your other arm, to where your hand rests on her jacket. Her very cool jacket. Her very cool white jacket. You draw it back as though you've touched a flame. Purple-brown marks are all over it. Gail's eyes enlarge. Her mouth enlarges. Her whole being seems to enlarge, elemental. You won't remember what she says, the exact force of the hurricane, the names, the curses, the rage, her friends rising from behind her like sea beasts, talons rearing, overpowering you, circling you – you fear being eaten! – and will forever picture those fingerprints on her jacket as you back*      *a*

                                      *w*

                   *a*

*y*     into the gig without Julie spotting us NOW WATCH to see where she and Gavin go *fuck is she doing with him??!* take Nadine elsewhere and and and and and and and and and and Adult here man I feel Adult and Awkward knowwhatimean? and and and and and and and COKE'S KICKING IN! Whooh! smiling at Nadine *Charlie have you taken coke?* then drifffft to the bar smiling smiling at girls smiling emptily at girls for no reason ?smiling? for some reason WHO NEEDS REASONS there's Julie *Julie!* I gasp hug *My god it's so good to see you!* then she says *Charlie your jacket it's so uh so very* Tartan? I say *Yeah tartan* WELL THAT'S WHAT'S ON THE WAY *IN* JULIE *Okay cool Charlie I believe you* and we stand stand looking at each other stand

stand looking she says *Uh didn't you say you were visiting your sister again tonight?* She cancelled *So who are you here with?* Some assholes *I see uh* Julie's hand on my arm hazysmilingdrunk *Weren't Y'all is Fantasy Island great?* Totally I say then Cool then Yeah Yeah Yeah Yeah Yeah but I didn't think you'd know who they were Julie and she's NOT HAPPY with that nope nope *Oh is that cos I'm OLD Charlie? I can't listen to music for YOUNG people any more?* but I say Not what I meant Julie just um just cos you've never um mentioned them y'know um um y'know um

weak        surely        coming back        ready? coke        can't be        down al

'Listen,' Julie said, 'I'm not all Joni Mitchell and Leonard Cohen. I do like modern bands too.'

'I'm sorry,' Charlie said. 'Forget it. Who are you here with?'

'Gavin.'

'Gavin.'

'Gavin,' she said. 'I still want to be friends with him. That okay?'

'It obviously is for Gavin.'

'What's that supposed to mean?'

'Zilch,' he said. 'Nowt. *Nada.*'

He was trying not to sound irked, but he was. He was irked. That was the sound Gavin made in his head. *Irk.* Like the dying buzz of a fly. Julie said, 'Let's stop this sniping, Charlie,' and leaned into him and kissed him, which irritated him, a little, that she wasn't sensitive enough to tell that he was irked, he was irked, or that he was

S   K   U   L   L      F   U   C   K   E   D

'We could have a wee *cuddle?*' she whispered. He smelled the booze on her breath. Her woman's body, pressed into him, pressing with all its lonely bar-stool experience. 'A wee *fumble*, Charlie, what do you say?'

'Well,' he said, 'Let me deliver this drink.'

Charlie delivered the drink.

'Nadine,' he said, 'I've seen some people I work with. Just going to stand with them for a while.'

'Oh,' said Nadine. 'Can I come?'

'Uh,' he said. 'I'll just get you back here.'

'Okay,' she said. 'But don't leave me here alone all night.'

'Of course not,' he said. 'I'm taking you home, remember?'

Nadine rolled her eyes.

Charlie went to the toilet and did some more coke. He found Julie and Gavin, and he was still pissed off with Gavin because of some incident surrounding pupils who'd been in detention which Gavin was supposed to cover and didn't cover cos he said he was busy marking and Charlie covered it and the kids were little brats and gave him cheek all afternoon and when he went to the staffroom there was Gavin having coffee – *coffee!* – definitely not marking, unless you counted the round *coffee-marks* he was making on the table.

'Charlie,' said Gavin. Like a host.

'Gavin,' said Charlie. Like a guest.

'Heard you got stuck with that detention class,' grinned Gavin.

Charlie cracked peanut-shells in his mind. 'That's right.'

'Nightmare.'

'They were,' said Charlie. 'Weren't you supposed to be taking them?'

'Marking,' said Gavin.

'Marking,' said Charlie. 'Right.'

Charlie looked at the stage. Roadies were either setting something up or dismantling it, he couldn't tell which. Julie's eyes flicked between them. Charlie cackled: coke. Sniffed. 'Sorry.'

'For what?' Julie said.

'Um.' He didn't know. 'I don't know. Gavin, my man. Wasn't aware you liked Sons and Daughters.'

'Yeah,' said Gavin. 'Got into them on their first album.'

'That right?' said Charlie. 'I got into them with *Love the Cup*. The EP.'

'Before their first album?'

'*Yeah*,' said Charlie.

'Hm. I don't know that one.'

'Where's your poetry chess now?'

'Eh?' said Gavin.

'Don't you just hate it when everyone else is into something you like?'

'Know what you mean,' said Gavin.

com ing *Whooh!*

back up

Sons! And! Daughters! roooooooaaaaaaaar from the crowd Yeah! I shout Whooh! I shout Sons! I shout Daughters! Gavin looks at me I say Hey Julie have to get back to my other friends THEY'RE ASSHOLES but what can you do? shrug Julie crestfallen *Oh well come back later Charlie we could get a taxi* and Gavin watch watch *watches* me as I go then hey! Nadine! swaying crush of bodies sweatsheen !excitement! thebandarebeltingout*HITS* horny guys AN ARMY OF THEM checking out Nadine scare them away with a with a with a with a LOOK! we dance to the band and Adele from Sons and Daughters sings *I am innocent!* then screams over buzzsaw guitars I AM INN-O-CENT! the band thumping *yeah* man *So sexy aren't they?* says Nadine Yeah I say *Which girl do you fancy most?* she says *The cool studious bass player or the hungry writhing singer?* I think the men are sexy *The men ARE sexy Charlie YEAH look at the way the guitarist goes at it like he's just not afraid of anything* and this ? somehow ? why ? I don't know ? means ? something? THAT THE GUITARIST FROM SONS AND DAUGHTERS DOES NOT SEEM TO BE AFRAID OF ANYTHING ALL THAT SEX ART GUITARBLOOD ENERGY *THESE PEOPLE REALLY FUCKING MEAN IT!!!* and bodies crush rub exqui sit ely getting hard COKE! COKE! want COKE! I'm saying to Nadine can't wait to meet your friend Dawn and she smiles says *She's looking forward to meeting you Charlie* and I say Bet her nipples taste like maraschino cherries Nadine says *'Scuse me?* shitNadinebettergetbacktomycolleagues *You're supposed to be here with me Charlie* I know! I know! and onstage the singer's prowling growling that deepsexmenace Julie !grins! pulls me through the crowd I kiss her

mmm mmmmmwah mm mwhh mmmm mmmwah mm wammm mmmm wwmmm mwah mmmww wwwmah mmmm m m m m mmwah hhhhmmmm mw ammmm aaa mmmm mm m mmmmm m m m mmmmmmmm m m m m m mmmmmmmm m m mmmmmmmm glance past her to Gavin spectacles fixed on a band *!!!he claims he's been into since their first album but has never mentioned before!!!* everytime I kiss Julie I look at Gavin he's not looking at me so I LOOK at Gavin *he's still not looking at me* HOUSE LIGHTS crowd crowd exiting crowd crowd Nadine's chin aloft searching for me SHE IS SEARCHING FOR ME she'll take my arm say something like *Okay Charlie your place or mine?* and Julie will say *Who's this?* and Nadine will say *Who's this?* and Gavin will point dramatically naming suspects – *She's the girl whose arse he felt at Jupito and I've MET his sister Julie AND THAT'S NOT FUCKING HER!!!!!!!!!!!!!!!!!!!!!!!!!!!!!!* whoah

breathe       breathe

WHOAH       brea

whoah       breathe

oah

'Right,' Julie said. 'Shall we head to the taxi queue, Mr Bain?'

'Uh,' Charlie said.

Nadine spotted him, approached. He turned to Gavin.

'What?' said Charlie.

'Hm?' said Gavin.

'You bastard,' said Charlie.

'Eh?' said Gavin. 'Why am I a bastard?'

'You know you should've taken that detention,' he said. 'And what did I find you doing? Marking? No. Drinking fucking *coffee*.'

Julie made confused noises, which Charlie wasn't even listening to: performance performance performance.

'Hang on,' said Gavin. 'I told you the reason for that. I was—'

Charlie punched him. Gavin's hands flew to his nose. Julie shrieked, then her arms were around Charlie's chest, hauling him off. Nadine arrived, hanging back, SHOCKED BY THE POWER!!!!!!
breathe        breathe        breathe        breathe        breathe

'Know what?' shouted Charlie to Gavin, sprawled on the floor of the ABC, holding his nose, holding his bleeding nose — ha! — 'You're not worth it.' Everyone was staring.

Charlie made his face into something and started to walk away, people scattering like sheep from a passing locomotive as he did so, looking from Nadine to Julie, neither aware of the involvement — the *existence* — of the other, these two women who both loved him — separately — in their own ways — in their own special ways — these women who both had cunts — who knew him — who knew him separately — loved him, *loved* him — who lived in different space-time continuums — did different jobs and had dreamed in separate bedrooms of *things*, beautiful *things*, monstrous *things* — brought together into this reality — but each of them — strangely, and this was the crux of it — each of them unaware — *unaware of who he really was*

– and for a second he thought he saw purple-brown iodine marks on their faces clothes necks mouths arms legs hands

                                        and then he was running

**Always introduce the topic of sex** in a humorous manner. This plants an image in the mind of your seductee, allows her to visualise the two of you **together,** but is not threatening. You may then begin the process of **massaging** her inhibitions, over the course of the evening ratcheting up the images. By the end of the night you should both be **talking absolute filth,** allowing you to lead her comfortably *into* absolute filth. In her mind, it will be as though you've had it already.

**Brother, you are *working* it.**

ft he   r?

*He is your father.*

                                                            *it is*

*Dad?*

*know straight away it is your father. It is your father with That Woman.*
*That Gretchen.*

    *Her name like something bad-tasting.*

    *You take the train with your pals into the city centre for the Saturday*
*Mooch: you buy comics, hunt for computer games and chart albums and*
*football tops and trackies and trainers, sometimes sneaking a look at*
*pornos in WH Smiths, giggling, drinking Fanta, belching, checking out*
*girls gathered in gangs of girls' colours and makeup and glances your*
*way. Acne is on the rise in your skin. You've tried soap and water,*
*Clearasil, little sterilised cotton pads. Nothing works. Your pals have the*
*patter, can approach, pause, cock their heads, and release these girls'*
*laughter like doves from a magician's hat. You sit with your spots and*
*your trainers and your can, burping dismally.*

    *This particular day. This Saturday. There are only so many sports-*
*shops and games-shops to go into, only so many assistants to wind up,*
*only so many jokes to tell and retell and re-retell. You are all stoating*
*down Sauchiehall Street. You are ribbing each other. You are following*
*some lassies. You are all comparing trainers – smart? casual? smart-*
*casual? – and you are walking, head down, hands in your pockets, and*

the very thought, the very interrupted thought is: did Deborah say she was going to record the footb—

Standing in front of a hotel is your father. It comes back: the handsome hair, the confident Confidence. Like the sheen from an advertisement. Your father worked in advertising for a while, actually – he used to try out jingles and slogans on you and Deborah – but you've heard that since he's become head of a design company. The last time you saw your father he was in your kitchen, talking to your mother, and your mother was biting her lip and her arms were crossed and your father was leaning in – appealing, his features soft – and she was trying to whisper to your dad because you and Deborah were there, listening, and she was shaking her head with disbelief.

But your father is here. Now. In your thirteen-year-old life. In the middle of the street. This street. In Glasgow. In Scotland. On Planet Earth. Near the end of the Twentieth Century. But Scotland unmoors itself from the universe at the sight of your father – floating, spectral, detached in space. There must be an almost magnetic presence, *some triumphant physic willing this*, and you hang at the edge of the force-field of your father. He's still talking, smiling, his hand on the arm of That Woman. Gretchen. She is nodding, also smiling, shrugging occasionally and touching his face. She is thin, her bare arms like saplings, and your father's hand cups her elbow. Your pals have walked on. They aren't even aware you've stopped. In these moments before Gretchen notices you and says, 'Can I help you?' and your father turns and sees, you feel a stillness and purity of waiting, an anticipation, beautifully poised, something close, you imagine, to those seconds before death. It is happening. They are there. Together. Unalterable. Gothic.

'Oh, hi,' your father says. 'Charlie!'

You want to say, 'Hi, Dad.' You will it and will it, then when you open your mouth it says, 'Hi, Dad.'

*For a while it is a breeze.*

'What you doing in the town today, son?' 'Oh, just having a mooch.' 'What you been buying?' 'Computer games.' 'Computer games, is it?' 'Yeah.' 'Surprised you're not at home listening to the match.' 'Deborah's taping it.' 'How is Deborah?' 'She's fine, *damned* and in primary five.' 'God almighty, the high school already? And your mother? She keeping all right?' 'Not too well, Dad.' 'Brilliant. I don't mean brilliant. Em, you know what I mean. Oh. Charlie? Em. This is. Gretchen.'

*Then it all unravels. You've had it too easy. It is not why the cosmos has arranged this.*

'Very good to meet you, Charlie,' says Gretchen, and offers her hand. 'Your dad's told me a lot about you.'

You stare down at that hand, lined and elegant. Stare down at it, then back up at Gretchen. You look her in the eye and slowly shake your head. A panic flaps in Gretchen's eyes for a second, something coming home to roost. She says, 'I understand,' then crosses her arms. Your father's gaze churns.

'Charlie,' he growls, 'that isn't very polite.'

You shrug. 'Know what else isn't polite? Leaving your family.'

Your father speaks in tremors, the same signs of imminent danger he'd used the times when you were wee and you and Deborah had painted the cat green or played American football with a vase.

'Gretchen is my partner now,' he says. 'Gretchen. Do you understand?' 'And I'm your son.'

'You're a twelve-year-old boy,' your father says. 'Your mother clearly hasn't learned you any manners.'

'Or you any grammar,' you say. 'It's "taught".'

His eyes.

'James,' That Woman says, touching his shoulder – in front of you! 'It's fine. Really. Charlie has a right to be upset.' Her voice is posh. Clear. Like water.

*'And I'm thirteen,' you say.*

*'What?'*

*'Not twelve.'*

*Your father stands, chiselled and defined and implacable – the gym? – and you survey him, your gaze becoming blades.*

*'Son.' Your father sighs.*

*Look, this isn't necessary. Maybe if you and Gretchen...*

*... got to know each other...*

*... you...*

*... might...*

*?'*

*Your head is buzzing like a saw.*

*'What I'm saying, son, is that things happen between a husband and wife, that, em, might not make sense to the children, but, em... What I'm trying to say is ... Sorry. Basically. Uh. Sorry.'*

*He frowns.*

*'Gimme a hug,' your father says, and your being squeaks. Your thoughts pause – half candy, half Kalashnikov – then you lean in and hug your father, face to his sternum, and the whole moment creaks like a leather jacket.*

*'It was nice to meet you, Charlie,' Gretchen says.*

*'     ,' you say.*

*Your father shakes your hand. You expect electricity, your hair to become static or something. But it doesn't.*

*'I'll give you a ring,' says your father. 'We'll meet up. The three of us.'*

*'Me, you and Debs?'*

*'Uh, yeah. We could do that too. Say hi to her,' he says. 'And your mum.'*

*'I will.'*

*'Okay,' your father says, as Glasgow begins to unfreeze and move again. 'I'll see you around some time, son.'*

*'Sure,' you say, dreaming.*

*''Bye,' says Gretchen.* reSist

*You nod.*

*Then your father leads her into the velvet swank of the hotel, as if leading a pedigree towards a show, and you are standing on the street, disturbed, entranced, slow, wondering what will happen if you run after them, arms outstretched, and say please? Please! But you do not. You do not try to catch up with your pals either. You go home. You go Home. Back to the same Home he'd left to chase women with*

*accents like water* resist resist reSIST! *Deborah has taped the footie and your mum is making tea, and your mum sees your face and says, 'What's wrong?' and you say, 'Nothing,' and she looks at you and looks at you and you say, 'Nothing!' And she says, 'You saw him, didn't you? You saw him with That Woman?' And you nod and when you go to Deborah's room she tuts and says, 'What's up with your face? Taped it, didn't I?' and you just say, 'Yeah,' and she says, 'A thanks would be appreciated,' and you say, 'Shut your mouth,' and she flinches, and you*

*say, 'Deborah…' then you try to hug her and she's like, 'Oh just piss off,
Charlie,' and you stand and stare at her, then go to your room and put in
the tape and watch the game — Rangers win one–nil — and think about
that crystal-cool splash of Gretchen's accent. Dousing, beautiful, cleansi n*

g

ns       in    g    *Clea* ns    g       in    g

*cl*  e         *a*      ns  nsi  *sin*

*l*    *clea* n*si*                  *i*

n    a                              g    sin

                                    *sin*

                    *s i n*

| | |
|---|---|
| He stood in front of the class. | Silent. |
| His arms were folded. | Waiting. |
| This was a tried and tested technique. | When they were rowdy. |
| Instead of yelling. | You do the opposite. |
| You stand. | Like this. |
| Watching. | Unperturbed. |
| For as long as it takes. | Until they notice. |
| And it will spread. | Ssh. |
| Sssssssssssssh. | Sir's waiting. |
| And the noise drops. | Completely. |
| And every single one of them. | Is staring at you. |
| And you say: | 'Thank you, class. |
| Respect. | That's all I ask.' |

Then he got on with teaching the first-years about Similes and Metaphors, cos the first-years were great and Similes and Metaphors were easy, for him and them, the things they came up with, man. The freakishness of their imaginations. Nuclear. He wrote on the board, 'The sun is as bright as . . .' and hands went up. 'The sun!' 'Well, John,' he said, 'the sun *is* as bright as the sun, but still, uh, it's not really a simile.' 'As bright as bells?' said another. 'Not bad.' Charlie winked. 'Make one thing seem like another. As Ezra Pound said, boys and girls, *Make it new.*' 'As bright as a toilet,' said a kid at the back. 'A toilet?' 'Aye,' the kid said. 'Ma maw cleans the toilet till it gleams.' Charlie paused, smiled. 'Okay . . .' he said. 'Fine . . .' And maybe it was. The sun was a toilet. The moon was an arse of the whitest hue. Thunder was God's almighty fart. He liked the way the kids thought, sideways, up and down, round the bend. Not yet HOUSE PRICES. Not yet BANK CHARGES. Not yet JOB

    or DIVORCE

    or PROZAC

    or CUSTODY

It's fucking boring being an adult, let's be honest with the wee ones. Since we're teaching *litruchur* here – Great Art, my dear! – let's remind them how it is made: James Joyce's genius was that he managed to keep thinking like a kid for ever: the synapses snapping the syntax crackling the *whoosh* the yes! the oh! the unborn consciousness of the human race forged in the smithy of his soul and all that.

Charlie told them the one about the frog in a blender. They laughed.

The pictures of Bolshevik propaganda art on his classroom walls. Look at the optimism in them! Look at this, kids! A revolution! An actual revolution! When the masses rose up and overthrew their oppressors! Can you imagine it now? Can you imagine people getting off their XCubes and GameStations and PlayBoxes long enough to do it? Those men and women really believed that poverty and inequality were coming to an end, that they were building a new bright dawn for humankind!

The horror.

The horror.

When Baldy Paulson made his start-of-term speech he'd surveyed the assembly hall, eyed these same kids and quoted Edison.

'"Genius", boys and girls,' he'd said, '"is one per cent inspiration and ninety-nine per cent perspiration."' That old chestnut. So long fallen off the tree it was mouldy. No, Charlie had thought. Genius is 99 per cent inspiration. Bawbag. Don't give them all that Young Enterprise work-ethic shite we drill into them to make them effective drones for industry the numeracy the literacy the computing skills let's all pull together and help the company achieve its goals targets strategy for the coming quarter secure new markets all forging ahead as one big family aye but who keeps the fucking profits?

Charlie wrote on the board: *Genius is staying a child for as long as possible.*

'Copy it down,' he instructed.

The kids liked it. Giggled.

'You create your own destiny, boys and girls. Society will try to trap you and use you for its own ends. But you must not let it. You must defeat it. You must *Become*.'

'Become what, sir?'

'Whatever you were born to be, Darren. Whatever your destiny is. In your case, probably a mob boss.'

'Cool!'

'And in mine, sir?'

'A unicorn, Denise.'

'A unicorn!'

176

They stared at him, grinning. Their futures twinkled. Ageing could only degrade them, surely, would degrade the Earth, would degrade all things eventually. And the icecaps would melt. And the seas would rise. And the land would be washed away.

Poetry.

He started to write the word on the board, but then the door opened and it was Baldy Paulson and Charlie thrust his hand away as though caught graffiti-ing.

'Mr Bain?' said Paulson, and coughed. The cough added emphasis the same way a gun did.

'Yes?'

'Wondering if we might have a word soon. My office?'

'Sure,' Charlie said, wondering what other chestnuts Paulson would have warming there.

When he entered Paulson's office, Gavin was waiting, and Charlie knew immediately the roasting chestnuts would be his own.

All Charlie saw was the bruise. Bruise! it said. *Bruuuuise*. Like a comic-book ghoul.

'Sit down,' said Paulson.

He was a socialist. He wanted to rebel. But he sat.

Gavin crossed his legs away from Charlie, pointedly, as Paulson began his speech. 'I'm sorry that we have to have a chat like this, Mr Bain, but it has come to my attention that a *contretemps* occurred between you and Gavin at the weekend. Is it true?'

Charlie inspected his fingers. *Contretemps*. For fucksakes.

'Gavin has told me his side of the story: that you launched an unprovoked assault on him at a concert venue. With all due respect to Gavin, I find it difficult to believe.'

Charlie didn't make a move.

'Now I'd like to know your side.'

177

He remembered being pulled into the headmaster's office when he was wee, having smacked a kid who'd called him a 'girly boy'. Booming voice. Big man. Charlie wondering. Simply wondering.

He shifted in his seat, cleared his throat. 'Well,' he said, 'that won't be difficult. I did launch an unprovoked assault on Gavin. I was drunk and, er, depressed. Gavin was the collateral damage from that. But it's no excuse, I know.'

'It's not,' said Paulson. 'I appreciate your candour, Mr Bain, but that doesn't explain anything. Why on earth did you feel it necessary to attack another member of staff?'

'Out of school hours,' said Charlie.

'I'm sorry?'

'And school grounds.'

Paulson summoned gravitas. It rushed into him like an Old Testament spirit. 'I hardly think that's the point,' he said, teeth gritted so hard Charlie felt sure they'd split. 'You assaulted a colleague for no good reason, Mr Bain. The locale is not the issue. Is that not the case?'

'Yes, you're right,' Charlie stated. 'It is not the case.'

Gavin was staring at him.

'Y'know, I'm sorry,' said Charlie, and turned to Gavin – 'Sorry, Gavin. I shouldn't have done it and, y'know, you didn't deserve it. But I hardly see what issue this is of the school's. It was an argument between two friends, which took place at the weekend, off the school grounds. So – with respect – I don't think it's any of the school's concern.'

'Charlie . . .' said Gavin.

'Well,' said Paulson, Moses surging inside him, 'may I – with respect – *disagree*?'

'You may,' said Charlie.

'And warn you to be *very careful*, Mr Bain? Thankfully Gavin will not be pressing charges, preferring as he does for me to deal with this in-house. But I'm sure his mind can be changed if he feels you are insufficiently remorseful.'

'I am sufficiently remorseful,' he said, then turned to Gavin. 'Do you feel it?'

Gavin's bruise stared, aghast. 'Not really.'

Charlie said, 'See what I'm dealing with?'

'Mr Bain,' Paulson said, 'I don't think you realise the seriousness of the situation.'

'Can I ask you something?'

Paulson nodded.

'Why are you addressing me as Mr Bain and him as Gavin?'

'What?'

Charlie shrugged as if to say: There it is.

'Mr *Bain*,' said Paulson, 'the local authority is not involved here. That doesn't have to remain the case for very long.'

Charlie looked at Baldy Paulson, the big cross hanging behind his desk, the picture of Christ that gazed forlornly at whichever evildoer had been sent to the headmaster, and he instantly wanted to embrace Satan.

He glanced around the room:

Plant pots. Books. Windows.

what in the name of fuck was he doi

'No,' Charlie said. 'Um. There's no need to do that.' He offered his hand. 'I'm sorry, mate. I was out of order.'

Gavin looked at him. Charlie felt like Gretchen, facing his own unshaken hand. Shake it, Charlie thought. Shake it or so help me God I'll beat you again.

Gavin shook Charlie's hand limply.

'Sir,' Charlie said, 'you're right. This is stupid. Accept my apologies. This situation's all wrong. I'm on the defensive.'

Paulson studied Charlie, his handshake. The entire structure of ethics.

'Indeed.'

'I was drunk,' said Charlie, 'and depressed.'

'You've said.'

'This world,' Charlie sighed, 'will be a better place one day.'

'What?'

'Won't happen again, sir.'

A case shutting.

They all nodded.

'That's it, Mr Bain.'

Charlie stood and thought about bowing, but didn't. He just left the room with Gavin, buttoning up his shirtsleeves as he left. Julie was waiting outside, gnawing at a nail. Gavin stopped, locked gazes with her, then carried on down the corridor without saying a word. She removed the nail from her mouth, unfurled her curiosity in a rush: 'C'mon, c'mon, what did he say? What did he say? Well?'

'I am, thanks.'

'I didn't mean that.'

'I didn't mean to hit Gavin.'

'Oh, really?' she said. 'I'd hate to see you punch someone and *mean* it.'

'C'mon, I hit like a blancmange,' he said. 'He's hardly got a mark.'

'Apart from the massive bruise?'

'So what's a bruise?' Charlie flicked his hand.

'It's a lesion on the skin caused by the application of force. It indicates *actual ruptured blood vessels*.'

'People need to grow up about these things.'

'They certainly do,' said Julie. She crossed her arms, intimidating something, but not him.

'Bruises are relative.'

'*Relatives* are relative. Bruises are bruising.'

He studied her disapproval. The slopes of her face. She suddenly seemed much older than him, telling him off like this, and he felt like one of her pupils for a second. Then she leaned in, touched his hand. 'Listen, why don't you come round tonight and we can talk about it?' she said. 'I'm worried about you, Charlie.'

'Why?'

'Punching Gavin?' she said. 'That's not like you.'

He thought: That's because I am *not* me. Similes, see? One object can be *like* another without *being* it. You're an English teacher, Julie, you should understand this. He looked at his shoes – silver smart-casuals, which even one of the kids had said they liked – then glanced up the corridor. Monise was trotting towards them, folder clutched like protective armour. Her eyes were low, the darting looks of a maiden in bandit country.

'Emo!' mooed a group of boys. Charlie shot a cattle-prod look and they clopped off.

'Thanks, sir,' said Monise.

'No probs,' he said. 'How's the writing going, Monise?'

She shrugged. 'They lied,' she said. 'There's only one way to skin a cat. And I can't find it.'

'Now *that*,' he said, 'was a good bit of writing.'

Monise suppressed a smile and clutched her folder.

Julie looked at her watch. 'Sorry, Mr Bain and I were talking about something, Monise, could you just—'

'What about the characters?' he said. 'You found them yet?'

'Hm. They seem to be heading somewhere I didn't intend for them to go.'

'Where's that?'

Julie clicked her face shut.

'I dunno,' said Monise, 'but something's going to happen between them. Like you were saying: what's *actually* going on between these people?'

'Monise,' said Julie, 'this isn't a good—'

'It can't really be about guitars,' said Charlie.

'Exactly,' said Monise. Her closed, cautious, Goth-running-the-gauntlet walk had been replaced by the nascent chattiness of girl-in-a-milkshake-bar. 'I'm trying to get away from that repression you talked about in the writing. The uptightness.'

'Free things up,' he said.

'Open things out.'

'Then move on to the big themes?'

'Death,' she said.

'Life,' he said.

'Love,' she said, looking at him.

He felt his eyebrows furrow.

'Anyway,' sighed Julie, bits of patience detaching in her voice, 'I'll have to go, Mr Bain, I've a class to teach. We'll speak about this later?'

'Yeah . . .' murmured Charlie.

Julie went one way, heels clicking; Monise went the other, shoes scuffing. Charlie placed his hands in his pockets and seemed to feel himself de-solidify for a second, become immaterial and weightless. Then Baldy Paulson's door opened and he came out, saw Charlie standing there and said, 'Was there anything else, Mr Bain?'

'No, Bal— uh, Mr Paulson,' Charlie said, and walked away.

*s*     *E*     *e*     *R*

*h*          *r*

s h                    *E*              er

b           l              iz a *R*                              d

    *B*           z                    *Z*

b                l    i        *Z*    z

              a                              *R*

              b                              d

*sheer blizzard*

                    *of transactions*

*and*

*book*                              *ings*                    *and*

                              *wedding fairs*

                                   *and choices of*

*wedding dresses*

                                        *wedding cars*

*wedding favours*

          *churches*

reception venues

menus

and guests

that you want to invite

guests

who really should be invited

guests

who

under no circumstances will be invited

but expect to be invited

You know how it is.

These all mean Yvonne has to have everything spread out before her at all times, at every moment of each day, can feel the whole quivering, delicate thing in her grasp, like a spider fiddling silk, attuned to the flex of a thousand strands and their potential, imminent collapse. This is in addition to her job in the nursing home, wiping, cleaning and chatting to *absent memories, mummies sitting up in chairs and spilling food onto themselves.*

*She comes into the flat, throws down her stuff, and after barely a kiss and a cup of tea and a sketch of a work conversation – 'Oh, honey, listen to this. Today at school there was a – and then he – so I said –' – she's straight onto the phone calling caterers, bagpipers, chauffeurs, hotels. 'No, I asked for it at four o'clock' 'What am I expected to do, get out and push?' 'But I already paid that deposit.' You run a bath, full of scented things and minerals, and when she has finished with the wedding, with the budget, with the calculator, you lead her towards it.*

*'Thanks, baby.' She groans, placing a foot into the heat. As she lowers herself in gingerly, you see her exhale the stress as though it's a cloud of black vapour.*

*You have infinite patience, but you have just started your first teaching post and have yourself too much to think about, too much work being shovelled onto your young, just-above-the-line-of-soil shoulders. Nothing you can do convinces her to feel good about herself, her own place in the world (wiping, cleaning, chatting to old people, cleaning, wiping, bringing food, chatting to old people, wiping, bringing food, cleaning) or the vast ranks of wedding arrangements ganging up and haranguing her.*

*'It's okay,' you say. 'It's the marriage that's important, not the wedding.'*

*'I wish I could believe that,' she says.*

*'Stay with me, honey,' you say.*

*'I would,' she says, 'but I don't know where you are. You're always working.'*

*But it was true. The work of a student teacher is staggering, sits there, teetering in a giant pile in your imagination. You come home from school and announce, 'Honey, I'm home!' and she runs to kiss you at the door like in a 1950s marriage and leads you by the hand to the kitchen*

*where she has a glass of wine always waiting for you and you take her
through the minutiae of your day and she listens and then kisses your
head and says, 'Oh, honey, my conscientious little teacher boy,' and then
you look at her and say, 'And I have so much marking and planning to
do tonight,' and she says, 'Okay, well, why don't you go into the spare
room and blitz it?' and you do. You shut yourself away in there and
stare at children's names and lesson plans and Intended Outcomes and
guidelines on 'Differentiation in the Classroom' and sometimes she
comes in and tries to talk to you – 'So, you know Meg from my work,
well, she was asking what we wanted for a wedding present and I said
one of those juicer things? That I showed you in the Argos catalogue?' –
while you are lost in the construction of the futures of seventy-six
children! You look up at her and the ghost of a scene from* The Shining
*plays in your head:*

Wendy, let me explain something to you. Every time you come in here
you DISTRACT me. And it takes TIME to get BACK to where I WAS.
So let's make a new rule. Whenever you hear me TYPING (*does
exaggerated typing*) that means I'm WORKING. THAT means you
don't come in! Understand!

*It's one of her favourite films. You know that were you to play the
scene to her, she'd understand, she would get it, she'd realise just how
gigantic your workload is and how you just can't afford to be thinking
about, like, WEDDING PLANS. I mean, what? The concept is paper-
thin, flattened beneath endless reports and jotters and essays, like a
crushed flower.*

*But instead you murmur an appropriate response and run your hands
up and down her thighs and say, 'Can we talk about it when I'm
finished?' and she nods and mutters, 'But you're never finished, are you?'
and you drum your fingers on the desk and say, 'Please?' and she drifts*

*out moodily and shuts the door and when eventually you come to bed you find her snoring, with a copy of* New Bride *or* Dream Wedding *sprawled across her chest and you kiss her head and switch off the light and slide into bed beside her.*

*A variation on these events is played out each night of your teaching practice.*

*Your teaching practice lasts for a year.*

*Along the way, you medium-busy yourself with organising a stag night, mainly peopled with guys from work, as your male acquaintances are few. You struggle to find a Best Man, but settle on a cousin who used to knock around with you when you were wee. You choose songs for the DJ to play, along with a list of songs he'd better not even think about on pain of death ('YMCA', 'Angels', anything by Oasis) and this is the entirety of your contribution to the wedding.*

*You send an invite to your father but he doesn't repl*y

Charlie arrived home and his mother was hobbling around the kitchen, making her own dinner. For some reason, she'd started placing wind-chimes all over the house, and when he opened the door the wind-chimes chimed. All of them. Like a shop full of clocks.

He placed his briefcase down in the kitchen.

'You need to do something about those things.' He winced.

'Why?' she said. 'I like the sound.'

'It's like Santa's car-boot sale in here.'

'They're not all wind-chimes. That one,' she said, pointing to a web-like monstrosity, 'is a dreamcatcher.'

'A dreamcatcher?' he said. 'How does that work?'

'Well,' his mum said, opening the oven door and removing a joint of meat, 'you place it near yourself when you go to sleep and it catches all of your bad dreams as they come in the window.'

'Like a burglar alarm?'

'A *Native American* burglar alarm,' she said, carving. 'All very spiritual.'

'So what's it doing in here? Do you sleep in the kitchen now?'

'Charlie,' she said, 'I could sleep outside on the washing-line and you wouldn't notice.'

'What's that supposed to mean?'

'You're never here! I see Deborah more often than I see you!'

He looked at the steaming fist of the joint. 'Have you cooked? I'm supposed to cook. Why did you cook?'

'I got hungry,' she said, 'waiting.'

Last Monday: trawling the bars of Ashton Lane. He'd chatted up two student girls and gone home with one. Her bedroom smelled of jasmine. Inverted left nipple. Celtic tattoo above her arse. Tuesday: he'd stayed over at Julie's. They'd watched sitcoms on DVD, then tried to have sex in the bath. Water sloshing. Cramped laughing. Wednesday: stayed in his room, took some speed and marked, marked, ticked, crossed, until the sun came up, which he'd stared at, dry-eyed and flexing fingers. Thursday: thirty lengths of the pool, chatting to a pretty lawyer in the sauna. They'd gone for a drink after. Kissed at her car. Hair like sunshine. Hadn't texted her yet. Friday: Nadine and Julie and Gavin at the ABC.

Gavin – fuck ye! Doof!

The shame spread like a red-wine stain over his memory.

'I was in on Wednesday,' he said.

'You were in your *room* on Wednesday. That doesn't mean you were *in*.'

'Thought you wanted me to find my own place anyway.'

'I suspect you have,' his mother said, ladling roast potatoes onto the plate.

'I haven't,' he said. 'I told you I need to be with you, didn't I? I love you, Mum. I'm here to take care of you.'

She handed him his dinner and a glass of milk. 'Obviously,' she said.

That night, when he was reading, he heard a giant hum at the edge of his consciousness. Like a plane approaching. As the seconds passed the hum intensified into a roar. He went to the window. It was directly overhead – rumbling like a giant wasp trapped in the clouds – but he could see no lights and he'd never heard such a din from these flightpaths before. It lasted minutes, filling the sky. He wondered if, beyond the horizon, a fleet of jumbo-jet planes were poised to hit the city. Eventually the roar passed, but it still took the noise several minutes to fade beyond the Campsie hills.

The next day he went into one of those New Age shops – floaty music, incense, books on Buddhism – and bought a dreamcatcher, which he later placed above his bed.

**The secret desires in men** come out as they feel themselves **alone** and **free** from the screen of cynicism they don in public. That **deep, creative wish** to be more than merely an obedient worker appears, and men are **romantic, noble, courageous, poetic** in the secrecy of darkness. I once heard a man, a foul-tongued man, reciting the Song of Solomon to the darkness, like the rustle of the sea breaking against a ship's forefoot. Alone, man becomes what he would be were he not forced into a mould by the **system** he lives in.

# Ext. King Street, Glasgow. Day

*Camera follows* CHARLIE *down the street. He is listening to his iPod –
the song 'A Brighter Beat' by Malcolm Middleton. He looks through the
window of the 13th Note and sees* NADINE *with another girl he presumes
to be* DAWN. *They are chatting excitedly. A bottle of wine sits in an ice
bucket between them.*

# Int. 13th Note. Day

CHARLIE *approaches the table.*

CHARLIE:      Hey, girls.

NADINE:       Hey, boy.

CHARLIE:      Superstar DJs?

NADINE:       Here we go!

CHARLIE:      Again.

NADINE:       Charlie, this is Dawn. My friend from the art school I
              told you about?

              CHARLIE *and* DAWN *shake hands. She has a brilliant big
              smile, and dreadlocks. Blonde dreadlocks. A subliminal
              image: the creature from the film* Predator. CHARLIE *sits
              down.*

DAWN:         Can I just say? Loving the tartan jacket.

              CHARLIE *looks at* NADINE.

NADINE:       *Real* men don't wear tartan jackets.

CHARLIE:      'Real men'. Huh. I don't even know what that means.
              Those kind of men wear fake tan. *Real* men use

193

|          | whatever it takes to get the job done. Dawn, does this jacket make me look like a dick? |
|----------|----------------------------------------------------------------------------------------|
| DAWN:    | No. |
| CHARLIE: | Thank you. |
| DAWN:    | It just makes you look gay. |
|          | NADINE *fires a 'Ha!' at* CHARLIE. |
| CHARLIE: | Well, then. Real men look gay. |
| NADINE:  | Nice one, Raeburn. |
| CHARLIE: | Hang on … Dawn Raeburn? I know that name. |
| NADINE:  | Remember that video installation at the CCA during the Glasgow International? |
| CHARLIE: | Oh, yeah. The one with the girl being all the different pop-culture icons? Playing in multi-coloured sand? |
| NADINE:  | *boudoir*. |
| CHARLIE: | That was *you*? |
| DAWN:    | My greatest hit. |
| NADINE:  | There's talk of her being nominated for the Turner Prize. |
| CHARLIE: | Holy shit! Congratulations! |
| DAWN:    | Oh, God, we're not going to speak about that, are we? I came up here to get away from it, Nadine. (*Hides face*) 'There is no art, there is only Zuul.' |
| CHARLIE: | *Ghostbusters.* |
| DAWN:    | Correct. (*She and* CHARLIE *clink glasses.*) Admit it. When you came in and saw the dreadlocks you thought of *Predator.* |
| CHARLIE: | I did! How did you know? |
| DAWN:    | Men your age always do. It's my *way in.* (*Pause.*) Although sometimes I get Jar-Jar Binks. |
| NADINE:  | Might've guessed you pair would hit it off. You *live* in films, the both of you. |

CHARLIE: Actually, sometimes I do. Y'know, while I'm talking to people? In my head I'm seeing it happen in a movie.

DAWN: Me too! Like you imagine you're the lead actor in the film of your life?

CHARLIE: Yeah. *Yeah.* I can see that in your video installations, actually. That's how you conceptualise yourself, isn't it?

NADINE: Oh, God, it's started...

DAWN: Interesting. Explain.

CHARLIE: That's what I took from your piece *boudoir*. You're there, Dawn Raeburn. Onscreen. Presenting yourself as the ultimate object. As though your life and your film are indistinguishable.

NADINE: Well, *someone*'s been paying attention. I thought you hated conceptual art, Charlie.

CHARLIE: Not all of it.

NADINE: What you *said* was that you wanted to walk into the Tate Modern and take a big piss over everything. Then if anyone complained you'd tell them you were making an art statement.

CHARLIE: So, Dawn, did you see that last Jim Lambie installation?

NADINE: (*Dismissively*) Gaudy, shallow, kitsch.

DAWN: Oh, I dunno, Nadine. Sometimes that's good. I like his work, it's fun. The best art can feel just like playing. The best *anything* feels just like playing.

CHARLIE: Exactly. The best *sex* feels just like playing.

NADINE: (*Tuts*) Down, boy.

DAWN: Actually, Nadine, these are *exactly* the things I wanted to say in *boudoir*. It's supposed to be a big joyful celebration of the body. All that colour and fun. Sand. We play in sand. As children. And pop music is like

195

playing too, so I wanted to throw all of this ephemera together: style, sex, fashion, music, childishness. See what it did to the signification of all them.

*Insert montage from* boudoir. *Dawn Raeburn writhing around in blue, orange, red, purple sand, to the Goldfrapp song 'Strict Machine'.*

*She touches her breasts, pinches her nipples. Runs her hands up and down her body. Coloured sand is flying about everywhere. Big handfuls of it! Being chucked into the air! She is squealing and excited! Whooh! she says. Wheeh! Now she is David Bowie. Now she is Debbie Harry. Now she is Marlene Dietrich. Now she is Madonna. Now she is Johnny Rotten.*

*Now she is completely naked and masturbating against an angelic white background. As she brings herself to orgasm a huge man in red body paint with a muscled back walks into shot and stands over her, in a pastiche of William Blake's* The Great Red Dragon and the Woman Clothed with Sun.

*Cut back to* CHARLIE's *face, distracted. He catches* NADINE *looking over her glass of wine at him.*

NADINE: Are you imagining you're in a film right *now*, Charlie?

Nadine paid the driver, fingers twirling around in her purse. 'Keep the change, keep the change,' she said, hand flapping a generous dismissal. The driver examined the twenty-pence tip. As the women spilled from the taxi, swaying, Charlie handed the driver a pound coin.

'Coupla firecrackers you've got there, pal,' said the driver.

'Well, y'know,' said Charlie, 'they're artists.'

196

'Piss artists,' muttered the driver.

Charlie stared at the man. A working man. A man who got up for work. A man who came home from work. 'Tell me,' he said, 'what do you think of conceptual art?'

The man snorted. 'Like bricks in the middle of a room? Like lightbulbs flickin' on and off?'

'Aye.'

'Pretentious pish.'

'What about teachers?'

'Teachers,' the driver said. 'Mean, like, schoolteachers?'

'Aye.'

'They've got it hard,' shrugged the driver. 'Weans these days. The cheek of them. They don't even want to learn. I seen some sights driving the taxis, son, but there's nothing could persuade me to try that job. Those people are saints.'

'Hmm.'

'How come, like? You a teacher?'

Charlie sighed. 'Probably.'

In the flat, Dawn made a joint while Nadine poured gin-and-tonics. Charlie tried to engage Dawn in banter, but her chat was punctuated by the brief silences of a focused joint-roller.

'So you knew Nadine at the art school?' said Charlie.

'We established this,' said Dawn, crumbling the hash.

'Just making conversation.'

'You shouldn't have to *make* conversation,' said Dawn. 'Conversation should just happen, freely.'

'Like playing?'

She smiled up at him over her joint. Nadine came back into the room with three big, spilling glasses. 'Drink drink drink drink drink,' she said. Dawn licked the skins, ignoring her.

*

Later, they watched a thunderstorm outside. Gigantic forks split the sky. They all went ooh with every Gothic slash of lightning. Nadine squealed at the thundercracks. Dawn blew hash-smoke at the sky and said, 'Cool.' They passed the joint between them while they watched rain flash down roofs, gurgling in gutters, the pavements boiling with water. People ran past with newspapers over their heads. In the tenements opposite, faces huddled at windows. The sky felt huge. They felt the universe around them, wet and angry and plentiful. 'Let's go out in it!' said Dawn.

the

the stag

the stag night

*!!!the stag night!!!*

*kicks off the way stag nights usually kick off.*
*They hire a stripper! Which displeases you immensely.*
*First of all, it's sexist.*

*Second,*
*who would want to cavort with a stripper?*
*When you're getting married the next week! Pledging infinite fidelity.*

*Third,*
*why pay when you could easily get someone to take them off*

*for*

*free.*

*The boys roar!*

198

'Sounds like a challenge!' And so

when the stag party creeps into town you demonstrate:

with all of them watching you stroll to the other side of the bar to a
hen party

also winding itself into an apocalyptic frenzy.

Girls with devil-horns encouraging the bride to

down it! down it! down it!

You introduce yourself and your party

stags and hens meet

merge, react like chemicals, hormones –

there is an explosion of dancing, shards of flirting –

and before the end of the night

you are kissing one of the

y u  a e  ki ss g  on  of  th

*Final fling!*

*C'mon!*

Yvonne would almost agree with it!

*after all*

*on her hen night*

*she probably*

*did it?*

*too?*

*didn't she?*

They ran back in from the rain, laughing like children and shaking themselves. His head dripped, and cloudspill clung to his shirt. 'Whooh!' grinned Dawn, running her hands through her hair. 'Did you feel that? Did you *feel* that? Whooh!' Nadine caught his eye. He smiled at her, as if to say: *You were right. I do like her.*

'That was *fun*,' said Charlie.

'Some of the looks we got ...' said Dawn.

'I can guess why,' said Nadine.

'Why?'

Nadine pointed to Dawn's top. Her small nipples were clearly visible through her damp T-shirt. Nadine glanced at Charlie. He looked away.

'Man,' said Dawn, 'just feeling yourself out there among that ... electricity ... and thunder ... and *danger*.'

'And that *rain*,' said Charlie.

Dawn carefully peeled the wet material from her breasts. 'This is what we do. This is what makes us human.'

'Yeah,' said Charlie.

'This is what people have forgotten.'

'*Yeah*,' said Charlie.

Dawn turned away from them, and ripped her top up over her

dreadlocks. Rainwater lashed from them. She had no bra. As the top covered her face, he glanced at her breasts and torso, rippling with tattoos. He wasn't quick enough to tear his gaze away from her body, though: she *just* caught him – damn. Her top hit the floorboards with a slap. She turned, walked into the bathroom and shut the door behind her. He heard it lock. Then the sound of towelling.

When he looked at Nadine she was standing with her arms folded, staring at the door, nails tapping her skin.

Later that night, all fluffy in their dressing-gowns and dryness, they drank more gin and watched an arthouse film, *The Lives of Others*, about Communist East Germany. When Charlie complained at their fag smoke, Nadine said, 'At last. At *last*. An ally against the Smoke Fascist. Go and live in Communist Berlin, whydoncha?' Then they both turned and blew smoke in his face and he coughed and flapped his arm like a weak bird. Dawn cried at the end of the film and said, 'Those poor bastards,' while Nadine flicked an eyebrow in her direction and said, 'Looks like someone's had too much gin.'

'What an unfeeling *cyborg* you are, Nadine,' said Charlie.

'Yeah,' said Dawn, then hissed, '*Communist.*'

'Okay, so we're all Communists,' said Nadine, 'but there's a recession on, guys. C'mon. The Left is totally back *in*.'

They watched some porn, sniggering at it. The film was set in a school. Teacher was a woman. The class were unnaturally muscled boys, tanned and coiffed, each of them. She was teaching, unsurprisingly, Sex Education. Now this is the clitoris. Miss, what's a clitoris? Well, why don't I show you up close? I find practical experiment much more effective than theory. Teacher's blouse was lost, never to be seen again. She had, predictably, breasts. Her knickers also became irrelevant to the lesson. She had a vagina. Her class all had penises, sizeable penises. There were few twists of narrative logic.

Charlie and Dawn interrupted with hoots and cackles, ironic patter. Nadine sat with legs crossed, sampling her wine like a bird, and studying the film as though it were Fellini.

During the scene where three of them fucked the teacher, it was Dawn who said quietly, 'That's hot.'

There was silence in the room for the rest of the film.

'Tired, Nadine?' said Charlie, when it ended.

'No,' said Nadine, yawning.

'If you're tired you should totally go to bed,' said Dawn. 'Don't let either of us stop you.'

'I'll be fine.'

Nadine stayed up with them until Dawn stretched and decided that she, too, was ready for bed. As her yawn snapped shut she glanced at Charlie. 'Where am I sleeping?'

'In the spare room.'

Charlie said, 'Can I—'

'I'll phone you a taxi,' said Nadine.

'I never discuss my mistresses
or my tailors.'

Leonard Cohen

Charlie stubbed out the joint as Julie lay down alongside him. His eyes were resting on the TV screen; his feet were resting on the coffee-table.

'Are you watching this?' she said.

'Um,' he said, 'not really.'

On the telly were crocodiles. Crocodiles indolent in the sun, like he and Julie right then: all bellies and yawns and slow, slow blinks. Regular now that after school he'd go round to Julie's for dinner and telly. He'd had to phone his mum and tell her he wouldn't be home till late, if at all, and she'd said, 'Fine,' a quick syringe of guilt, and the conversation thereafter had walked woozily.

'So . . .' he'd said, blowing out air '. . . how was your day?'

'How was my day? I carry you for nine months, go through agony more excruciating than you can ever imagine, for that? How's my day?'

'Just being polite, Mum.'

'Polite? I raised you like my own son!'

'I am your own son.'

'Exactly, Charlie. *Exactly.*'

Julie moved on the couch, spread her legs over his, smiled up at him with a low wattage of contentment. She had the sweet, full-cheeked face of a child's toy, a Teletubby or Care Bear. He wondered if she'd make a giggling noise when he tickled her. She farted.

He examined his attraction to Julie. He could pan for it in his heart and there it was: gold or fool's gold, he couldn't tell which. Julie was growing on him, but also growing *on* him, around him, like a plant. The sex they had was vigorous, fierce, and afterwards she'd spend a long time curling herself into cooling corners of him, her whole being spaced and blissful, staring into his eyes, checking the sex she'd experienced against the emotions he displayed, a traffic warden of the heart. She was older than him, closer to being washed away in that great blank truth about mortality, clinging to the raft of youth.

But for how long?

He tried to hide within himself. He could construct some makeshift effigy of affection, he found, which he would manoeuvre in these moments for her. Julie's body was warm and full. It nourished him. Other times he choked on the tendrils of her: she'd twist her feelings into him, and scrape the cavities of his soul with her *needs*.

'I need you to understand what it's like for a woman my age.'

'I need to spend quality time with you.'

'I need you in my pussy.'

'I need affection.'

Needles.

The television made sounds. Julie looked at him, touched his face. 'What are you thinking about?' she asked.

*Whether or not I have dandruff,* he nearly said. *Guantánamo Bay,* he nearly said. *Palestine, Iraq, thousands dead,* he nearly said. *Corporations like huge lumbering beasts, breathing fire and laying waste to the earth. Julie!* he wanted to say. *I really want a threesome! I'll be as big as a horse! Giving it humph! humph!* He wanted to say: *Does Hell exist? Or is it the absence of life? Is the eternal void merely a lack of love?* He wanted to say: *The colour of the sky the first night I walked Yvonne home was like a peeled peach and she held me at the front door of her flat and her kiss was the fondest of any I have ever known.*

'Julie,' he said.

'Hmm?'

'I think I'm falling in love with you.'

Julie almost leaped from her sprawled position. Her cat scattered, her tea spilled. It made a bloom on the rug that took its time to spread and he felt it seeping warmly between his toes.

'Are you sure?' she said.

'I'm falling in love with you,' he repeated.

The more he said it the truer it became.

She took his face in her hands and her gaze was Krakatoa. Her fingers trembled. 'Don't say these things now, because I've been hurt before. You know I have. Do you really love me, Charlie?'

'Julie,' he said, trying it out, 'I love Julie Carell.'

It was fact now. Once said, it became irrefutable, physical. One could invest in facts. They were true: that was the point about a fact. You didn't need to *feel* it. Loving Julie Carell was in everyone's best interests. He was not unhappy about it.

She threw her arms around him. 'Oh, Charlie,' she said, 'I love you too.'

He nodded and said, 'Yup,' and then, 'Uh-huh,' while she clutched and shook him and he thought he saw for a second, as he held her, small purple fingerprints on her back, like marks left by iodine, but her hair was in the way – in his face and everything – and she was sobbing and hugging him so hard that they fell off the couch. They landed in the spilled tea. The two of them laughed. In the spilled tea. She touched his face. They went to bed and had sex. It was good. It was good.

He was going with his mum and Deborah for the check-up. His sister pushed wee Elizabeth in her buggy and Charlie helped their mum out of the car.

'I feel like the Queen when you do that for me,' she said.

He bowed. 'Ma'am.'

She held out her hand and Charlie kissed it, then she waved him away. 'Begone. Now treat your sister like a princess.'

Charlie took off his jacket and made to lay it down, then whipped it away and cackled an as-if.

Deborah scowled.

'Oh, there's the Face!' said Charlie. 'Mum, remember her Face?'

'Certainly do. I can feel myself turn to stone as we speak.'

'You are not my family,' said Deborah. 'I was adopted. Must've been.'

'Actually,' said their mother, 'you were found on the doorstep. I didn't want you, but little Charlie thought you were *so cute*. "Can we keep her, Mum? Can we?"'

Deborah made the Face and tried to kick Charlie.

'Hey, what are you trying to kick me for? She's the one who said it. I'm the one who wanted to save you!'

'Kiss my child,' said Deborah. 'Now.'

Charlie scrunched his face into wee Elizabeth's and went num-num-num-num. Elizabeth pushed him away and *mwehed*.

'See?' said Deborah. 'That's what happens when you slight her mother.'

'Ah, you're the royalty here, wee yin,' said Charlie. 'All hail, Queen Elizabeth!'

Deborah – finally – smiled.

The two of them side by side, he and Deborah, fully grown. How had their lives become this? The two of them playing football in the garden, her in goal because she was a *girl* and *girls* had to go in *goals*. *Nyaah!* And now they were Adults. With Responsibilities. In Big Coats. And Big Gloves. Which they clapped – Big Claps! – to keep Elizabeth happy. Big Clap! Yeeees, good girl!

Wee Elizabeth's wee face stared from scarf and hat: wee wee wee wee wee. Occasionally she'd point. 'Doggy,' she'd say, and they'd all have to say, 'Doggy.' 'Doggy?' she'd say, and they'd all have to say, 'No, that's a horsy.' 'Horsy.' She'd sniff, disappointed. Things and names of things, but soon: sentences, shapes, numbers. Boys, cars, booze. And here it all starts with the difference between a dog and a horse.

'What do you want her to be when she grows up?' Charlie said.

'I want her to be happy,' said their mother.

'I want her to be a high priestess,' said Deborah. 'Learn black fucking magic!'

'That's what you wanted to do when you were about thirteen,' said their mother. 'Remember you used to subscribe to all those pagan magazines?'

Charlie smirked. 'Said you were going to be the most powerful woman in the world.'

'I know.' Deborah smiled, stroking Elizabeth's head. 'And it worked.'

They arrived at the hospital and Deborah was taken in for a scan while he and his mum waited, and he fed coins into a coffee-machine, which refused to give him coffee, a drab scam. He banged its side and a nurse glanced and he smiled and thought about giving her the patter, but remembered that nurses worked with death.

Nothing sexy about death.

He'd once read a book about serial killers, had rifled, sickened, through the whole gamut of them – Jack, Ted, Fred, Harold, names banal as a soap-opera cast – and their gradual transgressions: the spying on a cousin changing, the theft of her underwear, its mysterious, licentious scent, the torturing of dogs (they deserved it: weren't human), the porn, the following of someone home, the torturing of prostitutes (they deserved it: weren't human), the dizzying, accumulating orchestra of sin rising to a pitch until the living among trophies, bone-chairs, pots of blood, locks of hair, curtains made from skin became chintz and commonplace.

That was how it happened. They just got deeper and deeper in.

He shivered. 'Coffee, Mum?'

'No thanks,' she said, squeezing her chest.

'What's the matter?'

'Nothing.'

He looked her up and down, then took his coffee – at last! He read some posters about prostate disease and lung cancer and HIV. The waiting room yawned. Elizabeth chased a toy cat.

'Why's Jordan not here?' he said.

'Working.'

'He's always working.'

'So are you.'

'But I don't have kids.'

His mother shook her head.

'What?'

'He's a good dad,' she said.

'He's an *asshole*.'

'Why do you say it all American like that? And he's father to your niece, so get used to it. And watch your language in front of Elizabeth.'

He tasted the hospital coffee. It tasted like hospital coffee.

'He should be here for the scan,' said Charlie. 'I'm the baby's uncle and I'm here.'

His mother was rubbing her chest, wincing.

'Sore?' he said.

She breathed in sharply. 'Yes,' she said, then, 'Oh, God,' then, 'Charlie?'

Elizabeth stopped playing and looked up.

'What's the matter?'

'Christ!' she said. 'Fuck!' she said.

*

By the time Deborah had discovered where they'd been taken, the doctor was leading him through a prognosis. 'Hm,' Charlie said, and, 'Uh-huh,' then, 'I see.' But he couldn't see. He couldn't see a sentence in which 'another' and 'heart attack' appeared sequentially, how the laws of grammar could allow that. Then Deborah was running towards him, all panicked arms and trailing handbag. 'What's going on, Charlie? What's happened to Mum?'

'She's had another heart attack,' he said. There it was. That sentence again!

'What?' Deborah said. 'Where is she? I want to see her.'

Deborah started walking up and down, shushing Elizabeth, even though Elizabeth wasn't saying anything, just patting her mother's face. 'It's all that wine,' she said, 'and the butter.' She threw out harassed hands. 'And salt, probably. Yes, *salt*, Charlie. And *you*'re meant to be watching her.'

'This is *my* fault?'

'Yes,' she said. 'No. I don't know. Sorry, I shouldn't have said that. I'll have to phone Jordan. Take the bairn.' She handed Elizabeth back and the baby slapped his cheeks, delighted. He bounced her. He kissed her face. She leaned back and watched him with big Disney eyes.

'What?'

Elizabeth stuck out her lip.

'It's okay, honey,' he said. 'She's only fifty eight.' He started bouncing her again, saw doctors and nurses with gurneys and worries. 'Only fifty-eight,' he repeated, testing the strength of the number, its resilience, before Deborah returned, shaking her head.

'Couldn't get a hold of him,' she said. 'Usually has his mobile on too.'

Charlie fumbled through appropriate things to say, a whole cupboardful, rejecting shopworn platitudes as if they were used shoes or burst tennis racquets. 'It's a mild heart attack,' he said, and that felt

211

good in his hand, fit for purpose. *Mild* had just the correct, light heft. The doctors, in fact, had hit him with it; it hadn't hurt too much. Like a padded baseball bat used in school, it had bounced off him, briefly stunning. *Mild*.

When Deborah took Elizabeth from him again he felt her absence against his chest, phantasmal. Then his mother was being wheeled to them and her face was granite until she saw Elizabeth, who ran to her. Charlie kissed his mum. He kissed her years. Elizabeth was trying to clamber onto the wheelchair and for a long time none of them said anything at all, simply watched Elizabeth climb, then reach her gran's lap and sit there, and grin.

'Mum,' Deborah said, 'it's got to change.'

Their mother touched Elizabeth's head.

'Charlie,' Deborah said, 'it's *all* got to change.'

You're my little sister, he nearly said. I make the rules here!

But he didn't say anything. Just nodded while she instructed him.

w

*w*

*w*

*ed*

*ddi*

*ng?*

*w e*

*d    d    i*

*n    g    ?*

*w e d d i n g ?*

*W E D D I N G !*

# C H A R L I E !
# W E D D I N G!

ou are    by Deborah

d din g!

We d ng!

woken,    shaken awake from a dream

the dream you were having. About
snakes. A pit of snakes. And there is Deborah's faceful of glee. She looks
the way she did when she would wake you on your birthday when the
two of you were kids. 'Charlie!' she'd say, bouncing on your bed. 'It's
your birthday!'

'Okay,' you groan, 'I'm getting up.'

You arrive with your cousin in the rain, grinning as you emerge from
the limousines. Stand at the altar, cracking jokes with your Best Man.
Your mother is there, smiling and frocked, and you notice the absence of
your father by her side. Deborah is there too, with her new boyfriend,
Jordan, who looks too old for her. Your cousin's parents. And that's the
sum total of your family. Her side of the church is gelatinous with
hatted aunties, uncles, brothers, sisters, half-brothers, half-sisters and
their step-fathers and -mothers, cousins and cousins of cousins, half-
cousins, parents, godparents, godchildren.

Then she arrives.

The music commences, and you feel a rush in your blood and air fills
your cheeks. Your heart thuds, battle-hardening. She appears, trailing
satin and something borrowed and something blue, and beauty, and is
suddenly by your side looking more stunning than you think you have
ever seen her. You glance at each other during the service and giggle.
When you slip the ring onto her finger, expelling the last few months in
a puff of hard, compressed breath, and the minister says, 'You may now

213

kiss the bride,' and the church erupts into applause, you hold her hands and lean in to kiss her and meet her gaze. It's all over: the saving, the staying in, the planning, the anger and stress and fuss and depression and constant self-questioning. You've done it. She's got you this far. You've got her this far. And now you can get on with the simple business of being married.

In the limousine going from the church you bicker – there was something about the service she didn't like, something the minister messed up or had said in the rehearsal and wasn't supposed to say again today – 'I mean what the fuck's a rehearsal for? We were just wasting our time that night?' Yvonne cranes to look out of the window, back at whatever the mistake was, waving and clapping at her, mockingly. You can see the tendons in her neck stretched.

'Honey,' you say, patting her hand, 'forget it. Relax.'

'And I never invited that Gavin fella from your work, but he's turned up anyway! I don't like him. Gives me the creeps. I hope he's not expecting to come to the reception.'

'Leave it,' you say.

She nods and sits. You rub her hand with your fingers. She fidgets and shifts. She checks her wedding dress for marks.

'I told your sister to lift my train. Didn't I tell your sister to lift my train?'

'You did,' you mutter.

'Well, how come I've got dirt on the hem?'

'For fucksake!' you cry and drop her hand.

She stops. Her face changes, a tiny tic of shock. 'Sorry,' you say, and shake your head, but want to say IT'S MY DAY TOO, REMEMBER?!!! 'I didn't mean to shout. I'm sorry.'

'Doesn't matter,' she says quietly, and turns her head away, to where the rain – waiting for most of the day – has begun to *drip dr  p  d  p drip down the win  o  w.*

    *i*     *r*        *d*

 *i*

   *i*

      *p*

He was meeting Monise for coffee in Offshore and didn't know why.
All day the thought had brewed: why had he arranged this for a
Saturday? Because she was a star pupil and needed encouragement. If
you could find a way to inspire you should take it. But why a Saturday?
This bubbled, fizzed. Because there was simply not time enough in the
school week. Roar. Whoosh. What was the problem? He was currently
trying to squeeze their conversations into lunchtimes, which he
needed, quite frankly, to recover from the classes.
burble whoosh shoom

He flicked the thought's off-switch when she arrived. Monise
glanced around, saw him, and stuttered to the table with her eyes
down. She got halfway there and drew her hair behind her ear in
Monise-like fashion, then pointed at the queue and he nodded.

'Black coffee,' she said, when she returned with the drinks.

'How did you know?'

'It's what you drink at school.'

'Indeed.' He smiled. 'What other little details have you been jotting
down about my character, Miss Ferguson?'

She poured sugar into her coffee, stirred. 'I've noticed the shirts
you wear on Fridays are never ironed. I'm guessing it's because you're
too tired by the end of the week to bother. Your shirts on Mondays are
immaculate, though, so that must be what you spend your Sunday
night doing.'

'Um . . .'

'In class you always ask me to answer questions last.'

'I do?'

215

'Yeah. Why is that?'

'I dunno,' he said. 'Usually because the others fumble about and you can cut right through. But I have to give them a chance first.'

'Well,' she said, 'Simon's pretty good too.'

'Hm,' said Charlie.

'Oh, and the combination for your briefcase is 666.'

'It is!'

'You're not a Satanist, are you?'

'Moo ha ha ha ha!' he went.

'Just because it's easy to remember?'

'Too easy,' he said, 'since you've remembered it.'

'Right,' she said. 'But horror movies are my secret shame. From my dodgy depressive past.' She grinned. But he thought of her at school – dressed in black and mascara – then thought of her at home, only last year, scratching sharply at her wrists. He'd read the report. But she seemed over that now. If you ever get over something like that. Life was a Grand National race: you only got over the biggest things last.

'Oh, and you're good friends with Miss Carell.'

His mind twitched. 'You think?'

'Yeah,' she said. 'I always see you pair talking and laughing in the corridor.'

'Well spotted.'

'It's nice. We like it.'

'We?'

'Yeah,' she said. 'The Kids.'

'The Kids are all right, I hear.'

'Oh no they're not.' She scowled. 'They're *foul*. Fucked-up brats that we are.' She paused. ''Scuse my French.'

He frowned. 'Anyway,' he said, 'Miss Carell and I are just close friends.'

'Of course,' Monise said. 'I mean, doesn't she go out with Mr Prentice anyway?'

Charlie stared at her. 'She used to.'

'Oh,' she said. 'I thought they still did.'

'What makes you say that?'

'Simon told me he saw her get into his car yesterday.'

'Miss Carell?' he said. 'In Gavin Prentice's car?' He studied this. 'Where were they going?'

'Dunno.'

'Did they kiss?'

'What? No. I don't think so.'

'So why do you think they're going out?' the coffee in his blood insisted. 'That could mean nothing, Monise. He's just getting into her car. Why did you bring this up? What's this about?'

Monise shrank a little. 'No reason, Mr Bain. It's not a line of enquiry, just what Simon told me.'

'What business is it of Simon's?'

'None,' she said. 'Look, I'm sorry I mentioned it. I didn't mean anything by it.'

'Monise,' he sighed, 'that's how gossip starts.'

'I know,' she said, 'I'm sorry, Mr Bain. Forget I said it.'

'I'm friends with Miss Carell and so is Mr Prentice. That is all.'

'Okay. I know that now. I wasn't implying.'

She seemed chastened as a puppy, and he was starting to feel like a domineering handler. Simon's fault not hers. Gavin's fault, in fact. Or Julie's? Cars? Huh? Caffeine drummed. The smell of coffee decorated the silence, but he didn't want her to see him contemplating all this too closely, so he opened his briefcase:

666

Took out her manuscript.

'Yikes,' she said.

'What?'

'Did I really write all that?'

217

'You did,' he said. 'Superbly.'

'Is it good?' she said. 'Tell me.' She covered her face. 'No, don't tell me! Tell me. No, don't!'

They dipped into her novel. Rippled through it. Stopped on lines and images and fished for significance. She was still trying to find her characters, locate them among all the paragraphs about guitars and frets and notes. He attempted to slice through all the feedback and white noise and ask her: what did an adolescent girl see in a sixty-year-old man? A surrogate father? An artist-mentor? Monise's ideas felt under-produced, still in demo form. Further: what would a sixty-year-old see in *her*? It didn't seem like simple lust to Charlie, a vampiric preying. Something spiritual was taking place. Monise and Charlie talked, and along the way discovered that the protagonist — fifteen and furious at the world — felt older in almost every sense than her mentor. The guy had learned, from his wife's death, to come to terms with the beauty of existence, to love it in all its blank indifference and vast, cosmic farce. If only he'd realised it decades earlier! This was the Tragedy. She, however, who was young enough to enjoy it, hated life, hated youth, *hissed* at it. This, too, was the Tragedy.

It wasn't that this guy wanted her and she wanted him. He wanted to *be* her; she wanted to *be* him.

Monise touched her coffee cup and said, 'That's the reason I sympathise with her, Mr Bain. I don't like being young either.'

'What?' Charlie said. 'Why?'

'Being young is so . . .' She drew in a breath, which rose to a tsunami. 'It's all fads and bands and *cool* and gangs and *did you see Ashley with Jack?* And chatting online about *nothing* and being seen at the right party, and there's no *poetry*, Mr Bain. There's no *beauty*. There's no *truth*. Adulthood has depth to it,' she said. 'Integrity. Intelligence.'

He took this in, felt it tick and rotate in his system, but something about it angered him. He shifted in his seat. 'No,' he said. 'You're wrong, Monise.'

She snorted.

'Look, I also remember never wanting to become an adult.'

'Really?'

'Yeah. Thought it'd be a betrayal. All that *Catcher in the Rye* stuff. The adult world seemed fake, sickening, full of resignation and . . .' He looked around the coffee-shop — its relaxed atmosphere! Its laid-back appeal! '. . . regret,' he said.

'And is it?' said Monise.

'If you let it be.'

'And have you?'

He stared into chocolaty swirls, angel folds. 'Um . . .'

'Sorry, Mr Bain,' she said. 'You don't have to answer that.'

'No,' he said. 'It's fine. What I'd argue is . . .' He stirred his coffee, watched the foam sink and churn. 'Think about sex, Monise.'

'Sex?'

'When you're young,' he said, 'especially when you're a virgin, it's this great symbolic thing. It's huge and terrifying and enticing. It's like giving someone a part of yourself and taking a part of them in return. There's an exchange at a really deep level.'

'And now?'

He shook his head.

'Oh,' she said.

Neither of them spoke for a while.

'How can you stand it?' she said.

'I fell in love once, Monise. And it ended horribly. Going through something like that . . . scars you. You try not to let it, but it makes you cynical and frightened and a little bit . . .'

She was staring.

'Colder.'

She nodded. Her head dropped. 'My mum and dad have divorced.'

Say nothing and let it come.

'Mum just drinks now. And Dad . . .' She flicked her hand. 'Well, we don't see Dad any more.'

'Hm,' he said.

She had fingers clutched round her mug of coffee.

'Adulthood is sadness,' he said.

She thinned her gaze. 'Not for me,' she said. 'No way.'

'Good,' he said. 'Make me proud of you.'

'You will be. Wait and see. I'm going to do amazing things, Mr Bain.'

'Oh, Monise,' he said.

'They won't get me.'

'For me it's too late,' he said, 'but you . . .'

'Too late? What do you mean?'

'Nothing.'

They chatted about school a little bit – the politics of popularity, the in-bands, the in-clothes, the in-crowd, the insidiousness of it. She shivered, went, 'Eech,' and brought things instead round to Chaucer, Shakespeare, Milton. Bethan. Jenny. 'What about Simon?' he said.

'Simon's sweet,' Monise said, and her eyes drifted for a second.

'Sweet as in . . . ?'

'Sweet,' she shrugged, 'he's sweet. He's a sweet boy.'

He could see nothing sweet about Simon. Arrogant, yes. Disrespectful, yes. But Monise had her poet's way of looking at the world and Charlie was content to let her have this image of sweet little Simon with a cherry on top.

They finished their coffees and rounded off their angst with a few perfunctory oh-wells and that's-lifes, then made their way to the door.

They were chat-weary, all smiles and lets-do-this-agains and then: a formal handshake.

'Oh, don't be daft,' she said, and hugged him.

He did not put his arms around her.

'It's been great, Mr Bain.'

'You are,' he said, 'a spectacular young adult.'

*Young adult*, he chose. Not *young woman* or *young lady* and certainly not *girl*.

'Don't use the A-word!' she said.

'Keep questioning *everything*.'

'I'll try, Mr Bain.'

'That wasn't a question.'

'I'll try, Mr Bain?'

'Charlie,' he said.

'Charlie.'

She grinned. Then she was off, heading into who-knew-what-she-did, and he stood there, settled and well, before walking up Gibson Street, and all the people he saw were pregnant with hope and for a few seconds even global capitalism seemed weak, teetering, defeatable, like a giant candy statue about to fall, break, *be eaten by the people*!

Because the future was Monise.

**It's about her desire, remember,** not yours. If it becomes all about what you want she'll grow bored. The point is to turn her on, then leave her satisfied and **wanting more,** not regretting an experience she could have had with any average joe. This can only be done by building the **anticipation:** taking time to ask what she likes, what her fantasies are and where her partners have gone wrong before. You are promising to be an exception. Explain in **exciting** detail what you are going to do to her. If you can say without embarrassment the things you will do together you will radiate **sexual confidence** and enact a self-fulfilling prophecy: by behaving as though great sex is imminent it becomes so.

Give women the **fantasy.** Be who they want you to be. Think of it as a **persona,** a role you play. Think of yourself in the third person, for example, a 'He' that you become when talking to women. Never, ever be Yourself. 'You' are probably a loser. So 'You' will lose.

**He will not.**

There was the bliss of the afterglow. Like whalesong, deep and submarine and lowing. It expanded through your body. It was opiate, addictive, a premonition of death. And it happened to everyone. This was the democratic beauty of sex: it could happen to anyone. This heaven. That sex could not, could never be, disconnected from love was evident in those alchemical moments after orgasm when the body turned to gold. If you'd both fucking *come*, that is. Charlie bunched the covers in his fist and turned away. Julie's fingers were making braille through his chest hair. 'Charlie,' she said, 'it's okay. I still enjoyed it. Women don't need an orgasm every time.'

'Course they do,' he said.

She settled her head on him, kissed his skin.

When he'd been a younger man it had been a matter of just *finding entry*. The vagina was a rogue, shifting, unmapped terrain: folds upon folds, and hidden mysteries, and soft, accidental places where pressure would produce either moans of ecstasy or complaint. It was pot luck whether or not she felt anything at all. But as he'd grown older he'd learned, gleaned, experimented, become a cartographer of sorts. A woman's body, when desire was focused through the lens of experience, warmed and rippled, became indistinguishable from his own flesh: he could touch it in places (knowing *when*, knowing *why*) and predict the sensations he would elicit. And he studied those stations that, when revealed, or stroked, or skated over with the backs of hands, or tickled, or licked, or bitten, or merely breathed upon, brought a sigh or flutter or a sudden cry. There were plazas of ecstasy he couldn't even have guessed existed when younger: shoulder, shoulder-blades, neck, eyelids, cheeks, fingers, the soles of feet, the backs of legs, the inner thighs, the undersides of breasts, earlobes, crenellated waistlines, the smooth, alien planes of hip-bones. The body was a landscape of erotic republics, which each required the student of its lore, language and materials to become an expert. He loved it. He loved *touch*. And some women – weaned on a diet of hopeful fumbles and rabbit-like eagerness – were surprised when he merely wanted to stroke their skin.

He watched their eyes close, their steady breathing, their hands fall back against sheets.

'I'm not used to this,' they'd gasp. 'Usually guys just want to . . . y'know . . .'

He would say nothing. Perhaps smile and continue to caress.

'That feels . . .' they'd say. 'Oh . . .'

He would not remove her knickers until the last moment. He would leave her exposed and wanting while she smiled, wriggled, gasped.

When he entered her he would enter partially, move gently. Let them need each other. Deny.

And then he would penetrate. Fuck. And she would take in breath and soften and arch, as though on a chemical rush, and the feeling of it would ripple along his cock: that deep, roaring moment between them.

He would enter fully but barely move.

Soon *she* would be thrusting, encouraging him in.

They would take a long, long while and they would build up to orgasm: the clutching, the scratching, the rhythmic, submerged pressure.

And after that? If she didn't come? He was gutted.

He'd curl into a foetal position, irritated, extinguished. He'd lie sullen and silent and it would not dissipate until they did it again, and she orgasmed, and then, *then* he could leaven himself of that responsibility: they'd finally joined souls, ascended, met on that very highest plane.

Whatever the hell her name was.

Charlie got up to get a drink of water, padding across the floor, moody as a cat. 'You want one?' he said to Julie.

She nodded and looked at him, pulling the covers around her breasts like a film star following the Hayes Code.

They drank water, which was cold, gulping off-rhythm with each other.

His penis felt small and silly.

'Still okay, though?' he said.

'It was *lovely*,' said Julie. 'Beautiful. I just didn't come, that's all.'

He nodded.

'But it's not a big deal,' she said. 'Really.'

'You can touch yourself.'

'Charlie. It's *fine*. C'mere.'

He burrowed back into the bed, into a world of sheets and Julie's warm body. Two creatures. There *was* a difference between sex with a stranger and with someone who loved you, and it was simply this: forgiveness. You could get away with crap sex, lazy sex, bored sex, all the flaws of performance in the world, and it did not matter, because you were still loved and you were still loved and you were still loved.

'Julie,' he said, 'can I ask you something?'

'Sure,' she said, snuggling.

'Monise Ferguson told me Gavin's been giving you lifts in his car.'

He felt her stiffen.

'And why does Monise Ferguson say that?'

'You've been seen,' he said.

'I've been "seen"?' she said, raising her head. '*That* doesn't sound like an accusation.'

'But have you?'

'That's none of your business.'

'Really?' he said. 'That your ex-boyfriend might be taking you into his car? And you haven't told me? In fact, Monise seemed pretty sure that you and Gavin were still together.'

'Well, she's mistaken.'

'I know that,' he said. 'I told her that.'

'Charlie,' said Julie, 'don't you see what's happening here? Monise has a wee crush on you. She's trying to make you jealous.'

'No,' he said. 'That's not her style.'

'I've been a teenage girl,' she said. 'Believe me, it's what they do. She might not know she's doing it, but she's doing it.'

'You still haven't denied this.'

'Denied what?' she said. 'Getting a lift in a car?'

'You and Gavin don't live anywhere near each other. It's not as though he can drop you on the way.'

'What are you doing speaking to Monise Ferguson about this anyway? She's a pupil.'

'She brought it up.'

'But why does she think she's close enough to you that she can bring it up?'

Charlie folded his arms. 'Don't turn this into something about me.'

'Look,' she said, 'let's just stop talking about it, Charlie. I don't like where it's going.'

'Still haven't told me where it *is* going,' he muttered.

After a while she said, 'All this because you didn't make me come.'

He got up and went to the bathroom. There, he pissed and stared into the mirror. When he returned he said, 'Julie, let's move in together.'

Julie flumped back on the bed. 'What are you talking about?'

'Let's move in,' he said. 'Let's start a life together.'

'Charlie,' she said, 'one minute you accuse me of having it off with Gavin, the next you're asking me to move in with you?'

'Yeah,' he said. 'Never mind that. Pupils stirring it.'

'And what about your mother?' she said. 'She's just had another heart attack.'

'Oh,' he said, 'I forgot about that.'

Julie propped herself up on her elbows. She moved hair out of her face. 'You forgot about it?'

'I did,' he said. 'We can't move in. I have to look after my mum.'

She shook her head. The hair fell back in front of her face and Charlie couldn't see her eyes again. Then she rose from the bed and started to dress: knickers, bra, jeans. He liked to watch women dress and undress, observing the rituals they undertook before and after each day, reminding him that, beneath their clothes, people he would never see naked were naked. There were laws and banks and businesses and armies and institutions and great, dreaming dictatorships but they were all nude and horny underneath.

he needed          to take better care of his mother

and his stomach was getting flab  b   y

Julie rolled down her T-shirt and looked at him. Her gaze was a hard barrier for a second, but she lowered it when she saw him sprawled there, pink and defenceless, like a peeled prawn. She sat down on the bed. 'Charlie,' she said.

'Mmm?' he said, closed his eyes beneath her hand.

'Just do the right thing by me,' she said. 'Okay?'

'Always,' he said, and kissed her wrist, and she let him, looking at him.

*you*

*and*

# Ross

right    *walkin*

       *walkin*

         *walkin through the woods after*
*school, just come out De Niro's Fish and Grill and Ross with the chicken*
*supper and you're getting stuck into a pizza, trying to stay out the house*
*like cos it's not good, not so good just now, not with Mum and Dad the*
*way they are. Ross is like Celtic have NO CHANCE this year, Charlie.*
*Ten points behind Rangers and it's not even Christmas? You're like,*
*yeah, but there's still plenty time for them to catch up and he's, like,*
*never! With that defence?*

 *It's not the best.*

 *Naw, says Ross. It's definitely not the best! Hey by the way. Munch*
*munch. Swallow. Seen Gordon's dad's new car?*

 *Naw, you say. Heard it's smart as.*

 *You're trying to use your best patter cos that's the way Ross talks.*
*Cool as. Smart as. Naw instead of no. Tasty. Shady. Nae danger. You've*
*got to keep in with someone like Ross at your school. Stops the other ones*
*picking on you. He was transferred to your school from Drumchapel and*
*went in with his fists – nae messin! But for some reason he likes you, lets*
*you hang out with him. Oot with him. He's the hardest boy in your year.*

 *Goes dead fast! says Ross. And it's got all these cool gadgets and stuff.*
*That right?*

 *Aye, says Ross. Like electric windows and sunroof and this voice that*
*tells you if one of the doors is open.*

*It talks to you?*

*More than that, mate! Gordon's dad dropped the two of us off at football training last week tellin ye, Gordon could've charged them all for a look. Straight over to it, they were, lookin in and Gordon's like, Roll up roll up! Fifty pence for the gadget show! Can't mind what else it does, but it does all of this cool as fuck stuff like.*

*Sounds cool, you say. Em. As fuck.*

*Totally is.*

*How did the training go? you say. Getting into the first team?*

*Naw, he says. Gordon probably is, though.*

*Pisser.*

*Jammy bastard.*

*Hey, Charlie, what's the latest wi yer mum and dad?*

*Ach, you just say.*

*And there's silence for a while.*

*You walk through the woods and there's birds singing and squirrels darting about and big leaves up above are swaying and there's the sound of nature. Ross steals one of your chips and you say, I asked if you wanted any! He says, Aye but it's only when you see somebody else's that you want them. And Ross is looking about the place and he says, I'm fuckin tense man. How come? you say, and he says, No gettin intay the football team and that wee shite Gordon making it, him and his big flash car, and that Mrs McAlpine earlier. You hear her? Nae other cunt had done their homework and I'm the one that gets picked on? Aye, you say, she's totally got it in for you man. Too right, Ross says. Bitch.*

*You munch on your pizza. Loads of pepperoni. Magic.*

*The tits on her, though, says Ross.*

*Aye, you say, thinking: This pizza's something else.*

*Love to ride her, says Ross, big-titted cow that she is.*

*McAlpine? you say.*

*Would you not?*

*Nup! you say. She's ancient! She's about thirty-five, man.*

*So what? he says. Bet she'd be a great ride. The wee skirts and them tight blouses and everythin. Bet she bangs like a fuckin toilet door.*

*Want some of this? you say, thinking: Who'd want to shag a toilet door?*

*Nah man. Telling you, she wants it. She wants it tight.*

It's like something's possessed him. He's nodding, but he's not there, his eyes narrow and his hands stuffed right into his pockets, shifting around. He keeps looking off to the side of the path through the woods.

*C'mere, he says.*

*Where?*

*Want to show you somethin.*

*What is it?*

*You'll like it.*

He takes you through this wee hidden bit between the trees, well away from the main path, and you have to push past branches and over jaggy nettles. *Where we going? you say.* But he doesn't say anything, just charges ahead through the trees. Then you get to this clearing that has a burned-out fire in the middle and empty lager cans lying about and plastic bags and stuff, and Ross is going into the bushes.

*What's this, man? you say.*

He's lifting out the damp magazine, holding it between his thumb and finger like a surgeon.

*Scud mag? you say.*

*Aye, he says proudly.*

*I've never seen one.*

*Aye but, Charlie, he goes, you've never even shagged before.*

*Aye I have.*

*Bet you've never even touched a lassie's fanny.*

*Have so!*

*Who?*

*Em. What's her name? Gretna.*

*Gretna? Gretna who?*

*Gretna Green.*

*Piss off! You're makin this up!*

*Naw I'm no!*

*So what did her fanny feel like, then?*

*Felt like em. Felt like em kinda like em*

Ross brings the scud mag and lays it flat on a log. Hangs there like wet washing. *Kinda like what?*

*Like fannies feel. Y'know. Like hairy and em. Soft.*

*Was it wet?*

*Wet? No way! Eeuh!*

*It's better when it's wet. Get more fingers up.*

That wasn't a problem, you assure Ross.

*How many fingers you get up her?*

*Aw man. About eight?*

*Eight!*

*Or nine,* you say. *Probably ten. Lost count I had that many fingers up her.*

*Hm,* he says giving you this 'Aye, right' look. *Anyway, want to see?* He points at the scud mag.

*Em,* you say. *Obviously, aye. I love scud mags like.*

*Thought you said you'd never seen one.*

*Aye, but I know loads of folk who have.*

So you flick through the porno, even though the pages are damp and you can't see some of the pictures. Pages are stuck together and there's dirt and stuff on it. Neither of you says anything, just flick through. Sometimes you say Go back to that one, and Ross will say Whoah look at her and you'll say What's she doing with that? Why's she putting it

*there? It makes you feel a bit queasy but good at the same time. Funny*
*that. You read out bits of the stories – 'my pork sword lanced her*
*sopping honey-pot' – and you're like, Have they not had their tea or*
*something? But Ross doesn't laugh. He's got his hand in his jeans and*
*he's muttering under his breath. Tellin ye, Charlie, that McAlpine she's*
*asking for it. Asking for it good and fuckin tight. Then he takes his willy*
*out and strokes it and you've got your willy out and you're doing the*
*same and you're both going aye She wants it She wants it She wants it*
*and you don't even know what it is she's supposed to want but soon it*
*doesn't matter*

*cos then all the good feelings start oh! oh! oh!*

Departmental meeting.

Or, as someone had written on the door: *Depart! Mental meeting!*
Twelve English teachers seated in small groups, all with their own
lives neatly tucked away because they were HARD AT WORK. A
patchwork of ages and rages. The young, thrusting, trusting ones,
fresh from teacher-training. The arsenal of the can't-be-arsed,
shuffling towards pensions. A marking – yaaawn – moderation
meeting. The pupils' work second-marked so as to preserve the
integrity of the system blah blah blah. Scones. Coffee. Crumbs
scattered like the decapitated heads of tiny soldiers. Charlie had been
paired with Gavin as second-marker for the Advanced Higher group.
They'd done Bethan and Jenny's creative-writing folios. 58, 65. Gavin's
bruise was fading, its slight yellowish tinge now merely that of a
buttercup held to the face. Julie stranded at another table. She seemed
a bit lost, mussing over papers with some irrelevant colleague, while
he and Gavin's bruise faced off.

'Sooooo,' said Charlie, handing him another manuscript, 'Simon
Wray.'

Gavin leafed through Simon's folio, hemmed and hawed. 'Strong poetry. Very good facility with rhythm and line-breaks. Fresh imagery. Found the stories captivating and charming, especially the one about the man who wakes up to realise he's turned into a frisbee.'

'Really?' said Charlie. 'You didn't find that juvenile?'

'Not at all,' said Gavin. 'Thought it asked some serious questions.'

'About frisbees?'

'In fact, I think you've undermarked it. You've given it sixty-four.'

'Yeah.'

'That's a mid B.'

'Yeah.'

'This is higher than a mid B.'

'What is it, then?'

'I think it's around the seventy-two mark. Probably a low A.'

Charlie sipped hot sweet coffee. It burned his lip. 'Well,' he said, 'I don't know how much experience you've had of Mr Simon Wray, but he is frequently late to class. His attitude is lackadaisical. He interrupts discussions to talk about his favourite bands. And he wears the most *ridiculous* clothes.'

Gavin scratched his hair. 'With all due respect, Charlie, we're not grading his fashion sense.'

'Just as well.' Julie looked over at them. He caught her eye, winked. Gavin saw it.

'Seventy-two,' said Gavin, firmly. 'Low A.'

Charlie considered arguing the point, but realised grades going up reflected well on him. He swallowed his coffee. 'Okay,' he said. 'Seventy-two.'

Gavin wrote '72' on Simon's folio and circled it, then pulled the next folio from the pile.

'Monise Ferguson.'

Charlie grinned.

'THINGS TO DO WHILE WAITING FOR SOMEONE MORE POWERFUL THAN YOU TO SPEAK.'

Charlie bit into a scone. 'Good title, isn't it?'

Gavin took a deep breath. 'Well,' he said, 'you've given it an eighty. That's a high A.'

'Yeah,' said Charlie.

Gavin read aloud Charlie's comments. 'Exceptional vision . . . Considerable maturity . . . Uses a range of literary devices . . . Originality of concept . . .'

'It's all there,' said Charlie. Julie had risen and was asking the other marking teams if they wanted coffee – 'Coffee? Coffee?' Charlie wanted her to sit here, and listen to praise about Monise Ferguson, recognise the work they'd done together and how she might, y'know, change the world.

Gavin winced. 'With all due respect, Charlie, I don't think it is.'

Charlie shrugged. 'Yeah, she stumbles here and there. I still think there's a little too much about guitars in it, but—'

'I think you've been incredibly generous. This really isn't as good as you believe.'

Charlie stared at Gavin. Gavin stared at Charlie. The thin glass wall of Gavin's spectacles separated them. 'So what's wrong with it?' Charlie said eventually.

'Well,' said Gavin, 'the characters are wooden. I mean I just don't believe for a second in this relationship between the old man and the young girl—'

'Oh, I think it's *highly* believable.'

'Let me finish,' said Gavin, raising his hand. 'I thought the language was fairly flat and limited, especially in comparison to something like Simon's.'

'*Simon's?*'

236

'Let me finish!' Gavin barked, and the rest of them paused their discussions and looked round at the two of them. Charlie shifted in his seat. They knew, as he did, that to bring into question the marking of another teacher was to bring into question everything they did, who they were, the essence of their professionalism, the entire structure of a teacher's being, values, *existence*. Charlie sipped hot, *hot* coffee and listened. 'Structurally loose and baggy . . . Dialogue stilted and forced . . .'

Each was a piece of chest-hair ripped.

'So what mark would you give it?'

'Fifty-eight.'

'*Fifty-eight?*' said Charlie. 'That's a high C!'

'That's the mark I'm giving it.'

Glances were flicked at them.

'No way,' said Charlie. 'No *way*. You've taught Monise Ferguson before, Gavin, you know how good she is.'

'I do indeed. And this is far from her best work. I don't know what's happened to her this year. With all due respect—'

'You keep saying that,' said Charlie, 'but I don't really *see* this respect supposedly due.'

Gavin linked his hands together, pressed them.

'Carry on,' said Charlie.

'For a start, I think your closeness to this girl is getting in the way of your better judgement.'

'Is it really?'

The whole room was looking at Charlie, their stares like water pressure on a deep-sea craft.

'Let's look at the assessment criteria . . .' said Gavin.

'Let's not,' said Charlie.

'Sorry?'

'You should be. Think I can't see what's going on here?'

Gavin sat back and let his bruise do the talking. 'Oh, and what's that?'

'This isn't about Monise Ferguson.'

'What's it about, then?' Gavin adjusted his glasses. 'Go on. This should be good.'

Charlie pulled back the bow. He looked around the room. The eyes of his colleagues were on him, Julie's on him, full, imploring *No no no*. He pointed the bow at Gavin. Gavin sat quietly, staring at it. Then, straining, Charlie let the arrow fall to the ground. 'I think we both need a third party.'

'Indeed we do,' said Gavin.

Lolita The Night of the Hunter The Lord of the Rings 12 Angry Men Doctor Zhivago On the Road The Searchers Things Fall Apart Il Gattopardo The Tin Drum Naked Lunch Catch-22 The Prime of Miss Jean Brodie Labyrinths The Golden Notebook The Seventh Seal Pale Fire Le Notti di Cabiria A Clockwork Orange Tou **am** One Day in the Life of Ivan Denisovitch Bharat Mata Ellington at **i in** Newport La Dolce Vita Jules et Jim The Atomic Mr Basie The Bell Jar Vert **here** ouse Rock Manon des Sources V Birth of the Cool Strange Fru **?** Negro Kind of Blue Wide Sargasso Sea A Love Supreme In Cold Blood A Bout de Souffle Master i Margarita Psycho Cien Años de Soledad The Haunting Il Saggiatore Sasom i en Spegel La Disparition Breakfast at Tiffany's Highway 61 Revisited The French Lieutenant's Woman My Generation Repulsion Rabbit, Rest Portnoy's Complaint Revolver Slaughterhouse Five Pet Sounds Who's Afraid of Virginia Woolf? Blonde on Blonde The Atrocity Exhibition Scorpio Rising Sgt. Pepper's Lonely Hearts Club Band Gravity's Rainbow Dr Strangelove The Velvet Underground and N **sorry?** to the Music of Time Forever Changes Persona The Sea, The Sea Disraeli Gears Csillagosok, Katonak Piper at the Gates of Dawn 2001: A Space Odyssey Electric Ladyland Lawrence of Arabia The Book of Laughter and Forgetting **see** Upon a Time in t
**me in**
**here?**

*On average, you will have sex 423 times in your lifetime. You will fall in love three times. If you are one of the 70 per cent of people who get married, it will last 11.5 years. You will drink 72,452 cups of tea, take thirty thousand tablets. Your skeleton, and all of your cells, will be renewed every ten years, meaning that the oldest thing in your body right now is your first memory.* **do you?**

*How easily you forget everything in the slow, steady sleep of married life: working, eating, television, pillow-talk about taxes and bills and silly comments from other married couples at dinner parties that have pissed you off.*

*She's stopped making punk compilations.*

*Your first trip to Ikea: imminent.*

*You push the trolley – smoothly and efficiently – while she looks at Besta Inreda TV storage units with sliding doors, Karlstad three-seat sofas with long covers, a clean white Hemnes wooden bed-frame, the Idealisk kitchen utensil series, the Lillangen wash-basin cabinet.*

*'What do you think of this, darling?' she says, holding up Hensvik children's storage boxes.*

*You look at her quizzically, as if through a telescope at life on a distant planet.*

*The checkout girl is sparky – green and purple hair-dye and a nose-ring – and she banters with you. Larks. 'Oh, this,' she says, stroking an art print of Edvard Munch's* The Scream. *'This I had on my wall at uni. This was how I felt most of the time there.'*

*'Uni's where we met, isn't it, darling?' says Yvonne, squeezing your hand.*

*'This,' you tell the checkout girl, 'is how I felt most of the time in here.'*

*The checkout girl laughs and when you reach for the next item you see Yvonne staring at you through a frown, as though you've just graffitied her* bedroom        bedroom        be r  oom      b d   o   m

*How at first you get on with things and smile at each other and hug each other and go out for meals together, get the deposit on the house down, start paying into a pension scheme, sell after a couple of years to take advantage of the market boom, buy a bigger house in preparation for the first baby.*

*The first baby. It is just presumed.*

*How you grow so used to the permanent presence of each other's company that you become mere appendages, incapable of independent thought: a joint mind, like a twin-valve engine, focused simply on the getting by, the getting on, the making and saving and spending of money.*

*The appliances. The upgrade of appliances. The upgrade of stereos, televisions, dishwashers.*

*Your life will be over in one and a half billion blinks of the eye.*

*How you second-guess the way she'll react, the way your words will break down in her consciousness.*

*How you just do not say things that might need said.*

*How the love from the pupils in your classes replaces the monotony of the two of you and no one else. Where have all your friends gone? Where has all of your youth gone? Did you spend it all at once on the honeymoon? Was that all you were allowed? You're still both in your mid-twenties. Why does everything feel so old?*

*One time, when you and Yvonne are having sex, your leg muscles seize up. There you are, folded into yourself with ecstasy, when a pain from your calf pierces the bliss and you cry out. She squeezes her thighs tighter around you, mistaking your agony for joy, and, for a few seconds, a few transcendental, juddering seconds, you experience both pleasure and pain at once, spasming simultaneously. You are reduced to binary elements. Your self as you know it, the facts of your person – Charles Bain aged twenty-four, MA (Hons) Upper Second, in English Literature in twin pulses of sensation.*

*Pain*

*Pleasure*

*Pain*

*Pleasure*

*Pain*

ohnny Cash at Folsom Prison Satyricon (You Make me Feel) Like a Natural Woman Z Music from Big Pink Easy Rider Astral Weeks Kes The White Album Five Easy Pieces Trout Mask Replica Woodstock Abbey Road Performance A Confederacy of Dunces Tommy **Boo!** Harold and Maude Five Leaves Left Deliverance Dusty in Memphis Solaris Songs From a Room The Godfather Hot Rats Paranoid Badlands Bitches Brew Don't Look Now What's Going On Riders on the Storm Stairway to Heaven

subway, stoned, he watched a young Rastafarian surfing the train. The kid stood in the middle of the aisle, let go of the straps and tried to keep his balance as the train shunted from side to side. He placed his arms at either side of himself, leaning in and out of the G-force. Then when the train stopped and the doors opened he ran for the escalator and rode the rail up. He perched there until he met his girlfriend at the top and they embraced and smooched. Charlie stood on the escalator, slowly rising, hands in his pockets.

Outside, Glasgow was shimmering. Dusk. Summer arriving in a pastel sky. Pink. Yellow. People drifting past. He walked down Great Western Road and cut across into Kelvingrove Park. The day was cooling. He put his hands deep into his coat pockets and watched couples sauntering past.

He took out his phone and flicked through the address book. He stared at her name. He stared at her name. He stared at it and stared at it until it just became a jumble of letters, jagged shapes, hieroglyphics. Then he sat down on a bench and glanced up and down the street. He inhaled. He exhaled. He chose 'send message'.

Hey monise wot u up2?

... ten seconds ...

Mr bain? She seemed surprised. Nice to hear from u. Not doing much. Readin that book you recommended. Its gr8!

Which one?

Confessions of a Justified Sinner.

Ah Scotland's finest ever novel. The duality of man! Glad ur likin it.

Yeh it's mindbending. Everything ok wit u mr bain?

He stared at the phone. He looked around the park at couples walking, chatting, discussing future homes with each other to be filled with pretty things and little dogs and kids with full, rosy-cheeked smiles and eating disorders. He'd given her his number the Saturday they'd met in town for a coffee, and there'd been a brief, functional exchange beforehand. Now it was:

Yeh monise im cool. :-) C u at school. And its Charlie not Mr Bain.

OK charlie. Well as long as everythings alright. C u 2morro.

Now it was open. Permitted. They took to it quickly. On nights that were black and rumbling and rainy, the deep, heavy taste of red wine and marijuana in his mouth, the Jesus and Mary Chain playing, guitar feedback and candy, he'd find himself drifting towards the phone.

Dont u think sumtimes it doesnt mk sense?

Wot?

Life. Growin old.

Ur not old! Anyway we all grow old but u dont have 2 grow up.

:-)

Why? Wots wrong?

Nothin. Thanks 4 the support.

No probs. Always here mr bain. Wot are we doing at school 2morro btw?

Ah. Do you like James Kelman?

KELMAN?!!

James Kelman: a great Scottish novelist and conspicuously *not* on the school curriculum. They'd been doing some outstanding work, his class, even lazy, showboating Simon, and he was sure they could handle it. He gave out an extract from Kelman's novel *How Late It Was, How Late*, along with his essay 'Élitism in English Literature', which explained everything. Charlie smiled at Monise. Monise raised her eyebrows: *Kelman, eh?* He flashed a response: *I'm sure you can take him on, Monise.*

'This isn't on the syllabus,' said Simon, suspiciously.

'No,' said Charlie, handing out sheets. 'I thought I'd introduce you to some new ideas.'

Simon frowned: it was the exams. What a system were exams. Memorising instead of learning.

'Today,' Charlie said, 'we will learn instead of memorising. Like *artists*.'

The class seemed untouched by his description of them as *artists*. Simon had once said something about wanting to be a writer, but Charlie suspected this was just to impress the others. Bethan was borrowing a pen. Jenny had started to read already. Monise and Simon were whispering to each other, which Charlie silenced with a glance.

He read the story in a really broad Glaswegian accent, which made him sound hard.

He looked up at the end and moved a questioning gaze round the table. 'Any responses?'

There were none.

Jenny was still frowning.

'Bethan?'

Bethan reached for a stray curl, curled it while talking, in a voice

243

that also curled. 'Weeeeeell . . .' she said. 'It's veeeeery . . .' She stopped. 'It's hard to read.'

'As opposed to what?' said Charlie, sipping his tea. 'Chaucer?'

Jenny was still frowning.

'Jenny, did you cope with the language?'

Jenny nodded. 'I could cope just fine with the Glaswegian,' she said. 'It's the . . .'

Charlie waited.

Jenny waited.

'Storyline?' said Charlie, eventually. 'But I think Kelman is reacting against a type of narrative that is overly plotted with dramatic events, because life isn't like that. He's a realist and—'

'The swearing,' said Jenny.

Charlie blinked at her.

'It's not the dialect,' Jenny said, 'or the plot. It's the swearing. I mean, is it really necessary?'

Charlie longed, suddenly, for a class of the roughest Easterhouse kids, their ASBOs sported like acne, dripping with attitude and bling.

'Surely,' he said, 'you've heard words of this sort before?'

'But not in English class,' said Jenny. 'It's not written in *English* for a start.'

'So it doesn't count?'

'Well, it's not exactly the prettiest language I've ever read,' she said, folding her arms.

He wondered about their parents, what they did for a living. He'd never considered asking. How many sons or daughters here of lawyers, dentists, doctors, teachers? And where were the oil-stained bairns of mechanics? Squirrelled beneath the cars of lawyers, dentists, doctors and teachers, that was where.

Jenny was warming up now. 'I mean look at this,' she said. 'The C-word. On nearly every page. I object to that. It's sexist.'

'I *hate* that word,' muttered Bethan.

'Oh, so do I,' said Monise. 'It's horrible.'

'Not in many parts of Glasgow,' said Charlie. 'It's everyday speech.'

'*I* don't use it every day,' said Jenny.

'What other words do you object to?' said Charlie. 'Fanny? Minge?' Simon laughed.

'They're just comical,' said Bethan.

'Pussy?' he said.

The class fidgeted now.

'Monise?' he said. She'd been silent.

'What?' said Monise.

'Do you object to the word "pussy"?'

She reddened and stared at the table. 'Well,' she said. 'If,' she said. 'Um,' she said.

He was off: 'But we object to "cunt" because it has a hard, Anglo-Saxon sound, right? And yet it means exactly the same as those other words.'

Silence bubbled. Theirs boiled over first. 'It is offensive to women,' said Simon.

'Oh, is it really?' said Charlie, innards roaming. 'Does it occur to you that the more people use this word — especially women — the less taboo it will become? That by shying away from it you just give it that kind of power?'

'Yes, I know, but—'

'This is about *class*,' said Charlie, pressing his finger into the desk. 'Not sex. In many places of Glasgow this word is freely used. "Wait till you meet this guy, he's a great cunt." "How ye doin, ya cunt? No seen ye for ages." That's not swearing. It's a gesture of friendship and community. If a husband and wife use the C-word in an intimate way, it's clearly not swearing either: it is the language of love. Romantic language, erotic language. Do you have a problem with the word "vagina"?'

'Of course not,' said Jenny.

'In these same places in Glasgow,' said Charlie, 'you would never use that word in front of your mates. For them, it would have all the taboo that "cunt" has for you…'

'Mr Bain, will you stop saying it?'

'…so the effect of these words is simply dependent on their social context. Do you see what I mean? And given that it's the middle classes who have an issue with the word "cunt", it shows the power they have to fix and define meanings.' He was now *standing*. 'Why is your meaning the correct one? It's a political act against the establishment to use the word "cunt".'

The class were flat and still and small.

'Ya cunts!' He laughed.

They were looking at their desks.

'C'mon,' he said to Bethan, who would not raise her eyes. 'Say it.'

'No,' she said quietly.

'Say it!' he instructed, then sang: 'It's just a word. Cunt cunt cunt cunt cunt!'

One of the girls gazed at the ceiling and breathed out. Monise was staring at him. He met it, tried to read it: nothing. Then he waited, thought, and? Okay. Fine. Okay. He requested that they take out their copies of *Hamlet*. They did so.

'Now this,' he sighed, 'will be in the exam …'

nsformer The Rise and Fall of Ziggy Stardust and the Spiders from Mars Exile on Main Street Tubular Bells The Exorcist Imagine Dark Side of the Moon El Espiritu de la Colmena Catch a Fire Perfect Day

That Saturday he woke late. It was already afternoon. He went into the bathroom cabinet and there were his mother's pills. Racks of them now. Diuretics: furosemide and chlorothiazide. Beta-blockers: propranorol and bisoprolol. Calcium-channel blockers: bepridil and nicardipine. And, of course, the ones she'd always been on, for depression: Librium, Xanax, Prozac. It was a Willy Wonka's Chocolate Factory of uppers and downers.

He went into his bedroom and lit his hash-pipe.

Smoke rotated gently in lungs.

Then he shaved, careful with the up strokes. But there was that bit between his ear and jaw-line he couldn't reach. And when he wiped the mirror he left fingermarks. Five of them. He stared at the prints, then wiped again, but they didn't go away. He wiped and wiped but they still wouldn't go away.

Charlie went downstairs. His mother was sunning herself in the garden, whisky in one hand and a bit of cake on a plate on the grass. She moved her head when she heard him, then moved it back, and the sun flashed off her dark glasses. Her face seemed stoic, lethally preoccupied. She looked like a mad scientist or supervillain, concocting schemes in an underground fortress. He thought of the panoply of drugs upstairs in the bathroom – was she going to tip them into the city's water supply?

Earlier she'd put down the phone when he'd walked into the room.

'Nice day,' he said.

His mother nodded and sipped her whisky.

'Want me to take you out to the park or something? We could go and pick up Elizabeth. She could run around a bit.'

'Jordan's at work,' she said.

'We don't need him.'

His mother's eyebrow rose far enough for Charlie to see it above her shades.

He took off his shoes and socks. The hard soil and the thin, green tickle. The sun beat against his chest. He removed his T-shirt too and sat down on the step. Elizabeth's toys were strewn around the garden: their pink, plastic smiles. Each toy seemed to be saying *I wuv you!*

'How you feeling, Mum?'

'Fine, son.'

'Not think you should be laying off the drink?' he said.

She looked down at the glass. The liquid was brownish and ordinary as a penny. She sloshed it round. It could prove or disprove nothing. 'Not really,' she said.

He breathed in. He breathed out.

'What's the cake?' he said.

She didn't move her head, pinned by the sun's rays. 'Sultana,' she said. 'It's healthy.'

'Sultana cake is not healthy.'

'Sultana cake is healthy.'

'It's full of sugar.'

'It's full of sultanas.'

She raised the whisky to her lips and drained the glass. Then she shook it at him. He stared at her. She turned her head to him. 'Could I have another drink, please?'

'No,' he said.

'Why?'

'Because you're recovering from two heart attacks.'

'*Mild* heart attacks.'

'The next one won't be.'

'Yes,' his mother said, 'so I plan to enjoy myself before it.'

'*Mum.*'

'Charlie,' she said, 'I don't need my son to tell me what I can and can't have.'

'I promised Deborah I'd take better care of you.'

'You promised Deborah,' she said, 'not me.' His mother shook the glass again.

Charlie took the glass from her and went to the kitchen.

'Nearly summer,' his mother said.

He poured her a whisky and put some ice in it.

'Put some ice in it.'

He took it to her and she said thanks and they both sat in the sun that was not quite summer sun. The silence bathed them. There was only the sound of her sipping. Swallowing. Charlie started whistling a song. Then he went inside and dialled 1471 on the phone to discover that an Edinburgh number had called last. But he didn't know anyone in Edinburgh, and neither did his mother, except

except his

except his fa

Charlie put down the phone. Dreamy. Adolescent. Soon he was padding upstairs to his bedroom, the room that had been his, which had remained unchanged since his early twenties, before he'd married Yvonne. He lay on the bed. He lay on the bed for a long time. Someone texted him. The lawyer woman he'd met in the sauna at the gym. He ignored it. He studied the ceiling. The fingerprints there. Before he knew it, he was flicking through Bluetooth porn on his phone: some teenage barmaid, who worked in the city, was playing with herself. It had gone from phone to phone in a blur. Now every guy in Glasgow had seen it. His skin was hot and the light made him sleepy. This girl was someone he could once have hung around with at lunchtimes, could have sat beside on the school bus. She could have been fun and have made jokes and recommended bands and given him advice on girls, even though he might secretly have pined for her, even though she might secretly have known it. She would have been his naïve little crush. But here he was at thirty, and why was desire perceived to darken as it aged? The same basic chemical element it always was? He'd read about a female teacher in America who'd slept with an underage boy and avoided jail because she was gorgeous. The defence attorney's premise had run: 'Why send a young, beautiful, intelligent woman to jail for fulfilling every boy's fantasy?' And the jury had agreed. But did young girls too not have fantasies for older men?

so what was the pro

what was the proble

ipples and blonde hair round her cu

Afterwards he cleaned up his shame, deleted the clip from his phone, and set about planning a lesson on *Hamlet*. It was for his seniors. Their exams were coming up, everyone was stressed this time of year, teachers and pupils. Charlie wanted to go to Australia, backpacking; such people were free and beautiful

This world.

**Mine your past** for material. Previous erotic experience can stimulate her excitement, and back-story equals **maturity.** Mentioning a divorce, for example, will imply a depth that may be absent in younger men, and also hint at **vulnerability.** But be careful not to come across as damaged goods. Don't dwell on heartbreak too long, except to show sympathy with hers, as this will establish a **connection.** Over-emphasising painful break-ups, however, will make you seem **defeated** or lonely, and take you into the 'friends' zone. Brush aside your failures. Appear **positive** at all times.

**Go get 'em, tiger!**

'Ladies' men don't exist, because it is the woman, ultimately, who chooses.

*y*

*ou have*

*known your* And besides, no one, male or female, ever truly

*mother's friend,*

*Maureen, since you were wee —* masters the heart.'

*used to take you and Deborah to the*

*beach at Girvan, and you always thought,* Leonard

*as Maureen lifted you onto the roundabout* Cohen

*or swings, that she smelled like perfume and fauns.*

*A rich and dazed scent. Even when you were wee you'd find excuses to induce her to pick you up. You were tired, you couldn't reach her, or, your favourite: you were a wounded fox, mewling in the forest. And she'd bend down and say, 'Aw, is the poor fox cub okay?' and you'd sniff and whimper, and Maureen would say to Deborah, 'Shall we take him to the vet?' Deborah would just wave a wee flag and stick her tongue out. Then Maureen would lift and cuddle you and go, 'Is that better? Does it still hurt, little fox?' And you'd shake your head and burrow into her soft jumper, her array of smells, her dense curls, her woodland-scented womanhood.*

*Hogmanay. For Auld Lang Syne, my dear, for Auld Lang Syne. We'll tak' a cup o' kindness yet for boozing and bawling and dancing and falling about. She corners you in the kitchen, her face lined with age and marriage. 'My God, Charlie, you've grown into a good-looking boy, haven't you?' You shrug and blush and she says, 'No more wounded fox cub, eh?' and you're mortified by the memory. 'Uni now, is it? Hear you got yourself a wee girlfriend there?' Then her husband comes into the*

*kitchen, staggers, burps, reaches for another beer, and she is quiet again.*
*She still smells good, even through the fug of fags and booze and party:*
*cuts a swathe of sensuality through these tired, drunk, rubber grown-ups.*

*The evening lurches, the music enlarges, and you notice Maureen*
*staring at you every so often. You squirm beneath her gaze and adjust*
*your jeans.*

*she slips into the bathroom after you*

*'What is it?' you say, standing there, waiting to pee.*

*You don't say a word when she places her hands on your chest,*
*breathing onto your neck. Her perfume is narcotic: you are little, with*
*her arms around you, and you are wounded again, mewling softly. But*
*you are also grown and nearly adult and bristling. She runs her hands*
*down your chest and over you. Her fingers find your cock; it stiffens. You*
*exhale. Soon her lips are on your lips and your trousers are at your*
*ankles and she is straddling you on the floor, forty years and the*
*wreckage of her marriage roaring in her fuck. Yes she takes you hard*
*Yes and leaves none of the child behind and you both emerge from the*
*bathroom Yes kiss at the top of the stairs, then descend Yes fleet-footed,*
*into the carnage of the party Yes Charlie Yes raw Yes! Yes Charlie! Yes*
*Charlie! Yes! YES!* 'Yes, Charlie, you can order a starter if you like, but
I'm not going to have one,' said Julie, pointing to her stomach. And he
knew she was looking for a compliment. He provided it, on cue.

'As if you need to worry about that,' he said, and she gave a little
*faux*-shy smile.

'Well, that's very nice of you, but all the same.' She patted her
stomach again.

These little man-woman rituals.

He feared she'd brought him out to dinner tonight for a reason, for
The Reason. She'd been stepping up the pace, constantly asking how
his mother was, for example, whether or not she could cope on her
own, and if she could then, y'know, maybe it was time to, y'know, cut

the thread. Charlie consistently answered, 'She can't.' And the conversation was gutted. Julie was wanting to spend more time with him, asking who was texting whenever his phone beeped, suggesting he move favourite DVDs to her flat, buy a new toothbrush. And a razor? For when he was staying over? You'd be as well leaving some clothes too, Charlie, since you spend so much time here, ha ha. He had a password for her lap-top. A key for her door. It was starting. Startling. This cruising for intimacy. This creeping-up over the heart. He could feel her age — those eleven years between them — start casually to colonise him. She was forty-one. He was a bare-arse out of his twenties.

What did she want?

What did he want?

'I'll have the steak, please,' he said. The waiter snapped the menu from him: clean, crisp.

'And how would you like that done, sir?'

'Rare,' he said.

Julie ordered salad. Their differences woke and stretched. Then started bawling.

'So,' said Julie, 'how's your mother? She managing when you're not there?'

Charlie stared at her. There was love. Yes, there was love. So he let it go. Instead he brought up Gavin's *ridiculous* assessment of Monise Ferguson's folio.

'I mean a high C? Can you believe that?'

'She didn't get it, though,' Julie said. 'You agreed on a mid B.'

'But that's not what he *wanted* to give her! You've taught Monise before, Julie, you know how good she is.'

'Well,' said Julie, 'she usually gets the marks, yes. But she's a bit of a robot.'

'A what?'

'Y'know,' said Julie, 'one of those kids who listens to every bit of advice you give, then follows it To. The. Letter.'

'Julie,' said Charlie, 'Monise Ferguson is not a robot.'

'She has pushy parents. Pushy parents produce robots.'

'Julie, what are you talking about?' he said. 'Do you know what she's been through at this school? Not only for being the smartest kid in the year, but for how she feels, how she *questions* things? And her commitment to her art is extraordinary, despite what Gavin says. It's how she expresses herself. People like her, her very existence is evidence that ... the bad guys ... haven't won ... yet.'

'Okay, she's not a robot.'

'She's *far* from being a robot. Robots just don't ... *feel* the way Monise *feels*.'

' "Feels"?' said Julie. 'Feels what? What are you talking about, "feels"?'

'Nothing. Never mind. You wouldn't understand.'

'Understand *what*, Charlie?'

'She's not a robot. No way is she a robot.'

Julie sipped her drink and placed her hand over his. 'Look, you obviously recognise something in her. And that's great. Maybe she reminds you of yourself when you were that age, I dunno. We all get close to certain pupils, Charlie, that's the nature of teaching. We wouldn't be human if we didn't.'

'We'd be robots,' muttered Charlie, 'like Monise.'

'But we can't let it cloud our objectivity.'

'Oh,' said Charlie. 'Like it hasn't clouded Gavin's?'

'What do you mean?'

'You know what that little charade was really about.'

Their food arrived, and they lapsed into silence. Then she started eating her meal, hurriedly jabbing her salad. 'He's a professional teacher, Charlie.'

'He's professionally *jealous*.'

'*You* punched *him*, remember.'

'Listen,' said Charlie. 'Listen.' He stopped. 'I just . . . want to do something true and . . . right in this world. Do you understand? And Monise . . . she's . . . a good kid . . . different from the others. She's. *Good*. And I can. I can really *help* her, Julie, I under*stand* this girl. She's . . .'

He touched his knife and fork. For a moment, he wasn't sure what they were for. The ambient hum of the restaurant. Its clarity. Its clarity.

'Charlie,' said Julie, 'I was reading something recently.'

'What?' he said, cutting his steak.

'A book about divorce.'

He stopped cutting his steak.

'You see, I've been trying to work out how it has affected me. How it has affected you. Why divorcees find it difficult to commit to other people. Why divorced people are more likely to suffer from *depression*, Charlie.'

He placed down his knife and fork and dabbed at his mouth with his napkin.

'You see, when you get divorced, you lose your external-memory system.'

'Explain what that means.'

'Okay.' She spoke as though she was before a PowerPoint slide. 'Once you were able to discuss your experiences with your partner, and you'd reach a shared understanding about them. You could count on access to memory storage inside your partner's head, like a hard drive. But after your divorce, it's gone. Wiped.'

'So?'

'Well, Charlie, doesn't the loss of those memories feel like losing a part of your own mind?'

'You think I'm losing my mind?'

'Jesus Christ,' she said, 'that's not what I'm saying. It's a metaphor. I'm trying to work out why you're acting this way.'

'Which way?'

'You're so very . . .'

She let the the sentence hang and didn't finish it and he was left cutting into meat, into rich, bleeding muscle, sifting through the possibilities of what he was *so very* of, as though he'd been told a prophecy by a g  h    o  s     t

     g    h         os    ts                      t

 h                              o        st

        o            s           t s

 h  o                                       g h o s

*like a*         *ghost*  *she*       *walked*     *the*     *floors*

     *sound of*       *feet*   *on*        *hard blond wood*

ssshp

                                  ssshp

'Charlie,'    *she'd say*                             *I'm bored.'*

       *We don't have fun any more,*

                                       *Charlie.'*

                          *We used to dance.'*

'Why don't we go out dancing?'

                              *Have you got too much work on?'*

*sound of*        *feet*        *on blond*

                   *wood*        *floor*

*ssshp*                        *sshp*

             *shhp*

'It's like we're

                   *passing out of existence.'*

'Don't you think,

           *Charlie?'*

                     *'Charlie?'*

'Remind me why we got married.'

                   *Remind me why*

we're going to this?' said Nadine, doing that cute thing of wrinkling her nose, which she did when considering something, like a muffin she wanted to eat, or clothes she knew would go with clothes she knew.

'I've read this guy's book,' said Charlie. 'Just wanna see what he's like in the flesh.'

'Let me get this straight,' said Dawn, binning banana peel as they headed up Sauchiehall Street. 'He's the world's greatest seducer?'

'So he says.' Nadine snorted, lit a fag.

'So everyone says,' shrugged Charlie.

'And this book,' said Dawn. 'It's like – what? Three hundred pages of boasting?'

'Kinda,' said Charlie. 'But I also think his journey's pretty interesting. This guy went from being an *über*-geek to America's greatest pick-up artist.'

'So *he* says.' Nadine puffed briskly as the bookshop loomed.

'Nadine,' Charlie tutted, 'so *everyone* says.'

'You admire it,' said Dawn, smirk ticking, 'don't you?'

'I admire its *purity*,' he said, not missing a beat.

Dawn grinned. '*Alien*.'

'Eh?' said Nadine.

'Ian Holm,' said Charlie, 'Sigourney Weaver.'

'Eh?' said Nadine, glancing between the two of them.

Charlie and Dawn laughed. '*In space*,' he announced, '*no one can hear Nadine . . .*'

'What,' said Nadine, single fingernail picking the air, 'the *fuck* are you pair talking about?'


Bookshop basement: full of slick, groomed, bald guys in their thirties. Glesga patter-merchants morphed into LA stars. A *lot* of uni students. Also: leather jackets. Tans. Biceps. Baseball caps. All the testosterone ripped from Glasgow by the hands of a bare-chested god, dumped here – lightning! clay! – sculpted into these bodies. Formal rows. Pecs like brick. Do me justice, lads. Yes, O Great One.

'Men . . .' said Nadine, and though Charlie didn't know what she meant, the word was airy on her lips, had room in it. She headed towards a free seat, scything through the tripwires of glances.

Dawn shuffled in Nadine's wake, with hoodie and dreadlocks. 'Is it safe?' she whispered to Charlie.

'Laurence Olivier. Dustin Hoffman. *Marathon Man*.'

'Uh, yeah,' she said. 'But *is it*?'

All had turned to see *WOMEN!!!* enter. Charlie could feel their monstrous, male, dinner-plate eyes sizing him up. What does he got? Huh? What does this chump got? How can we take him down? Huh? How do we wrestle his puny little psyche to the ground? The military sweep over his clothes, haircut, estimated age. How easy or difficult it would be to prise these women from Charlie's side. All of this felt, as he passed them, like pulsing threat. He was Damon Albarn at a Gallagher wedding.

He, Dawn, Nadine sat, on mannequin display. He squirmed and wished he'd picked up a glass of the free wine, just to relax him a little. So many men, with their big garbage-crusher hearts grinding all around him. He thought about taking Nadine and Dawn away, away, upstairs, to the art section, flick with them through glossy coffee-table books, let them teach him about Giotto, Rembrandt, Mondrian, 'Oh, Charlie, you don't *know* this stuff? You pretty little Philistine.' He suddenly didn't want to be in the presence of this man who could, as he boasted, sleep with any woman anywhere – because if that was true then he could sleep with *these* women *here*.

But then the Master Seducer came onstage, and he was no monolith.

Skinny frame, skinny tie, shirt, jumper. Tiny. The room sat up to greet him. He blinked once. 'So, guys.' His small, still voice. 'I tried a life experiment. I decided I was going to do something every day that would take me outside of my comfort zone. It changed everything. And that's where this book came from: *The Master Seducer In You*.'

*GQ* haircuts nodded. He coughed and read through sheets of paper, occasionally holding one up and saying, 'What do *you* think, guys?

'Dear Master Seducer, I'm worried about my looks. My five-year-old baby girl said I was ugly. How do I convince people I'm not?'

'How cool is this. Guys are working *The Master Seducer* rules in Uganda.

'Should you or should you not masturbate before a date? Okay, let's take a vote.'

Geeks wanting to be boys. Boys wanting to be men. Men wanting to be kings. Kings wanting to be gods. This man knew his followers. He recognised the look in their eyes, the histories that fluttered there like torn flags, the dismal, washed-out setbacks and knockbacks. He bantered with them, easy, brought them out of themselves, and their souls quivered, then stilled like whimpering dogs before him.

He smiled *constantly*.

'Pish,' said Nadine, with each piece of advice he shed. 'Pish pish pish.' Her crosses on his page.

'Look at *this* guy,' Dawn whispered to Charlie, pointing to a long red boutique coat with the collars turned up.

'Peacock,' Charlie said.

'Come again?'

'It's a method of attracting women. You stand out from the crowd by dressing outrageously.'

'Wow,' said Dawn. 'Even his *shoelaces* are peacocking.'

The peacock saw them looking. Smiled at Dawn.

'Yikes!' said Dawn. 'Did you bring the garlic and crucifix?'

Nadine was staring at the stage, eyes narrowed and fingers clicking over her chin. 'He's not such a big deal.'

'That's what they all say,' Charlie whispered, 'before he fucks them.'

The Master Seducer told a sexy story about one of his encounters. Himself and another man, a club late at night. A woman in her fifties.

Smoking. The sex that had curled from her lungs. The two of them kissing her breasts and how she'd stroked their heads and *growled*. 'This is what we do, guys. We awaken women who have forgotten their sexuality.'

'Oh, please,' said Nadine.

'I want this to be the beginnings of a men's self-help movement.' His voice so . . . ordinary. Ikea-built. But everyone listening. Even Nadine, even Dawn: art itself seeing what it could reshape and sculpt and make sense of here. 'Those old-style men's help groups, what was that shit? Guys in woods trying to commune with the "ancient gods"? No. We're doing this for women too. We're finally giving them what they've always wanted from men. That's the difference.'

'Bloody hell,' said Nadine. 'He really believes this.'

Dawn was chewing one of her dreadlocks.

Charlie looked round. The focus in the men, leaning forwards and listening. The Master Seducer had seduced them too. All these alpha males, these wannabes, kicked and slapped by rejection all their lives. Their vast backlog of revenge fucks glistening, just waiting to hatch and shriek.

'"Dear Master Seducer. What do I do when I approach a group and they shut me out and go into a girl-conference with each other, then I'm left standing?" Okay, dude, well, you go off and approach someone else. Do *not* decrease your value. Come back with a new girl, and your value will be increased.'

Assent murmured beneath baseball caps

'"Dear Master Seducer. This girl cancelled on me by text, so I froze her out by not texting her back, but she never texted me back either." Buddy, you really did freeze her out. Not all behaviour has to be punished. You just make yourself seem bitter and controlling . . .

'Anything a guy says to a girl translates as "How about some dick"? Brothers, you have to come in under the radar . . .

'If you're going to do better with women you have to control the surface details of grooming, presence, posture, et cetera . . .

'I've got six other books under contract . . .

'Here's why you should never buy a woman a drink . . .'

A couple of pretty, studenty girls, who'd wandered into the basement and started listening, were now flicking through the book.

Charlie found himself inspecting his fingers, the strange purple smudges on the tips.

Nadine said: 'I can't listen to this shit. Let's go.'

Dawn said: 'I wanna hear more.'

Charlie said: 'Anyone got coke back at theirs?'

On Nadine's walls dresses, decades old, hung there like ghosts. She had an ancient record-player in a wooden box, stylus resting on a scratched LP. *Moods for Candlelight.* A stack of 78s lay beside it, waiting for the fond hand of some nicotine-stained Tom Waits character to bring them to life. Nadine slammed shut the box, chopped up some coke on it, bent, sniffed jerkily. She rose – whoosh! – and rubbed at her nose. 'I mean,' she said, bright, quick, glittering like a stick of glam rock, 'their *ridiculous* nicknames. "Presence!" "Cobra!" "Stealth"! You want to just fucking say to them, y'know, YOUSE ARE NOT NINJAS. Going up to women with practised lines and routines. Are we, are we, like, computer programs? Just punch in the right code and we, like, we, like, open our legs? Do they think that shit will work?'

'It does work,' said Dawn. The bean-bag moulded itself round her lazing form. 'He wouldn't be so famous if it didn't work.'

'Wouldn't work on me,' Nadine mehhed.

Charlie laughed.

'What's so funny?'

'Nadine,' he said, 'you use routines from that book *all the time.*'

'You just don't know you're doing it.' Dawn scratched her exposed navel-ring.

Nadine looked at each of them and straightened her back, cat-like. 'I do not. Guys want to fuck me cos I'm *sexy*.'

'But what's sexy,' said Dawn, smiling at the word, 'when you break it down? Really. Attraction is based on certain laws. Like economics. Like physics. There are ways men and women can be, things they can do, which increase their attractiveness to the opposite sex. That's obvious.'

'Why do we bother getting dressed up?' said Charlie. 'Why do we dance?'

'I *like* getting dressed up,' said Nadine. 'I *like* dancing.'

'You like the attention it brings,' smirked Dawn.

'Fuck off, the pair of you.'

'Think about it,' said Charlie, 'if you lived alone in a Highland cabin for a year, you wouldn't dress like an indie pixie.'

'Indie pixie.' Dawn nodded, deep and philosophical, as though Charlie had exposed the essence of things. Nadine's fag waved dismissively.

Ross Clark's song 'Silversword' was playing. Whoah-oh-oh-oh-oh! Do you like me? Whoah-oh-oh-oh-oh! I don't mind! Dawn's iPod plugged into Nadine's docking station (the Magnificent Bastard, she called it, after a cock she'd once described to Charlie). Charlie bent forwards to the coffee-table, sniffed a line off a magazine. Scarlett Johannson's sculpted cream face smiled up at him. She seemed to approve. He was glad. Thanks, Scarlett. No problem, Charlie, I don't judge.

'That is fucked up,' said Nadine.

'What are we talking about?' said Charlie, and rubbed his nose.

'Oh, my God,' said Nadine. 'Right. Listen. Right. Last night. Did anyone see that programme? Called, like, *Women Up Close*? Or, like,

*Girl Trouble*? Or, like, *Look At My Big Fadge*?'

'What was it about?' said Dawn, rubbing specks of coke into her gums.

'Oh, my God,' said Nadine. 'Oh, my God. Right. Right. It was about like vaginas? Like how they *work*? Up close? And, Jesus, they were on show, like, *all the time*. Is this what we call programming now? Is that what we call – I'm sorry – *women's* programming? Tasteless. Tacky. There's this sexy "patient" and she's up on a chair and there's like this blonde lady-doctor talking about like the labia minora and the perineum and she's pointing to this poor woman's . . . her . . .'

'Foo-foo,' said Dawn.

Nadine paused. 'Foo-foo?'

'Yeah,' said Dawn. 'Foo-foo. Flower. Front bottom.'

'Eech,' said Nadine, then shook as though she was covered with goo.

'Ha ha,' said Charlie.

'What did you call your thing when you were a kid, Charlie?' said Dawn. She was gazing up at him with red-rimmed eyes.

'My wee man.'

'Your wee man.' Dawn laughed, lay back on the floor. 'Ha! Brilliant.'

'Can we stop talking about this?' said Nadine.

'Why?' said Charlie.

'I just don't think it's appropriate to talk about children's names for their genitals.'

'Just a laugh,' said Dawn. 'Here. Charlie. Pass me some more of that . . . um . . .'

'Charlie?' he said, handing her the bag.

'Charlie.' She grinned. Then she chopped out more lines with the side of a credit card.

'What was I talking about?' said Nadine, hands poised spinily.

'Y'know,' said Dawn, and stopped for so long that Charlie thought she'd forgotten her thread, 'for years I thought I had a "clutterbox".'

'A clutterbox?' said Charlie. 'What the hell is that?'

'My mum was a doctor,' she said, 'and she gave me Claire Rayner's *Body Book* to teach me about the birds and the bees. Had pictures of naked people all the way through it, but I just drew clothes on them. Mum patiently explained to me what all the parts of my body were called. Including my "clutterbox".'

'And where exactly,' said Charlie, 'is your clutterbox?'

'Charlie. Please,' said Nadine.

'On my flower.' Dawn snickered.

'Dawn,' said Nadine, '*please*.'

'Oh, what, Nadine?' Dawn smiled. 'Never been touched on your flower?'

Charlie started to laugh, but something about the way Nadine stiffened stopped him. She was upright, eyes alert, and he could see the coke like forked lightning in her system. Then she exhaled and started smoothing her hands down over her thighs – once, twice, thrice – quickly. 'Listen,' she said, 'I know you'll think this strange and maybe unreasonable, and it's not that I don't have a sense of humour, but I'm asking the two of you. Very calmly. This is not a discussion I find funny. So can we please leave it?'

Dawn looked to Charlie quizzically.

'If you don't mind.'

Charlie nodded. 'Sure,' he said.

Dawn stopped chopping the coke and shrugged. 'Whatever.'

Nadine folded, then unfolded her arms and tried to smile. 'Right,' she said. 'Good. What shall we do now?'

The three of them swapped silent suggestions with their eyes, until Dawn said: 'Let's dress up!'

267

**You may have to 'play gay'.** On a night out, most men resort to boorish, aggressive and chauvinistic behaviour. You should take advantage of this by playing yourself as more feminine, **sensitive** and self-deprecating. This role, however, is played with far more conviction by gay than straight men. Women will often go clubbing with a gay man for that very reason. Gay men are thus, by virtue of their lack of threat, always already **'on the inside'** of any group of women. This is one of the reasons why it is a good idea to play gay (though **never** camp): in order to divest a group of women of their defences. **Sexual ambiguity** is your greatest weapon. This is why 95 per cent of straight men, recoiling in horror that they may be mistaken for a homosexual, are stupid.

**And sleeping alone.**

pull clothes from Nadine's wardrobe !!!DAISY AND GATSBY!!!
they're giggling teehee Nadine's bedroom revolving round us Hey will
I get the tartan jacket? but Dawn says *No let's play with hats!* Nadine
draping a featherboa round me *Charlie's Marc Bolan* yeah yeah yeah
YEAH YEAH YEAH YEAH they laugh clap as I pose in the mirror
then Dawn says *Some makeup! Yeah!* pulls out a box rrrraking through
MEANwhile Dawn trying on a sequined fedora with her dreadlocks
and the COKE makes her stunning preening in front of the mirror
pushing up breasts she says *Hey Charlie try on this coat* sure enough
man fits me *poifectly* seems to morph itself to me shhhhlp like
Spider-Man's black costume Dawn draws hands down my slimtapering
waist *Yes Charlie oh yes that suits you* looks me in the eye from
beneath her hat THE LOOK lingers till she finally dra aaa a ags it
away but it trails behind her we take pictures SAY SEX! with hats
scarves boa coats wigs ladies and gentlemen Miss Audrey Hepburn!
Mr Syd Barrett! Miss Louise Brooks! Nadine's bringing eyeliner to the
bed *Okay Charlie lie down open your eyes I'm going to apply this very
carefully* her soft big bed her longblack jacket featherboa and Silver
Surfer T-shirt Nadine con . . . cen . . . trates as she applies makeup
Dawn stares at me wee smile WINK just playing on her face Nadine's
saying *Right open your eyes wide* and my eyes are wide TRULY
WIDE OPEN she's drawing the pencil along the edge of them both
their faces !so close to mine! breath on me ?vodka? both mmmmm
kissabledistance descending angels then Dawn dabbing at my eyelids
with the eyeshadow Nadine's saying *Wow Charlie you look beautiful*
and soon the lipgloss feels so soft on my mouth a melted scented
energy a second just a *second* when ALL THREE OF OUR MINDS

SEEM TO HANG THERE SUSPENDED IN THE AIR then Dawn leans down kisses me my hand on her face Nadine's fingers on my nipple under my T-shirt we are GRINNING at each other full and big and bright as film stars then

## Int. Nadine's bedroom. Night.

*Soft light. The Twilight Sad's first album is playing, a line repeating itself, over and over: 'The kids are on fire in the bedroom . . .'*

NADINE *and* DAWN *are kneeling either side of* CHARLIE. *He is stroking his prick.* DAWN *stares down at it, tongue licking over her lips.* NADINE *has her hand on* CHARLIE's *face, staring into his eyes.*

DAWN: Look at it, Nadine. Look at how hard he is.

NADINE: Enjoying this?

CHARLIE *groans.*

DAWN: Wank yourself. Wank your big cock for us, Charlie.

CHARLIE *raises his hips, strokes faster.* NADINE *puts her finger in his mouth. He starts to suck on it. She grins. He smiles back at her.*

DAWN: God, yes, that's beautiful. What a beautiful prick.

DAWN *starts touching her breasts beneath her top.* NADINE *smooths her palm over* CHARLIE's *chest, his thighs. Then she looks at his hard-on, places her hand over his cock and masturbates it.*

DAWN: That's it. Stroke him. Can you feel how hard he is?

NADINE *moans and takes over from him, her fingers spidery, stroking him gently.* CHARLIE *touches* DAWN's *leg. She has lifted up her top now and is pinching and pulling at her nipples.* CHARLIE's *eyes travel over her tattoo – a red Chinese dragon that ripples the length of her body.*

272

*Her skin shifts beneath the ink. The dragon seems to be alive, part of her.*

DAWN: I want his cock in my mouth. Let's lick it. I want to taste him.

*They bend down and both start to kiss* CHARLIE's *hard-on, soft, gentle kisses over the shaft.* DAWN *runs her bottom lip up it.* CHARLIE *gasps. Then they kiss each other, tongues flickering on the head of his cock.* DAWN *takes* NADINE's *face in her hands and kisses harder.* NADINE *whimpers.*

DAWN: You are a fucking sexy bitch, Nadine.

NADINE: Oh, God.

DAWN: Look at her, Charlie. Look at how hot she is. Show him your beautiful tits. Go on.

*NADINE unbuttons her shirt and removes her bra, staring at* CHARLIE. *He stares back at her, then reaches up and touches her nipples. His fingertips leave purple stains. As he moves them down her soft, rolling side to touch her ass the stains trail over her body, like watery ink.* DAWN *kisses* NADINE *while she wanks his cock, then* DAWN *bends and kisses* NADINE's *nipples, bites them, licks them.* NADINE *grips* DAWN's *hair and moans deeply.*

*CHARLIE moves from beneath them, then positions himself behind* DAWN, *runs his hands over her. Her tattoos meld with the purple marks from his fingers.* DAWN *sits upright between them and* NADINE *kisses her on the mouth again.* CHARLIE *slips his hand into* DAWN's *jeans, starts playing with her clit.* DAWN *gasps and bucks against him suddenly.*

DAWN: That feels good. Play with my pussy, Charlie. Yes. Yes.

NADINE:      Is she wet?

CHARLIE:     God, yes.

DAWN:        Fuck me. Take my jeans off and fuck me.

*They stop while* CHARLIE *takes* DAWN's *jeans off. During this,* NADINE *runs her hand over her breasts and watches.* DAWN *bends over, and* CHARLIE *hooks her knickers to the side, slides his cock into her.*

NADINE:      Aren't you going to wear a —

DAWN:        Oh, God yes. GOD, yes, Charlie, that feels good. That feels so good. Fuck me. FUCK me.

CHARLIE:     Yes.

NADINE *retreats to a chair in the corner of the room and watches* CHARLIE *and* DAWN. *She takes off her knickers and lifts her skirt up to her waist. Then she places one leg up on the arm of the chair and starts to masturbate.* CHARLIE *stares into her eyes while he grips* DAWN's *ass and slides his cock in and out of her.*

DAWN:        Are you watching him fuck me, Nadine? Is it turning you on?

NADINE *starts masturbating faster.*

DAWN:        Look at her, Charlie. Look what it's doing to her. She's wanking herself because of us. Because of *us.*

CHARLIE:     Yes.

*There is only the sound of moaning while* CHARLIE *and* DAWN *fuck and* NADINE *plays with her own clit. Soon,* NADINE *is pushing two fingers inside herself, grinding her pussy against her hand. She comes, loudly, the chair rocking beneath her. Then she collapses into it, fingertips trailing lazily over her nipples.*

DAWN:        Get on your back, Charlie. I want to ride your cock.

CHARLIE *does so.* DAWN *flicks the head of his cock over*

*her clit for a few seconds then eases herself onto it.*

CHARLIE: Oh, yes.

*DAWN fucks CHARLIE, nails dragging down his chest.*
*NADINE watches this for a while.*

DAWN: Fuck me. Fuck my pussy.

CHARLIE: Yes. Oh, yes.

*NADINE picks up her knickers from the floor, slides them back up her legs. She leans forwards, places her chin in her hand, and watches DAWN bend down and kiss CHARLIE on the mouth. Then CHARLIE turns DAWN over onto her back and starts to fuck her hard, slamming into her. DAWN wraps her legs around him.*

DAWN: Yes, Charlie. Yes. Yes. Come in me. Come in me. Come in my cunt. Do it.

CHARLIE: I'm coming. I'm COMING. Oh, God. Oh, GOD.

*DAWN grips him with her legs. CHARLIE bucks and roars.*
*NADINE sighs, then picks up her skirt and leaves the room.*

'I don't think much about death, but in a certain stage in your life it becomes very clear that your time is not unlimited. Tennessee Williams said: "Life is a fairly well-written play, except for the third act." I'm maybe at the third act, where you have the benefit of the experience of the first two. But how it ends is nobody's business and is generally accompanied by disagreeable circumstances.'

Leonard Cohen

'Mr Bain, I've had a complaint from one of your sixth-years.'

Charlie exhaled, standing with his hands behind his back, trying not to bounce up and down on his heels.

'Last week,' Paulson continued, reading from a piece of paper, 'you used an extract by James Kelman, which included extreme profanity. You used obscene sexual language in a discussion about the text. Before you rounded it all off by calling the class . . .' Paulson looked up at him.

'Cunts.'

Paulson placed the sheet of paper on the desk and stared at Charlie through the kind of sober-framed spectacles that would be worn only by someone who wanted to stare through sober-framed spectacles.

'Would you mind telling me the context for all of this?'

'Certainly,' said Charlie. 'I was making a point about semantics.'

Paulson said nothing. Paulson said everything.

Charlie cleared his throat. 'I was trying to explain to the class the political motivations behind what is considered "obscene" language.'

The staffroom had been bustling that morning – teachers causing a bottleneck of suits as the bell rang, which Charlie, making himself little and shrew-like, had tried to pass through – but Paulson had still sinisterly sensed him in the crowd, descended upon him like a bird of prey and hissed: 'My office, please.'

The Bald Eagle scratched his chin with his talons. 'And you couldn't have used a different word? "Bastard" perhaps?'

'Or "poo" maybe?' said Charlie.

'Don't try to be funny,' said Paulson. 'This is very serious.'

'Censorship usually is.'

279

'And don't try to dress it up as a political debate either.'

'Well, what about a literary one?' said Charlie, growing in confidence now. 'Chaucer wrote in what was considered low, vulgar language instead of high Latin. Dante wrote in common Italian. Would you let me teach them?'

'Not if they said cunt!'

Charlie nodded. 'We were examining the political assumptions behind language. The fact of the matter is, we would not be having this discussion were those political assumptions not currently present.'

'Mr Bain, you called four pupils the most obscene sexual swear-word there is! There is nothing else to be said! Can you imagine how this would look in the papers? "Teacher Tells Children They're Cunts!"'

'They're not children.' Charlie sighed. 'They're nearly adults, for godsakes. And they hear that kind of language all the time.'

'Not from teachers.'

'Who was it that complained?' said Charlie.

'That's confidential.'

'Was it Simon? I bet it was Simon.'

'Mr Bain.' Paulson stood. Charlie had forgotten how tall he was. He loomed like an obelisk, going all *2001: A Space Odyssey* on Charlie's ass. Charlie squawked and screeched, monkey-like, adjusted his tie. 'May I remind you that you've already received a verbal warning for your assault on another teacher –'

'Off the school grounds.'

'– and that in a period during which you should be trying to repair your reputation you seem to be hell-bent on completely destroying it.'

This was incredible. Attempting to expand the mental horizons of pupils, encouraging them to question the invisible structures that surrounded them, was bringing him into direct confrontation with the authorities? He didn't know why this even surprised him. That was the system. That was the system as it existed. Built to repress, to weigh down, to stare through binoculars, to stultify, to measure and probe and demand, to invade and take and rummage through bins and hold to the light with a magnifying-glass, then grin. *We have found the proof we need, sir. A dissident is among us.*

'This is very disappointing,' Charlie said.

'You're not joking,' Paulson spluttered.

'Am I receiving a written warning?'

'You certainly are.'

'I might have to involve my union in this.'

'By all means,' Paulson said. 'Your union rep is Gavin Prentice, I believe.'

Charlie paused. The room expanded. They were in Nuremberg. He was staring Fascism in the face. History would judge. History wanted justice.

He wanted to yell *CUNT!* at the top of his voice.

He stood there. Charlie stood there waiting for History to clear his name. History didn't do anything. Come on, History! What are you waiting for? History coughed politely, looked at its watch, and remembered it had another appointment, absolving drowned witches and Hollywood stars from the McCarthy era.

'Charlie,' Paulson said. This was the first time Paulson had called him Charlie. His own name a weapon used against him. 'Is everything all right?'

'All right?'

'I mean at home. I'm aware that your mother hasn't been well. Are you ... coping?'

'Coping?' Charlie said. 'Of course.'

'It's a stressful job. I've been there. It's difficult keeping things together sometimes, I know.'

Charlie considered this. 'It's a stressful life, sir.'

Paulson nodded. 'Well. Just try to do your best, son. That's all I ask. And for godsakes keep your nose clean from now on.'

'I will.'

Son?

icnic at Hanging Rock Solid Air Salo o le Centoventi Giorante di Sodoma For Your Pleasure One Flew Over the Cuckoo's Nest Here **let** e Warm Jets Revolution Will Not Be Televised Physical Graffiti Bohemia dy Carrie Born to Run The Hissing of Summer Lawns All the Presid **me** Men Tonight's the Night Blood on the Tracks Horses Shine on Yo Diamond The Man Who Fell to Earth Star Wars Dancing Close Encoun **in!** the Third Kind Midnight's Children Annie Hall Lanark Eraserhead Mar on Suspiria Hejira The Deer Hunter Songs in the Key of Life Alien Riddley Walker Last Tango in Paris Never Mind the Bollocks Here's the Sex Pistols Music for Airports Unknown Pleasures Apocalypse Now London Calling The Wall Ghost Town Trans-Europe Express Manhattan My Aim is True The Shining My Life in the Bush of Ghosts The Elephant Man White Noise Raging Bull L'Amant E.T: The Extra-Terrestrial Bladerunner Gandhi Murmur Once Upon a Time in America Brazil Swordfishtrombones Shoah Neuromancer Blue Velvet The Handmaid's Tale Full Metal Jacket Watchmen Akira Fairytale of New York Hounds of Love Psychoca

Charlie strode to Simon's common room with all the authority of a prosecutor. Son. Kids in his way got out of his way. Son. He entered the common room without knocking. The rule of law was null and Son void here. Simon was sitting with a caravan of girls, arranged round him Son and laughing Son at whatever he'd said. Monise was one of them. They all turned as Charlie leaned into the room.

'Mr Bain?'

'Simon,' he said, 'can I see you outside?'

'Sure,' said Simon, picking up his bag. 'Remember,' he said, and made a funny voice, '*I'm only a phone call away.*' The girls cackled. It didn't sound all that funny.

Charlie shut the door. 'I know what you're doing.'

'Mr Bain?'

'Don't give me that,' Charlie snapped. 'Was it you who told Paulson I said cunt?'

Simon shook his head, cheeks ripening. 'No.'

'Does that word offend you, Simon?'

'*No.*'

'What about *fud*?'

'Look, sir,' said Simon, 'I was playing devil's advocate. I thought that's what you wanted. An open debate.'

Charlie focused his gaze. He wished he, too, had sober-framed glasses to narrow it through, the way Paulson did. It would have added just that extra presence to his suit and shirt and tie, that *soupçon* of gravitas. Instead he had to be simply 'Mr Bain' and hope that performance was enough. 'Of course,' Charlie said. 'Open debate.'

'Which didn't have the outcome you wanted.'

'What?'

Simon looked impossibly small and youthful, impossibly strong and tall.

'The class disagreed with you. So you didn't really want an open debate at all. You wanted *us* to agree with *you*.'

'The class didn't disagree with me,' Charlie said. 'You disagreed with me.'

'Everyone disagreed with you.'

'Did not.'

'Did so.'

Charlie opened the common room door. 'Monise,' he said.

Monise glanced up from her books.

'Can you come here for a second?'

She did.

Charlie closed the door again. 'Monise,' Charlie said, looking at

Simon, 'would you care to refresh Simon's memory about the debate we had in class last week.'

'Which one?'

'The one about cunts.'

'Oh,' said Monise. 'That one.'

'That one.'

'What do you want me to uh—'

'Did or did you not agree with me that day?'

Monise scratched her arm. 'You mean about whether or not we should be using the, uh, C-word?'

'Yes,' said Charlie, enunciating, '*cunt.*'

'No, I didn't.'

'Didn't what?' said Charlie, looking at her.

'Didn't agree with you. I didn't think it was appropriate for the classroom.'

Charlie placed his hands on his hips.

'I didn't think it was appropriate then and I don't think it's appropriate now.'

The universe rippled beyond his comprehension.

'Monise,' he said, 'do you know who complained to Mr Paulson?'

'Yes,' she said. 'Me.'

'*You?*'

'At the request of the female members of the class. I'm staff-student rep.'

'*You* did?' he said. His voice sounded too high and squeaky.

'She didn't want to,' said Simon, 'but she's staff-student rep. She had to take the complaint forward.'

Charlie looked at Simon. Simon shrugged. Simon's cheeks were ruddy-pink, as though he enjoyed healthy outdoor exercise. The corridor echoed with the ghosts of Confrontations Past, decades of them. The balance of power quivering eternally.

'So it wasn't you?' Charlie said.

Simon shook his head. 'The language didn't bother me, Mr Bain,' he said. 'I was just playing devil's advocate.'

Charlie nodded. 'Aye,' he mumbled. 'Aye, that's just . . . what I . . . wanted.'

'Sorry,' Simon said.

''Sall right,' Charlie managed.

'I had to put in a complaint, Mr Bain,' she said. 'It's my duty. The girls felt pretty strongly about it.'

'I understand,' he said, lifting his gaze from the floor.

Simon glanced at Monise, then said, 'You okay, Mr Bain?'

He nodded. The floor the floor the floor.

Monise pushed her glasses further up her nose.

He clutched his folder.

Simon's eyes were flitting between the two of them.

Charlie scratched his neck.

'Okay,' he said. 'I'm sorry.'

'We're not looking for apologies,' said Simon.

'Aren't you?'

'Actually,' Simon said, 'it was one of your best lessons.'

'You think so?'

'Yeah, Mr Bain. All that stuff about politics and language and stuff. It was really stimulating.'

Charlie nodded again. Shrugged. 'Well,' he said, 'I'll be, uh, seeing you both.'

'Take care of yourself,' said Monise, her gaze softening.

He raised his eyebrows, then made off down the corridor, trailing bits of himself. When he rounded the corner he coughed and smoothed his hair and straightened his tie. He stared down the corridor. He stared for a few seconds. Then he saw a kid spitting on the floor and picked up the pace towards him. 'You, boy!'

*where*     THE *whisper fro*         *whisp*

      *once*

*m t he e mpty spaces in your flat. Where once the whisper was* Money, *now it is* Kids. *Something clicks, long-legged, into the room each time there's been an argument, sits poised behind the couch and through its mandibles hisses: Chiiiiiildren. Yvonne watches Supernanny and says things to you like, 'Do you think that would work? Do you think we'll ever have a kid like that? What would we do? Do you think we should buy a home near a good school?'* Spectral beings drifting through the universe waiting to be born, *waiting to rush into the room and jump on the bed and wake you; they're out there, in space, shaking their heads and watching the two of you come to a decision: Next year? The year after? Ever, Charlie? Ever?*

     *Just those words 'good' and 'school'.*

     *'Don't you think we'd be good parents? Don't you want to be a father?'*

     *Good Parents.*

     *Good Father.*

     *Good People.*

     *Like a vampire has walked into the room, a respectable, bourgeois vampire.*

     *It's her birthday. For her birthday you take her to a hotel in the Highlands: big roaring fire in the lobby, deer's heads on the walls, everything is tartan. The two of you get drunk on the train on the way up, and things start to become liquid again; you come back to each other, those kids you were at university. She's on good form. Giggling plenty. She's off on a riff about how much she hates jazz music, she's doing an impression of Dizzy Gillespie or Miles Davis, playing a plastic fork, her eyes and her cheeks bulging as she goes off on an imaginary jazz-muso wank-off. She's funny. She's quicksilver. That girl. That girl you fell in love with. That* Midsummer Night's Dream.

286

When you get to the hotel you fuck immediately. Drunkenly. With claws and teeth and an unsheathed, canine lust. The look in her eyes. The need. As though she has summoned a figment of you.

'Charlie, yes. Oh, Charlie. Charlie, my love.'

She still wants you. Some part of you. And some part of you is overjoyed — weeps! — to discover this.

But then something happens during the sex. The wrong thing is said, or you fuck too long without looking her in the eye, or maybe she just doesn't come. Whatever it is, it snags on your expanding lust and rips at it, and everything deflates, and before you know it she's saying, 'Get off me. Just get off me, Charlie,' and you're lying next to her and she's staring into space and she's shaking her head and the sweat on your skin is cooling and you reach out to touch her and she rolls away from you.

'What is it, Yvonne? What's the matter?'

'I've just realised,' she murmurs, 'that I'm stuck with you now.'

'What?' you say. 'Could you repeat that?'

'Nothing.'

And the two of you lie there for a while in silence, then you each shower in turn, and you eat a beautiful meal in a beautiful restaurant, with the minimum of fuss, and you look round at all the couples — none of them talking to each other.

There's an edge creeping into things, a shark cruising beneath the surface of each conversation you have about yourselves: the wedding debt, the student loans, your disinterest in housework, her disinterest in books. In the coldest hours, after another argument, as you lie, sulking and drunk, on the couch in the front room, you stare at the dark and start to come to Conclusions. About Marriage. About Possession. Look at this sick fucking middle-class materialistic life we create for ourselves, you think. This boxing-ring. This toxic career of acquisition. This elaborate peacock display we make of our lives. In a truly free society, *people would need no possessions, no wealth, and so could love freely — surely.*

*That's how you begin to justify your affairs.*

*You're not sure why, but something strange has happened in the last few years: women have started to find you attractive. When you and Yvonne go out you're constantly surprised by glances, and second glances, and third glances, from eyes that would never once have turned your way. It makes you fidget, blush, embarrassed. You even start to feel a little harassed by this attention, by the compliments Yvonne tells you she's had from workmates who've only just met you.*

*Why has this come now? Why did this have to happen when you're married? The number of girls at school that you asked out, as though you were simply walking along a line saying, 'You? You? You?' faced each time with bored shakes of the head. And now women are queuing up to flirt with you?!*

*No. No. No. No.*

*Not so annoying that you don't flirt back, though.*

*You learn to enjoy it, become adept at it.*

*At parties, with colleagues, on trains, in shops.*

*You flirt with waitresses who come over to take your order.*

*'What?' you say, when you find your wife looking at you.*

*You flirt with her friends.*

*You flirt with her family.*

*You flirt with those colleagues who'd told her you were cute.*

*It becomes so natural eventually, this new-found power, that you fail even to recognise it as flirting. You start to wonder if you could seduce a woman: someone you'd just met in formal circumstances, if you could tempt them into bed. You'd stop before it ever got that far, of course. You'd never do that to Yvonne. That's the kind of thing your father did. No! No, you'd never have an affair. Just an experiment.*

*just*

*to*

*see*

*if*

*you*

Turns out you can. At the school Christmas party, introduced to the
wife of your head of department (he leaves you alone together, and
disappears to talk shop with senior members of staff – an implied insult
to you both), a woman in her forties, to whom you direct your attention.
Learned talk of the Middle East moves quickly to the lives of her
grown-up children, to a documentary on TV about a touring erotic
revue (you're turning this conversation, dropping in hints and
innuendo, to which she smiles), then she tells a naughty story about
something she did when she was a young woman, in a department-store
changing-room. The quickness of it. The naughtiness of it. The pilot
light that appears in her eyes as she remembers. It's a signal. You're
sure it is. You feint and flick and weave around her growing attraction
to you – 'This is turning me on, actually,' you say – parry away
her own surprise at being desired. 'You're a very confident young man,
aren't you?' she smiles, glancing above the rim of her glass. Before you
know it – flushed, the drink rushing to her head – she's told you how
often she likes to masturbate. 'Oh, gosh,' she says, hand to her chest,
giggling, 'oh, my God, you don't want to hear this!' 'But I do,' you say.
The volume of your conversation drops to whisper level – you can't be
sure who's listening, but you're damn sure she is – so you both have to
lean, breathing each other in. It shuts the last remaining gaps of
propriety.

289

*You tell her how much you want her. She n    arrows her eyes and growls at the back of her throat and says something like, 'Of c    ourse, my husband would toootally have you fired.' 'It'd be worth it.' 'I think it    would, you know.' God, the attraction of fucking the wife of your boss. No!    You draw back. It's enough to know. You're startled by yourself, and    she says, 'For what?' You return home to Yvonne, drunk and di    sgusted with everything, and she is    he pleased to see you, is please    d to notice that return of lust into*

*he    your eyes. She puts down    her magazine and says, 'Some one's horny,' and virtua    lly carries you to bed so you ca n vent all your volcani    c frustration on this woman y ou love. Three or fo    ur times! Rifling through a pa    was rade of images. A    nd the next day you bo th phone in sick    to work, go walking in    a*

*was    Kelvingrove P    ark and sit down on a bench. T    ogether you stare    series*

*a    at the d    ucks on the    of rive    r all*

*ghost    d ay    ghosts*

His mother was dozing in front of *Newsnight. Snoozenight.* She looked like a little old baby. He stood staring at her for a while. She snored, unperturbed by reality. What did the dream life of his mother involve? Being a horse? Charging across the night plains of Arizona? He bent over and kissed her head. 'I love you.'

A programme came on television. *How To Have Sex When You're Married.* The presenters made a husband and wife rate each other out of ten for attractiveness, sexual performance and emotional understanding. The couple faced each other, faced each other in their thirties, faced down the amount of years they'd been together. While tearful music played, they showed their litany of twos, threes and fours, written on large pieces of card.

The wife said to him, 'We've been honest here today. It can only get better now.'

Later, the same woman spoke to camera, panda-eyed and sniffing. 'He thinks I'm a two?' she said. 'A *two*?'

His mother whimpered in her sleep. He touched her hands and remembered sitting on her knee, learning to read *Chicken Licken* while she clapped and encouraged him and his dad prowled the room, barking at one of his 'team'. Occasionally, his dad would stop and look at him and smile. Occasionally. 'And Chicken Licken said, "I'm going to see the king because the sky is falling in!"'

'Clever boy, Charlie!'

A psychologist commented, 'Megan keeps quiet because she wants to distance herself from Lewis's constant demands. She needs time alone to look inside and take care of herself. And so . . .'

'Oh, Mum. My mother.'

One of the presenters brought out a vibrator for the wife and told her to rediscover her sexuality. Charlie immediately changed channels.

His mother snuffled awake, smiled to see him. 'Oh,' she said. 'Charlie? Was I asleep?'

'I disagree,' said Nadine, stubbing out the last of the joint. 'Feminism is an absolute. It is non-negotiable. If you are not a feminist then you are not interested in humanity.'

Nadine's pristine Kelvinbridge flat: the space and dust of it echoing around them. Colour slashes across the walls and Glasvegas rumbling, dark and artful and grand, in the background.

It had come up again. *The Master Seducer In You.* Dawn didn't think there was anything wrong with it; Nadine did. She really did. Thought it was setting relations between men and women back forty years, had rolled out the jargon – 'patriarchy', 'objectification', 'solidarity' – which, boulder-like, rumbled through her argument. Dawn thought it simply told men how to speak to women in a way that women found exciting – so where was the harm? 'Get a grip, Nadine,' was her most used sentence: weak as a blade of grass as theory, but it utterly disabled Nadine's defences, every time, sliding between the joints of her argument.

Charlie was still hankering after another threesome, but Nadine was too edgy. After the last time, their history had clearly caught up with her. Their friendship clicked its jaw whenever he referred to the threesome. She'd shut down every text or conversation heading in that direction: What I loved, Nadine, was when we—

I looked up at you and Dawn while I was playing with myse—
Nadine?
Yo yo yo!
Sorry, Nadine, have I fucked up? x
A kiss, Charlie, that's better. x

She wasn't looking him in the eye very much, and when she did it was as though she suspected he'd stolen her purse, but couldn't prove it. It made him wonder how much coke she was doing, so he was glad when Dawn had decided to roll a joint instead. But all it had done was make Nadine more paranoid, argumentative, her hands twitching at her sides like spiders. The mong had not relaxed anything. Bat wings now cloaked their conversation and he could barely breathe beneath
how do you be part of societ

'Of course,' said Dawn, starting to roll another joint, 'that goes without saying, Nadine. But let's not pretend that the world would be a much more beautiful place if only women ruled it. That's a sentimental fantasy. We wield power over each other just as effectively as men do over us.'

Dawn was goading her. He could see it. Word had come through that Dawn Raeburn had not made the Turner Prize long list so she hadn't been in the best of moods herself. A secret competitiveness seemed to bristle when she'd received the phone call — 'Who's on the list? *Him*? A fucking *portrait* painter?' — and it hadn't settled yet.

Dreadlocks: dangerous.

Stonerboy.

'No,' said Nadine. 'Women don't rape other women. Women don't pay prostitutes to have sex with them. Women don't stone each other to death for adultery. Women don't sexually abuse children. Men have both the power *and* the will to do these things.'

'Nadine,' said Dawn, shaking her head, 'listen. Are you seriously this naïve?'

'Naïve?' said Nadine. 'Feminism is *naïve*?'

Dawn licked the edge of the skins. 'Why do you keep presuming I'm not a feminist?'

Nadine crossed her legs. 'Why are you so down on female power?'

'I'm down on *all* power, Nadine. It doesn't matter to me whether or not the bully wears a skirt or trousers.'

'Bullying? Feminism is *bullying* now?'

Charlie considered asking them if they wanted tea. Something. Anything. Nothing.

'You're not *listening* to me,' said Dawn. 'Don't you remember being a little girl? Was any world more brutal than ours? Don't you remember the insidious torments, the sophisticated little cruelties we visited upon each other? Think about the tyranny of those popular girls, who could cast out on a whim anyone who was different from them. I mean, there was a girl at our school who was called "It" and "Thing" by the entire hockey team.'

'Never seen the film *Carrie*?' said Charlie.

Both looked at him.

'Dawn,' said Nadine, with a sigh, 'I also remember *those* girls who would do anything the popular boys wanted. Jane Buchanan, Charlie? The most glamorous girl in our year?'

'What about her?' said Dawn, turning to Charlie. He had the immediate feeling of judgement, as though *he* had done something to Jane Buchanan.

'Well . . .' He smoked, shrugged. 'All these rumours went round the school about her sucking off two guys in the PE changing-rooms. She got drunk at the end-of-year party and admitted it. It immediately became the talk of the party. All the guys were like, She admitted it! I just heard her! The whole football team laughed about it openly in front of her, virtually pointed at her.'

Nadine shivered. 'It was horrible.'

'It *was* horrible,' said Charlie. 'The worst thing was you could see her trying to deal with it. She realised she'd made this huge mistake by admitting it, but knew she couldn't take it back. She had this terrible fixed smile on her face as they said these things about her, *while she was there*, as if she was playing along with the joke, when she was clearly this wounded deer, scurrying to different corners of the party to escape the laughter. But she was trapped, just completely unable to avoid that word.'

'What word?'

'*Slut*,' enunciated Nadine. Then she ran her fingers over her forehead. 'Fuck was in that joint?'

'Just weed,' said Dawn.

'That's how they *get* us, Dawn. Do you understand?'

'With weed?'

'With *words*. That's how they control our behaviour.'

'So what happened to her?'

'She drank bleach,' said Nadine.

Dawn nodded slowly. She stopped her joint-making and looked from Charlie to Nadine and back. The flat gave up its still, pure, arty-

Glasgow space for them to fill with smoke, with fight.

'So,' said Nadine, 'hierarchy. Defined by sex.'

Dawn frowned. 'Why don't you ask one of the unpopular boys if they think they had all the power? The nerds and geeks? The fat boys? The spotty boys?'

'What,' said Nadine, with her teeth, 'do *they* have to do with anything?'

'Point made,' said Dawn.

Nadine shook her head and folded her arms. But her hands wouldn't let her. They started twitching, fingers flexing. She tried sitting on them. Then she released them again.

'I didn't have any power over girls when I was at school,' said Charlie.

'Hmph,' said Nadine. '*That* explains a lot.'

Dawn glanced over the half-made joint.

'Hey,' said Charlie, 'I deserved that how?'

Nadine dismissed him with a flick of her hand. Dawn tried to send him a smile, then went back to rolling the joint.

'Right,' said Nadine, flustered. 'Right. Right. Didn't you just listen to that story, Dawn? Don't you understand what it means?'

'No,' said Dawn. '*You* don't. Because they were boys, they were just bastard oppressors to you, rather than children so terrified of peer pressure, of their own place in the pecking order, that they *had* to laugh openly at this girl. A girl who'd done this in the first place to become more popular. It's *all* power games, Nadine. We're all trapped by it. Men *and* women. That's the system.'

Charlie checked his phone, put it down. Messages from Julie, Monise, his mother and some random he'd kissed at the Arches.

Myriad siren calls.

'What I'm saying . . .' Nadine pressed her fingers to her head. 'You two. This fucking weed. What I'm *saying* is that girls *need* a feminist awareness at that age. They're not conscious of what's being done to them.'

Dawn laughed. 'Jesus Christ, Nadine. You only talk about women in terms of what's being *done* to them. Do you know how patronising that is? And how blind? You think women are the only ones who have things *done* to them? Like we haven't sat together and laughed at perfectly decent men who have tiny cocks? Something that's not even their fault? What did *they* ever do to us, except try to make love to us with their tiny pricks? They're considered *sport* among women. They're fair game.'

'Hardly the same as rape.'

'Stop using that as the ultimate difference.'

'But it *is* the ultimate difference, Dawn! That's the power disparity right there that you're just failing to—'

Then Nadine stopped and went, 'Oh God oh God oh God oh God. I'm too stoned for this.'

'Nadine,' said Dawn, 'seriously. Just listen for a few minutes to women in a coffee shop anywhere in the world. Read their emails. Are they accepting of other people? Are they interested in fairness? Chances are they're ripping apart some other woman who isn't there to defend herself. The hierarchies between us are *rigidly* controlled, Nadine. *We* do it. We do it to *ourselves*. It's just too easy to blame men. It's like these idiots who think that if Scotland broke away from England everything would be fine cos at least we'd be getting shat on by Edinburgh instead of London. Power is power is power. End of sto—'

'But women don't rape!' screamed Nadine.

Dawn froze and her eyes locked on Nadine's. Any stonedness still lazing around stood upright.

'No no no no no no,' said Nadine, standing, chopping both hands by the side of her head, as if trying to swat a wasp.

'Nadine . . .' said Charlie.

'No no no no no NO.'

'Are you okay?'

'No, Charlie,' said Nadine, 'I'm not okay. I'm not okay. She's. You're. The two of you just. You've never.'

'Whoah, Nadine, settle down,' said Charlie.

'Don't touch me!' she shouted, hands flitting like trapped birds.

'It's all right, Nadine,' said Charlie. 'Calm down. We're just having a debate.'

Nadine placed her hand on her chest. Her mouth opened, she gulped for air.

'Nadine . . .' said Dawn.

'Sit down,' said Charlie. 'Please.'

Nadine started to hyperventilate.

'Charlie,' said Dawn, rising, knocking over the tray, scattering the weed, 'she's having a panic attack.'

'No no no no NO!' Nadine squealed, then gulped for air again, and as Charlie and Dawn placed their hands on her, tried to reassure her, she started to kick and thrash and flail. 'Get the fuck off me!' she barked. 'Get the *fuck* off me!'

After a while they calmed Nadine and got her to bed – Zoey Van Goey's album *The Cage Was Unlocked All Along* trilling beatifically on the iPod – and she'd looked up at him, then said, with softness and utter clarity, 'The darkness is rising, Charlie. It's coming back to claim us both.'

'Nadine,' he said, 'you're stoned, honey, just let it pass.'

'Everything's been too pretty for too long,' she said. He touched her face and tried to shush her; she moved her skin against his palm. Her eyes were wet. Then she closed them and turned over and he kissed her head and she whimpered.

*

The hallway seemed huge. The bike propped up was a giant's bike, not Nadine's, surely. Everything was suddenly JUST TOO BIG TO TAKE IN. All along the wall pictures of damaged women, given a mercury tint by Nadine, preened like silver ghosts.

Monroe. Winehouse. Plath.

'She's way gone,' he whispered, shaking his head. 'She's worse on that than she is on coke.'

'Oh, come on, Charlie,' said Dawn. 'There's more to it than that. Where did all this *rage* come from?'

'You think it's . . . y'know . . . that night?' said Charlie. His eye kept flicking to the bedroom. 'Think she regrets it?'

'Possibly,' said Dawn. 'But I think it's something else. Something deeper.'

'Like what?'

'You tell me,' said Dawn. 'You've known her a lot longer than I have.'

Charlie sifted through a folio of memories of Nadine – way back into childhood – and wasn't sure if it was because he was stoned but all he could find was a series of colours, clothes and songs. There was something there. He remembered something in his childhood, when the two of them were little kids, playing near the swings. A secret she'd told him – 'Swear, Charlie, swear the most excellent promise that you can make' – but which he couldn't touch when he reached for it. Whenever he tried to hold onto an emotional experience of her it dissolved beneath his grasp, lovely but insubstantial, and he suddenly felt (the weed talking, *surely*, the weed) that it was the dozens of men who'd shared her bed who had really known her all along.

He missed the work he and Monise did. He missed doctoring and nursing words with her, like two colleagues, professional in tone, on the late shift in the casualty room. The two of them there, trying out variations of similes ('Janet strode through the campus, scarf folded over her shoulder like a ...' 'Leather bookmark?' she said. 'Regal sash,' he said. 'Thank you, Doctor'). She was getting closer now to what was at the heart of the novel: her young protagonist and the aged mentor had shared a lingering, erotic look as he'd arranged her fingers around a chord. The girl's mouth had clicked as her lips parted, gazing at him, her heart tapping. The music she played thereafter was troubled and frantic; the prose Monise wrote this in was rhythmic and quick. Her style was becoming her self. Her self was becoming her style. She was being freed, growing out of herself, as if from a chrysalis. In between working on the story, Monise would tell him more about her parents' divorce and Charlie would listen. *Let it come.* He'd talk about the experience of breaking up with Yvonne. She would listen. *Let it go.* Then they'd discuss new Glasgow indie bands – Be A Familiar and Errors and Isosceles and Frightened Rabbit. She was cool. She was a cool cool girl, and he wondered why none of the kids in her year could see it. Perhaps, like a developing photograph, the true Monise Ferguson was still a few years in the exposure. And then they'd be all over her. For now, though, it was just him, in the darkroom with her, prodding and teasing her image into the light. Whenever she left after these sessions he felt clean and useful, part of a system operating at the optimum. He felt like a good teacher. Yes, a pretty good teacher.

But today Monise was there in his class, eating the cake she'd made, and there was a solid awkwardness. She swallowed, said: 'I feel awful about the complaint, Mr Bain, but you understand I had to do it?'

'Of course,' he said, arms folded. 'Don't worry about it. I'm going to speak to the class about it today, in fact.'

'I hope it's not going to affect anything between us.'

'The work's too important.'

'I mean at a personal level,' she said.

'No,' he said.

She nodded.

She dabbed her lips with a napkin.

Eventually she said, 'So are you and Miss Carell, uh, going out?'

He blinked. To his great surprise he said: 'That's right, yes.'

'I think that's great, Mr Bain,' Monise said, and smoothed her hair from her face, then did it again. 'Seriously. Miss Carell's a really nice woman.'

'It's a really nice world,' he said.

He kept to his word. When the class came – arranged around Simon and laughing, *always laughing around Simon!* – he sat them down and apologised. Not for the story, he said. The story was a work of art and merited the language. But he was sorry, he said, for trying to make them all say the C-word and sorry if he'd made anyone feel uncomfortable. Bethan and Jenny mused and sat and sighed like actresses faced with a truculent director. Then they nodded and said, 'We accept your apology,' and he became the good guy again. Good guy in the blink of an eye. It was as easy as that. Simon looked at him. *What?* Charlie thought. *You can shut up, Simon, ya cun* no

No                             NO

At the end of the session Monise handed him an envelope. 'This is for you,' she said.

'But it's not my birthday.'

'It's an invite to an end-of-year party,' she said, pushing it towards him, 'to celebrate the exams finishing. We're hoping you'll come.'

'Thank you,' he said. 'I'll try. Where is it?'

'It's at Simon's house.'

'Well, why hasn't Simon invited me?'

Monise shrugged.

'Hm,' said Charlie.

Monise shrugged again. He stared down at the envelope. He was glad to be invited.

'Sorry again about the C-word thing.'

Monise nodded.

'You going?'

'Of course,' she said.

'Then I'm going.'


At the end of the school day he headed round to Julie's classroom — full! and lifelike! and wanting to share it with her! perhaps take her out for dinner! To make up for the last one they'd had, when he'd brooded and glowered and spilled himself all over the table. But she wasn't there. She'd already lifted her coat and gone. He went to her window, which looked out over the car park, to see Gavin holding open the passenger door for her, Julie getting in.

Gavin glanced up, noticed Charlie, and his eyes began to smile beneath those spectacles.

**You must be able to work the men.** Your understanding of the male psyche must be as complete and functioning as that of the female one. You never know when you may have to call on this resource. If a guy is convinced you are on the level he can **recommend** or introduce you to his female companions, thus disabling their defences. It is worth **cultivating** male friendships for these opportunities alone. However, in order to **out-manoeuvre** a competitor you must be quicker, sharper and more **confident** than him. This means analysing the **patterns** of male behaviour as surely as you'd analyse women's, recognising yourself and your own actions in them. For, despite whatever lofty or noble virtues they might ascribe to themselves, they surely seek the same as you: **female attention.** Your strategy will involve understanding the **motivations** of these men and using this against them. If your competitor is boorish and laddish, you must be **feminine,** exposing his stupidity. If he is intellectual, then play the everyman, exposing his pretensions. It is all about using the other guy's 'role' against him. Think about it in terms of the **marketplace:** you must be different from your **competitors,** offering something new and exciting, instead of the same old predictable product. To tempt the **consumer.** As such, you must ensure that she is more attracted to your **'role'** than his.

***Sell* yourself!**

The water was warm but growing cold. He and Julie had been in the bath for about an hour. They'd drunk a whole bottle of wine, their speech starting to career and topple. Julie was submerged, just her face peeping above the water line. She raised her lips, her cheeks full. She sent a long stream of water arcing across the bath to hit him in the face. She laughed. He picked up his penis and angled it towards her. 'Don't you dare,' she said.

'Why no?' his penis said, Scottishly. 'Dae whit I like.'

It did a wee Highland dance to demonstrate this.

Julie grinned. 'Make it say something else.'

His penis bent and shrugged. 'I dinnay perform for free, ye ken.'

She giggled, clapped.

'You got some noive, lady,' his penis said, rolling its hips in indignation, head quivering.

She said, 'All right, enough with the cock voices.'

His penis grunted and disappeared back under water: it had a business to run.

Julie laid her foot on Charlie's shoulder. Her toes wiggled beside his ear. 'I can't wait for you to move in,' she said, 'if your knob's going to address me every night.'

'Not every night,' he said, 'Royal Variety Performances mainly. He's very selective.'

'That is one discerning cock.'

'You'd like to think so, wouldn't you?'

Her toes wiggled some more. 'So when *are* you moving in?'

He sniffed. 'Why don't we wait till the end of the school year? Once the exams are out the way.'

305

'That makes sense,' she said. 'More sense than your knob talks.'

'Hey!' his penis said, breaking the water.

'Sorry, Willy.'

'Sir William tae you,' it harrumphed.

'You know this is the last throw of the dice for me, Charlie,' she said, stroking his leg. 'You know that, don't you?'

Charlie nodded.

Leonard Cohen grumbled on the stereo, with his mouthful of woe. Leonard Cohen made certain things tolerable. He made late nights marking school work, with the cold and dark massing outside, and a single lamp-light and malt whisky his only company, tolerable. He made the painful times, the times of toast crumbs in the bed and cats mewling out their stringy lungs, tolerable. He made the wondering and wondering and wondering tolerable. He made the post-coital moments, when Charlie couldn't look a woman in the eye, tolerable.

Leonard Cohen was rumpled. He was old. He was almost ugly. His voice, at its best, croaked and groaned and strained. Charlie sometimes hated Cohen because he reminded Charlie that he, too, would age, then die. But women had loved the man. Many women – ones he'd met and ones he'd never met – had loved him in their souls.

*And the woman always chooses.*

Well. Julie had chosen Charlie. Julie Carell had chosen Charlie Bain.

Not. Gavin.

Humankind, thought Charlie, as the bathwater lapped against his chest and Julie smiled into his eyes. We have evolved into this startling species. The vast civilisation we have built around ourselves. A dreaming animal that became a race of gods. Our laws, science, reason, art, infinite network of codes, fashions, languages, ideas, cultures, evolving, *evolving*, a tapestry upon a tapestry. And that great irresolvable conflict in every adult life, between security and freedom.

Security. To *have*.

Freedom. To *live*.

What kind of educational programme was it all anyway? Where were the lesson plans? The intended outcomes? The assessment criteria? What sort of lackadaisical teacher had drawn up this world?

'I've got marking to do,' said Julie. 'Let's get out of the bath.'

'Let's not,' said Charlie, and draped his arms around her.

Nadine: No Charlie. I don't know wot I think about this anymore.

Dawn: She's just saying that to make us both paranoid about the whole 3some thing.

Nadine: Im sure dawn will go out with you. Im sure she'd LOVE that.

Dawn: Yeah id come out but nadine's being really weird so I'm not sure.

Nadine: You love it dont you. Is this what you wanted? This SHIT?

Dawn: I think shes losing it.

Nadine: Things are just gettin 2 complicated charlie. Thats all I'm sayin. We need to help each other.

When Nadine opened the door to him the very first thing she said was: 'Have you fucked her?'

The speed of her attack. Raptor-like.

He came into the hall and took off his coat and scarf. 'Jesus Christ, Nadine, let me get in the door a second, will you?'

'Have you fucked her?'

Charlie folded his arms. 'You were there when I did, Nadine.'

Nadine folded her arms. 'Have you *since*?'

307

'What? Nadine? I haven't, like, even *seen* Dawn since that last night when you freaked out.'

'Do you love her?'

'Do I *love* her?' Charlie threw up his hands. 'No, of course I don't *love* her. She's a friend. A friend of *yours*, as it happens.'

'A friend you have threesomes with, *as it happens.*'

'Well, er, yes.'

'And what about me, Charlie?' she said. 'Am I that kind of friend?'

'Nadine, have you been crying?'

'I don't *cry*.'

'Look,' he said, 'just calm down, it's fine.'

'*Don't* tell me to calm down. I want to know what's happening between you and her.'

Charlie led Nadine into the living-room, past her studio. He caught a glimpse of a painting she'd been working on. Big, dark, jagged shapes. Like *Guernica*. On the coffee-table in the living-room was a tray with lines of coke on it.

'Want one?' she said.

'Are you kidding? No.'

She bent and hoovered one up, sat back, gasping.

This was not going to be good. She had Scarface in her eyes.

Nadine sat down, sniffing. 'It's what that night was all about, wasn't it? You didn't want me there at all. You just wanted to fuck her with another girl watching. Is that it? Nadine'll do it. She's a *slut*.'

'No, Nadine,' he said. 'That's not what it was about. I thought we all had a beautiful time together. I just don't see where this has come from.'

Nadine cackled. A deep, unearthly cackle. It chilled him.

'Oh, really. So I wasn't just a body to you? You didn't treat me like just another one of Them? One of those women you sleep with and

308

throw away? The two of you forgot I was *there*. I left the room and you didn't even notice.'

'I was having an orgasm at the time, Nadine.'

Nadine thinned her gaze. 'Quite.'

'Let me put some tea on and we'll talk about this.'

'Ha!' said Nadine. 'Tea!' Then she started rubbing her nose.

Charlie went into the kitchen. It was a mess. The sink overflowed with dishes, like a big riotous trash-compactor. The metal teeth of knives, fish-slices pointing outwards from its gurgling maw. There were ashtrays everywhere. Dirty clothes draped over the backs of chairs. He took milk from the fridge. It was the freshest thing in there. The whole room looked like a bad art installation.

While waiting for the kettle, he stood with his hands on the counter and breathed. The only point of sanity in the room. *Him*. What did *that* say?

He came back with the tea and she muttered, 'Thanks.' He didn't really want to go into the threesome – a big KEEP OUT sign hung over that conversation – so he told her about the trouble he'd been in at school, the argument he'd had with the class about Kelman. She listened to him with, against all expectations, sympathy, nodding and saying, 'Uh-huh,' and 'That must've been horrible,' when he talked about being hauled in front of Paulson. He mused about contacting his union (Gavin Prentice Gavin Prentice Gavin Prentice). 'Of course you should,' she said. 'All that just for swearing?' But when she asked which words in particular, and he swallowed and answered, her face hardened.

'You used the C-word?'

'Uh, yeah.'

'To schoolgirls?'

'I did, yeah.'

'What's wrong with you, Charlie?'

'I know,' he said. 'But there was, like, a political context for it, I wasn't just. You see, it's about how meanings are fixed and controlled by—'

Nadine was staring. Nadine was staring right into the back of his brain.

'Let's forget it.' Charlie sighed. 'Look, Nadine, what's this all about? I'm so worried about you.'

She sipped her tea. Then she stood and went to the window and looked out over the clean, pretty West End of Glasgow. Eventually she said, 'I thought it was me you liked. That entire time. Even as we were taking off our clothes. I still thought it was me.'

'I do like you,' Charlie said, 'but as a friend. We're friends, Nadine, y'know—'

'Remember you said in Barcelona—'

'You must've known we were never going to—'

'At the fountain. You told me you loved me.'

They both stopped.

'Yes,' he said. 'I remember what I said in Barcelona. But I'd just split from my wife, Nadine. My head was a complete mess.'

'And now?'

'Clear.'

'Really?'

'Like glass.'

'So do you like me?'

'Yes, I do. I do like you.'

'Not Dawn?'

'Yeah, I like Dawn too.'

'But you don't love her?'

'No, I don't love *Dawn*. Of course not. I hardly know her.' Then he inhaled and said, 'But I don't love you either.'

Was this evil? Genuine, punishable *evil*? He wasn't quite sure.

'Love, Nadine? What do you mean by love?'

He could put something in his mouth and say, Tastes like liquorice. Hey! Is there aniseed in this? And they'd show him the bottle or packet or box and say, Yes, you're right. Aniseed.

'Love's a meaningless term, Nadine. Love's only ever just an interpretation of events.'

So difficult to tell if your own actions contained good or evil, unless checking with someone else.

Nadine stared at him over her mug as she drank. Shards lined the path to her thoughts. He tiptoed through them. She put down the mug. That they were drinking tea. That they were here, drinking tea, with all that vast history exposed. The calm way they were finally talking about it. Over tea. This was Nadine now. Tea. She stared at the remnants in her mug when she spoke, as though it were poisoned. 'She's manipulative, Charlie. She plays people off against each other. She used me to get you into bed.'

'I'm sorry, Nadine, but I just don't believe that's true.'

Nadine gave a small smile. 'No, you wouldn't, would you? Not if she was doing it properly.' She shook her head. 'Let's go out in the rain.'

'What?'

'She's so fucking transparent. Her *clothes* certainly were.'

'Nadine...'

'No wonder she admires all that *Master Seducer* shit. She's an expert. She played *you*.'

'And you,' he said, 'didn't you and Dawn when you were at art school actually...'

'Actually, what?'

'Actually...'

'Well,' she sniffed, 'that's what I mean. The little jealousy games she used to play with me after that. Flirting and kissing other people in front of me. Men *and* women. I hate that, Charlie. I don't believe in using people like that.'

'Me either,' he said.

Then both of them laughed.

'Aye.' She shook her head. 'We're above all that.'

Charlie sighed. He felt weak and ruined, as though the two of them had been exiled from the aristocracy, raising a toast to old times – when they ruled, when they fucking *ruled* – with the very last of the expensive brandy. Nadine tapped the table, raised her smile, dropped her smile. She fidgeted. 'Oh, Charlie, what's happened to us?'

Charlie frowned. 'Nadine,' he said.

'What?'

'Is there something else?'

'What do you mean?'

'Something,' he said, 'darker.' He paused. 'Did someone do something to you?'

Her stare shrank. Her whole being seemed to contract, like a sea anemone touched by an incautious diver. She placed her mug on the table. 'Charlie, listen to me. Don't try fucking with my head. Understand? Because I'm better at this than you. And I will *eat* you.'

Charlie put down his tea and rubbed his chin. 'Now that,' he said, 'was pretty sexy.'

snake-like supple twining herself round me kisses HARD FAST ANGRY WOLVEN hair in my face stares a challenge BITES ME Nadine does not want to be stroked or caressed NO almost dares me to enter her Almost DARES me with her TEETH sex with the lace cut off Yes No stalk her to the bedroom she walks walks walks backwards staaaaaaring beckoning stripping as she goes shirt bra panties lies back on the bed topless fingers on her tits STARING opens her legs can see up her skirt her pussy winking at me *Show me your cock Charlie* and I look right into her eyes and I unzip myself and wank right there in front of her and she looks at it hungry greedy DON'T TRY FUCKING WITH MY HEAD CHARLIE BECAUSE I AM BETTER AT THIS THAN YOU AND I WILL *EAT* YOU sliiiiides forwards on the bed licks up down my cock slow soft like it's the first she's ever tasted grrrooooowwl *I want you in my cunt* push fingers into her roughly *yes Charlie yes* so wet so fucking wet *Take me you dirty bastard Just let your cock take me* but I'm thinking

Can't it be sweet love?

Can't we do it slowly and gently?

I say *I'll fuck you yeah is this the way you like it* THIS IS WHAT WE HAVE BECOME mind pouring oil-like from my head thick black unstoppable THIS IS HOW WE WILL CHEAT DEATH *Ooooooh yes that feels so gooooood* says Nadine *You've ALWAYS wanted to do this Charlie haven't you You've always wanted to FUCK me* and I say Yeah that's right But I haven't always wanted to do this and so ADMIT THAT YOUR HEART IS NOT IN THIS Want to kiss her hold her tell her it'll all be okay instead of That's right and yeah and Do you want it hard Do you want it hard Do you want it hard Do you want it ha

what                             happ ening                    m          ?

is                              to          e

'Come on,' Nadine said, turning onto her front and lifting her ass, 'fuck me, you filthy bastard.'

Charlie entered her, picked up the pace of his thrusts, then slackened. 'Nadine,' he said.

'What?' she said.

'Please don't call me a bastard.'

'Push your cock deep into my cunt,' she said.

'No.'

'What?'

313

'Nadine, this isn't right.'

'It's a bit late for that.'

'No. I mean,' he said, 'do we need to do it like this?'

'Like what?'

'So aggressive? It's beginning to make me feel a little . . . dirty.'

'That's kind of the *point*.'

'Don't you want me to hold you? Or stroke you?'

'No.'

'Don't you want me to be a bit more . . . gentle?'

'*No.*'

'Well, can I make a suggestion?'

'What?' Nadine sighed and ran her hands through her hair.

'Can we not call it your . . .'

'My what?'

'Your, um . . .'

'My cunt?'

'Yes,' he said.

'Oh. Suddenly you don't like the word?'

He looked down at the bedclothes. There were purple fingerprints all over them. 'I thought you found it offensive,' he said.

'What exactly,' she said, 'are you trying to do here, Charlie?'

She turned and stared at him for a beat, then stood and picked up her knickers, with all the routine air of someone picking bits of lint from an office floor. She searched for her skirt, wandering the room, topless and furious. Her tits were just tits now. Hanging from her. Two protrusions used to feed children. He watched her, feeling bemused and sort of prissy, wanted to cover his nudity from her. 'What's the matter?' he said.

'I warned you,' she said. 'I warned you about fucking with my head.'

'Please come back to bed.'

'Shut up,' she said.

'Nadine, don't speak to me that way.'

She faced him, half-naked. There was a kind of sense in her voice, a calm presentation of fact. 'I thought you were a friend,' she said.

'I am a friend,' he said.

'You're not!' she shrieked, and he flinched. 'You're just like the rest of them!' She grabbed his hair, pulled her face to his. 'You just want to fuck me. That's all I'm *for*.'

'Nadine?' he said.

'What?'

'Please let go of my hair.'

'Why should I?'

'It's very sore.'

'Oh, is it?' she said. 'Is it sore now?' She pulled harder.

'Ow,' he said.

She let him go; his head jerked back as if on a spring. He rubbed at his hair and tried to disappear from her. Time filled the room like sand. She was pressing her feet into socks now, eyes streaming with tears. She did up the buttons on her shirt, fumbling, swearing, dropping her hands, useless.

'Oh, Nadine,' he said.

She said nothing.

He shook his head and said: 'When did it stop being fun?'

She didn't look at him. 'I don't want to see you again,' she said.

'Okay.'

'You know,' she said, 'you used to be different at school. I liked you because you were a sweet guy. You didn't stop talking. You made me laugh.'

He got out of bed, started gathering up his own clothes.

'Now I realise the reason you don't stop talking is actually because you've got nothing to say.'

315

He nodded. He dressed. 'Good luck, Nadine,' he said.

He paused at the door, then turned around. She'd reached a hand out to the wall as though to steady herself. The other was at her face.

'I'll always think of you as a good friend, Nadine. You mean a lot to me.'

She raised her gaze and her eyes did not blink. 'You too, Charlie.' She sighed. 'You too. That's why this friendship has to end.'

'No, it doesn't.'

She dropped her head. 'We are both fully equipped to destroy each other,' she said. 'Utterly. I'd leave now if I were you.'

He turned to go.

'I love you, Charlie,' she said.

He paused. And then he closed the door behind him.

That Monday at school, Baldy Paulson's assembly speech lasted half an hour and took in such conceits as chastity, God's Plan For Us, the Revelation of St Matthew the Divine, and the new homework-timetabling system. Charlie cracked knuckles throughout, felt the satisfying crunch of cartilage. Gavin, sitting next to him, chuckled every so often.

'What's so funny?' said Charlie.

'The only way I can get through this,' Gavin whispered, 'is that every time he mentions the Almighty, I imagine he's talking about a heavy metal band.'

'Let us praise the Almighty,' announced Paulson.

Charlie and Gavin sniggered. Charlie did the Devil Horns. Julie glanced along the row at them and they quietened, smirking at each other, before Gavin went, 'Raawwk!' and Charlie hooted.

Paulson stopped his speech and looked at them.

'Daniel Watson, wheesht,' said Charlie, to a bemused Daniel Watson.

Paulson lowered his leonine gaze, continued: 'Because the Almighty has decreed . . .'

Later Gavin came rushing into Charlie's room. 'Oh, man, how busted were we?' he said. 'That was so funny.'

Charlie grinned. 'Aye, and Paulson hauled up Daniel Watson for it afterwards.'

'Ach, he'd probably done something anyway,' said Gavin. 'Little pest.'

They shook their heads and smiled, as the the ghosts of pests running through the room briefly animated them.

'Hey,' said Gavin, 'I was thinking. This situation is stupid. Me, you and Julie can be friends. There's no problem. Let's put it behind us.'

Charlie felt his whole system contract and relax at the same time. 'Uh,' he said, 'well. I'm glad you think so. That's very mature of you, Gavin.'

Gavin folded his arms. Various permutations of the word 'mature' folded theirs.

'Yeah,' said Gavin, 'it's nothing I can't deal with.'

'I'm glad,' Charlie finally managed to grind out.

'In fact, I was thinking we could all go for a drink together. Y'know, as pals.'

Charlie's mouth clicked when he opened it. He wetted his lips. 'Uh,' he said. 'You mean. Me, you and—'

'Julie. Yes.'

'Just the three of us?'

'That a problem?'

'Well,' said Charlie, 'it's, uh. A little. Unusual.'

'How so? We all three of us work together every day.'

'I suppose.'

317

'Look,' said Gavin, 'if you're uncomfortable with it, then why don't you bring along someone else?'

'Like who?'

'I dunno. Friend of Julie's. Friend of yours. What about that Nadine?'

'Na,' said Charlie, 'dine.'

'*Yeah.*' Gavin nodded, and Charlie saw him detach and drift into imagining. 'Yeah, bring her! Is she single?'

*sick   with      dripping   with      guilt   guilt   guilt*

*What you have done rises like bile from the memory. It lasts and lasts and lasts. You and Yvonne having an evening meal or cuddled together watching telly and it surfaces from your stomach. The thought of you with that other woman. Yvonne's eyes. Her smile. The way she pats you on the arse when you're cooking together. You are nauseous with it. Sick with          Dripping with*

*'How we doing, Charlie?' says Yvonne, as you walk through the Kelvingrove Museum one Sunday.*

*'What do you mean?' you say.*

*'Nothing,' she says. She is looking up at a woolly mammoth.*

*You walk together past giant dinosaur bones, Egyptian mummies, Inca gods. The vastness of history and its dust traces in the present.*

*'I used to want to be an Egyptian princess,' she says.*

*'Did you really?'*

*'Yeah. Used to imagine people worshipping me. Drawing hieroglyphic pictures of me. Burying me in a tomb with gold and sapphires. Like Cleopatra.' She mused. 'Probably not going to happen now.'*

*'Ach, there's still time,' you say.*

*She shrugs.*

*She seems so vague, these days. Sometimes at night you wake up and find the bed empty, and you go to the living-room and find her on the couch, asleep in front of the telly, her skin cold. You stroke her hair. You say, 'I still love you, Yvonne. I'm with you.' She murmurs. Then you pull a cover over her and go back to bed. Other times, while you're marking, you feel her drifting through the house like a spectre, spaced out or fretting. She starts leaving you notes about the house, sometimes functional ('Lift a finger, Charlie, and load the dishwasher like I asked you'), other times entreating ('Charlie, I think we need to talk. Are we still capable of that?'), and one time – so stark and cryptic that you were too afraid to ever refer to it – she'd written:* 'Does *Hell exist?'*

*It was the word she'd underlined that scared you most. 'Does.' The ink fretting on it, a metaphysical knot she'd been working at awhile.*

*Sundays. Day trips. Time together. You must make this. The note flaps in the breeze of your mind, its papery concept. You must find her again. You must journey down and find her.*

*Sundays in the museum.*

*You both drift through the Kelvingrove, musing and standing and pointing out things to each other politely. In this big empty cathedral-space your chatter is tiny, insect wings pattering against a vast nothingness. The Egyptian princess flickers in her eyes, casts a golden pall.*

*'They didn't do things by halves,' Yvonne says, 'those ancients. Burying them with gold and jewels and everything.'*

*'Bit of a waste, though.'*

*'Not if it's the only way to reach the afterlife.'*

god
please
help
me

*You laugh. 'I thought you didn't believe in Heaven or Hell?'*

*Her gaze locks on you, like fingers snapping in front of your face. She almost spits. 'I believe in punishment and reward.'*

*And as her eyes release you, and she wanders away into the museum, you actually feel a shiver go down your spine. All of the mischief you remember in her – the imp-like thing who chatted to you in your*

*English lecture, who spotted an urban fox with you, a wintry moonlight creature feeling like the quick of the two of you – all of it, you realise, is dying, is being shed from her.*

*As though she is passing into the afterlife.*

*The sister of a teaching colleague you meet on a works night out. A woman you find in a chatroom on the internet. Another chatroom, another woman, all this password-locked away from Yvonne, and on and on and on, and it begins to shock you less and less. The more women you take, claim, fuck, the more your self empties into them. Your moral centre begins to feel like a mirage. You can't cleanse the horror of what you're doing. You catch yourself grieving while queuing for a coffee in Starbucks and as the girl behind the counter says, 'Two pounds fifty,' and you smile at her and she blushes and the smooth, slow words of seduction are poised there on your tongue like honey, you think: I can no longer stop myself.*

*You now see what all of these rules governing behaviour are for. Homogenising. Inducing conformity. To establish a hive-mind. To protect* the system, the soci℮ty itself, *structured to benefit its strongest, most ruthless and predatory members. You can harness a civilisation – its rules and codes and cultural traditions – and make these perform to your advantage. You can study the runes of social transaction, learn them, exploit them. You are only carrying out nature's wil*

*nat ure s wi*

*only carrying out nature's will*

*Marriage. Mortgage. Family. Status. All superstitious magic. They have been brought into place to stupefy, to ensure the survival of the colony. What is love but certain chemical elements in the brain combining to produce an illusion, so as to stimulate procreation among the species? Does the illusion matter? You can steer a course from the*

*ways in which you inhabit it, quietly, without anyone noticing: working*
*yourself into a quiet corner – still making the required noises – then*
*glancing round and silently slipping through a door conveniently left*
*unlocked. You are free to act as you will. Whisper it:* you live outside all
of this! *It isn't cheating if you don't get caught. There is no wrong-*
*doing then. A tree falls in the woods and no one hears it; therefore the*
*tree does not fall.* QED. *You begin believing – the realisation of*
*it clear and pure and terrible – that being a 'nice guy' is simple lack of*
*opportunity to be a bad guy. You are unable to fathom your own*
*reasons for doing this. Hypocrisy becomes your new conviction.*
*Getting caught is a closed moral sphere all of its own. In the act itself*
*there is only clinical          self-regard*

                *ical, amoral          do this because you ca*

                              *you do this because you can*

*nothing but*

                              *the*

                    *will*

                              *to*

                                        *POWER*

They'd gone to a bar after work, a few of the teachers (neither Julie
nor Gavin had joined them, though Charlie had *definitely* seen them
leave separately) – slow, easy, after-school banter about PE teachers ('I
saw one of them marking today!' said Charlie, to many smug guffaws.

'Holding a pen! And pointing it at paper!'). Charlie came back with a round of doubles and they tasted and looked at him – Old Gus and shrew-like Beatrice McGrew and Peter the Probationer, who shrank further into his suit and polished shoes each day, and miserly Janet McLeod, clearly timing an exit with her imminent round – and someone said, 'Are these doubles?'

Charlie grinned. 'It's a Friday.' He saw them all glance at each other, like people in a bank realising they were hostage to a madman. A madman who celebrated (shiver) *Fridays*! 'Oh, come on,' he said.

They sipped until the PE-teacher banter expired, replaced by uncertainty about the Minister for Education's forthcoming report about standards. The Old and Shrew-like announced they'd seen all this before, had grown cynical on the vine; the Probationer shrugged oversized-suit shoulders, said he just wanted to teach kids. The Miser slipped away on cue: her round. Charlie felt surrounded by cardboard. He wanted to prod them and say, 'Are you real? Are there people in there beneath the Teachers?' but feared they'd fall backwards with a papery *floomp*.

Before the next round he'd ordered another double for himself.

Old Gus left.

Beatrice McGrew left.

Peter the Probationer stayed, drinking his (single!) vodka through a straw. At some point in the evening, Charlie placed his arm round the kid's clothy shoulders and said, 'You know the key to motivating them? You make the girls fancy you and the boys want to be you. After that they'll do anything you tell them.'

Peter nodded and smiled weakly. 'Well,' he said, 'I just wanna teach kids. I'm very excited about the opportunity the school has—'

'Ah, c'mon, kid,' said Charlie, 'don't give me that.' He leaned forward on his haunches, like a spindly trainer in a boxing movie.

'You do it the same reason everyone else does. You want to be adored, don't you?'

'Well, um, I want the respect of the kids, yes, but—'

'*I wanna be ad-o-red . . .*' Charlie sang, and chimed on air guitar. 'Hey, let's hit the jukebox!'

Charlie pulled Peter the Probationer up to the jukebox and they searched through classic albums, a panoply of genius. Peter made general sounds of appreciation, while Charlie gasped at the flicking magnificence. 'Look at this. *Blonde on Blonde, Dark Side of the Moon, Electric Ladyland, The Queen Is Dead.*' He leaned against the jukebox and ran his hands through his hair. In the corner of the bar, a pair of office workers, sipping through pink straws, were eyeing up him and Peter. 'I mean,' said Charlie, flashing them a Cruise-like grin, 'here's another reason why we become English teachers. It's our only way into the canon.'

'What do you mean?' said Peter, cueing up (Charlie was distressed to notice) some crappy dance track from the early nineties.

'We all want to write a classic, don't we?' Charlie pressed his face against the jukebox, its plasticky warmth. 'Something that'll imprint itself on the history of human consciousness. But we can't. We're too lazy or materialistic or scared or . . . unimaginative.'

He waved at the two office girls; they smiled and whispered to each other.

'So the best we can do is try to inspire the generation below us to do it.' He looked at his reflection in the light and whirl and buzz of the jukebox. Peter was selecting now (fuck was this kid on???) some generic American angst rock shit. 'But it makes us no better or worse than those Football Dads screaming at their sons on the touchlines or women who enter their daughters in beauty contests. We're trying to live through them to compensate for our own . . . fucking . . . inadequ . . .'

Peter turned to Charlie; Charlie was staring at the office girls' table. They were beckoning him over with a curled fingernail. 'What's that?' said Peter.

'Never mind,' he said, punting himself away from the jukebox.

Charlie was halfway towards them before he realised that Peter the Probationer worked in the same department as Julie. He turned in the middle of the bar and came back, rested his head and his fist against the jukebox again. 'Let me pick the next track, for fucksakes,' he said. 'One that *means* something.'

Something had driven him out of doors and kept him there, some radar pulse from outer space finding him. Drink – Drink – Drink. When Peter the Probationer drifted off eventually ('Stay! I command thee! Look, do you want to pass your probation or not?') Charlie headed straight to the table of the office girls, and gave them medium banter ('So, who's sexier – Han Solo or Indiana Jones?') and it turned into a bit of a laugh ('Cool times, ladies, cool times'), and one of them gave him her number and when she did so he kissed her hand and gave her Sexy Stare No. 16 and even her friend laughed and he thought about chasing the threesome, the mechanism of pursuit clicking and locking into place, the dog in him awakening, growling, and through the booze, their soft calves and the drop into their cleavages sang a smoky after-hours song to him (a grand piano, each girl sliding around the top of it), drank and flirted ('Girls, where you going? I thought we were going to a hotel room. I was heading to be Han Solo then Indiana Jones and you were going to tell me which one you'd rather fuck!') so late into the night he missed the last train back to his mum's, didn't he? Fuckshit. It smoothed out of the station like something retreating in a dream, and he watched it go.

Luckily, though? Everyone loved to see their big brother!

hic

houses on Deborah's estate looked the way they looked in children's pictures: two windows up top, two below, curtains bowing to each other. They even had chimneys. But Charlie was pretty sure they didn't have a fireplace. And he'd never seen smoke coming from those chimneys. What were the chimneys for? He'd ask Deborah. He'd ask Deborah!

He rang the bell.

The estate was secure and solid and content, despite the blue light that washed between night and morning. Secure cars, secure homes, secure gardens. Secure security.

He rang the doorbell again, leaned on it.

The sleepy dud dud dud of stairs descended.

Jordan opened the door. Jordan opened the door to his twitching, hiccuping brother-in-law, and in the face of that disarray, how did Jordan look? Secure.

'Charlie,' he said, 'what kind of time do you call this?'

'I call this time . . .' Charlie shrugged '. . . Fred?'

'Hardy har. What's the matter?'

'Nothing's the matter,' Charlie said. 'Can I stay here tonight?'

'You mean what's left of tonight?'

'I missed the last train,' he said. 'Shitload for a taxi home.' Why was it even under discussion? Charlie wanted to stay and here was his own brother-in-law, husband to Charlie's sister, father to Charlie's niece, questioning his, er, questioning his

Charlie burped.

'Are you wasted?' said Jordan.

'No,' said Charlie. 'It's just the drink.'

Jordan shook his head and looked him over. Charlie wondered if this was how he dealt with all subordinates: his employees, his suppliers, even his daughter. Grow strong, young Elizabeth, thought

325

Charlie. Grow strong and unsheath your blade and decapitate this fucking

Charlie, as you speak, he is allowing you access to his home. He is holding open the door for you. He is stepping aside to permit you entry. You are drunk and it is two a.m. and you are fleeing from a failed threesome and the man is offering refuge.

'There's the couch,' said Jordan, hands in the pockets of his dressing-gown, a lived-in, suburban dressing-gown. 'I'll get you a blanket. Don't wake the baby.'

The *baby*. She has a name, you. You. It's? He couldn't quite remem-remem—

Burp!

Charlie crashed against the coffee-table, then tried to hold it steady as though on a lurching ship. Jordan shook his head managerially and climbed the stairs. With effort, Charlie took himself from a standing position to a horizontal one. It seemed an incredibly complex manoeuvre. His brain felt as though it had been graffitied. He heard someone come into the room and to his surprise it was not Jordan or Deborah but Elizabeth. She was in pyjamas, staring at him, with her watercolour-brown eyes. 'Oh, hello, Twinkles,' said Charlie. 'Gosh, I didn't mean to wake you.'

'Unca Chally,' said Elizabeth, then lifted her hand to show him a pink plastic toy. 'Mendeez,' she said.

'Is that Mendeez?' was all he could reply.

'*Men*deez,' she repeated.

'Oh,' he said. '*Men*deez.'

The world of children: bejewelled and fanciful, the size of a universe, a place impossible for grown-ups to venture into. But he reckoned he could make it there. He reckoned he'd be welcomed, accepted even, could perhaps settle down there. Buy a toy car and a toy house, with toy chimneys that billowed toy smoke.

Deborah came into the room, exhausted of niceties. He could see the first swellings of her pregnancy. 'What do you want?'

'There's a fine greeting.'

'What do you want, Charlie?'

'Asylum, Debs,' he mumbled. 'I seek asylum.'

Deborah looked at him there, scrawled on her couch like a felt-tip-pen mark. 'Watch Elizabeth,' she said. 'I'll get you a blanket.'

'That's what Jordan said.' He gestured to Elizabeth. 'Come on, Twinkles, come see your uncle Charlie.'

Elizabeth took hesitant steps towards him. She proffered the pink toy. 'Mendeez,' she said.

'Mendeez,' he said, lifting her onto his lap. 'What a lovely name.'

Elizabeth placed the toy in his hand. He stared into her eyes. Neither of them said anything for a bit.

'I think Mummy and Daddy might be a little angry with me,' he said. Elizabeth looked back at him. 'I think it's because I'm a wee bit drunk.'

Elizabeth reached up and touched his nose.

'I've got to tell you something, Twinkles,' he said. 'Can you keep a secret?'

Elizabeth touched his cheeks.

'I think my soul is in danger.'

She patted him and laughed.

'I can't feel anything any more,' he said. 'It's very worrying.'

Her eyes were brown and smiling.

'I'm capable of inflicting harm on a massive scale, and I don't even care. Isn't that awful?'

She had little milk teeth, which he could see whenever she smiled. He bounced her on his knee until she started to squirm, then set her down, and she tottered to the coffee-table, slapped it once or twice. Deborah came back into the room, unfolding the blanket. She spread it over him. His little sister. 'What are you like?' she said. Then she sat down in the chair opposite him, watched him scratch and roll to get comfortable. 'This really isn't good, Charlie,' she said. 'It's no good for me, it's no good for Elizabeth, and it's no good for . . .' She patted her stomach.

'I know, Debs,' he said. 'I know that. But just answer me one question.'

'What's that?'

'What's the chimney for?'

'Eh?'

'The one on top of your house. What's it for? You don't have a fireplace.'

She stared at him. She shrugged through a fog of weariness. 'Charlie, it's . . . decorative or something. I don't know. Who cares?'

Who cares? Who cares! Houses being built with chimneys but no fireplace! Designed for the modern couple, to appeal nostalgically to yesteryear! It was everything that was fucking wrong with the world! But Charlie just purred and shifted on the couch, kittenish. 'This is a nice life you've made,' he said.

'How's Mum?' said Deborah.

'Not you as well.'

'What do you mean?'

'That's all I get from Julie.'

'Who's Julie?'

'Never mind,' he said. Then: 'But if she ever asks – you and me went out together a few weeks ago and you were *really* upset.'

Deborah clenched her jaw. Then she said, 'Are you taking good care of her, Charlie?'

'Julie?' he said. 'Course I am.'

'I mean Mum.'

'Oh,' he said. 'She won't listen to me, Debs. She's still eating all the wrong foods. Still drinking way more than is good for her.'

Deborah raised her eyebrow.

'Very funny,' he said.

Elizabeth was arranging a line of animals. She came teetering back to Charlie, holding out the plastic toy again. 'Mendeez,' she said.

'Mendeez?' said Charlie. 'What does this mean?'

'It means *mendies*,' said Deborah. 'It means it's broken. She wants it mended.'

Elizabeth started patting Charlie's hand urgently. 'Mendies,' she said. 'Mendies!'

'Mendies,' Charlie mumbled, looking down at her little form, her eyes, the tiny majesty of her teeth. There was silence in the room while Elizabeth blinked at him, then Deborah stood and swung her daughter upwards. 'Right,' she said. 'Let's get you back to sleep, madam.' Jordan was standing in the doorway, solid, impassive, silent, like a figure in a nightmare. Charlie was pleased to see that Elizabeth protested.

'Night, Charles,' said Jordan. Secure secure secure.

'Night,' said Charlie, and whispered, '*fuckwit*,' before pulling the covers up to his chin.

'Help yourself to breakfast,' said Deborah. 'We'll be driving over to see Mum at lunchtime so we can give you a lift home.'

'Thanks,' said Charlie, before she shut the door. He smiled and tucked himself into the covers, wriggling with warmth. But as he reached to switch off the light he noticed something. It flashed against his brain. Elizabeth must have been playing with purple paint. There were fingerprints on the blanket, the couch, the floor, his clothes.

*how can you wreak such a wanton path and expect Yvonne not to notice?*
*Your trail has not been one of secrecy, but of smoke and ambulance*

*sirens and news helicopters, rising from the city. She confronts you with it one Sunday, out of the blue, over a coffee, on your balcony overlooking the street. Busy traffic. The two of you have been reading through the morning papers. Armies mass in your separate imaginations. There's a lull and she looks down at her lap and something flickers in her face and you see her thoughts heavy, freighted. And she comes out with it. She doesn't look at you but she says, 'I don't know what you think you're doing, but you've obviously had your fun, and now I would like it to stop, Charlie. Okay? Just make it stop.'*

*Your first thought is: That's why she's been so quiet recently. And she has. Eerily, unnaturally moody, drifting across hardwood floors, her face rigid and turned away from you.*

*You don't even bother denying it. You simply ask, 'How did you find out?'*

*She shakes her head and frowns. 'I didn't.'*

*You sip your coffee and purse your lips. Blood floods your skin. You're on the verge of rage, incredulous at this deceit. 'Oldest trick in the book,' you say.*

*She says: 'Not as old as adultery.'*

*but of course it doesn't stop*

*it is who you are now*

*what you do*

Thank God for Julie: good, big, strong, warm-hearted Julie! Julie was magnificent. Her love seemed to be made of pulleys and ropes and weights: it *held*. The room was shot through with bolts of morning and the two of them felt sumptuous and lovely, rolling around in the wreckage of Sunday papers. She'd made him breakfast: toast, scrambled eggs (with salmon), bacon, beans, square sausage, crumpets (*lashings* of butter, like a picnic in an Enid Blyton novel), Cheerios, tea and orange juice. This was the other thing they liked to do apart from have sex: eat. And tell jokes. Julie Carell was puns and bad jokes sometimes. 'Hey, Charlie, don't you like your tomatoes? What's tomatta with them?' And 'What did the tank driver say at Tiananmen Square? I could murder a Chinese!' And when he failed to laugh she'd put her fingers at either corner of his mouth and lift them and say, 'That's better,' then they'd kiss and it'd be all right. Yes, it'd be all right. It'd somehow even become a good joke, *simply because she wanted so much for him to laugh at it*. And because she was also a teacher she understood when he had to take time to mark or prepare lessons. This was how it happened at her house. He'd come over and they'd get their schoolwork out of the way, labouring silently at either end of the couch, sipping tea and occasionally smiling, and then they'd put it away, and eat or have sex or bathe or tell each other jokes or go for a walk or go to the pictures (to see comedy, only comedy), then come back and snuggle and sleep and wake and tell each other what dreams they'd had, interpret them for each other, then he'd drive them to school and they'd return and do their work, perched on opposite ends of the couch, smiling at each other occasionally like a proper couple and, yes, he was growing used to it and, yes, he could imagine moving in with another woman and, no, he wouldn't rule out kids.

Yes, he would.

No, he wouldn't.

It worked, what he and Julie had. It just worked. Even when drunk, it worked: the true test. He was preparing *Hamlet* for the sixth-years, those rebellious sixth-years. He'd won them back after the C-word farrago. Like some cocksure charisma-wagon in the movies, he'd gained their trust again. He could do anything. He could do anything when Julie was there, beside him. Julie put down her books and crept across the couch and snatched the play from him, then kissed him right the way down to his toes and back up again.

'I love you,' he said, when she reappeared in front of his face.

'I,' she said, 'love' (kiss) 'you' (kiss) 'too.'

'This is fun,' she said.

'Let's do it,' he said. 'Let's move in together.'

Her eyes flickered. 'But ... your mum.'

'Mum's doing fine,' he said. 'She knew when I moved back in with her it wasn't going to be permanent. She must have known I was going to find someone eventually.'

Julie's gaze roamed his face. 'Serious?'

'Yeah. Let's do it.'

'But, uh ...'

'What?'

'You think you're over everything that happened before? With Yvonne?'

'Yes,' he said. 'I'm over all of that.'

Summer was coming. It was warm outside. The West End yawned, stretched, looked around, and was pleased with itself. He made his way to Ashton Lane. People draped outside bars on their way home from work. The froth on the top lip, the optimistic shorts. Charlie avoided them, went into where it was dark. Dawn was already there in Brel, tapping her wine glass before he could reach the table, and he nodded and went straight to the bar. Came back with a new bottle.

'A whole bottle?' she said. 'I didn't realise it was *that* kind of night.'

'Every night is that kind of night.'

'And you expect to teach in the morning?'

'I expect to do no such thing,' he said. 'Now. Nadine.'

Dawn sighed and poured. 'I don't know,' she said. 'I just don't know about that girl any more. Did you get anything from her?'

'Only that she's totally paranoid.'

'About what?'

'You. Me. Every man she's ever slept with.'

Dawn shook her head. 'I should have seen this coming.'

'How so?'

'We used to go out on the pull together, at the art school club nights.'

'Back when Franz Ferdinand were playing there?'

'They were,' said Dawn, wide-eyed suddenly. 'Yeah. They *were*. Cool as fuck.'

There was a silence while the two of them watched skinny ties and sharp haircuts slash guitars in unison, felt the noughties emerge, new and glistening around them.

Now here the decade was, nearly over.

'Anyway,' Dawn said, 'we were always successful. Made a good double-act. Kinda like the two of you except . . .'

'Except . . .'

Dawn smirked. 'We could do things together that you and her probably can't. Y'know. To attract guys.'

'Riiiiight.'

Dawn shrugged. 'Guys are simple like that. Stupid.'

Charlie's fingers drummed on the table. 'So . . . ?'

'So.' She filled both their glasses. 'I think there are two types of people who sleep around, Charlie. There are those who can do it and it doesn't affect them any way but positively. They're totally in

334

control of it, and are doing it because they *want* to do it, not because of any neediness or desperation. They don't *need* to see themselves validated in the eyes of others. They make connections with their sexual partners – as many as they like – through sex. It's just another method of communication for them. It's, y'know, healthy. *Fun*.'

Charlie shifted in his seat, sipped the wine. 'And the rest?'

'The rest . . .' said Dawn, and shook her head slowly.

He nodded. 'So which is Nadine?'

'I think you know.'

'And which am I?'

Dawn touched the skin of her wine with a finger, licked it. 'I think you know.' He stared at her. Dawn met the force of his gaze. Then said: 'She loves you, Charlie.'

He looked into his glass. He glanced round the bar. 'You know, there's something there. Just at the edge of my memory. I can't quite grasp it. Something she told me when we were little kids.'

'What?'

He frowned and rubbed his nose. 'I dunno. Too long ago. It's just sitting there . . . this dark and strange . . . thing.' He looked into his glass. Eventually he said, 'Tell me about your tattoo.'

'The dragon? You recognise it?'

'Should I?'

'You ever see that William Blake painting *The Great Red Dragon and the Woman Clothed With Sun*?'

'Yeah. You reference it in *boudoir*, don't you? The bit where you're masturbating. But isn't that the one –'

'– that the killer from the movie *Manhunter* is obsessed with. Based on the Thomas Harris book –'

'– *Red Dragon*. Which was the prequel to –'

'– *Silence of the Lambs*.'

335

They clinked wine glasses. Dawn winked.

'What about it?'

'Well,' she said, 'it's my favourite painting. It's based on a line in the Book of Revelation, and it shows this giant, muscled Satan standing over the body of this woman who's, uh . . .'

'Clothed with sun?'

'Right. And according to Revelation he's about to devour her. Cos it's the end of the world and she's, y'know, about to give birth to the saviour or something.'

Charlie waved a hand. 'They're always doing that. Those women clothed with sun.'

Dawn smiled. 'But I never really thought that. I always thought that Satan was kind of in love with her. She didn't love him back, cos she was terrified of him. You can see that in her face. But I always thought that Satan was a little . . . well . . . jealous.'

'Of what?' said Charlie.

Dawn rested her chin in her hand and looked out at the rehearsal for summer. 'Of her light,' she said. 'It's what he fell away from, after all.'

Charlie drank his wine. She didn't move her face from the window. 'So why did you get the dragon tattooed? Why not her?'

She brought her eyes back to his. There was density in them. He felt it. She sipped. 'Because I'd rather be clothed in *sin* than *sun*.'

He stared at her until their gazes became heavy, too heavy for them to hold. Then he glanced away, and as he did, something caught his glance, held it there. He couldn't drag his eyes back to Dawn's once he'd seen it.

Jordan. Entering the bar.

Jordan didn't drink in the West End, thought it was full of 'left-wing, arty fuckwits'. The implied adjunct: *Like you, Charlie.* But that

336

was unmistakably his big shirt and big walk, that broad tanned face that smelled of a daily shave. With a woman on his arm who was not clothed in sun. Black cocktail dress.

'Charlie?' said Dawn.

'Hang on. Sshh.'

'Who are you staring at?'

Charlie was thirteen years old and his father was outside the hotel. Charlie was thirty and here was his brother-in-law with a woman not his wife. Not Charlie's sister. Not Deborah.

'Charlie?'

'Ssh, he hasn't seen me yet.'

'Who hasn't seen you?'

Jordan crossed the room arm-in-arm with his mystery partner – with her louche, ain't-nothing-like-a-dame air – and reached the bar and Charlie felt floaty and wondering and focused and sharp all at once. Jordan was not wearing his wedding ring. Charlie asked Dawn if he could have a couple of minutes. 'Yeah, uh, sure,' she said. Then he went outside and phoned his sister. Deborah at home with baby-and-a-half.

Click. 'Hello?'

'Where's Jordan?' he said immediately.

'What do you want him for?'

'A quote for a car.'

'What car?'

'Noddy's toy car, Debs. Put him on.'

'He's not in.'

'Where is he?'

'At the pub watching the football.'

'With?'

'Does it *matter*?'

'Humour me.'

'Some of the guys from his golf club,' she said. 'They've got a sweepstake on.'

'Did he tell you who was playing?'

'Um, Chelsea and Arsenal. They've got a sweepstake on.'

'You said that.'

'So go to the pub if you want him! Stop bothering me!'

'Okay,' said Charlie, his mind grabbing at the cosmos.

'Do you want to speak to Elizabeth?'

'Put her on.'

Charlie heard Deborah fumble and clutch for Elizabeth and didn't waste any time: he walked back into the bar, through the sudden, sodden bloom of noise, and Elizabeth was saying, 'Unce Chally. Postman Pat. Me's playin,' and Charlie was saying, 'That's great, honey, that's great. Hold on a second, I'm just going to put someone on the phone for you,' and he was tapping Jordan on the shoulder and Jordan was turning and seeing him there, seeing the phone held out like a stick or a threat or a trick-or-treat, and his eyebrows were furrowing and he said, 'Charlie? Who is it? What's—' and Charlie was shaking the phone, the phone, *take the fucking phone*, and Jordan lifted it to his ear and said, 'Hello? What? Elizabeth? That you? . . . Daddy's here, yes. Is you playing with Postman Pat? . . . Oh, that's great. Aye. Okay . . . Uncle Charlie, yes, that's right. I'm just going to speak to him now. Okay, 'bye, honey.'

And he was handing it back to Charlie. And Charlie was looking at Jordan. And the woman was looking at Jordan. And Dawn, who'd drifted to Charlie's side, was looking at Jordan and saying, 'Charlie, what's going on?' and the woman was saying, 'Yes, what's going on?' and looking at Jordan.

'What's up, Charles?' said Jordan.

'You tell me,' said Charlie.

'Who was that on the phone, darling?' the woman said.

Jordan glanced from the woman to Charlie. The security he'd exuded at two in the morning: gone. Jordan looked stark and shocked and spaghettied, as though an army had deserted him on the battlefield.

Darling.

'Tell her,' said Charlie. 'Tell her who I am.'

'He's my brother-in-law,' Jordan mumbled.

The woman sized Charlie up, thoughts orbiting thoughts. 'So he's,' she said, 'your . . . sister's . . . husband?'

Charlie laughed and shook his head. Now Jordan was ringing the doorbell on *his* house at two a.m., and Charlie was pissed off. Yes, Charlie was pissed thoroughly off. 'No,' said Charlie. 'He's *my* sister's husband.'

The woman joined dots. 'And on the phone was?'

'My niece,' said Charlie.

A collapse of the scaffolding in the way – Charlie's, Jordan's, the woman's, Dawn's – all was plainly seen now.

'So that makes her . . .' said the woman.

'My daughter,' said Jordan.

The woman nodded and looked at the floor. 'You total bastard.'

'Look,' said Jordan, eviscerated.

'She's got a point,' said Charlie. 'Your wife is at home pregnant.'

'I can't believe this,' she hissed. '*Pregnant?*'

'Charlie,' said Dawn, 'maybe you should deal with it in the morning.'

'He'll be less guilty then?'

Charlie was the irritant Jordan's gaze hardened around, like a pearl around grit. 'Guilty?' Jordan said. 'Listen, I know *exactly* what went on in your marriage. You're no saint, Charles.'

St Charles.

Charlie shook his head. Jordan took a step towards him, lowered his voice to a hush. 'Charlie, listen,' he said. 'Deborah doesn't have to find out about this. Think about the new baby. Think about Elizabeth. Let's be reasonable here. You know the score. We're both men.'

He knew the score all right. Game, set, match.

Charlie looked at Dawn, fidgeting, poised to flee towards the sphere into which Nadine had disappeared. The woman looked ruined, her simple investment crashing in one big stock-exchange disaster.

'No,' Charlie said. 'We are not men.'

He and Dawn walked from the bar. Dawn was rubbing his arm, pressed into the silence. They just walked. Where were they heading? He didn't know. Who was that woman? He didn't know. Was he going to tell his sister?

'I don't know!' he said.

'Right,' said Dawn. 'Sorry. You okay?'

He grunted.

'Look,' she said, 'I don't want to send you home like this. I'm staying not far from here. Why don't you come and we can talk about it?'

'Sure. Whatever.'

They were walking arm-in-arm. He was a bullet. He was a battle cat. They reached the crossroads at the bottom of Byres Road, at the other side of which was Dawn's flat.

'No,' said Charlie. Stopped.

'What?' said Dawn. 'Come to mine. Let's talk it through.'

'We should not do this.'

'It's okay,' she said, and tugged him into the road.

He retreated back to the kerb.

'Dawn,' he said.

'Charlie,' she said, 'you're upset. We'll just have a cup of tea and a chat.'

'We won't,' he said. 'We'll have sex. I won't be able to stop myself.'

'Is this about Nadine?'

'Why does everything have to be about Nadine?'

'Is it?'

'Maybe it's about Iraq!'

'What?'

'Oh, I dunno. I just don't know any more.'

He had his own desire tied up on a chair in Room 101: it had to learn. It could not go around having sex with anyone just because it felt like it! What would happen to society if everyone did that? Anarchy in the UK, that was what! If it was ever going to end – what he had done to Yvonne, what he was doing to Julie, what Jordan was doing to his sister, what men were doing to this goddamn world, all of them with dicks, let us remind ourselves, healthy swinging dicks – it would end here. Here in letting go and saying *no*. We have dicks but we are still men. We can be men despite having dicks.

Dawn sighed and looked down the street. 'Um,' she said. 'Okay. Maybe we shouldn't.'

He paused. 'Or maybe we should.'

'I don't know, Charlie,' she said, and scratched her shoulder. 'I don't want to make you feel uncomfortable.'

He was strapped between horses by his arms and legs. The horses, whipped, were straining. He closed his eyes. He summoned strength. He gritted teeth. Gnnnnngh.

'Look,' he said, 'I'll come back and just have one cup of tea, okay?'

'Okay.'

\*

It was mind-blowing. She sucked his cock. He licked her like a dog. They masturbated in front of each other. She asked him to fuck her in the arse. He fucked her in the arse. He came on her face. It was incredible, horrible, porno, gorgeous, exhausting, demeaning, exhilarating, awful, *awful*, no No NO, you *idiot*.

It was beautiful.

And he was going to do this again and again and again and again, he realised, until it killed him.

When he woke Dawn was wide awake, hands behind her head, staring at the ceiling.

'Hey,' he said, and moved towards her. He raised his fingers and placed them against her cheek. They left purple marks. Dawn closed her eyes. 'You didn't sleep?'

'Not much, no.'

'How come?' he said.

She shrugged.

He didn't know whether to kiss her or not. He reached over and kissed her eye at the corner. Her mouth made some shape or other.

'That was great last night,' he said.

'Glad you enjoyed it.'

He tried a few comforting manoeuvres: placing his leg over hers, his face snuggling into her neck, his arm across her chest. Her breasts were squashy beneath his elbow. He couldn't gain purchase on her body. His legs slid from hers. His arm felt dull and block-like on her chest. Nothing was said for a while. Nothing swelled to fill the room.

'Want to watch TV?' she said.

'Yeah.'

For half an hour they watched a drama aimed at teenagers. Everyone in it looked lovely and cloned. Cloned from a clone of a clone. Their problems revolved around who 'liked' who and who 'dissed' who and who was 'making a go of it with the caff and that'.

'Want that cup of tea?' Dawn said, when it finished.

'Might be nice. Finally! Ha ha.'

She didn't laugh.

She rose and put on her dressing-gown. Before she did he saw her arse, the tattoo of the dragon's tail above it. Her blonde dreadlocks were like gold in the morning light. She went into the next room — pad pad pad — and he heard a kettle boil. He was alone in the bed. He was alone in the bed. She came back carrying two cups of tea.

'Ta,' he said.

'How you getting home?'

'Taxi,' he said.

'Want me to phone one?'

'Would you mind?'

'Do you know you cried in your sleep, by the way?'

'What?' he said. 'Did I?'

'Yep. Real tears.'

'Oh,' said Charlie.

'Can I ask you something?'

'Sure.'

'Do you have a girlfriend?'

Charlie didn't say anything.

'Thought so.'

Dawn phoned the taxi, spoke the address politely. After what felt like thirty seconds — in which neither of them said much — it rang to tell them it was there.

Automated message.

He dressed quickly. She watched telly while he did so. Then she went to the door with him, through into the wee corridor.

'Take good care of Nadine,' she said.

343

'If she'll let me,' he said.

He leaned over and kissed her on the lips. She reacted too late, and started to kiss just as he was withdrawing. He nodded. 'Okay,' he said, and moved into the stairwell.

'Well, see ya.'

'Um,' he said, 'maybe I should—'

She closed the door.

Sunday over breakfast in a cafe somewhere on Kelvinside, the papers spread before him and Julie. They read them and looked up and smiled at each other. Sometimes they touched noses. She squealed and wrinkled her eyes with delight. Julie, over forty and childlike. They'd made sleepy morning love an hour earlier, the kind that felt like being brought slowly to life and leaves behind gratitude. Then they'd put on clothes and coats and escaped out for lunch and Sunday supplements. Charlie looked around the café, at the middle classes, at the arts grads, at the young, twitchingly hipster couples. Three bald men in Celtic scarves banged on the window outside. The café looked up. One of them took off his scarf and started waving it, tongue licking the window, then said something that the glass muted, and they joggled on, a green and white hydra. A faint smile ghosted Charlie's face.

'What?' said Julie.

'Y'know,' said Charlie, leaning into her dreamily, 'I *believe* in Glasgow.'

Julie took in the gentle fizz of intellects around them. 'Have to remember, Charlie,' she said, 'this is only a wee middle-class sliver of it. This is a city with the highest knife crime in Europe, with the lowest life expectancy, with bitter sectarian hatreds. This is a miserable place for ninety per cent of the people who live here.'

'Yeah,' he said, 'but even that means there's something *different* about the other ten per cent. About *us*.'

'What do you mean?'

'Well, it's not as simple as "pretentious arseholes swanning around like we own the place", is it? It's not like London. Our posh aren't *posh*-posh. You can still feel reality humming, even in the West End. The middle classes who migrate here aren't afraid of that.'

'I've been afraid of this city before.'

'Yes, but that makes it all the more vital. Its arts immigrants take a risk in moving here in the first place, so they're more likely to be boundary breakers and radicals.'

Nadine pulsed and twined through his thoughts, directing his speech. Continue, she purred, vindicate us. Make us *famous*.

'Otherwise they'd move to fucking Edinburgh, wouldn't they? Where they hide reality away for the tourists. That's why this city has a different energy, Julie. That's why it's so *alive*. Poverty is its life force.'

Julie placed her cutlery down, cleared her throat. 'Charlie, listen to what you're saying. As a socialist.'

He made shapes with his hand, conjured the planet for her. 'Our small nation has etched tiny pictures of itself on the world's consciousness. We're part of a global dream humans have about themselves. Scotland can exist fully if we dream hard enough, Julie. I just can't relate to that Scottish deep-fried-chip-on-the-shoulder. *Trainspotting* was wrong: it feels fucking *great* being Scottish. We're *becoming* something, Julie. I can feel it. We're getting dressed up.'

'As what, exactly?'

'I dunno, but England doesn't have to take it *personally*. It can be an amicable divorce. We could even get back into bed together for a quick fuck every so often!'

'Are you stoned?'

'A little.'

Julie squeezed his hand then kissed him. 'Oh, Charlie,' she said, 'I love you to bits. You're so sweet. So naïve.'

'Naïve?'

'Yes,' she said. 'See the ninety per cent of the city that isn't like *us*? To them we're still going to seem like pretentious arseholes swanning round like we own the place.'

'You think?'

'Charlie, for people who just get up in the morning and go to work and come home and try and feed their families? They don't care about the city's "energy".'

'Thought you didn't believe in socialism,' he mumbled. 'You sound like Gavin.'

She raised an eyebrow so sharp he could have cut steak with it.

'Tell me,' Julie,' he said, 'why did you become a teacher?'

Julie drank her coffee. It was swallowed down into layers of thought. 'I always wanted to be in a position where I could teach some manners and respect to young people. A lot of them don't get strong guidance at home. I wanted a job where, as a woman, I'd be treated like a professional, not just some servile bit of skirt. Though some of the men in our school wouldn't know what professionalism means.'

Charlie dropped his spoon into his coffee. It made a sugar-brown splash. 'What does it mean?' he said.

'Oh, y'know,' said Julie, 'doing the job to the best of your ability. Being reliable, dedicated, businesslike about things.'

He grimaced. '*Business*like?'

'What?'

'I dunno,' said Charlie. 'There's just something about the word "professional" that I'm not impressed by.'

'That's the standard any pupil or parent should expect from us.'

We could have torn this city to pieces! Nadine shrieked in his head.

I know, honey.

Destroy this woman, Charlie. Destroy everything she represents.

'Yeah,' said Charlie, 'but, Julie, *anyone* can do that. Anyone can turn up on time, and punch in, and tick all the right boxes and make notes at the meetings and take "decisive action" and all that. It doesn't mean you have an ounce of soul.'

'Soul?' said Julie. 'What does that have to do with teaching?'

Charlie blinked at her. 'Are you kidding? That's the *only* thing it should be about. Soul and love. Obeying and impressing your superiors? Learning how to become a lapdog? That "professionalism" you talk about is machinery and acquiescence and passivity. It has nothing to do with art! I mean, the words you use, Julie. Teaching young people "manners" and "respect"? That's *anti*-art in its very nature. A "professional artist" is a contradiction in terms. "Professionalism" is the death of humanity! It must be resisted at all costs! And guess what else, Julie? The kids know it! The kids *know* the ones who are in it for "the job" and the ones who *feel* it. That's just not the way we truly inspire young people.'

'Hmm.'

Take *that* and party!

'So why did you want to become a teacher, Charlie?' she said.

He mused and stirred his coffee.

'I like being looked at.'

*This waiting room.*

*It makes you wait.*

*This is what it does.*

*It has olive green walls, gossip magazines on the counter, and a song from the eighties playing. Something about someone's love. Sent from above. The only thing that seems different to you are the leaflets lying around which feature the word 'lifestyle' and the posters on the wall for the Gay, Lesbian and Transsexual Society.*

*It makes you wait.*

*Across the room sits a young woman, pretty, with an iPod. She could be a student. You think about giving her the patter but don't.*

*'Mr Bain?'*

*You stand. 'Yes.'*

*'This way, please.'*

*You are taken through a corridor into a consultation room. The woman sits at a desk with a computer on it and reads from a file.*

*'Charles Bain?'*

*'Yes.'*

*'And it's for the test?'*

*'Yes.'*

*So far you've said nothing but yes. Like some think-positive salesman. She smiles. 'Just a form to fill out first, get some info about your ... history.'*

*'Okay,' you say. Eventually.*

*'Right. What age are you?'*

*'Twenty-eight.'*

*'And you live in Glasgow?'*

*'Yes.'*

*'Do you have intercourse exclusively with one sex?'*

*'Yes,' he said. 'Women.'*

*'You've never slept with men?'*

*'Never.' You emphasise this.*

*'How many sexual partners have you had in the last twelve months?'*

*You think. Your mind is a collage of indistinct names and faces, sheets covering chests and necks, hair being pushed out of eyes, noses being rubbed, dipped looks. You try to make it cohere into a pattern, a scheme, a giant mural. Clarify faces, put them to names, places, times:*

*Naomi. Nurse. Approached her in the Loft. She laughed a lot. Liked to be bitten on her nipples and kept calling you 'babe'. Petra. German exchange student. Her walls showed photos of her friends and her family and she pointed everybody out to you and told you a little story about each of them, but you interrupted her with a kiss halfway through one about her brother (he liked hang-gliding, and once nearly—) and she had a little tattoo of a love-heart above her pubic hair. Jackie. Lifeguard. Got talking to her at the local pool, but she wouldn't talk for long cos she had to watch the bathers. So when you'd spotted her in the car park you'd hailed her and introduced yourself: Recognise me with my clothes on? She was flat-chested but gave incredible head and she'd talked in her sleep about flamingoes. Hannah. From the bakery. Daragh. Northern Irish. Her living room had Republican posters on the walls, which surprised you since you'd presumed the entire evening that she was Protestant. Pauline. Divorcee. Met her over the internet. Better-looking than in her photo, but smoked and talked incessantly about her dogs, and kept wanting you to dance with her in her living room.*

*'Six,' you say. 'No. Wait.'*

*Christine. Barmaid in your local. Married. When you were making love she kept saying, 'All the way, all the way, all the way,' for some reason. Paula. Socialist. Met her on an anti-nuclear march at Faslane. She was hoarse from the march, which was funny afterwards, in bed, since she could only speak in a cracked whisper. Kate. Parent to one of your pupils. You'd made chat about her son's performance, then asked for her number, 'in case there are any problems'. Powerful thighs. Fucking powerful thighs.*

*'Eight?' you say. 'No. Wait.'*

*Tanya. Insurance clerk. Long fingernails. Jessica. Worked for your bank. Wouldn't look you in the eye whenever you went into the branch after that. Louise. Skinny. Kept asking to try it in different ways, all*

*ways. 'Can we try it another way?' she'd request, halfway through the
last way she'd wanted to try it.*

'Thirteen?' you say.

*Erin. Worked in a comic-book store. Looked bored in bed. Vicky.
Hairdresser. Constantly fiddled with your hair. Henrietta. Loved hats.
Kept wanting you to lick her neck.*

'Twenty?' you say.

*Carrie. You made jokes about the film. She'd never even heard of it.
She didn't orgasm.*

'Twenty-five?'

*Maeve. Hippie. Room reeked of marijuana.*

'Thirty?'

*Nadine. Barcelona.*

'You don't know exactly, Mr Bain?'

'Somewhere between twenty and thirty.'

'And how many of those did you have unprotected sex with?'

'Maybe four.'

'Maybe four?'

'Probably nearer eight.'

She writes this down in her file.

'Look,' you say, 'I just want to make sure I'm in the clear.'

'Yes,' she says, looking up at you, 'I know that, Mr Bain. That's why
you're here.' She tries to smile in an I'm-not-judging-you way. But still.
'Did all of these encounters take place in the UK?'

'No,' you say. 'One was in France.'

'With a French woman?'

'She was Polish, actually.' You feel almost proud of this achievement
for a second, but then suddenly you're small inside it.

'Ever take drugs?'

'The same ones as everyone else,' you say. 'Coke.' She writes this
down. 'Sometimes ecstasy.' She writes this too. 'And speed.'

'Anything else?'

'Grass. Obviously.'

She breathes in and then out.

'How many units of alcohol do you drink a week, Mr Bain?'

'How many in a drink?'

'There are two units in a pint. One in a measure of spirit or a glass of wine.'

'Oh, let's see,' you say, and throw some numbers in your head. Great big comedy foam numbers. Nothing lands to make a sum.

'The recommended weekly amount for a man is twenty-one units.'

'Right,' you say, 'I'm probably double that.'

She writes this down.

'Do you have a regular partner, Mr Bain?'

After a while you say: 'Not since I separated from my wife.'

'How recently?'

'Two years ago.'

'And did you have unprotected sex with her?'

You almost tell her, Don't you think that's a little personal? *But you answer her.*

'And when was the last time you had unprotected sex with anyone?'

You speed-dial through the images. Martha. Behind a night-club. She'd pulled you into her before you could protest, then instinct had just taken over

and over                                     and over

and over

'Three weeks ago,' you say.

'Oh,' she says, and puts down her pen. 'Mr Bain, there's actually a twelve-week waiting period between the sex and the possibility of anything showing up in our tests.'

'What do you mean?'

'The virus can take twelve weeks to manifest itself.'

'So...' you say '... I'll have to wait another nine weeks before the test?'
'Afraid so.'

You say nothing, look around the room — its olive green complexion and neatly typed notices — and eventually say, 'Can I make another appointment?' Even though you can't imagine the world still existing nine weeks from now. You try to imagine what the life of this woman is like. Who she is. The things she worries about. The names she has given to her cats. The colour of the carpet in her living-room. What she wanted to be when she was little. Whether or not she's afraid of flying. Whether or not she believes in God, in punishment and reward.

'The good news,' she says, 'is we can use this information for the test. You won't have to go through it again.'

'And if I sleep with anyone else before then?'
'Wear a condom.'

He awoke to shouts from downstairs. Deborah's voice. His mother's voice. Muffled, small stains of noise spreading on a cloth of silence. Knew instantly what it was about: awareness sliced through the fog of sleep.

Charlie had been drinking the previous night. He fumbled among the covers, their jungle-warmth, trying to find his head somewhere. There it was, on his shoulders, where he'd left it. He touched his temples, reached for a drink of water, drank the water, looked down at the bedsheets covered with fingerprints again, hand-prints, purple like bruises. He stood, put on his dressing-gown, then bundled up the covers and sheets and hauled them sleepily to the washing-machine.

He hadn't seen Deborah like this for a long time, not since a boy in school — Robert Torrance — had broken her heart and bragged about it, forcing Charlie to reluctant, shaking action: Robert Torrance was six feet tall.

Adulthood, he now realised, was just adolescence with the stakes raised.

Deborah looked rank and stark and clumsy with upset. She anchored the middle of the living-room and it revolved around her: Elizabeth tottering back and forth from her mother's centre of gravity, even Deborah's cat, brought for some bizarre reason, was scattering with every barked remark. There was something manic in her stance, all jagged and askew, hands on hips creating isosceles triangles. When Charlie entered the room his mother looked at him, a how-do-we-deal-with-this? appeal in her eyes. Charlie frowned.

'Did you know anything about this?' Deborah said. Even the flick of her head towards him seemed sharp.

He didn't want to answer, in case she was only blowing her top at a rise in petrol prices or something.

'About what?'

'About my husband being an asshole.'

'Oh, yeah,' he said. 'I knew about that.'

'Did you know he's been sleeping around with some bint?'

Jordan had confessed, or been found out. Mountains cascaded from Charlie's shoulders, rivers of flowing stone. 'Thank God,' he said.

'What?'

'He admitted it?'

'Elizabeth told me.'

'*Elizabeth* told you?'

She nodded. She breathed in. She let it out: 'After you phoned the other night Elizabeth came off the phone and was like Daddy Daddy I said no it wasn't Daddy it was Uncle Charlie but she was like Daddy on phone Daddy on phone so when Jordan got in I said to him were you talking to Elizabeth on the phone earlier and he said, So Charlie's told you, then.'

'Oh,' said Charlie.

'So I know you know.'

'I was going to give Jordan time to tell you,' he said, 'before I did.'

'Oh, Charlie.' Deborah threw her arms round him so suddenly it startled him, buried her face in his shoulder. It took him a while to realise that he felt like the elder of them again. For the first time in a long time he put his arms around her. It felt good. Like he was a big brother. 'What the hell am I going to do now, Charlie?'

'You'll get through it,' he said. 'I did.'

He looked over Deborah's shoulder to his mum. She was shaking her head, darkly. Charlie closed in tighter to Deborah; she wept. Elizabeth tugged at their legs and Deborah detached, immediately, on Mum-automatic. 'It's okay, sweetie,' she said. 'It's okay. Mummy's fine.'

'Why did you bring the cat?' said Charlie.

'I don't want it staying in that house with *him*. Who knows what he'll do to it.'

'I think the cat's quite safe, Debs.'

'It's female.' She snorted. 'I wouldn't take the chance.'

Deborah started walking up and down with Elizabeth nestled in her arms. Her belly protruded beneath a smock. The cat followed. They were a bizarre little family troupe of performers. 'What am I going to do?' she said. 'Where am I going to go?' she said. 'I'm going to be a single mum,' she said. 'I'm going to be a single mother of two,' she said.

'You can always come here,' said their mother.

'There isn't the room,' said Deborah. 'Not for an extra three.'

'I'll be moving out soon,' said Charlie.

The weight in the room tipped: daughter to son.

'Moving out?' said Deborah.

'You're moving out?' said their mother. 'To where?'

'I've met a girl,' Charlie admitted, feeling all of fifteen. *Girl?*

'Where did you meet her?' said his mother. What did she fear — the docks?

'She works beside me, remember?' said Charlie. 'She's a teacher.'

The room was quiet for a minute, except for Elizabeth saying, 'Tee-cha. Tee-cha.' There was simply too much volume of thought, filling up the room like a thick mist.

'Not the forty-year-old?' said their mother.

'No,' he said. 'The forty-one-year-old.'

'All change,' said Deborah.

'Tee-cha!' said Elizabeth.

'Miaow,' said the cat.

'You're moving out?' said his mother. 'Definitely?'

'I'm thirty,' said Charlie.

'You're starting again,' said Deborah. 'I'm splitting up.'

'I've split up before,' said Charlie, 'and started again.'

'Me too,' said their mother.

'No offence,' said Deborah, 'but I don't exactly want to end up like either of you.'

'What's that supposed to mean?' said Charlie and his mother, at the same time.

'I can't take this,' said Deborah.

'Tee-cha,' said Elizabeth.

'Gaagh!' said Deborah.

Then the three of them were embracing in the centre of the room, and Elizabeth was watching a pyramid of bodies melt.

Nadine gone. Yvonne gone.

But he had his mother. And Deborah. And Elizabeth. He still had them. They still had him. They all still had each other.

*

355

the Queen is Dead Sign o' the Times Appetite for Destruction The Joshua Tree Surfer Rosa It Takes a Nation of Millions to Hold us Back Blue Monday I am the Resurrection Disintegration Straight Outta Compton Fear of a Black Planet Do the Right Thing El Amor en los Tiempos del Colera Sex Lies and Videotape Losing my Religion Beloved Libra Loveless Foucault's Pendulum Goodfellas Smells Like Teen Spirit Spiderland The Trick is to Keep Breathing Unforgiven American Psycho Achtung Baby Generation X Unfinished Sympathy Reservoir Dogs Screamadelica The Remains of the Day C'est Arrivé Près de Chez Vous The Secret History Ba Wang Bie Ji The Virgin Suicides Schindler's List Parklife A Suitable Boy Heavenly Creatures Dog Man Star Pulp Fiction How Late It Was, How Late The Holy Bible Heat What's the Story (Morning Glory)? Se7en Grace Common People Trainspotting Fargo Odelay Der Vorleser Bitter Sweet Symphony Infinite Jest Ladies and Gentlemen, We are Floating in Space Festen Fat of the Land Underworld OK Computer Seta Music Has the Right to Children The God of Small Things The Soft Bulletin Happiness Atomised Agaetis Byrjun Disgrace Fight Club House of Leaves Magnolia La Fiesta del Chivo The Blair Witch Project Kid A The Corrections Felt Mountain Amores Perros Is

This it? Atonement Wo Hu Cang Long White Teeth Memento A Heartbreaking Work of Staggering Genius Elephant Dancer in the Dark Up the Bracket Cloud Atlas Sen to Chihiro No Kamikakushi Mulholland Drive Hable Con Ella Der Untergang Volta Everything is Illuminated Cache The Damned United Neon Bible Das Leben Der Anderen In Rainbows El Labarinto del Fauno There Will Be Blood Then We Came To The End *of the night and you sleep with a witch. A real, genuine, self-confessed witch. You are in some Goth-punk club — you can't remember why, except that's where the drink has taken you this fine Glasgow evening — she's dancing, you're dancing, and you like her whole set-up: the kohl round the eyes, the tight black clothes, the way she writhes on the dance-floor, tantric.*

*'Let's go back to mine.'*

*Her bedroom is the perfectly normal, studenty bedroom of a woman in her twenties — film posters, prints, clothes all over the place — except for the crystal ball on her dressing-table.*

*'That doesn't work,' she says.*

*'Pity,' you say. 'Was hoping you could tell my future.'*

*'I can,' she says, and throws you onto the bed.*

*Afterwards, lying on top of the covers, talking, she admits she's a witch. You prickle a bit and she grins. 'Relax,' she says. 'It's not like you think.'*

*'I'm not ready to die!'*

*'Don't talk daft,' she says. 'We don't stand round stirring pots and consorting with bats.'*

*'What do you do?'*

357

'We just worship the Earth,' she says. 'Nature, the seasons, the animals, the plants. It's very healthy. It's all about fertility.'

'But,' you say, looking at your shrink-wrapped dick, 'we used a condom.'

She shakes her head and rolls her eyes, a quirk Gothicised by mascara. 'I don't mean that. Mankind is destroying the Earth,' she says. 'Pagans are trying to commune with it.'

'So you don't worship,' you gulp, 'evil?'

vonne crashed on the sofa weeping bottle of vodka and pil

'No!' She laughs. 'It wouldn't make sense to a pagan. There's a very basic rule: whatever good or bad you do in the world will come back to you trebled.'

'Oh.'

'Yup,' she says, leaning over to kiss you again, her hand twitching below your waist. 'So you, Charlie Bain, must have been a very good boy ...'

As days went by he became caught up in the storm of Deborah and Jordan, what seemed like a global economic crisis watched with mounting horror on the news, involving him mainly in baby-sitting while Deborah attended summit meetings with Jordan. He didn't mind baby-sitting Elizabeth. He and his mother sat smiling in the living-room while she entertained them – dancing or mimicking adverts or pulling her jumper over her head – and they exchanged deep, damp looks as Elizabeth cavorted. But it was all shot through, like warm waters threaded by cold currents, with the knowledge of what was happening beyond: Deborah's whole life falling apart. Elizabeth was the One True Thing here, the simple fact of her running around the room naked made her seem like some mythical creature appeared within their lives, a unicorn or pixie, that brings villagers from homes to gawp, amazed, and, looking at it, become forgetful. But sooner or later – the creature vanished or banished – they go back to their lives, heads bowed.

Nadine was gone. Yvonne was gone. Still true.

But he still had Monise. And his classes. And his family. And Julie. Stiller. Truer.

He wanted to glut himself on the love from those kids; wanted to move in with Julie Carell; wanted to become friends with Monise – sweet, smart Monise – as soon as she'd left school. But the exams were in the way of all of these things. The kids were stressed, he and Julie were stressed, and any contact he had with Monise, and with all of her class, was strictly regulated by work. The furrowed brows of the girls, pens jammed into the sides of their mouths. Monise's smile floated at him across the classroom. She was going to walk it.

Simon's sarcastic remarks each time Charlie offered a practical exam tip. What was it with this kid? He'd arrived in Charlie's class as a slightly shy but affable young man, but the hot-house of attention from those girls had brought him into bloom. Now everywhere he went he did so with a rank of laughing females, tugging at his cheeks and tousling his hair, Monise chief among them. Why did Monise persist in mothering Simon? He was a big boy, he could take care of himself. But she continued to talk about him as if he was a tiny child lost and alone in the city. The words she used, 'sweet', 'so intelligent', 'the soul of a poet', 'very respectful towards women', seemed to describe someone else entirely – Percy Bysshe Shelley perhaps, or Nelson Mandela – not this vague and pimply and impertinent young man. Because of this, there was arrogance in everything Simon did: his walk, head high and eyes brimming with challenge; his voice, not so adolescent and apologetic now but firm and clear and direct and refusing to taper away at the end of a sentence, set up in opposition to Charlie's own. Simon simply disagreed with everything that Charlie had to say. Textbook Alpha Male. Charlie was the dominant ape in the group and Simon, in order to ingratiate himself further with the girls, had to take every opportunity to make Charlie look ridiculous, or stupid, or old. Especially old. Did Simon not even realise that he, too, would age, would grow into something alien to himself, would also criss-cross blindly across his life towards death? Charlie remembered being Simon's age. He and Nadine preening with the sentience of youth, the way they'd regarded the male teachers as though they were some kind of endangered species, fumbling with the knowledge of their extinction, wondering how they'd become like that, so soiled and shopworn and withdrawn, with their solacing cups of coffee and hot, furtive looks at the girls in Charlie's class.

At Nadine.

'Yuck,' she'd scribbled on Charlie's jotter, after yet another of their glances down her cleavage. 'Age has a *cock*.'

But this had chilled him in a way she could never understand. He'd realised dimly that he was linked to these men by biology, the way one recognises a vague, trapped humanity in bears, walruses, elephants. Fundamentally, though, they are not *like you*. They are animals. With neither logic nor speech. When he was at school and uni, Charlie had exulted in youth – dancing, drinking, the music papers and afternoons asleep – made a statement of it, invested in it. Being young was a politic in itself! Charlie would never grow up and become a Man, with all the slow, stupid, dwindling, blunting, fading and compromise that entailed becoming a Man. He'd find some way of avoiding that fate, perhaps cryogenically freezing himself, waking in a future world where ageing had been abolished and everyone was a beautiful stripling of a thing, or by extinguishing himself in some heroic, romantic act that the poets would write about!

hree-quarters of suicides are male suici

The future he'd woken into was Julie: a future of walks in the woods with Julie. His future was what he was doing right then –

walking in the woods with Julie, through the wet, breathing trees, her dog nosing ahead of them into comical confrontations with nature. Dog meet Rabbit. Dog meet match. He and Julie were both wearing rain-slicker jackets and wellington boots. They were holding hands and smiling at each other, the smudged way you did when you were in love. Her hair was a little damp across her forehead. She was pretty and sensible and smart. His death did not seem imminent when he looked at her.

'What are you smiling at?' said Julie.

'Nothing,' grinned Charlie.

The dog returned to their feet, carrying a branch and seeming to laugh. It dropped the branch and Charlie clapped its ears, saying, 'Good boy,' and bunched up his lips and said, 'Oh, yes, you is a handsome boy, isn't you?' Julie was watching with a smile on her face. A deft little smile. A meaningless little smile. They felt like a family, the three of them.

Nadine became the White Witch from Narnia in his head. She walked alongside them, pointing a sharp wand and cackling. Oh, Charlie, you fool. You are me. I am you. We cannot make happiness such as this last.

Please, Nadine . . .

Soon, Charlie, all will become winter and never Christmas. And I will have my revenge.

They walked over the mulch and tenderness of the earth, and Julie said, 'What's happening with your sister?'

Charlie shook his head. 'He's begging her to stay, but she's moving out. Says she can't trust him again.'

'And what about this other woman?'

Charlie threw a stick. The dog went after it, pantingly happy. 'You have to remember, this other woman thinks of my *sister* as the other woman. She didn't know Jordan was married.'

'So she's dumped him too?'

Dumped, he thought. What a way to end human intimacy, with a *dump*. It was how you ended a bowel movement, not a relationship.

'Well,' he said, 'what does the other woman usually do when she finds out he's married?'

'Your poor sister,' said Julie. 'If any man ever cheated on me again . . .'

'Hm,' he said.

Cheating? he thought. *Cheating?* There was no such thing. If two people wanted to have sex with each other they should be allowed to. The world was such a sad fucking place that moments of joy had to be taken, cherished. For him, there was no longer such a thing as saying no. It was inconceivable now. What would be the point when he'd said yes so often? Desire was the most natural condition in the world. It was hard-wired into the meat and sinew of the body. Evolution had bred it for the purpose of species propagation, gene survival. Desire could never be such a thing as depraved or immoral. Desire was *pure*. Desire was *being*. 'Cheating' was in denying that! The cheating was on nature!

ohmyGodthisiswhatitfeelslike

E                    V                    I                    L

That's *better*, hissed Nadine. Give *in*. Feels *good*, doesn't it, my love . . . ?

Julie whistled at the dog, who was trotting through the undergrowth, snuffling. Then she said, 'Are you excited about moving in?'

'I am,' he said.

He was.

'We should set a date for it.'

'The exams end this Friday,' he said, 'so what about Saturday?'

'Wow,' she said. 'So soon?'

362

'Sooner the better.'

'Okay,' she said. 'Saturday.'

'Day before the pupils' party.'

'You're going to that?'

'I've been invited.'

'So have I,' she said, 'but it doesn't mean I'll be going.'

'Why not?'

'It's a party for the pupils. What are we going to do there? Talk to them about mortgages?'

'Don't be daft,' he scoffed. 'Inviting us was a lovely gesture. Come with me. Just to show face. Then we can go somewhere and celebrate moving in together.'

'Okay,' she said.

Then he said: 'Is Gavin going?'

'I don't know. I don't think so.'

'He'd better not be.'

'Oh, Charlie, give it up. You *boys.*'

Charlie placed his arm around her shoulders and she leaned into him. They watched the dog dive and leap through the undergrowth, emerge grinning and shaking its fur of rain. It sniffed and laughed and ran towards them. He and Julie patted it togethe *y   ou*

ogether         you      y   *u*      together         y   o         *you*
*ou like nadine fisher*

*nadinefishers nice!*

*Shes got longlong hair and*
*a My Little Pony bike and*
*even though you don't like pink shes got a better bike than you.*

*Yours is yellow.*

*Sometimes you and Nadine go with your mummies to the canal and catch the butterflies in the jar and watch them flap about or sometimes beetles or even caterpillars yuk! Nadine's not scared of beasties not like other girls. When you play doctors and nurses she always wants to go doctor. And even though she makes you take your pants off she never takes her pants off. Says her mummy told her not to. Not in front of boys.*

*No fair.*

*Right then, Charlie, I'm the nurse. What's wrong with you?*

*I've got a sore head.*

*Okay take your pants off.*

*She has a good look but she can't work out what's wrong with your head.*

*Then you go and play on the swings. Nadine pretends to be an eagle and you pretend to be a giant called Sam.*

*You like being in her class at school. Nadine plays nice.*

*One day your mummies buy you ice-cream. Your mummies stand there and smile, watchin you eatin the lovely ice-cream, lickin n dribblin. Aw says Nadine's mummy, they could be boyfriend and girlfriend!*

*You'd like to be Nadine's boyfriend.*

*You would be a nice boyfriend.*

*Maybe you should ask to be her boyfriend?*

*You seen Daddy give Mummy a card and it was for Vantenines Day. He said I luv you here's your card. And Mummy said Aw thanks and she opened it and it was a big red luv heart and she sat it on top of the telly. Mummy looked pleased. Later they shouted n shouted but you membered Mummy looked pleased with the card at the time and so the card must have been a Good Thing.*

*Mummy had got you some paper to cut n make shapes. You go and pull out the paper from the drawer. There's still some red left. You get a pencil and draw a luv heart on it and you are leaning on the bed so it's a wee bit wonky. Then you lean on your sticker book and finish it. You get the plastic scissors and cut round the luv heart. Then you write N for*

*Nadine and F for Fisher. You're good at writing, Mrs McLintoch said so.*

*You go to the garden and out the gate. You walk round to Nadine's garden and there she is. She's holdin a hose and a wee stream of water is fallin into the bushes. She says hiya Charlie. What's that you've got in your hand?*

*Something I made, you say.*

*What is it?*

*I made it for you.*

*Yeah but what is it?*

*A Vantenines Card.*

*A Valentines Card?*

*No Nadine it's Van-ten-ines.*

*Charlie uh uh. It's Va-len-tines.*

*No it's not!*

*Yeah it is! I heard my mummy say it and Mrs McLintoch in school. Valentines day was yesterday.*

*You shake your head.*

*You must be daft, she says.*

*I am not daft.*

*Vantenines! Who's it for anyway?*

*Um, you say. It was for you. But if you're going to be all bossy.*

*I'm not bossy. Give it here!*

*No!*

*Give me it!*

*You are so bossy!*

*She grabs the card and tries to pull but she just gets a wee corner and it tears off. You're tearing it! you say.*

*Well give it to me!*

*No!*

*If you don't give it to me, I won't show you my pants ever again.*

*You stop pulling.*

*Take your pants off next time, you say. And I'll give you the card.*

*I don't want it* that *much.*

*All right okay, you say. And you hand her the card. It's all wrinkled and tore from when she tried to grab it and you tried to pull it back.*

*She looks at it. Then she looks at the other side.*

*What shape's that supposed to be anyway?*

*It's a luv heart.*

*She laughs. It doesn't look anything like one!*

*Not now you've tried to grab it.*

*What does it say?*

*It says N. F.*

*For Nadine Fisher?*

*Yes.*

*What did you write that for?*

*Cos it's your name.*

*But why did you write my name?*

*Cos I want to be your boyfriend.*

*Do you?*

*Yes Nadine. I Luv You. It says it there.*

*She looks at the card. You stuck glitter on the inside n it's glitterin.*

*I don't want a boyfriend.*

*Don't you?*

*Not at the moment no.*

*Do you luv me?*

*She shakes her head.*

*Oh right, you say. Do you want to keep the card anyway?*

*She shakes her head again. Why don't you keep it? she says. If you find another girl and her name starts with N.F. you can give it to her.*

*Okay.*

*You try to think of other girls whose names start with N.F. You can't think of any.*

*Right then.*

*Do you still want to play on the swings tomorrow?*

*Yeah, she says. If my mummy lets me. She says I swing too high.*

*You do swing too high.*

*Maybe a wee bit. It's fun.*

But then Nadine's dad comes out. You don't like Nadine's dad. It's like everything's not fun when he's around cos he's always angry and Nadine told you one time about something weird that he did one night but she made you promise the most excellent promise in the world not to tell so you won't. He comes out and he stands behind her, that's all he does, and her mouth goes wee and she won't look at you and she says right, Charlie I'd better go. Her dad turns round and goes back into the house and it's like the sun comes back out again. Except not for Nadine.

*See you at the park?*

*Okay then, Charlie. Bye.*

*She's in a hurry now.*

*Bye. Oh. Nadine? Can I get a kiss?*

*Hm, she says. She looks in the house. Then she says okay quick then.*

*Thanks.*

*Just one though. I'm not supposed to let boys kiss me.*

*She leans over and kisses you on the cheek.*

*Okay then. Bye Nadine.*

*Bye Charlie.*

Bye Charlie

Bye Charlie

Bye Charlie

Bye Charlie

Bye Charlie

*Bye Charlie*

*Bye Charlie*

*Bye Charlie*

*Bye Charlie*

*Bye Charlie*

*Bye Charlie*

*Bye Charlie*

His mother was yearning for something.

At nights he'd pour her the single gin and tonic he thought it was safe for her to drink. Then he'd sit in his bedroom with his hands behind his head, watching the ceiling fan spin (he barely had the energy for marking these days, something listless pressing, *pressing*), tugging the cord so that it went at different speeds, while his mother sat in the living-room reading stories of dashing cads in breeches, handsome bastards with moustaches, upright young men with fortunes, and virtuous, trusting young women simply trying to make their way in this godforsaken world. She'd switched from crime novels – 'Bored with them, Charlie, I can guess them too easy' – to romance.

'But surely you can guess how romances are going to end?' he said.

She smiled and looked out into the garden, where birds hopped and cats prowled. 'I like knowing that, though.'

His mother was yearning for something.

'We might need to think about getting you some home help,' he said, giving her a cup of tea, 'couple of days a week.'

'Yeah,' she said.

'Just so you're not exerting yourself. Tidying up and going to the shops.'

'Deborah can help me.'

'She's definitely moving back in, then?'

'She is, yes.'

His mother sat in her reclining chair, in front of the television, and he started making supper. She asked him for another gin and tonic. He refused. Her eyes were glassy and far-away. Her mouth seemed poised on the brink of saying something, which she'd retreat from when he asked if she was okay. She wanted another gin and tonic.

'Mum, I'm not going to give you a gin and tonic.'

Eventually, partway through the adverts, she said, 'I've been back in touch with your father.'

Charlie's spirit clenched.

'What do you want to do that for?'

His mother shrugged. 'For Deborah's sake, I think. She's going to be on her own soon. She never really knew your dad. She should have the right to a relationship with him. Especially now that Jordan's let her down.'

'Oh, and you think he's not going to?'

'She doesn't hate him the way you hate him, Charlie.'

He shook his head. 'If he wanted to know Deborah he's had plenty opportunity in the last fifteen years. He was invited to both our weddings, remember?'

'No,' she said. 'It was me told him not to go.'

Charlie scratched his thigh. 'You told him not to go?'

'Yeah.'

'Why?'

'I didn't want to see him.'

'And you do now?'

'He's never even met Elizabeth. It'd be good for her and the new baby to know their grandfather.'

'Good for who?'

His mother didn't say anything. She turned her attention back to the telly.

'Don't you think she's got enough to deal with? Her marriage is breaking up. She's got Elizabeth to take care of. And she's pregnant.'

'I know,' his mother said. 'This is for the future. When it's all settled down.'

'The future.' Charlie snorted. 'What's *that*?'

His mother made a face.

'Let me guess: he's split up with her.'

She nodded. 'He's hit rock-bottom, Charlie.'

'And the money's gone, is that it? That why he's crawling back? You miss him, don't you?' Charlie almost snarled. '*That*'s what this is about.'

'Of course I do,' she said. 'I was married to him for twelve years. Son, I've had two heart attacks. I want to let sleeping dogs lie before it's too late.'

'Sleeping dogs wake up and bite you on the arse.'

His mother looked into her tea-cup, as though reading the leaves. 'You're too hard on him, Charlie. It pains me to say it, but he did love her. He *loved* that woman. It wasn't a wanton, careless thing that he did.'

Charlie stared at the rug: how carefully woven. Look at how carefully woven a rug is. The skill and intricacy it must take. The dedication. Oh, fuck off, rug.

'Neither me nor him's going to last for ever, son. I'd like to be friends with him again. You don't forget someone you married just like *that*.' She snapped her fingers. 'Do you never miss Yvonne, despite what she did?'

He raised his head. Then he went into the kitchen and made her a gin and tonic and returned and handed it to her. She sipped gratefully.

'Mum?' he said.

She looked at him.

'Mum, it wasn't Yvonne who cheated on me. It was the other way round.'

She swallowed and set down her glass.

'I was the one having the affairs. She didn't do anything wrong.'

His mother looked at him in the disapproving way Scottish women looked at Scottish men.

'Thought I'd clear that one up,' Charlie said.

His mother lifted the drink to her lips again and swallowed. Then she set the glass back down and said, 'This family's still got a helluva lot to sort out.'


School, that Friday, was awash with the excitement of exams being over. It whooshed down corridors, cleansing and churning, lifting the kids into its sway, making them squeal and clap and splash among the newness. He was helping to invigilate the last exam, standing at the front of the hall with his arms crossed, catching the eyes of colleagues that said, Nearly done. *Nearly done!* Minutes were dragged through glue. He was restless. Rows and columns of kids hummed with the sound of their future.

The chief invigilator called time.

The school term was over.

He took in the exam papers. He was liberating the slaves. He was Abraham Lincoln, striding through a cotton-field! With each exam paper he lifted another kid sighed and flumped, grateful for their emancipation. He was big and tall. Sideburned! He was doing good in the world. He wanted to do good in the world! He wanted to help these kids. A generation fizzed, texted, immediately. Their hive mind was alive. He met Julie Carell's eye and she said, *Free!* She said, Here it begins, Charlie. Our Life Together. He grinned at her. There was no doubt any more. He wanted this.

Then Monise was by his side, standing expectantly like a job interviewee. 'Oh, hi, Monise.'

'Hi, Mr Bain,' she said, then expelled it: 'OhthankGodthat'sover!'

'How do you think you got on?'

She shrugged disingenuously: she'd surfed through it. 'It's done,' she said.

'All of it,' he said.

'School,' she said.

'Over,' he said.

'For good,' she said.

'You're a proper grown-up now.'

'Frightening.'

'Make your own decisions.'

'It's my life.'

They looked at each other and smiled.

'You still coming to Simon's party tomorrow night?'

'Of course.'

'Good,' she said. 'It'll be great to see you.'

'And properly relax.'

'And have a chat.'

'Without having to worry about the teacher-pupil thing.'

'Uh…' she said.

'Gets in the way, doesn't it?'

She hesitated a little, then nodded. Then she clutched her folder close to her chest and said, 'Anyway, eight p.m.? See you there, Mr Bain.'

'It's Charlie.'

'Right.'

He had some of his stuff packed in the hall: books, clothes, CDs. He sat in the living-room with his mum and Deborah – she was visibly pregnant now – watching Elizabeth line up her toy horses, move them, then line them up again. It was nearly eleven a.m. The appointed hour. Deborah said, 'So when are we going to meet this mystery woman, Charlie?'

Charlie said, 'What do you want to meet her for?' Both his mum and Deborah laughed and said at once, 'Because she's your girlfriend!'

The doorbell rang and it was the man with the hired van to help him take the gear. He answered the door to summer in full bloom, and soon he was loading up the van and Deborah and his mother and Elizabeth were waving and he made small-talk with the driver. They unloaded the stuff at the other end: into Novar Drive. Into Novar Drive in Hyndland. Into posh, clean, middle-class Novar Drive, which curved like a D. Even the *shape* of it was literary. And there was Julie, standing outside the flat waiting for him, smiling.

'Hi,' she said.

'Hi,' he said.

They kissed.

It was the second time he'd done this, merged his life with a woman's, like some kind of recurring past, a ghost drama played out every midnight.

Then they were embracing tightly and she was whispering in his ear, 'Are you sure you want to do this?' and he was saying, 'Definitely,' and kissing her again. Then they were unloading the van and taking upstairs the accoutrements of his life, the meagre possessions he'd managed to accumulate in thirty years, and they were dumping them sweatily in the centre of the living-room and grinning at each other as they passed on the stairs, and when they were finished and he'd paid the driver, tipping him generously, they sat on the couch and drank tea, and looked at the piles of boxes, books, DVDs, heaps of clothes rudely shoved into Julie's life – this mingling – and they shone with excitement and cuddled, then had sex and, afterwards, their limbs seeming to flow around each other, their smiles the smiles of the strong and happy, they told each other that they loved each other. He took a note of it. Love. His people would be interested in the concept. Perhaps, back on his home planet, it could be used as a foodstuff. Or to fuel trains. What was this Love? He put his fingers in its mouth and stared at its teeth.

'My Julie.'

'My Charlie.'

My Charlie.

My Nadine.

*To Whom It May Concern,*

*I am writing this letter in order to confirm that I have chosen to leave my wife, and that, as compensation for the four years she has devoted to myself and our marriage, I agree to leave the contents of our home to her to do with as she wishes. The only exceptions to this are listed as follows: a portable television; a CD player; a computer; and my own personal collection of clothes, books, CDs and DVDs.*

*I also agree that we are in debt for the amount of £7500, of which I agree to pay to her the sum £3250. This will be paid directly to my wife's account in either a lump sum or by eight monthly instalments of £400, followed by one final payment of £245.*

*Yours faithfully*

*Charles Bain*

*You sign it and place it in a return envelope on your mother's phone table near the front door, the front door of a house you haven't lived in since you were seventeen. You are twenty-six. You'd arrived here, with those things — a portable television, a CD player, a computer, and your own personal collection of clothes, books, CDs and DVDs — in the back of a hired van. When you'd opened the door your mother had seen the look on your face and known something terrible had happened and you'd sat both her and Deborah down and broken in two and said, 'I'm sorry, Mum. I'm so sorry. I wanted to show you that I was a good man. That there are decent husbands out there.' And she'd held you there for a long, long time, as you'd roared the inside out.*

*There is also a second envelope from Yvonne. You inhale and wait and then tear it open. It is headed simply INSTRUCTIONS.*

1. *Redirect your mail to your mother's address. I'm getting sick of it arriving here.*
2. *You need to seek professional help. This stems from your constant rejection by girls at school and from your parents' divorce. You need to deal with these issues now if you are ever to have a successful relationship with anybody. You are fast on your way to becoming your father, and I hope you realise this.*
3. *For godsakes learn from your mistakes. You cannot continue being so reckless with other people's lives. Please, God, do not do to another woman what you have done to me.*
4. *Find some friends who are men.*

*Even after your separation she is caring for you. Even after everything you've done to her (and make no mistake — you have destroyed her without mercy, with savagery, a job done so completely you almost took pride in it — her trust and faith so shot full of holes that she retreats to a job in Manchester to get as far away from you as possible), after all this, she is caring for you. She is still fulfilling her spousal duty towards you, the promises she made. She does not want to see you in pain. She has proven herself a better person than you, a thousand times over. She has proven you weak, selfish and vain; proven herself strong, generous and kind. You are the villain of this piece. How did that happen? How does the nice guy become the monster so definitely, so unequivocally?*

*It's not my fault!*

*It's all your fault.*

*I didn't know!*

*You knew all along.*

*I meant no harm!*

*You caused great harm.*

*I'm the victim!*

*You're the perpetrator.*

*An aftermath settles like volcanic ash across the land. A fundamental shift in your wife's understanding of you has taken place: she has broken through some barrier of perception and seen you for what you truly are. The devil. You have rewarded her loyalty to and love for you with contempt. She ceded power to you – in signing her heart over – and you have wielded that power casually, and fired upon her. Once that first betrayal had taken place, that first kiss of another woman, that taboo surmounted, you had more or less ceased to feel. There was no malicious intent, simply the inability to understand your own actions.*

*It is a shockingly dull epiphany.*

*And then the guilt sets in. Even as the venom of your divorce, expressed in polite, formal, legal prose, recedes into the past, the horror does not. Nightly you dream of yourself and Yvonne in a high place surrounded by woodland and snowfall, and you are holding her hands and imploring her to forgive you. You are saying the words, 'I'm so sorry,' over and over, and telling her that you were lost, you were so lost inside yourself that you did not know what you were doing, that you are wretched, wicked, but a man who wants to be good again, if she could only forgive you, and she says, 'Oh, Charlie,' and holds you and says, 'I forgive you,' and you wake, eyes damp, in the bedroom of your mother's house again, aged twenty-six.*

*On your own.*

*This is what you want.*

*This is who you are.*

When he headed off with Julie to Simon's party he was in an inordinately good mood. It was a warm night. Birds were singing. Long shadows on brilliant green lawns. All that kind of stuff. They held hands and smiled at each other, rubbed noses, stuffed full of coupleness. Julie said, 'We're not going to be staying.'

'Of course not. Just showing face.'

'Because it's, like, the pupils' party. We shouldn't really be there.'

He looked at her. 'Julie, it's okay. First of all, we've been invited. Second, the school term is over. They're on the brink of leaving. Third, some of these kids are eighteen now. They're proper adults.'

'Being eighteen doesn't make you a proper adult.'

'Well, they're certainly not children.'

'They *are* children, Charlie. Children who'll be drinking. And perhaps even taking drugs. We shouldn't stay for long.'

'Okay,' he said, palms up. 'One drink.'

'Don't *drink*.'

By the time they arrived the party was already ordering shots. It was already standing on tables. It was already hitching its skirt up and doing the can-can. Simon answered the door, and his big, sudden grin was a booze-soaked Welcome banner.

'Mr Bain!' he said, almost effeminately. 'Ms Carell! I'm so glad you *came*. Oh, c'mere,' he said, and kissed them both. 'Mwah! Mwah!' Julie laughed but Charlie took a hesitant step back. 'Oh, don't be silly!' said Simon. 'C'mon in. Everybody? The teachers are here!'

Julie and Charlie regarded each other nervously. Heads popped from doors, as though in some children's story, woodland creatures who find a boy and girl wandering in their kingdom. There were more grins. Bodies clamoured into the hallway to see them – teachers? here? – exotic visitors. Teachers out of school exuded a kind of glamour. Many had been the time when Charlie, drifting through supermarket aisles, had said hi to one of the kids, shopping with their parents, only to hear the cupped-hand whispering and catch the fascinated glance. At a party like this they were celebrity. They looked at each other and made a 'Well!' grimace. Soon they were being led into the living-room, where music was playing at toxic volume – PopUp's first album – and he and Julie were wincing against it, like proper old people. And there were faces. Kid faces. Smiling faces. Drunk faces. Curious faces. Faces he'd seen poking out of uniforms, on duty, at school, now – literally – letting hair down, hair that cascaded, tumbled, curled onto bare shoulders and over party outfits. Some of the girls, even the plain girls, looked stunning. And stunned.

'Mr Bain!'

'Mr Bain, you came!'

'Ms Carell!'

378

'Mr Bain and Ms Carell!'

'The Hollywood couple!'

'Come in! Come in!'

'Sit here!'

'Sit!'

'Sit sit sit!'

Julie was looking at him, eyes clam-wide. He shrugged. They sat. Soon some prescient sixth-year glided over to them, offering them drinks.

'No, thanks,' said Julie.

'Uh, vodka and Coke, please,' said Charlie, and the sixth-year disappeared again and he saw her hiss to someone who'd just arrived, 'You'll never guess who's here. Mr *Bain* and Ms *Carell.*'

'No!'

Julie leaned over to him and said, 'I thought we agreed we weren't drinking.'

'One's not going to do any harm, is it?' he said. 'We're celebrating. It's all good.'

Soon Julie and Charlie were jammed in the centre of the couch: one of the boys talking to him about music (he was in a band that played 'space jams'); Julie cornered by one of the girls, asking her about fashion ('Ms Carell, where did you buy those beautiful shoes?'). He could feel Julie, squeezed up beside him, squirm a little. He could tell she wasn't enjoying the attention, not from the kids, not in such a noisome, smoky, lax setting. Charlie could sense the instinct in her to control – fight the advancing tide of gleeful teens – and roar them back into place.

He, on the other hand, was having a ball. He was even playing keepy-uppy with it.

'*Clockwork Orange*, right?' he said, to the triptych of boys around him. '*Reservoir Dogs. Texas Chainsaw Massacre. Natural Born Killers.*

*The Exorcist.* I saw all those films when they were still *banned*.'

'Whoah, man,' said one of the boys, from beneath his fringe. 'They, like, banned shit back in the day?'

'Yeah,' said Charlie, trying not to bristle at 'back in the day'. 'I mean, you had to find a flea-pit somewhere that was showing it, or a dodgy pirate copy, then ring round all your mates. It was an *event.* Cos it was forbidden.'

'That must've been *cool.*'

'That's the problem with your generation,' Charlie said. 'Everything's allowed.'

'Man,' one of them said, scratching at acne, 'I wish they'd ban shit now.'

He folded his arms and nodded with all the wisdom of Gandalf. He never got the chance to speak to the kids like this. Monise, yes, but not the rest of them. About music. About films. If you wanted to know what was new you had to ask the young. They, in turn, were impressed at the names of the bands he'd seen live. The Strokes, for example. Julie had to deflect questions from a trilling posse of girls about herself and Charlie – how long they'd been going out! who asked who! any wedding bells, hmm? the patter of tiny feet? – and he liked it.

The Hollywood couple.

Soon he was on his third drink and talking to his star students in the kitchen. Jenny. Bethan. Monise. Monise had squealed and hugged him when he'd come in. He'd hugged her back, stiffly. After chatting to them, with cardboard in his voice, about how exams had gone ('Fine,' 'Shit,' 'Shitter,' they'd replied, descending the scales), he warmed up a little, told them what a great class they'd been ('And I mean a *great* class,' he said. 'I teach Advanced Higher every year, and you lot have been by *far* the best') and a few blushed and cooed and thank-you'd, and then the compliments were batted back his way. 'You've been an inspiration, Mr B', 'We couldn't have done it without you, Mr B', 'You've really pushed us, Mr B.' He shrugged and disabled them with a neat, 'You did all the work,' but couldn't prevent a couple slipping through and dissolving in his bloodstream, mixing with the alcohol. When Julie came into the kitchen he was flushed and beaming.

'Having fun?'

'I certainly am,' he said. 'This lot are being so nice to me.' He gestured towards the girls, who waved.

'Hi, you lot,' smiled Julie. 'On the lemonade, I hope?'

They all pretended to hide their glasses.

'You ready to go?' she said to Charlie.

He bunched his lips. 'Nah,' he said. 'Think I might stay a bit.'

There was something metrical in Julie's gaze. 'You think you might . . . stay?'

'Aye,' he said. 'I'm relaxed.'

She nodded. 'Are you still drinking?'

'Only my third.'

'Yeah, but have you seen the measures they're pouring you?'

'Julie,' he said, putting his hand on her shoulder, 'it's fine. It's the end of term. We've all been working very hard. Chill.'

Julie's shoulder wriggled from under his hand. 'Charlie,' she said, lowering her voice, 'we don't belong here. It wouldn't be professional to stay any longer—'

'Oh, fuck professional,' he said suddenly. 'I've been professional all my life. It's professionally *boring*.'

Julie stood completely still. Her eyes kept darting to the side, as though she was aware that some of the pupils were listening. 'Charlie,' she said, 'I'm leaving now. I would suggest that you do the same.'

He made puppy-dog eyes and lifted the drink to his lips.

She calibrated her gaze, mouth set to one side. 'Fine,' she said, then she was leaving the room, and he heard her make cheerful goodbye noises to pupils she encountered on her way to the front door. He turned back to his sixth-years. Monise and Bethan were drinking and grinning, but Jenny was not. She was looking at her lap and staring away whenever he tried to catch her eye. 'Now,' he said, 'who's for a chorus of the C-word?'

The girls groaned.

Jenny got up and left the room.

Monise moved in next to him.

The party was bleating and babbling. He'd forgotten what they were like, *proper* parties. Middle-class adults never had *proper* parties. What they did was get close friends together for 'nibbles' or 'drinks'. Everyone sat round a coffee- or dinner-table. Everyone was in each other's sightline and within earshot. One big homogenous dinner-party conversation was attempted, including all guests. Favourite topics were: house prices, the local school, plays, 'city breaks' and cars. No one said anything controversial. If anyone said anything controversial they were rebuked with the swift epithet: 'I'm sorry, but I find that offensive.' Nobody got too drunk. Nobody made a pass at anyone else. The middle classes.

Fucking capitalism.

# Int. Kitchen. Party

*Things are evolving into carnage. From the next room we can hear shouts and cackles, the occasional something-breaking. The music blasts out at eardrum-hammering volume. Frightened Rabbit.*

CHARLIE *is sitting with his sixth-year girls.* MONISE *by his side, thigh pressing against his thigh. He jokes and tells embarrassing stories about himself when he was younger.*

CHARLIE:        God, the amount of knock-backs. There wasn't a girl in the school who'd go out with me then.

MONISE:         Wow, that's so difficult to believe. Now that you're all grown-up and cool and … (*embarrassed pause*) … Well, y'know.

                *CHARLIE does a mock-bow. They laugh.*

CHARLIE:        Well, I had plenty friends who were girls. I was sweet, I was a nice guy, so at least I could always count on Nad—

BETHAN:         Who?

CHARLIE:        Never mind. Anyway. Uh. (*He raises his glass.*) To the fairer sex!

                *BETHAN and MONISE toast and they clink glasses. Enter SIMON, lording over his party like a junior Hugh Hefner. He is drenched in sweat and swilling a beer. He pats MONISE's shoulder. CHARLIE sees this.*

SIMON:          Having fun everyone? Good, good. (*Starts kissing the group.*) You, Mr Bain? Enjoying?

                *CHARLIE raises his glass.*

SIMON:          You don't get a kiss, I'm afraid.

                *CHARLIE shrugs and drinks. As he lowers the glass he thinks he catches SIMON making a face and gesturing towards him. A couple of other sixth-years squeeze into the group.*

RANDOM 1:       Mr Bain, we're totally going to miss you. Just wanted to say that.

CHARLIE:        Oh, thanks very much. That's really nice of you.

RANDOM 2:       Yeah, we were just talking about that time when James Harris called you a wanker under his breath, and you heard him and totally blew up.

| RANDOM 1: | We thought he was going to wet himself! |
|---|---|
| RANDOM 2: | Yeah, we'll miss you bawling at people in the corridor. |
| CHARLIE: | Uh-huh. And the way I inspired you too, right? I mean, it wasn't just me cracking skulls all the time. |
| RANDOM 1: | Oh, no, totally! Aye. Uh. You were totally like, uh… |
| RANDOM 2: | An influence. |
| RANDOM 1: | Probably. |
| | CHARLIE *rises and excuses himself to go to the bathroom.* |
| MONISE: | You're not going home, are you? |
| CHARLIE: | Little boys' room. |
| MONISE: | Come right back. |
| CHARLIE: | I will. |

# Int. Bathroom. Night.

*Submerged sounds of the party elsewhere. Underwater bassline.* CHARLIE *pisses triumphantly. He can see himself in the mirror.*

CHARLIE:
I'm *very* happy to receive this award and would *like* to thank my mother and my sister Deborah and my girlfriend Julie and, oh, Arab Strap and Mogwai and Belle and Sebastian for keeping the Scottish indie spirit alive all those years before I came along, and God and Satan and

*He shakes himself of urine, then stands in front of the mirror, his penis hanging from his trousers. He strokes it a little.*

*Then he tucks it away, and washes his hands.*

# Int. Landing. Top of the stairs.

JENNY *is there, waiting to get in.*

| | |
|---|---|
| CHARLIE: | Jennifer. |
| JENNY: | It's Jenny. |
| | CHARLIE *burps.* |
| JENNY: | Mr Bain, what are you doing here? |
| CHARLIE: | Well, I needed to go the bathroom and so I— |
| JENNY: | No, I mean what are you doing *still* here? At the party. |
| CHARLIE: | I have been invited, Jenny. |
| JENNY: | There are no other teachers here. |
| | CHARLIE *leans forward, holding onto the banister for support.* |
| CHARLIE: | That, Jenny, is because they're *squares.* |
| JENNY: | (*draws breath and folds her arms*) I think you should go home. |
| CHARLIE: | I think you should mind your own business. |
| | *He makes his way past her, but slips on the stairs a little. A gang at the bottom cheer. He holds up his hands to accept applause, and when he descends they pat him on the back and say, 'Cool, Mr B.' Or it might have been, 'Look at Mr B.' He isn't sure.* |

The party had moved into the garden. His sixth-year girls were there, sitting round the pond, smoking and smelling all suspicious. His phone beeped. It was Julie. Her text read, I think you should come home right NOW. No kiss. He stuffed it back into his pocket.

'Hey,' he said, and worked himself into the circle, sat cross-legged.

A couple of the kids looked at each other: should we hide the——? Do you think he'll——? He raised his hands. 'Look,' he said, 'it's cool. You guys do what you want. You're grown-ups now, and school's over.'

'Cheers, Mr B,' a couple nodded, smiling. 'Thanks, man.'

He sat listening to them talk while the joint was passed round. They were on about space aliens or something. The possibility of life on other planets. What passed for discourse.

'Hey, Mr Bain?' someone said.

'It's Charlie,' he said to the darkness.

'Hey, Charlie?' they said. 'Is it true you got in a fight with Mr Prentice?'

'Where did you hear that?' He wished he could see the speaker. He looked round for him, and his head felt heavy as though it had a bear's snout.

'Just heard that you punched Mr Prentice in a club.'

'I did,' Charlie said, and reproduced the scene. 'He came at me and he was all like yeah, yeah, I'm the big man. And I was like: That so? Then I was like doof-doof-doof. He hits the floor.' Charlie shrugged. 'Pansy.'

'Wow,' someone said.

'That's awesome.'

'Mr Prentice is a dick.'

'Cool, Mr B.'

Then the joint was being passed his way. It was being waggled in front of him. There was an arm at the other end of it, a thin, teenage arm. A face at the end of that, a pale, teenage face. It was Monise. 'Mr Bain?'

'Oh,' he said.

'Want some?' she said.

'Uh,' he said. 'Okay.'

He took it from her. It sat snugly between his fingers. He liked the way it felt.

'Have you done it before?' said Monise.

'What do you think?'

386

'Ha ha,' said Monise.

He sucked the end of the joint and watched the tip glow. He let the smoke sit in his lungs for a while, then exhaled. Smoke ribboned smoothly. The circle laughed. 'Check it out,' someone said. 'You can do it, Mr B!'

'I can,' he said, smiling. 'I can do anything I want.'

'You can do anything you want,' Monise said.

He nodded, dazed, staring at her. 'I'm a grown man. I don't need to ask anyone's permission.'

'No.'

'I can do what I like.'

'Yeah,' she said. 'We're all free people. That's what Kerouac would've said. Or Rimbaud.'

'Or Keats,' he said, 'or Byron.'

She nodded that mong-heavy way. 'Or Sartre or Wilde or Camus or Blake.'

'Yeah,' he said, feeling his brain detach and drift a little. Feeling his stomach set to jettison everything. 'Oh,' he said.

'What?'

''Scuse me.'

He stood. His limbs felt rubberised and dreamy. His vision sailed. He felt sick. Simon – being middle class, *typically* – had a large garden. It looked out over a burn, which Charlie could hear rushing and hissing. He made his way to the end of the garden, through a thicket of Narnian trees. The leaves were feathery in his hands. He could sense the pitch-sharp air. The music – throbbing its way through nature – felt effortless. His brain was pulling in two different directions. He bent over, breathed.

There was a rustling behind him: Monise.

'You okay?' she said, touching his back.

'That was quite a hit.'

'It's strong stuff if you're not used to it.'

'I'm used to it. But that was quite a hit.'

She rubbed his back. 'You going to be sick?'

'I think I'm okay.' He straightened up.

The two of them stood there in the dark. The moonlight broke on their faces. The sky was navy blue and throbbed with orange light pollution. The universe beyond, in all its endlessness. He felt like space itself.

'Isn't it beautiful?' said Monise.

'What?' said Charlie.

'Everything.'

He looked up at the sky. He looked at the burn. He looked at his hands, which seemed to swirl when he moved them. Monise, her face cool and serene. Her eyelashes blinked, slowly, stonedly. 'It is,' he said. 'Very beautiful.'

She smiled at him.

'I'm going to miss you,' he said.

'You too, Mr Bain.'

'I think you're a very good writer,' he said.

'I wouldn't be without you.'

'That's not true.'

'It is. You've helped me believe in myself.'

Charlie said, 'Well, y'know.'

'I feel more free now,' she said. 'I've grown.'

'You have,' he said. He stared at her. The world felt sugary. Raw.

'I let go,' she said, 'like you told me to.'

'I'm glad.'

She was still smiling woozily. He floated some happiness back to her. He touched her hand. A bat flickered above them. He placed his fingers on her cheek. She inhaled. The water made cool sounds. His vision was clear. His consciousness was perfect. Evolved. He'd reached the summit. His life would never contain more sweetness than this.

'We can do anything we want,' he whispered.

'Yes.'

'We decide our own destiny.'

'We do.'

He leaned in to kiss her. He touched her lips with his, brushed them across hers.

'Mr Bain . . .'

He placed his arms around her. She felt like a foal, soft and wriggling. He kissed her cheeks, her forehead.

'I'm . . .' she said '. . . not . . .'

'We should never deny our true natures,' he said.

She was pushing against him, lightly. 'Mr Bain, this is . . .'

'We have the right to be who we want,' he said. His hands moved to her waist. He kissed her neck. He took her fingers in his.

'Mr Bain, what if someone? Please. I'm not sure we should be . . .'

He lifted her top and pulled down the cup of her bra. She gasped.

'I keep telling you,' he said, 'it's Charlie.'

He bent and licked her nipple. Then raised his head and looked into her eyes. She was quivering, her breath held. His breath held.

Then he heard the swish of branches and the tramp of feet and Monise unfroze from his arms. 'What are you doing down here?' laughed Simon. 'Aren't you joining the—'

Simon stopped. Monise was there, poised for those few seconds beside him – everything completely still, crystallised – and then she was shaking him off and pulling up her bra, staring at him with confused eyes, staring at Simon, Simon staring at him, and even in the moonlight he could see his own fingerprints where he'd touched her.

# Sir takes drugs and makes pass at pupil

A teacher has been suspended after allegations that he took drugs at a school party and made advances on a 17-year-old girl.

According to onlookers, Charles Bain, 30, an English teacher at Renfield High, Glasgow, smoked **cannabis** at a party organised by pupils to celebrate the end of the school term. Reports claim he **lured** a pupil into the garden and tried to **kiss** and **grope** her. The girl, who cannot be named for legal reasons, is said to be 'very distressed'. Bain has been suspended for the duration of the inquiry by the local authority.

This is not Mr Bain's first brush with school bigwigs. Earlier in the year he was warned for his unpredictable conduct, which included **attacking** a fellow teacher and using **obscene** language in class.

A local authority spokesman said, 'We have suspended a teacher pending an investigation into an alleged incident at a party, involving **illicit** substances and **inappropriate** behaviour with a pupil.'

A school insider said, 'Mr Bain was a popular and friendly teacher, someone the kids looked up to. But since his divorce his behaviour has been increasingly **erratic**. This is just the final straw. We'll be **glad** to be rid of him now.'

Local parents, including those of the unnamed girl, are lining up to have Mr Bain dismissed permanently. One said, 'His life won't be worth living when we get hold of him. How dare he **abuse** the trust of a young woman, in this way!'

Mr Bain was unavailable for comment last night.

**Crackdown On Sleazy Sirs** – Editorial, p. 6

Do YOU have any school scandals? Call now. Cash offered.

wake into the memory of whathappenednext Monise running crying
Simon staring appalled *appalled* push through to EXPLAIN to Monise
EXPLAIN to her What Actually Happened too late man a BOMB's
exploded in the party Monise huddled sobbing the girls see me fire in
their eyes RAGE hold up my hands mumble Em no no didn't mean it
Monise burrows further into Jenny's chest *Keep him away* and Jenny
goes *Think you'd better leave Mr Bain* um okay hunt for my jacket
under pillowsbagscushions face burning Em um seen my jacket?
where's my jacket? 'scuse me that my jacket? not replying HOW
VERY STRANGE hunting hunting hunting through the party
narrowed eyes STARING Monise sobbing all I can think is Where's
my jacket? Where's my jacket? Where's my fucking jacket? behind the
couch OBVIOUSLY I shout Got it! make half-hearted attempts to em
smile ha ha move past folk towards the door but before I get there
stop in front of Monise try to say SOMETHING won't look at me
then Jenny armswrappedroundher hisses *Leave her alone* okay but I
didn't mean to *JUST GO* a scene from a film a text for study not
happening can't be happening weed still making everything faint
UNREAL a bizarre dream !!what a bizarrebizarre dream!! head to the
door feeling EYES on me then out into the cool night walking hands
stuffed into my pockets walking head down breathe walk Julie's flat
let myself in quiet ssh Julie sound asleep snooooooore in the dark
unconscious oblivious dreaming undress slide in beside her cold she
stirs *Finally* she says Uh-huh I say then *Should've been home hours ago*
I nod soon she's back asleep snooooooore I lie awake the dark the
darkness see SHADOWS Julie she breathes breathes beside me it's all
over now IMAGINE WHAT'S HAPPENING ELSEWHERE Monise
telling them about my hands on her body shocked faces of girls boys
shaking heads Disbelief kids phoning mums dads come pick me up
please BOO HOO HOO cars going home EVERY SINGLE ONE OF
THEM telling telling telling *Oh Mum you're not going to believe what*

*happened know Mr Bain the English teacher well I thought he was a nice guy* News spreading slowly sloooowly viruslike Taking Its Time making sure it stops at EVERY SINGLE HOME on the way Biblical Plague till it reaches this one here somebodysomewhere they'll phone *Julie have you heard* or *Is it true* or *Julie you didn't KNOW he hasn't TOLD you what he DID last night* IT IS INEVITABLE tell her yourself *first* before the phone rings or lie here staring at the ceiling Completely Awake for the first time in my life looking at midnight shadows FINGERPRINTS in the room I'm at the other side now Crossed Beyond as morning comes handsbehindmyhead staring at FINGERPRINTS Julie stirs turns sees me smiles sleepyhand reaches touches my face I flinch look at her she kisses me says *Somebody was a bad boy last night* I nod she says *You should've come home Charlie lucky not to get in trouble* I nod again she stretches yawns *You realise this is the first time we've woken up together since you moved in* I just nod Yes mouth completely dry lickmylips can't get moisture Julie says *So did the kids behave?* she looks at me says *What happened?* swallow balls of dry leaves say uh Julie there's something I have to tell you then the phone rings It's started It's started It's

What now how to explain this to Mum onlyleftyesterday she watched me go so did Deborah Elizabeth ON THIS VERY DOORSTEP waved me goodbye There'll always be a place for you here son littledidsheknow ha ha take my shoes off quietly ssh Mum Debs in the kitchen Debs making Sunday dinner stirring stirring telling Mum something about Jordan *he's only moved in with that fucking* I enter the kitchen both turn Hiya says Mum Elizabeth running squeals Unca Chally Unca Chally raises arms lift her MWAH pat her head she says *Pony* I say What's that you saw a pony? so where was that honey? points to the window *Onna road* she says On the road? Wow! put her down covered in FINGERPRINTS Mum Debs looking at me EYES then Mum says *Didn't expect to see you today Charlie you forgotten something ha ha* Em not quite *Well does this Julie not cook Sunday dinners* Uh it's not that Mum *So you've had a fight already* Well kind of then Debs stops stirring sauce flicking steamyhair from EYES turns looks SOMETHING'S WRONG they've known me too long *What's the matter* my sister says uh come into the living-room I say and please sit down.

Comparecontrast Julie's reaction to my family's Mum Debs looked Straight At Me listened did NOT interrupt though Deborah's hand strayed to Elizabeth then over her mouth eyebrows furrowed Mum TOTALLY STILL told it all calm as I could didn't leave a thing out I was drunk I was stoned I shouldn't have been there I misread the situation Never meant to scare her Never do that She's a great lassie my very best student I was close to her Would never frighten her like that I was drunk stoned justmisreadthesituation That's All when I stopped Debs Mum looked at each other TV show about antiques this tannedchap turning an old lamp round round in his hands ROUND ROUND like Aladdin tries to guess its value then Debs says *Oh Charlie* I bite my lip nod then I'm crying *You're still my brother* says Debs I'm stillnodding Mum's holding me I'm crying and crying and crying and crying and crying and crying and crying and crying and crying FROM BEYOND THE GRAVE so much crying Elizabeth doesn't like this UPSETTING HER so I stop dab eyes Debs staring at me despairing Mum too we talk about justwhatthehelltodo but Julie MY GIRLFRIEND JULIE had said *You disgust me Charlie thought you were a Good Man but you're not you're SCUM low-life dangerous SCUM get the fuck out my house GET THE FUCK OUT stay away from me GET OUT don't want to look at you DON'T TOUCH ME* so me Mum Debs talk into the night cos I know the worst is yet to come.

Don't wanna go to school Monday what am I supposed to do stay away for ever? no but the coward in me sure I'd like that ha ha walk

the corridors feel WHISPERS the EYES kids who'd usually say Hiya
Mr Bain don't say a thing lower gazes try to meet theirs
WHISPERING spreads spreads pause enter the staffroom
handonthedoor imagine Wild West pianoplayer stops everyone turns
looks at me barman drops drink !smash! BUT THAT'S NOT HOW IT
WORKS more subtle all in the wee glances Gossip never reveals itself
creeps like a tiny imp IN/OUT of conversation maketeawhydontcha
sit tremble try to hide maybe all the women will rush *YOU YA*
*BASTARD* jabbing jabbing the men just cough
therebutforthegraceofGod but no THIS IS STRANGE everyone minds
their own business I read a paper scanning for news about myself cross
legs uncross legs sip tea look round nobody catches my eye maybe
haven't even heard then GAVIN he comes sits down *Hey Charlie*
*how was your weekend* folds his arms looking right at me Uh it was
okay Y'know uh Quiet and he says *Didn't you go to the senior leaving*
*party* and I say *Yeah uh yeah I did* and he says *How did it go* arms
folded legs crossed staring straight at me those SPECTACLES
then hand on my shoulder big ole Hand of God know straight away
who it is That's why no one's said anything cos soon as I walked in
someone PROBABLY GAVIN picked up the phone That's Charlie Bain
arrived now sir *My office* says Paulson quietly in my ear patting my
shoulder. Gavin shakes his head looks at me IS THAT A SMILE OH
GOD I THINK IT IS *You fucked up* is all he says. Poetry chess.
Checkmate.
Don't even offer defence !!!What's the point at this late stage!!! ha ha
after thirty years ha ha stand hands behind my back listen to it Local
authority inquiry Possible police involvement Suspended indefinitely
If found guilty Dismissed without recompense Gross misconduct No
other school will hire you look at his AWARDS and CERTIFICATES
and FRAMED PHOTOS of himself with MPs *Remember hiring you*
*for this job Mr Bain* he says *You were so young and enthusiastic and*

*ambitious that really impressed me But something's happened to you and I don't know what Wish I could help son but you've crossed the line* I know sir *You're no longer that young man I admired* I know sir am I supposed to teach my classes today or not sir *That a joke?* he says *Go home Mr Bain your presence here is undesirable* float from the room EYES office staff all women FINGERPRINTS corridors walked a hundredthousandtimes now seething with EYES kids who used to love me Not Now everything strange alien heightened altered in the staffroom pigeonhole there's leaflets from the Union about Solidarity and PLAYING YOUR PART and !!!BEING STRONGER TOGETHER!!! envelope recognise handwriting Julie's it says

*Come round tonight and pick up your things. I won't be in. Post the key through the letter-box when you're finished and don't come back. Don't try and phone me either because I won't answer.*

Underneath she's written

*'He who acts like a beast avoids the pain of being a man.'*

crush letter throw it in bin pick up briefcase head home someone shouts a Word neverwanttohearitagain Simon walking towards me towards the school sees me coming TWO GRIZZLY BEARS met on an Alaskan plain we size each other up prepare for battle He stops I stop He looks into my eyes this young man UNAFRAID!

'Simon,' Charlie said.

'Mr Bain,' he replied.

Charlie's fingers clutched the handle of his briefcase. 'How's, uh, Monise?'

Simon shook his head like a nightclub bouncer. 'I really don't think you should be asking that, Mr Bain.'

Charlie looked down the street at an ice-cream van ladling out fat to a fat kid.

'She trusted you, Mr Bain. We all did.'

Beneath his teaching suit, Charlie was hot and sweaty and twitching. 'Simon,' he said, 'I didn't mean to upset her. Honestly, I didn't.' He placed his hands in his pockets to stop them shaking. 'I didn't ever want to hurt that wonderful girl.'

'Mr Bain, *please*.'

There were cherry-blossom trees lining the avenue they stood on, and Charlie thought for a second: Do cherries come from cherry-blossom trees? Will Simon have the answer to that? He considered asking, but then Simon said: 'You know we're together, don't you, Mr Bain? You know Monise is my girlfriend?'

Charlie nodded. 'Uh-huh, yes.' But he hadn't known! How could he have known? Something massive happened inside him. God, Simon and Monise! OF COURSE THEY'RE TOGETHER! How stupid. They were always going to be!

'Stay away from her.'

'Uh, I really don't think she'll want to see me anywa—'

'She doesn't.'

'Okay, I'll steer clear.'

'Good,' said Simon. 'Do that.'

Simon exhaled, swallowed, and Charlie was able to tell how scared Simon had been, how much of it had been necessary bravado. But then Simon did a very strange thing. He offered his hand and said, 'Good luck, Mr Bain.'

Charlie stared at it, thinking: Isn't it strange how things turn out? Isn't this the queerest of jokes? But he shook it politely, quietly, his tendons quivering. For godsakes, man, get out of there! Bail! Bail! Bail!

'Look, Simon,' Charlie whispered, 'I have to go, okay? I won't be coming back.'

'Okay, sure, Mr Bain.' Simon was looking away now. Perhaps at the cherry-blossom trees. Perhaps he was formulating answers about whether or not cherries came from them.

'Well, um, Simon, I hope you both do just fine.'

'Thanks.'

'Stick in there, son. You can both do whatever you set your mind to.'

OhmyGod, Charlie was becoming a Hollywood actor, an uncle giving advice to a bored nephew.

'And take good care of her.'

'Uh, I will,' said Simon, walking onwards now, patting Charlie once on the arm, but not looking at him.

'Goodbye, son.'

'Goodbye, Mr Bain.'

They both walked on, past each other: one of them into the future and the other towards history.

next day come downstairs newspaper SIR TAKES DRUGS AND MAKES PASS AT PUPIL Mum in kitchen silent Deborah's taken Elizabeth to the shops none of us knows what to say all day making dinner stirring soup just stir the soup !!EGGS!! hit the window wham wham wham wham Mum screams Straight out kids tearing away recognise them I yell but they're off giving me the finger shouting THAT WORD again Mum's shaking shaking breathing hard Are you all right? hold her close Mum it's okay calm down It'll be fine IT WON'T BE FINE Debs comes in lets Elizabeth's hand go toddles upto me happy but Debs the BAD LOOK on her face What's wrong? she shakes her head says *em Charlie don't go to the shops* Why? *well I don't think you're welcome* go out later bucket of warm water scrubscrub

eggs yuck man standing beside a car camera CLICKCLICKCLICK
CLICKCLICK climb down ladder walk towards him CLICK CLICK
then he's off into the car nyeeeeeow By ten that night my clean front
window well the brick put paid to that CRASH police they come take
notes but not really interested NOT REALLY because YOU'RE
STUPID IF YOU THINK THEY HAVEN'T READ THE PAPERS
TOO CHARLIE Mum Debs crisis-meeting Debs rubs her stomach
*Can't deal with this Not pregnant Not after what's happened with
Jordan maybe if I wasn't pregnant maybe but as it is NO* okay nod
Mum says *My heart can't take this son told by the doctor absolutely no
stress just can't have this* then I say it'll settle down People get upset
about things then forget *But Charlie you haven't seen the graffiti in the
underpass* IT'S ABOUT YOU haven't seen it yeah cos too scared to
leave the fucking house! Iraq in chaos Torture in Guantánamo
capitalism evolving into a globaltotalitarianregime RECESSION?
DEPRESSION? bombs exploding in Afghanistan !BOOM! and this?
*this? THIS?* is what gets folks upset THIS FUCKING TINY
INSIGNIFICANT DRAMA want to say WOMEN OF THE WORLD
LISTEN TO ME NOW you want a man to be dangerous and sexy and
roguish but you want him to be loyal and good and tender and loving
but that's just a BASIC CONTRADICTION isn't it yes it is Women of
the World YOU JUST CAN'T HAVE IT BOTH WAYS cos see us
sexydangerousfuckablerogues? !!!!WELL THIS IS THE SHIT WE
DO!!!! so tell you what Women of the World why don't you all just
have a wee huddle and make up your minds about what the *fuck* you
want from us But But But But But you know what you've done
Charlie oh yes you do Mum says *People are always going to remember
son* BUT WHAT THEY DON'T WANT TO SAY IS

'You don't want me here?' Charlie said, the moment suddenly one of
utter clarity. He could see everything. The pin-sharp colours. The

trembling of atoms in the air. The eyes of his mother and sister, looking at him. Looking away from him. 'Is that it? You don't want me here?'

His mother leaned forwards and took his hand. 'It's not that, Charlie. It's not a matter of not *wanting* you here. C'mon, son, we're *all* suffering.'

But they were right. Julie and Jordan's divorce. The baby on the way. His mother's heart attack. They couldn't take any more.

'So where am I supposed to go?'

His mother raised her eyes to Deborah's. She sat next to him, placed her arm around him, held him close, like a mother did. Like a mother did when her little boy was upset.

Then she said, 'Your father has a spare room.'

Never No way Not there get out head into the humidsummernight walk through the underpass GRAFFITI don't read it walk through the city cars traffic reflections on the Clyde beauty of this city walk think about all that has passed Mankind he is programmed yes or no Society it hardens its concrete coat of guilt Yet why operate against nature's perfect system bred evolved through millions of years natural selection for this specific purpose to attract mates REPLICATE himself He is streamlined designed for it no more immoral than a shark a hawk a virus DNA spawned proliferating with such precision as to mutate into this clean shape But the Society which sustained Man fixed him on its sticky web of interlocking morals DENIED this taught FIDELITY and MARRIAGE and HONOUR a flat-out refusal of the Law of Nature wild unjust in favour of this flavourless flat-pack civilisa

I am ravenous.

I need to be stopped.

I can't go on like this.

I am a space-ship. Hurtling. Hurtling. At the speed of light. Pieces of me are detaching.

Listen to me. I am my own masterpiece. Do you understand that I am evolving? That I am reaching my most perfect state? That I am becoming *art itself*?

hit a club called Inferno ha ha *Inferno* like in the Divine Comedy that weird bit when Dante reaches the centre of Hell !!where there's no gravity!! no longer sure if he's climbing or descending BECAUSE HE'S DOING BOTH weird that Friday-night packed with *mainly* men with *MANLY* MEN with REGULAR DRINKERS they glance my way I am one of them want to be Among them hey guys not usually interested in anything you'd have to say But noooooo But now the secrets to share the women the hearts we've broken the laughs we've had over it all ha ha ARE WE NOT MEN? want to live in a community of men men farming determined men tending the soil men Tequila the barman pours it sweetly thank you brother Cheers slam drink shakeshock Another slam ugh MAKE THIS A DOUBLE MY MAN feel it burn aah the night gradually circles circles circles downwards taking its time *Want to dance?* says the guy next to me Y'what? fairly short bald as a cue-ball tight-fitting T-shirt smiling Do I want to dance? *Yeah is that so strange?* Do you mean me? *Yeah* says the guy *Saw you standing there on your own thought y'know wonder if he'd like to dance* I say Okay um sure cos I like dancing as much as the next guy What's your name man? *Dave* Okay man I'm Charlie let's dance *We don't have to* No no I insist Dave let's hit the dance-floor Twisting the Night Away whooh bopping Dave's a good dancer This is fine y'know I'm y'know dancing with a guy and guess what man I'M ENJOYING IT here we are Just the Two of Us guys dancing just dancing just enjoying each other's company smiling y'know kinda feel At Home not scamming for an opportunity shelookingatmecanshefeelmelookingtoo? like being in the fucking

*field* man But here guys are clapping me cheering me We don't need
women We don't need women A FUCKING ALL-MALE WORLD
that's what we need whooh so drunk it's actually FUNKY another guy
joins in Bow to your partner sir then another then another Dave
smiling good old Dave MY MAIN MAN he says *Hey Charlie wanna
pill?* so I says Yeah man yeah fuck sure hands me one GULP cool
Dave grins we dance dance dance dance GRIN dance dance *Hey
Charlie wanna sit down* um maybe *Well what about over there* hm well
okay Head over to the couch His arm round me My arm round him
To the guys! I say *TO THE GUYS* clink ha ha cheers Dave. *So what's
a cute little boy like you doing in a place like this?* What's that Dave?
try to f fo fcus What's that you're saying there? *I said what's a cute
little boy like you doing in a place like this?* Ha ha good one Dave *No
really I mean it* Mean what? *Are you uh available?* Am I uh available?
What the hell you talking about Dave? *Oh sorry sorry I assumed you
were gay* You thought I was GAY? seriously? *Well yeah you're not uh
offended or anything are you?* What no way man I'm not offended but
well I'm just uh just a little uh surprised that's all *But Charlie it's a
GAY BAR* Oh oh right right GOT ME DAVE right right got me with
that one there oh OH HA HA HA good one then Dave he kisses me
shortfright but such a gentle pressure NOT HOW I'D THOUGHT IT
WOULD BE AT ALL not rough or brutal or spittle stubble But this
softness this softness Wow okay wow Dave I wasn't uh expecting that
*Oh sorry was it okay?* Uh uh I don't really have an answer for you
there Dave that's uh I'm not used to guys uh uh the guys I know don't
just do that I think you uh well I think you kinda went over the line
there Dave you're a good-looking man but y'know y'know but that
was way over the line there fella that was

    *FUCKING PRICKTEASE!*

    pushes me then storms off onto the dance-floor left sitting there
guys all looking at me so I picks up a drink DOWNS IT picks up

another DOWNS IT thinking maybe it's time to go brother but Stands there what you looking at eh? what you lot looking at? some kind of fucking mermaid on a rock singing into the emptiness into the vast grey sky here? that all I am to you? oh Jesus man I am FUCKED need to get out man !!!get some air!!! this is so not good *Hey mate gonnay get that guy outta here he's he's*

blooooogghhh

FUCKSAKES mate get him out

Right here you

next bar TEQUILA *aye sure pal* hey CHEERS THERE BAR-KEEP AND ALL MY LOVE TO THE MISSUS three pounds whooh! DOWN THE HATCH another *What d'you want?* ANOTHER! *Whoah pal I think you've had quite enough*

pleased to meet you!

whooh! whooh!

*aye right pal right okay we can all hear y*

Poetry Chess, everyone! How about a wee game of Poetry Chess?

*fuckin gonnay shut that guy up somebo*

okay, what's this one?

Which way I fly is Hell      myself am Hell

And in the lowest deep
a lower deep

        Still threatening to devour me opens wide,

          To which the Hell I suffer
            seems a Heaven.

anyone?

       *naw pal, we've nae idea*

           anyone?

           John Milton!

           *Paradise Lost*
           heh heh

          right there in yer faces!
          heh heh

*aye very good pal, ye're awfy clever*

    *ye've also had enough now get ou*

403

streetligh ?

where?

all right doll how's it goin fancy a bit of

aye same to you hen

fckn

better to reign in hell

than serve in heaven

sweetheart

'Scuse me hen?

'Scuse me

Kiss me!

Tease me!

Squeeze me!


*Naw pal cannay say that I will*

Ha ha, no I'm not looking for money doll it's


I just need you to tell me where

where i stay

No

ha ha

no

I didn't *suggest* I should stay with *you*

ya cheeky wee chickpea

See my girlfriend's dumped me and my mum's told me I can't live
with her any more and
I've lost my job and I'm divorced and I just I just I just

just want to be a nice guy again

I'm sayin
just a-wanna be a nice-a guy-a gain

eh?

That was it in Italian

Wha?

No doll

C'mere

No no it's all right I'm no

AYE ALL RIGHT calm down hen calm down

I'm going I'm going

'kay

hold-a yourself love


in the name of


                                                    Tut



                                    the mind is its own place
                                        and in itself


can make a hell of heaven
a heaven of hell

                        anyone?



                                                anyone?


Milton again, class


                                pay some attention



dozy shower

WELL WELL WELL WELL!

What've we got here!

*oh fuck no another one*

HEN party eh?

*Aye that's right pal*

Penny for the bride?

okay well here's a pound
you girls looking for a good time then?

*aye*

out on the pull?

*only the single ones*

Well I'm your man

BABY

I'M
YOUR
MAAAAAAAAAA

*oh jesus christ*

where's the lucky bride then

*jenna*
    *JENNA*

        *shout on jenna*

eh

that her

*what is it?*

You the Hen
hen?
*that's right aye*

Getting married eh

*that's what usually happens after a hen party*

yeah

409

Congratulations

That's brilliant

*cheers*

And you'll look beautiful honey

*yep*

beautiful

MWAH!

*aye all right all right*

So when you getting married

*next Saturday*

next Saturday eh

Still leaves plenty time then

I'm saying
still leaves plenty time then

*aye I heard ye*

don't kid on
you know what I mean

*no really*

No?

okay then

What about another wee kiss for the

No?

Not fancy a final fling?

had one on my stag ni

*look pal we've got places to go*

aye okay it's okay I'm no

mm

no c'mon a bigger kiss than that hen c'mon

*fucksake*

Aye all right all right what's the problem

just giving the bride a kiss like what's the

Hey

Hey

I got married once

You listening?

she looked

see on the day she looked so fuckin gorgeous

*yer all right pal*

*Listen*

*yer all right*

*Gonnay sober up somewhere buddy*

*ye'll be fine*

she was

she was

*just leave him*

*cannay just leave him look at him he's weepin*

*JUST LEAVE HIM*

*he's a jakey c'mon*

*wait a minute*

413

*Angie*

*that the guy*

*That no the guy in the news?*

*Teacher*

*attacked some wee lassie*

*Ho mate*

*Ho mate*

*what's your name?*

Charlie

*Charlie what?*

Charlie Bain

*Charlie Bain*

*that's him*

*that's him aye*

this cunt

this cunt here

*FUCKIN TELLIN YE ANGIE*

wee Elizabeth

just want to hold wee Elizabe

*HO SEE YOU*

see me what?

*SEE YOU YA FUCKIN*

wha?
no

NO

*YOU KEEP THE FUCK AWAY FAE WEE LASSIES IN FUTURE*

*ya fuckin*

*DICK*

no    don't    please

*FUC!*

*KIN!*

*BAST!*

*ARD!*

no

no

no

i'm sorry

please

don't want to be

this man any m

ladies

please


fore you go



forgive me



listen



c'mere girls c'mere



*get tae fuck ya dirty*

not going to be this man any m

begging you



forgive me

that's it okay im going

I'M GOING!

i hear you

Just hope the bride has a nice wedding eh

be fine hen

honest

on the day

you'll look beautiful

like a woman

clothed

with

sun

'There aren't too many genres of popular song, and one of the things I think we all love is a sad song. I don't know what the specific characteristic of it is but everybody has experienced the defeat of their lives. Nobody has a life that worked out the way they wanted it to. We all begin as the hero of our own dramas in centre stage and inevitably life moves us out of the centre stage, defeats the hero, overturns the plot and the strategy and we're left on the sidelines wondering why we no longer have a part – or *want* a part – in the whole damn thing. So everybody's experienced this, and when it's presented to us, the feeling moves from heart to heart and we feel less isolated and we feel part of the great human chain which is really involved with the recognition of defeat.'

Leonard Cohen

# Closing Credits

This was, for many reasons, a difficult book to write, and feedback or encouragement at various stages made it much more like an experience that sometimes didn't feel like eating my own head. I'd like to thank those who so freely gave. They are:

Adele Bethal, Nick Brooks, Jennifer Custer, Rodge Glass, Magi Gibson, Victoria Hobbs, Kirstin Innes, Tom Leonard, Wendy McCance, Bob McDevitt, Elaine McKergow, Ian Macpherson, Anna Miles, Ewan Morrison, Hazel Orme, Colette Paul, Lucy Reynolds, Euan Thorneycroft, Thomas Tobias and Gabrielle Trufant.

Thanks, as ever, to my mum, dad, brother and sister.

And to Bryce, Brandon and Lawson – little men. Treat well your mothers, wives and girlfriends.

# Acknowledgements

Some of the discussion which takes place about Chaucer on pages 49–55 is glossed from Nevill Coghill's 'Introduction' to *The Canterbury Tales*, published by Penguin Classics (1977), London.

The Leonard Cohen quotations on pages 41, 253 and 423 are from an interview in *Word* magazine in July 2007.

The Leonard Cohen quotation on pages 125, 203 and 277 are from an interview conducted by Nick Paton Walsh on 14 October 2001 in the *Observer*.

Julie's quotation on page 395 is from Aleister Crowley.

Some of Dawn's arguments about feminism on pages 291–3 are indebted to those made by Katie Roiphe in a feature entitled 'Democracy: Are Women More Democratic?' in the *Observer*, Sunday, 30 September 2007.

The lyric on page 17 is from 'Foxtrot Vandals' by Zoey Van Goey. Reproduced by permission. © Zoey Van Goey 2007. Song written by Brennan, Moore and McCarthy.

The lyric on page 87 is from 'Talking Back At The Voices' by Burnt Island. Reproduced by permission. © Burnt Island 2008. Song written by Rodge Glass.

The lyrics on page 265 are from 'Silversword' by Ross Clark. Reproduced by permission. © Ross Clark 2008.

The lyric on page 272 is from 'That Summer At Home I Had Become The Invisible Boy' by The Twilight Sad. Words by James Alexander Graham. Reproduced by kind permission of The Twilight Sad.